ABSOLUTE DOUBT

NEW YORK TIMES BESTSELLING AUTHOR

CHERRY-ADAIR

Have fun with River & Daklin

Cheers

Cherry Adair

D1600455

ISBN-13: 978-1937774387
ISBN-10: 1937774387

www.cherryadair.com
shop.cherryadair.com

REVIEW SNIPS

GIDEON. Gritty and action-packed from beginning to end, this is a classic Adair tale, so readers can be sure that the sex is sizzling and the danger relentless! ~Jill M. Smith Romantic Times 4 1/2 * top pick

Adair's BLUSH . . . sizzling chemistry adds to the heat of Bayou Cheniere, La., in Adair's knockout contemporary romantic thriller. ~Publishers Weekly starred review

UNDERTOW is full of action and suspense! Cherry Adair did such a great job making the reader feel as if they were part of the experience. I felt like I was right there diving into the water looking for the buried treasure with Zane and Teal. ~Hanging With Bells 4 Bells

HUSH Packed with plenty of unexpected plot twists and lots of sexy passion, Cherry's latest testosterone-rich, adrenaline-driven suspense novel is addictively readable. ~Chicago Tribune

WHITE HEAT "Scorching passion, gritty danger, and testosterone-fueled action blend flawlessly together in the latest addition to Adair's hot and suspenseful Men of T-FLAC series." ~Booklist

WHITE HEAT "...latest in Ms. Adair's T-FLAC series, roars out of the starting gate at a fast gallop and never breaks stride in a thrilling, no-holes-barred roller coaster ride of heart-pulsing suspense and hot romance featuring a delicious, to-die-for hunk..."

"Ms. Adair skillfully weaves an exciting tale of explosive action sprinkled with twisty surprises around a sensual love story laced with gobs of fiery desire. A must for readers who like their romantic suspense hot... and the heroes even hotter!" ~Romance Reader At Heart

HUSH delivers non-stop action, hair raising adventure, and titillating dialogue that will have readers poised on the edge of their seats waiting for what happens next. Ms. Adair has created a memorable couple whose antics are a pleasure to read about. Emotions run high in HUSH, making for an amazing read full of surprising twist and turns. ~ Fresh Fiction

HOT ICE is a sure thing! Ms. Adair's characters are well supported by the secondary T-FLAC operatives that assist in the mission. The villain is equally well developed as you come to learn how a man like Jose' Morales became so twisted, that you almost feel sorry for him...almost! Ms. Adair weaves in clever tools and ingenious methods to solve this assignment. There has also been great detail given to the locations/settings, which span many continents. And the ability to bring it all together in a pulse-pounding climax will leave the reader breathless and well satisfied by the time you close this book. ~All About Romance

ICE COLD Adair continues her wonderfully addictive series featuring the sexy men of T-FLAC with this fast paced and intricately plotted tale of danger, deception, and desire that is perfect for readers who like their romantic suspense adrenaline-rich and sizzlingly sexy. ~ Booklist

ACKNOWLEDGEMENT

To all my FTDB challenge acceptors - I knew you could do it.
Can't wait to watch you soar.

PROLOGUE

T-FLAC Compound
Montana
November

A sh? I--I'm in a shitload of trouble."

Holding the cell phone to his ear, gritting his teeth against knifelike stabs biting along the nerves of his shattered tibia, T-FLAC operative Asher Daklin flung his bum leg off the coffee table. He'd never heard that tone in his brother's voice, and he went from stupor to full alert as his defense physiology kicked into high gear. As it did when he defused an explosive, his pulse slowed and his focus became pinpoint.

Hyper-alert, his voice calm and even, he speed-limped to the front door. "Where are you?" Swinging his coat over his bare chest, he shoved his Glock 41 Gen 5 in the back of his sweatpants, then thought better of it and stuck it one of his jacket pockets. "*How* bad?"

By habit, his earpiece was in the bowl beside a full clip and his keys. He inserted the earpiece, then slipped the phone and clip into his other pocket. "Let me speak to your CO." Like himself, Josh was an operative, though still a rookie, with barely a year in the field.

"I'm solo on this."

Fuckit. A "shitload of trouble" could mean damn near anything when out in the field. Especially unsupervised. His brother could be anywhere. But he wouldn't be calling for help if he was in some shithole half way around the world, so he was somewhere here in Montana.

Left leg in a cast from ankle to mid-thigh, titanium pins holding the bone together and five weeks into recovery, Ash was more than ready to get back into the field. But not like this, damn it. Leaning against the wall for balance, he rammed his bare foot into his right boot. Ignoring the galaxy of stars obscuring his vision, he held onto the wall for balance as he bent to tie the laces on his boot.

Flickering light from the muted football game illuminated the bare walls, single bed, and sofa comprised by his crash pad, used only on the rare occasion he was between assignments. Or injured, as he was now. "Joshua? *Where?*"

"Bomb lab." The tightness in his brother's voice indicated his stress level, which jacked up Ash's heart rate and answered his second question. How bad?

Bomb lab bad. A jolt of adrenaline surged. No. No. Fucking no. "What did you do?"

"Peeled away some of the coating from the Nut. You said—"

"I said it's fucking *unstable*, and the only goddamn thing preventing it from going off is that protective barrier." Skinning

2

the thick outer layers off the explosive device was still just a test. A controlled—by *himself*—fucking test. "How long ago?" *How long to detonation?*

Pause. "Four minutes."

Even at a flat out run, his brother couldn't clear the blast zone in time. "What the fuck are you doing talking to me? Haul ass!"

"You know I won't make it."

No correct answer to that one. Ash's heart did a double tap as he looked around for his crutches in the blue glow of the T.V. The light passed through the almost empty bottle of Tovaritch Premium Russian Vodka on the coffee table next to an empty bag of Oreos. Breakfast, lunch, and dinner.

He had no goddamn business driving, let alone trying to save his idiot brother. Still, he considered grabbing the bottle to take with him, and then remembered he already had one in the truck. "Fuck, Josh—"

"Ream me out later, 'k?"

Rhetorical. There'd be no fucking later and they both knew it, but that didn't mean Ash wasn't going to move heaven and earth to reach him in time. "Damn straight I will." He hooked the lightweight crutches under his arms only because he could move faster with them than without. The apartment building was on T-FLAC property, isolated, private, off the grid. The lab was a ten-minute drive in this weather.

"I'll be there in three." *Only if he teleported. Fuck, fuck*

3

fuck. "Don't touch anything else until I get there, dipshit." Letting himself out of his apartment, Ash speed-hopped down the hallway to the elevator. "Which lab?" *Keep him talking, keep him calm.* He jabbed the button for the underground parking garage.

"B."

The dimly lit area was full. Operatives out on various assignments trusted their rides to T-FLAC's high-end security. "Breathe. It's small, so it might not detonate at all." The device, in this case the size of a pea, had an unknown blast field. However, it *would* detonate. "Get the fuck out of there. I'll meet you on the road. Go now, Joshua"

Ash unlocked his four-wheel-drive truck and climbed, crutches first, into the icy seat. The engine started with a roar. No time to warm up. Years of training and live combat kept him in control as he wheeled through the garage, then into the snowy street at eighty miles per.

"*Don't* come, Ash." Fear thickened Josh's voice. "Fucking hell. Sorry. I shouldn't've called you. This is my--"

"Who else would you call? What the hell were you thinking, numbnuts?" Snow collected on the rapidly swiping wipers, and his breath fogged the windows. Frigid air blasted through the vents, pebbling his skin. But he was reacting more to the imminent peril his brother was in than to the winter weather.

"I was thinking I could help you crack this one."

"Alone?" A mental countdown timer urged more speed. *Go go go!* Pedal to the metal, Ash ran the compound's lone stop sign.

Not another vehicle in sight, just open fields of crisp white snow on either side of the road, only visible because he had his headlights on bright. In the high beams, rapidly falling snow looked like heavy confetti as it came down in a slanted curtain. He might as well be the only man on the planet tonight. He passed the sign for Honey Winston's ranch where he'd spent a month after surgery, recuperating and going insane from sheer boredom.

Tire chains gripped the snowy road, but he felt as though he were going slo-mo. Fuck it. "On a Sunday at seven at fucking night?" He pushed the vehicle up to a hundred on the slick road. "Jesus, Josh,"

"Had nothing better to do."

"I'm the only person with access to that lab, Joshua. How'd you get in?" Since he didn't hear the distinctive beeps of the security locks on each door as his brother exited the lab, Ash knew he was staying put. Goddamn it.

Goddamn *him* for allowing Josh to see how he accessed the lab.

"My keen powers of observation, bro. I watched when you keyed the code a couple of weeks ago."

The kid was too damn smart and observant for his own good. Of he always did shit like that. Had from the time he was old enough to toddle after his older brother, following him, imitating Ash's signature moves, joining T-FLAC.

He should've known better than to show Josh what he was working on. "When I was showing off, you mean?" The

5

windshield wipers, now moving sluggishly, pushed a mountain of snow from side to side. *Thump-hurry-thump-hurry-thump-hurry.*

Not Josh. Please God. Not the only person on the planet I love, hell the only person on the planet who loves me back.

"You weren't showing off. I asked. Okay, I fucking begged. I want to learn from the best. You're the best. You'd be the best bomb disposal expert even if you weren't my favorite brother."

"I'm your only brother, dickhead." Maybe a miracle would occur and there'd be time to save Josh's ass. "Stick it in those white beads in the lead-lined box." The Upsalite was a promising, but as yet unproven, method of defusing a bomb. Just not *this* bomb. Not at this time.

"Does it work?"

"Do it, and we'll both find out." It fucking hadn't worked a few weeks ago, but if ever a miracle was needed, that time was now.

The tires slithered and slid as he rounded the corner and passed the nondescript single-story T-FLAC headquarters building where a few lights shone. The place looked empty on this snowy Sunday night.

Deceptive. All the action, the very heart of T-FLAC, was managed and run like a finely tuned Swiss watch, by the people manning the twelve floors underground. The hub of their telecommunication systems, computers, arsenals of weapons, satellites, and the ability to manage operatives worldwide were there, hidden from sight. He considered, and dismissed, calling in reinforcements. If he couldn't get there in time, they sure as shit wouldn't.

"Okay. It's in."

"Leave anyway."

Pause. "At least it's warm in here. You know I fucking hate the cold."

Better than being dead. "Get out! Now!"

The truck screamed past the hangars where planes, helicopters, and various vehicles were tucked behind an innocuous-looking forested berm behind the main building. HQ housed not only everything the operatives needed in the field, but also had a fully staffed hospital, with medical personal on duty 24/7, and temporary housing for personnel or government officials. It even held a safe room for the President of the United States, should the need arise.

T-FLAC HQ was as impenetrable as Fort Knox, which was why the bomb lab was in a satellite facility, five clicks away, surrounded by mile-thick berms covered with trees and dense vegetation.

"How's the leg?" Josh's voice shook, the sound putting the fear of God into Asher.

Ash got it. His brother needed to anchor himself to his voice. "Still broken." Pins held his femur together, the cast chafed his inner thigh, and his fucking skin *itched*. But those were the least of his problems.

Josh in the lab with quarter of a gram of the most powerful and volatile explosive in the world? That was a fucking problem.

"Tell me about E-1x."

"Already told you." Jesus, had it always taken this fucking long to get from point A to point B?

"Tell me again. Or regale me with the gory details of your love life."

He hadn't had a love life in three years. "We were called in to defuse an unfamiliar explosive device in Ben Talha, Algeria six months ago." Josh knew this. He'd avidly listened to the retelling of the discovery of E-1x several times. Ash had fuck-all to add to it. Still, he retold the events in a calm, unemotional voice, hoping Josh couldn't hear his own fear.

"We searched high and low for the device. We knew the explosive was located on the second floor of an abandoned building on the outskirts of the city. I saw, and dismissed, a misplaced Hawaiian kukui nut, not a bomb. Bad. Fucking. Mistake."

"How big a bang?"

"Hell, Joshua--"

"Tell me again. After all, it's no big whoop at this point, right?"

Yeah, no big whoop. Ash's chest hurt as the pressure inside built. He was always in control. Always able to function under pressure. Not this time. *Please, not Josh...* That one ounce of explosive, wrapped in its hard coating, had been responsible for taking out twenty city blocks, three schools, a hospital, a dozen office buildings, and almost six thousand men, women, and children. It had also killed eleven of T-FLAC's finest bomb disposal operatives, and shattered Ash's leg. "It was a big fucking bang. Happy now?"

"Not particularly." Josh's tone was dry. "*This* little guy isn't going to kill thousands of people."

No. Just the most important person in Asher Daklin's life

"You were damn lucky to get out of Ben Tahla with only an injury. It beat the crap out of the alternative, right?"

"I lost operatives and friends that day." And he'd vowed to figure out how defuse that type of bomb before more people were killed or injured. He'd never considered his baby brother would be one of them.

"Once we knew what to look for, it wasn't long before we found half a dozen Nuts in the nest of a known terrorist cell outside Paris. We returned home with the Nuts in a lead-lined, titanium box for me to play with while I recuperated. And because of the Ben Talha injury, I was able to spend considerable more time in the lab working on a solution to what's rapidly becoming a tango favorite."

"Due to its small size, ease of transportation, and powerful impact, right?" Josh didn't sound quite as terrified now, which bothered the crap out of Ash. His brother had gone from fear to acceptance.

Asher, however, had not. From here to the lab was a

9

straight shot. No curves or hills to slow him down even a millisecond. He pushed the engine as he methodically went through everything he knew about E-1x in his mind. Precious little. He had minutes to come up with a solution to a problem that he'd been working on with a full team of scientists and chemists for six fucking months.

"Boko Haram used it last week to annihilate a village in Baga, Nigeria," he absently told Josh as icy snow, kicked up by the tires, pelted the windshield. *Keep talking, business as usual.* "We suspect a suicide bomber carried one unnoticed on board that Russian airbus over Sinai the week before. More reports of its use come in every day."

"This shit's the tango's explosive of choice internationally now, right? Tell me about it."

"Fuckit it Josh. You *know* all this shit."

Josh's pause was filled with a shaky breath. "Just wanna hear your voice."

His brother's words struck his chest like a physical blow. Ash got it. He needed to hear Josh's voice, too. His brother *depended* on him. He was the kid's fucking hero.

Go go go. Already flooring the accelerator, Asher couldn't make the truck go any faster. "That inner off-white core is high density crystal packed with similar characteristics to Cubane's eight carbon atoms arranged at the corners of a cube, with one hydrogen atom attached to each carbon atom. Except this shit isn't manmade. We named it E-1x, based on its atomic structure, or the

Nut, for its appearance similar to that of a Hawaiian kukui nut--"

"Keep talking."

"The high-density substance packed inside the hard outer coating is found in nature. *Somewhere*. So far, we haven't ascertained its origins, or how the fuck to neutralize it. The methods in play to defuse and neutralize Cubane don't work worth shit on this natural substance."

Something else his brother knew; Every controlled experiment had ended with a big fucking bang.

Now Josh had opened Pandora's box. No going back.

"Are you geared up?" Taking the straightaway at high speed, his headlights sliced through the blackness. The tires shimmied before regaining traction.

"It won't protect me if it blows. I know. Love you, Ash."

"Christ. Don't get maudlin. I'll be there in two. I'll figure something out." There was nothing to figure out. He knew it, Josh knew it. Dread welled like black acid through his veins. "At the tree now." The tree was a massive, fifty-foot tall, hundred-year-old Douglas fir. Two long fucking minutes away. The seconds ticked in his head like the detonator on a timed bomb. *Go go go.*

"Stay back there." Dead calm.

*No, no, no, n*o. Ash's foot couldn't press on the accelerator any harder. "Fuck you, Joshua Daklin. Goddamn it, I'm almost there."

There was a loud pause before his brother said quietly, "Tell Mom I love her, and that I'm sorry about the whole grandchildren thing. You'll have to double up on that, big brother."

"Your mother doesn't want *my* grandchildren, bro. She wants yours. You'll give her plenty, and they'll all be as hardheaded as their father. Hang on, almost there." Snow sprayed in an arc as he did a wheelie at the foot of the steps of the bomb lab. "Pulling up now. Be with you in less than thirt—"

The world suddenly exploded into a bright ball of orange flames

ONE

Los Santos
Cosio
18 months later

I f Asher Daklin wasn't on a time-sensitive op, if his career wasn't already FUBAR, seeing the long, shapely legs of a beautiful blonde emerging from a red sports car would've intrigued him. But seeing said blonde and the Mustang convertible—circa 1990—in a tiny village in Cosio, in the middle of goddamned *nowhere*, put him on high alert. He'd seen the woman three hundred miles away, and nine hours earlier, refusing assistance with her luggage at the Santa de Pores airport.

She'd followed him over the mountain.

It was a six-hour trip. Where'd she been for the other three?

Undercover, and in character from the moment he'd landed in Cosio, Daklin's disguise was that of a bishop, there to "authenticate" an "apparition" for deeply religious, and even more unscrupulous radical, Francisco Xavier. The "apparition" was one of T-FLAC's making. It should be interesting to see the FX in person later tonight.

In the meantime, Daklin was trussed up like a Thanksgiving turkey in layered liturgical vestments of cassock, white rochet, and over that the black Chimere. Even at dusk, the temperature in the valley hovered in the mid-nineties; humidity, eighty percent. Sweat ran down the small of his back, making the layers of fabric stick to him like a shroud.

Bringing his parish priest with him, Francisco Xavier himself had personally come to collect *Bishop* Daklin from the airport earlier that morning in an air-conditioned four-wheel drive replete with snacks and bottles of iced water. He'd done the twelve hour round trip just so he could talk to Bishop Daklin about his apparition in private. *Nothing* in this small, poor village of Los Santos was private. All of Franco's vehicles, his home and his private chapel, had been bugged since the other five T-FLAC operatives had arrived a week earlier.

The only reason T-FLAC had given Daklin this one last chance was because he was the resident authority on E-1x. If not for that, his out of control drinking after Josh's death would've gotten his ass fired.

He couldn't afford to be distracted. He'd figured he could lay off the booze for the three days necessary to do this job. Only he hadn't anticipated this new temptation.

His instant cockstand, just *looking* at the blonde, reminded Daklin how long it had been since he'd had a good fuck. Even longer since he'd had one while sober. Either way, sober or drunk, it had been too damn long, and now, if things went as planned, it was too damned late to have one more. Too bad his fucking days were over. Hot, unwelcome need buzzed through his body as she approached. She carried herself with the self-confidence of a woman aware of her sex appeal and comfortable in her own skin. Sexy. Confident. Ultra-feminine.

She was an unnecessary complication in an already problematic, volatile situation. There was absolutely no reason for *anyone* to travel all this way to a jungle-surrounded village of five hundred people. There wasn't even a stop sign in the mining town and the only law was Francisco Xavier, who was about as law abiding as any terrorist, which was not at all.

The country of Cosio, nestled in the Qhapaq Mountains between Ecuador, Columbia, and Peru, had been a hot bed of terrorism until recently. And, no matter that *those* tangos had been cleaned out of the country, it was still a dangerous place.

Daklin resisted the useless action of gripping his left thigh. No point. The pain was *always* excruciating and unrelenting. Standing, sitting, walking. Night and day. It hurt like the fires of hell had scored bone and muscle. A constant, unrelenting reminder he was alive. Josh wasn't.

No painkillers, no booze. He deserved to remember. Every minute.

"Were you expecting her?" he asked his host, Francisco *call-me-Franco*-Xavier. Five-eleven, slicked back, silvering at the temples, black hair, religious fanatic. Xavier was seventy-two but looked fifty, thanks to two facelifts. In his crisp blue cotton shirt and black pants, he looked as refined and respectable as a bank president, not one of T-FLAC's top ten most wanted terrorists.

"I recommended she *not* come, Your Excellency." With a small, concerned frown, Xavier observed as the blonde exited the car and slammed the door. She gave a cheerful little wave to the three men waiting under the portico of Xavier's hacienda as she rounded the steaming hood of the vehicle. "I talked to her a few days ago. Her brother, Dr. Sullivan, was an employee. I informed her he left Los Santos several weeks ago."

Oliver Sullivan. He was the brainiac biochemist hired to do so much more than merely manufacture small explosives to aid in the mining of emeralds; because it wasn't emeralds they were pulling from the mountain at all. It was pure E-1x. Sullivan was just as culpable for thousands of deaths worldwide as Xavier himself. As yet, his bosses had no idea why Sullivan had left Los Santos.

They had enough intel to know there was a ticking time bomb, one programmed for seventy-two hours, somewhere. Daklin and his men had barely three days to unravel this clusterfuck before half the civilized, and probably a good portion of the *un*civilized, world blew up.

He was on shaky ground with this op. He'd been warned: One more fuck up and he'd be kicked out of T-FLAC for good.

Without T-FLAC, life as he knew it would be over. He'd be eighty-sixed. T-FLAC wouldn't be writing letters of recommendation for him. He'd be blacklisted from the world of special ops. Reputable private security companies wouldn't touch him. If he was lucky, he'd get a gig as a mall cop hoping to nab a fucking teenage shoplifter. With that kind of work, he wouldn't make it to the food court on day one. He'd die by noon—by his own hand.

At least the issue would be resolved in seventy-two hours, because this was one job he would not fuck up. Still, there was a ninety-nine point nine percent chance he wouldn't make it out of this op alive. His vindication would have to be posthumous.

Hell. He craved a drink so bad; his tongue touched his palate and tricked him into believing he could taste the smooth burn of alcohol. God, he wanted to drink himself numb, and watch his ninety-inch television in his dark apartment.

Ever since Josh's death, there hadn't been enough alcohol to quiet his brain, or bring him any measure of peace.

And now her.

Go the fuck away, Barbie.

"If she's anything like Oliver--" Father Marcus said, "she'll be focused and driven."

Marcus Cawcutt was a kind, decent, God-loving man. Looking at him now, nobody would've guessed he'd been a T-FLAC operative in his youth. A kind man who loved his flock, Marcus would do whatever it took to save both their souls and their physical bodies. Now in his late sixties, his salt and pepper hair perpetually mussed, he observed the young woman's progress with kindly brown eyes. "I'll talk to her. It was a long drive. She must be hot and thirsty."

She *was* hot, and *he* was thirsty.Fuck it.

Her wide smile was way too damned cheerful for someone who'd been driving a convertible, top down in this heat for hours. Big, soft eyes. Choppy, streaky, chin-length blonde hair and gorgeous, streamlined body. *"Buenas noches, señores."* Her accent was good, her voice husky and filled with warmth and good humor.

Wholesome, sophisticated, and downright lickable, despite the enervating heat, she looked as fresh as a dewy fucking daisy as she crunched across the gravel driveway in front of the portico. White shorts and thin, knee-high, crisscrossed straps on her flat-soled, gladiator-style sandals showcased her spectacular legs.

In any other city, at almost any-fucking-other-time, Daklin would've gladly undertaken the challenge to see whether her nod to bondage was merely a fashion statement or a promise.

As if there weren't enough explosive situations present, her appearance in this godforsaken pisshole of a village was guaranteed to work randy old Xavier into a lather.

Daklin exchanged a speaking look with Father Marcus before returning his gaze to Barbie.

A sheer, turquoise-colored, long-sleeved shirt, rolled up to her elbows, hung open over a white tank top that exposed the upper curve of her creamy breasts where a chunky turquoise necklace didn't quite fill in the area from throat to décolletage.

He wanted to fall on her like a starving lion and drag her off to his lair. Or toss her back in the car and order her to return to whichever fairy glade she'd come from.

18

Daklin considered the woman as dangerous as a heavily armed tango. He said mildly, "You have a flat tire."

Gray. Her eyes were a kitten gray with long dark lashes, and a gleam that told him nothing was going to get her down today. Not the heat, not the flat tire, and not a less than enthusiastic welcoming committee.

"I drove on it for four out of nine hours over mountain roads. There aren't many gas stations around." When she tucked a blonde strand behind her ears, diamond earrings sparkled in the early evening sun, disappearing as a red streak over the mountains. "I'll have to have it repaired before I head back, Father."

Daklin would repair it himself right now if it guaranteed she'd turn right around and head back. Except the mountains were no place for a woman. Hell, they were no place for *any* rational person, especially when driving alone and at night. Marauding guerrillas and other dangerous elements prowled the jungle on either side of the treacherously narrow, winding mountain road. The trip was hazardous enough during the day, but at night it would be certain suicide. *Shitfuckdamn.*

"Your Excellency," Daklin corrected, his tone cool, and just this side of 'fuck off, lady'. "Father Marcus here is called Father. As a bishop, I'm called Your Excellency or Bishop Daklin."

"River Sullivan." The open, friendly smile didn't dim. *Fuck.* She extended a slender, ringless hand. "I've never met a bishop before. And you must be Father Marcus and Senor Xavier?" She paused before shaking hands to wave away a fat, iridescent bug

19

hovering over her sweat-dampened cheek. Her gaze was direct and curious as it rested on each man's face. This woman clearly didn't have a nervous bone in her body. Would she be as bold in bed? Dumbass. Focus, for fucksake.

"I've heard so much about both of you."

Xavier extended his hand. "Call me Franco, please."

Daklin wanted to lick the sweat from her skin. He wanted to screw her until they both went blind. Damn it to hell, he *had* to get rid of her. Thank God his robes covered a multitude of sins. His weapons, and now, his inappropriately animated dick.

He stuck his hands into his pockets and left them there.

Shake, shake. Smiles all around. Franco and Marcus were clearly charmed, Daklin thought sourly. Marcus liked everyone. And Xavier, when he wasn't a psychopathic tango, was a lecherous dick, which Barbie would soon discover if she stayed long enough to spend any time alone with him.

"Come." Xavier offered his crooked elbow and she trustingly slipped her hand through it. "I'll have Ramse show you to your room." He snapped his fingers for his bodyguard. Ramse Ortiz was one of the T-FLAC operatives in town, and someone Daklin needed to talk to ASAP. "Since I wasn't expecting you, I'm afraid the only room available is the one your brother used on the rare occasions he came into town. Would you prefer refreshments sent up, or would you like to come downstairs for drinks? We don't eat for another hour."

"If I may, I'd like to take a shower first. Then I'd love to join you."

Dear God, was she fucking offering herself up as a goddamned sacrificial lamb? Why the hell would she willingly put the image of herself wet and naked into any red-blooded man's brain?

Barbie wanted a shower.

Well, fucking good for her.

Now all Daklin saw when he looked at her was her naked body under a transparent sheet of water. One glance at Xavier, who was licking his lips as he looked down at her and murmured, "Of course, you'd like a shower," told Daklin that Xavier's thoughts were boomeranging in the same direction. "Your arduous trip was in vain, I'm afraid. Your brother is no longer here, Miss Sullivan." Tension made his voice harsher than he intended. "I'd suggest you shower and get refreshments to go so you can get back on the road before full dark."

Yeah, he wanted her gone so badly that he'd have her put her life in jeopardy on the mountain roads. Because the chances of her survival here in Los Santos in the next few days were slim to none.

She turned her head to give him a puzzled look over her shoulder. "I've been driving on a tire rim for hours. Is there a mechanic in town, Your Excellency? Or perhaps, *you* can change the tire for me before I turn around and make another nine-hour trip in the dark, on my own, traveling on dangerous mountain roads with which I'm unfamiliar. When I'm *this* tired?"

Sassy. "It's a *six-hour* drive, Miss Sullivan. I'm sure Señor Xavier has someone competent to change your tire while you freshen up and pack a meal to take with you."

Oh, shit. Daklin had seen that stubborn jaw tilt before. From his brother, Josh. The lady was about to dig in her heels.

"It's a six-hour drive to someone familiar with how to get to and from the airport," she said pleasantly. "Unfortunately, my map and I had a difference of opinion. I'm sure if Señor Xavier wants me to leave, he wouldn't be so rude as to expect me to leave in the dead of night." She cast big, inquiring gray eyes up at Xavier.

Xavier patted her hand, which was still hooked over his arm. "Of course not, my dear. *Mi casa es tu casa.* Rest. Refresh yourself. I'll have your car in good repair by morning."

Yeah, good old Xavier didn't want her poking around either. That made Daklin's job easier.

She'd be easily dispatched come morning.

#

"Are you sure this Bishop is who he claims to be? His arrival, now, is highly suspect."

Franco's skin heated with annoyance. The disembodied voice had the effect of making his balls clench, which both annoyed and turned him on. He wished he dared activate the jamming signals so that he *couldn't* call. Yet he waited for the infrequent calls like a damned puppy being given a treat.

Still, mocking his faith was never part of their games--mind games his partner enjoyed playing, and physical games they both enjoyed. Master and slave. But that was only in the one room in the house where he was willing to take the submissive role. Everywhere else, Franco was *el jefe*, and his people both feared and respected him.

"I petitioned Rome," Franco told his partner, voice cold. "*They* sent him. I investigated him. I assure you, Bishop Daklin is exactly who he says he is. The Church does not lie."

"You're a fucking moron. What does authentication of your apparition do for us at this stage of our plan? What do you hope to gain?"

"God speaks to me through Mary. I want clarification. I *need* to be absolutely certain that the 12th at 3:33 p.m. is the correct date and time."

"Jesus, Mary, and Joseph. The date and time were of *your* choosing, for good reason, Franco. It's too late to change your fucking mind two days before the event. Everything's in motion." Franco heard the impatient tapping of a pen on the desk near the phone as the angry silence stretched out between them. "Speak with your Mary tonight and have her confirm that this is no mistake, if you must. Let your bishop tell you it's been fucking ordained. But allow me to clarify. Whether we get a wooden statue's blessing or not, our plans are progressing and there'll be no stopping them."

TWO

O liver really isn't here," River told her best friend, as she sat cross-legged on the massive bed. She'd spent five minutes on the phone regaling Carly with a dramatized retelling of the drive from hell over mountain and dale, mostly limping along on the rim of the flat tire.

"Good. Then you can turn around and come right back home." Carly's voice was as clear as if she was sitting in the room with River instead of half a world away in Portland, Oregon. "Honestly. You shouldn't even *be* there, Riv. Why subject yourself to all kinds of danger when your brother has repeatedly told you *not* to come?"

"I'm worried sick about him, Carly." River fell back against a mound of burgundy and gold brocade pillows and stared up at the elaborately painted beams on the ceiling twenty-feet overhead. "Where *is* he? Why did he leave? That, coupled with his growing depression, makes me think the worst. Ever since he was a teen, we worried about suicide. So when he told me about some woman he loved who'd died, coupled with the money he stuck in my account, then his abrupt disappearance. . ."

"He's too damned selfish to kill himself," her friend argued tartly.

True, but River automatically rushed to her brother's defense. "You don't kn--"

"Yeah, I *do*. I've been reading between the lines for as long as I've known you. He's a grown-ass man who doesn't give a shit about anyone but himself."

"That's not fair. His Asperger's--"

"Doesn't explain away all his unacceptable behaviors, River. You know that."

No it didn't, but *that* was a subject best left unspoken, even between best friends. "I cut him slack because he's the only family I have. And because it's part of my DNA to watch out for him." She'd promised their parents, albeit she'd done the 'watching out for' from a distance.

"You should concentrate on your own life instead of worrying about him."

"As soon as I know he's okay, I'll do just that. Apparently, there was an explosion at the mine around about the time he left. It's possible *that* had something to do with him leaving. I'll ask. If he still wants to be left alone after I find him, I'll be on the next flight home. Hell, I'm not even sure we'd recognize each other." She smoothed a hand over the rough brocaded bedcover. "Slight exaggeration, but we haven't seen each other in more than five years. Still, I always knew where he was. Now I *don't*."

Oliver hadn't come to her graduation, nor her wedding for her short-lived marriage. They didn't have the close relationship she'd always wished they'd had. The reasons were complicated.

His off-the-charts brilliance, combined with his Asperger's, made them very different people. There was also a ten-year age difference between them. He was her brother, and she loved him, but he was far from likable. He was difficult, taciturn, and moody; and those were his good qualities. Still, if he was in trouble, she wanted to help him. He was her only family, and that's what family did.

All she freaking-well had to do was *find* him.

"Just because he gave you all that money and disappeared isn't reason to think he'd *terminate* himself. Yeah, I guess it could be. Why didn't you tell me this when I was trying to dissuade you from going to a war-torn country halfway across the Universe?"

"Because I didn't want to put the thought out in the ether. I'm seriously worried that he's done something desperate. Not that I'd know what to do if I find him like that. But I have to try. He's always been a bit secretive, but he's never even *mentioned* this 'love of his life', Catherine, until three *weeks* ago. And she *died* years ago. That was our last damned conversation. I don't freaking know what to think."

Three years ago, River had been going through a divorce, and *El Beso,* her lingerie business was starting to take off, filling her life, 24/7. Maybe *that's* why Oliver hadn't mentioned his girlfriend's death? Maybe he didn't feel obligated to tell her anything about his life *at all*. His Sunday calls, as regular as clockwork, had gradually gotten shorter and shorter. His work seemed to have become an obsession. He didn't sleep. He frequently mentioned forgetting to eat.

"He's *never* missed a Sunday call. Not once in twelve years. Last Sunday was the third week in a row that I haven't heard from him. I invited him to visit me in Portland for a change of scenery, and he told me, in no uncertain terms, the place made him shudder. So I suggested coming to see him. And, as always, he told me flat out not to come."

"And yet-"

"Here I am. I always felt a little guilty at how relieved I was when he'd refused my offer. But this time, I had no choice."

"He's a practical guy, sweet pea," Carly reminded her. "Even if suicide was something he'd contemplate, it's been three years since the girlfriend died, right? If he'd wanted to do something, he would've done it before now, don't you think?"

"Not necessarily. Oliver's a planner. You know how he obsesses over the smallest detail. It makes him good at his job, but he tends to hyper-focus on something to the exclusion of everything else. It's absolutely possible that he'd planned his suicide, in minute detail, for years." River sat up, too filled with nervous energy to lie there contemplating a spider spinning a web near the ceiling.

"He *hasn't*," Carly said positively. "You're right there. He'll show up, and you'll see for yourself that he's absolutely *fine*. Maybe he's found a new love and taken her to Tahiti."

"Oliver doesn't *take* vacations. If he met someone, he's never mentioned her. But then, he never mentioned this other woman. Shit, I don't freaking know *what* to think. I'll look for clues. Maybe I'll find something. If this was the room Oliver used, there's no evidence he was ever here."

"That's not significant, Miss-There's-No-Obstacle-I-can't-Overcome. Maybe he only ever brought what he needed. Knowing how efficient and focused you are, I have every faith that you'll root out Oliver, do three years' worth of his laundry, and find a local restaurant to deliver his meals, all before noon tomorrow. My money's on you, girlfriend. What about his boss? Is he as creepy as Oliver said?"

"He's not creepy at all." River swung her legs over the side of the mattress, and hopped down to the floor. Going to the window, she held back the sheer white drape to look through the wide slats of the wooden shutters. She could see right down the middle of a town that apparently rolled up its streets when it got dark. There was no one outside, and just a few house lights spilled out over the cobbled streets. She let the drape drop back into place.

The silent military-type guy who'd shown her to her room had returned a few minutes later with her suitcase. River unzipped it, holding the phone against her shoulder. Flinging the case open, she pondered her outfit for the evening.

"Franco looks a bit like Sean Connery in his later Bond years," she told Carly as she shook out a dress modest enough to wear for dinner with a priest, a bishop, and a man who was possibly an aging Lothario. "Graying at the temples, very smooth and sophisticated." She unbuttoned her shorts and tugged down the zipper. "Clearly, telling me the poor man was lecherous and dangerous was Oliver's attempt to dissuade me from coming here."

Stepping out of her shorts, she sat down on the edge of the bed to unwind the straps of the sandal wrapped around her left calf, then did the same for the other one. She rubbed at the crisscrossed pink indentation on her left leg.

"The stuff he told you was pretty salacious and specific. Oliver doesn't have enough imagination to make up crap like that, so be on your toes," her friend argued. "What's the point in hanging around if Oliver's gone?"

River shrugged off her shirt, switching the phone to her other ear as she did so. "One thing at a time. Hang on." She peeled the tank top over her head. Dressed in only her bra and lacy thong, River paced the large bedroom. The breeze from a lazily circulating ceiling fan moved warm air and the spider web.

"Where'd Oliver get all that money he gave me, Carly? Five *million* dollars! Also, why give it to me unless he anticipated something terrible happening to him? He's been keeping so much from me. First, I hear he had a love of his life. Then I learn that she died tragically, more than three years ago. There are no freaking calls for *weeks*, and now he's supposedly left Los Santos without a word? Something's wrong, I just know it."

"Cosio's a war-torn country set in the middle of a jungle filled with natural predators," Carly added. "Maybe an animal?"

"Holy shit, don't put *that* terrifying thought into my head, for God's sake! What if Oliver knew he was going to die? Not suicide, but something else? A terminal illness?"

"If anyone can get to the bottom of this, my money's on you. What about the priest? Maybe Oliver gave a confession before he left?"

Despite her worry, River laughed. "We're not Catholic, and Oliver has always been tight-lipped about his job. Not because it's a secret, but because he knows nobody will understand what the hell he's saying. He wouldn't tell anyone, even a priest, anything."

"Then what are you going to do?"

"Ask around. Someone might know where he's gone. There's another man here, a bishop. He's steely-eyed and not particularly friendly, but I'll talk to both him and the village priest and see if they know anything."

"So the letch looks like James Bond, and the bishop is steely-eyed? Interesting. How old is he?"

"Francisco Xavier is about seventy."

"Nice try. The steely-eyed bishop?"

"Mid-thirties." River grinned. "Only you would romanticize this. One's a man of God and the other's old enough to be my father. I'm just here to find Oliver. Then I'll be home."

"Maybe there's a handsome stable master..."

"Bye, Carly!"

"Wait! Call me every day so I know you're okay."

"Of course I'll be okay. But yes, I'll call you."

30

Feeling better now that she'd touched base, River enjoyed the opulent marble bathroom as she took a cool shower, then dried her hair, and applied makeup.

Naked, she went back into the bedroom to dress. For a moment she pondered unpacking, but it sounded as if her host shared his humorless bishop buddy's desire for her to be on her way. She left the suitcase on the bench at the foot of the bed.

Perhaps there was a hotel in the village. She'd check first thing in the morning, because no matter how much anyone wanted her to leave, she wasn't going anywhere until she saw Oliver with her own two eyes. Her stomach rumbled loudly. She hadn't eaten anything since she got off the plane and that was hours ago. She needed to dress and go downstairs.

She hadn't packed with seduction in mind, though nobody would ever guess that by what she'd grabbed from her well-appointed lingerie drawer. She practiced what she preached, and advertised: the right underwear gave a woman confidence. So tonight, it would be the Abrazo, she decided. The 'hug' was a white lace and tulle, boned strapless bustier and matching bikini panties from her summer collection. The delicate bridal- inspired lingerie fastened with cunningly invisible clips from pubic bone to between the sheer white tulle cups of her demi bra. Slipping the matching low-rise briefs up her legs, she felt armed and ready for anything.

After stepping into a simple yellow and white glazed cotton sheath, River pulled it up and adjusted the bateau neckline so it just skimmed the curve of her shoulders. Not too sexy for dinner with two men of God and a possible ladies' man. Contorting, she did up the side zipper, then smoothed the fabric over her hips.

Sliding her bare feet into bone-colored, strappy high-heeled sandals, she took an assessing glance in the full-length mirror. Against the rich reds and golds, bullion and velvet of the room, she looked simple and elegant, and as freaking out of place as a nun in a brothel.

The same man who'd brought in her suitcase stood at the foot of the stairs, dressed all in black, apparently waiting for her. His hair was black, his eyes were black, and his mood looked almost as black. He and the no-nonsense bishop had personalities in common. What looked like a small machine gun was slung across his broad chest, and a handgun was stuck in his waistband. He didn't crack a smile as he indicated that she should follow him.

If the walls and tables weren't covered with religious paintings, artifacts, or tapestries, they were covered with silver-framed pictures of children. Xavier's children, she presumed. The guard pointed toward the room she should enter.

Her *"Gracias"* was met with slightly less than a smile before he preceded her into the room, then stepped to the side to stand in front of a tall, carved curio cabinet filled with more small framed paintings and religious artifacts.

The sitting room, lined with more ornate artwork and rich jewel colors, felt stuffy, and overcrowded with heavy Spanish Colonial style furniture. River was grateful for her bare legs and arms and hoped to hell her deodorant held up.

The three men got to their feet as she entered the room.

Bishop Tall and Surly took a ten second delay before *he* rose.

Resplendent in black robes, clerical collar, and a red sash with a heavy gold chain and cross, the bishop's latent energy, barely contained, seemed to pulse through him, even as he eventually got to his feet. Broad-shouldered, and at least six foot four, he had the tensile strength and lean musculature of a seasoned athlete.

Their eyes clashed across the room. Caught in the snare of mesmerizing pale blue fire, River was unable to look away. Goosebumps pebbled her skin and her heart started pounding as if she'd been running flat out. She'd never experienced such a weird physical response to a man before in her life. With effort she blinked, breaking the visual connection, although she found her reaction to him intriguing enough that it made her want to look again. River vowed to refrain from making eye contact. Better that way. Her heartbeat slowed dramatically when they weren't eyeball to eyeball.

He'd brushed back his hair, but it fell around his face to frame his features. River bet the slight wave in the glossy, dark strands brushing his collar pissed him off. Nothing soft for him, thank you very much. Instead of feminizing his strong features, his hair only made his strong face, with an aquiline nose, and dark brows over hooded eyes seem more masculine. The shadowy stubble on his chin suggested he probably had to shave twice a day. His well-shaped mouth remained unsmiling as he watched her approach.

His riveting, pale, crystal blue eyes promised untold delights to anyone who dared breech the darkness surrounding him. With his dark good looks and pale eyes, he looked like a fallen angel. How many women had succumbed to the smolder behind that clear blue? She wasn't that foolish. Fallen angels were wicked, and wicked didn't always translate into pleasurable.

She was pretty sure she wasn't seeing what she thought she was seeing. But, in her own defense, she was tired and worried, and the man was damn good looking. It was a minor detail that he was also a *bishop.*

Something about the way he held himself seemed more military than pious. Her gaze inexplicably dropped to his mouth, and the butterflies in her stomach turned to pterodactyls. *God.* What the hell *was* this? Her instant, visceral response to his sensual mouth made her think of sweaty tangled sheets and danger. It was ludicrous, considering the circumstances.

Dear God. I've lost my freaking mind.

Squaring her shoulders, River gave the men a cheerful smile. With any luck, one of them would lead her to Oliver. "Good evening, gentlemen."

"Miss Sullivan, you look as pretty as a rose in an English country garden." Walking toward her, Francisco Xavier extended his hand, palm up. Gallant and sweet. River took his cool, dry hand, hoping hers wasn't sweaty. "Will you join us in a pre-dinner drink?" He led her to an over-stuffed, tufted burgundy velvet sofa with a million buttons, releasing her when she sat down beside Father Marcus.

Bishop Daklin resumed his seat opposite them on a matching sofa. He looked aloof and mildly annoyed, and unlike the other two men, did not smile in greeting, or look even remotely pleased to see her. Any other time, any other man, River would've taken that as a challenge. But not here. And not him. *Definitely* not him. He didn't look like a man who participated in light flirtation. Not that being civil and cheerful constituted flirting.

The furniture was as hard as bumpy cement, stuffed with horsehair she suspected, but *she* still managed to smile. River amped up the cheer when his lips tightened in response.

The poor man didn't realize how much of a challenge he was presenting. She'd be like water dripping on a stone, wearing him down, even if she only dripped for a few hours.

Franco stood beside her. "What's your pleasure, Miss Sullivan?" Even with a heavy Spanish accent, River had no difficulty understanding him.

Finding my brother and getting back to my business. "Call me River. Something tall and cold, please." She shook her head at the irony of her words. All roads led to the bishop, it seemed. He was certainly tall, and his arctic-blue eyes, locked on her, were nothing if not cold.

She forced herself to look at the lit garden beyond the

French doors, away from those steely eyes that drew her gaze like a magnet.

As her host gave instructions to the guy standing like a statue at the doors, River turned to address Father Marcus, who was sitting beside her. "Oliver mentioned you with great fondness, Father." In the five years her brother had lived and worked in Los Santos, he'd mentioned Father Marcus, maybe *twice*. Both times in the most cursory, and disinterested way.

"I'm hoping something he might've said to you will enable me to find him."

"I wish I had something concrete to tell you, but like Franco, I'm only aware that your brother left Los Santos several weeks ago without so much a goodbye, let alone an explanation. I'm sorry, my dear."

River imagined she felt the icy hot weight of Bishop Daklin's gaze on her cheek. "I'm sorry, too. Thank you," she said as Franco handed her a tall glass of murky, pale yellow, lukewarm lemonade before returning to his seat beside the bishop across the wide marble and gold leafed coffee table.

Snap out of it. Why do I give a rat's ass one way or the other if he likes me or not? I don't. She blinked the priest back into focus. Father Marcus looked to be in his late sixties and had a kind smile and twinkling brown eyes. His round face was pink from the heat, and his short, untidy, salt and pepper hair was damp at the temples. He wore a short-sleeved black shirt and white clerical collar with dark jeans and black tennis shoes. Just looking at him made her feel hot, temperature-wise. With that thought, her glance automatically shot across the low coffee table to the bishop, who made her hot in a whole other way.

Covered from neck to toe in several layers of fabric, *he* wasn't even breaking a sweat. A prickling of awareness caused goose bumps to arise on her skin. Her heartbeat stuttered, then kicked into high gear. River's lungs forgot how to drag in air, and every drop of moisture in her mouth dried. Taking a gulp of her drink, she swallowed hard because *his* gaze was locked on *her* like a tractor beam set on high. *Laser blue* tractor beams poured over her like a hot, possessive touch. Pure electricity seemed to arc between them so powerfully, she wondered how the other two men in the room couldn't see it.

She *knew* it was one-sided, but it didn't make the sensation any less powerful. River's color rose as she felt every throb of her heartbeat on her lips, in the nerve endings of her nipples, and deep in the now moist juncture of her thighs.

The primitive sexual response was startling. She'd never in her life felt this instant physical response to *anyone*. Not even when she'd first met Devon, her ex-husband.

She hadn't had sex in years, so the irony of experiencing lust at first sight, for a *bishop,* wasn't lost on her. God should have rejected this man's vow of celibacy. There was no freaking way it benefitted humankind. Her business thrived on this very feeling of unbridled lust. Now, experiencing it for the first time, she finally understood the power of it. This man, a man she knew she could not have under any circumstances, could drive her to forget all of her inhibitions.

River took a deep breath to reel herself in. Was it pheromones? Some annoying chemical reaction over which she apparently had no control? Her gaze dropped to his mouth. Grim. Sensual. Her gaze rose as his lips tightened. Captivated, she held his gaze for several skittering heartbeats. She didn't expect men to fall on her like starving dogs, but this one was unresponsive to even her innocent smile. He didn't show the slightest bit of interest in her as a fellow human being, let alone as a woman.

She didn't expect him to appreciate her legs or her boobs or even her sharp mind. But couldn't he acknowledge that she was breathing, and occupying the same space on his planet? Was that too much to ask?

Apparently so. He looked down into his drink, as if it held the answers to the questions of the Universe.

"Oliver spent almost all of his time up at the plant." Father Marcus drew her attention. "He rarely came into town, and even then, he never stayed long."

She glanced over at Franco. "Yet he had a room here?"

"He did, yes. He used it when he came down from his lab for a meal and a night off. He has--*had*--rooms in the plant facility and preferred spending most of his time there."

"What did he do for you, Franco?" River asked. "I never understood what a biochemical engineer had to do with mining emeralds." Oliver had gone into a lengthy-for-him explanation.

River had understood about three words.

"Liseo would be able to explain more fully, but Dr. Sullivan was involved with the design and optimization of the processes used in extracting the stones from the ore."

"Are there other engineers or someone else who worked with him at the plant? Perhaps one of them knows something?"

"No, Dr. Sullivan was the only one working in the lab. He's a brilliant man, but didn't—- How do I say this politely? He didn't work well with others."

River smiled. "Oliver isn't very social. He's always preferred his own company, and when he's working on an exciting project, he focuses on it to the exclusion of anything else. I'm hoping he might have left something behind that would give me a clue as to his whereabouts."

"Unlikely, my dear. Oliver packed everything and took it with him when he left."

River frowned. "Then maybe there's something in his rooms up at the plant that will—"

Franco shook his head. "No, nothing. I asked my son, Lisco, to check."

Disappointment closed her throat. Another dead end. River took a cautious sip of overly sweet lemonade to moisten her suddenly dry mouth. "Did he say *anything* about leaving?" she addressed both Father Marcus and Franco. "Going somewhere else?"

"Not to me," the priest said, honest regret in his voice. "I'm sorry, my dear." He glanced over at their host. "Franco?"

"As I told you on the phone the other day, after the explosion, your brother just-" He waved a ringed hand. "Disappeared."

Frowning, River sat on the edge of the uncomfortable sofa. "Are you implying he was responsible for the accident? Was he hurt?" Oh, God. None of this made sense.

"I'm not implying anything. The accident was just that. An accident. And no, he was not injured."

"Five people *died* in that accident, Miss Sullivan," the bishop offered flatly. His deep voice held a thread of disdainful superiority that made her hackles rise. "Perhaps he felt responsible, and *guilt* drove him away."

River sucked in a breath, his words like a physical blow to her chest. Had the bastard really just said that? Despite the attraction for which she had absolutely no explanation, River was starting to reciprocate his obvious dislike. She turned just enough to bring him into focus. What the hell did he have to be so pissy about?

"Perhaps. That is, *if* he was responsible, which I highly doubt," she said, expending extra effort to keep her voice cool. She was too hot, too tired, too *scared* to tiptoe around a man who'd disliked her on sight for absolutely no damned reason.

The fact that her body found him appealing was driving her crazy. He wasn't *that* appealing. He was unpleasant and condescending and, honestly, a jerk.

"Regardless, Oliver *wouldn't* disappear. This was his dream job. I don't understand why he'd leave without telling anyone. Without telling *me*." Oh, shit, she felt the sting of tears behind her lids, and concentrated on forcing them back.

Those piercing blue eyes turned to permafrost. "Does your brother have any reason to avoid you, Miss Sullivan? A man isn't necessarily missing just because he doesn't check in with his sister."

Dickhead. Prickles of dislike tingled her skin as tension ratcheted between them. What was this guy's freaking problem? She was tempted to give the sanctimonious bishop the finger. Instead, she maintained eye contact and managed, with only a small bite in her tone, to say, "Do you believe in reincarnation, Bishop?"

Eyes locked, he arched a brow. "Why?"

"Because clearly we met in another life and I did something *exceedingly* unpleasant to you. *Your Excellency*."

THREE

As she spoke, Daklin watched her mouth. Lush. Succulent. Shaped for pleasure. She looked fresh and pretty in her yellow and white dress, her lightly muscled arms, and long legs, bare. Sizable diamonds in her ear lobes caught the light, winking between strands of silky-looking sunny blonde hair that brushed her stubborn jaw and draped seductively over one eye.

The acid of the lukewarm lemonade felt as rough as liquid sandpaper as it slid down his dry throat. A real bishop would stay silent and not take her bait. He wasn't a real bishop.

"Touché, Miss Sullivan," he said dryly. "I'll keep my opinions to myself." He didn't want to be sober right now, and sure as shit didn't like that this woman jacked up his blood pressure without even trying. He was *working*, goddamn it, and River Sullivan was in the wrong damned place, at the wrong fucking time. He maintained his poker face. Cheeks flushed with annoyance, gray eyes stormy, River Sullivan was fucking adorable in her bewilderment as to why every male in a thousand mile radius wasn't falling at her feet and salivating. Up to, and including, a bishop.

If he wasn't in character, if he wasn't *working*, if he wasn't already in his own brand of fucking hell, he'd be damned happy to test the limits of her flirtatious behavior. Or grab a bottle of Tovaritch, his go-to solution for avoidance.

Her smile faded, and her glistening gray eyes suddenly became more serious. "Please don't, Your Excellency. I prefer knowing up front what people are thinking. Guessing is problematic, and assumptions are dangerous. I'm a firm believer in openness and honesty. Isn't that also what the Church promotes?"

"You don't edit, do you, Miss Sullivan?"

"Edit what?"

"Is there any filter between your thoughts and your mouth?"

"Rarely, Your Excellency. That isn't a sin, is it?"

No excuse or apology. He guessed her flirty behavior was intrinsic to her personality. It didn't seem to be something she was putting on for show. *Angel, another time and place.*

Only there'd be no other time and place. Daklin knew, with pretty much one hundred percent certainty he'd never leave Los Santos. To do his job, he'd die here. He was okay with that. However, he'd make damn sure every last fucking gram of E-1x, Francisco Xavier, his explosive engineer, and his mystery partner, went with him.

Consuming every drop of that bitching, unopened bottle of Tovaritch Premium Russian Vodka he'd brought with him would be his final "fuck you." Fitting. In his world order, that wouldn't be considered falling off the wagon.

Good to have something to look forward to. Daklin caught Marcus's mirth-filled brown eyes and fleeting smile at his exchange with River. Before taking the cloth twelve years ago, Marcus Cawcutt had been one of T-FLAC's top operatives. Daklin bet Marcus had thought his life of intrigue and espionage was behind him when he'd been given Los Santos, Cosio as his parish.

Like it or not, Father Marcus was now back in the game, thanks to Ramse Ortiz's father, who lived in the village and who had reported suspicious activity around the mine to his son, to Marcus, and ultimately to T-FLAC. A middle-aged woman, dressed head to toe in black, slipped into the room. Head bowed, she stood beside Xavier's chair until he acknowledged her by waving her away. He got to his feet, sophisticated and urbane, the perfect host. "Dinner is served. Come."

Franco offered his arm to Barbie, and Daklin followed with Marcus. Ramse Ortiz and a second bodyguard—-this one *not* T-FLAC—-fell into step behind them. Xavier's paranoia fit into T-FLAC's plans very well. Having Ram in the house doubled their chances of discovering anything useful.

Her slender back straight, River's heels tapped musically on the tiled floor. Her legs looked a mile long in five inch fuck me heels. Damn it, the shoes were even sexier than the bondage sandals she'd worn earlier.

Shit. Josh would've ragged the shit out of him about lusting

44

over a woman while he was on an op. It was Daklin's number one rule: Work was work. Sex was something else. Josh wasn't, *hadn't been*, a stickler for his big brother's rules. He'd always joked that he wouldn't die in the field. He'd be killed by a jealous husband, an international tango, for screwing his trophy wife.

Instead, Josh had been blown to Kingdom Come because Ash had made the fatal mistake of revealing to his ever-curious brother his current project. It was information Josh hadn't needed to know, a mind-fuck of a puzzle that Daklin should've known would intrigue his brother. Selfishly, he'd wanted to bring Josh in on the problem as he worked to neutralize the explosive.

Josh's brilliance had flaws, one being that he didn't think intuitively, and quickly, through all the potential consequences of each decision. It was a goddamned fatal flaw for an explosive expert. Daklin should've known Josh would return to the lab, and he should've been watching to intercept him. Josh always tried to be the one to reach the finish line first.

Damn you for dying on me, Josh. I'll never fucking forgive myself. I'll also miss you until I take my last breath. Daklin rubbed his chest, trying to assuage the ever-present heaviness and pain. His fist brushed the heavy gold cross hanging on a chain around his neck. It was a reminder of what he was here to do. Avenge his brother. Redeem himself by eliminating E-1x. There was no time for attractive blondes with hopeful eyes.

Daklin was grateful to get out of the stifling heat of the sitting room. The vast dining room was marginally cooler with two

45

sets of French doors opened to the inner courtyard. The room was as overdone and ridiculously formal as the rest of the house. Xavier's wife, or a decorator, favored heavy Spanish Colonial-style furniture in dark woods, lush fabrics, and plenty of gold leaf. An odd choice, considering they were in the middle of a jungle. The twenty-foot tall ceilings, with heavy, intricately painted beams didn't mitigate the heat. Family pictures, both painted on canvas and photographs in silver frames, were stacked six deep on every flat surface.

Hot, irrationally irritated, and salivating for a real drink, Daklin found himself absently rubbing at the persistent ache in his left thigh. With relief, he pulled out a heavy, high-backed chair facing the open doors and sank onto the hard seat.

There were only four table settings, and they faced each other over the wide expanse of the table. Daklin and Xavier, opposite Marcus and Barbie.

A gentle, loam-scented breeze ruffled Barbie's rich sunny hair as she sat across from him. As she made small talk with Xavier, the earthy breeze also brought with it a fresh, sophisticated perfume evocative of crisp cotton sheets and cool ocean breezes.

Father Marcus rounded the table to sit beside her. He rearranged his silverware on the brightly woven tablemat after sitting down.

"How long have you been here, Your Excellency?" She wrapped her fingers around the stem of her water glass as her gaze shifted from Xavier to him.

Like her toenails, her fingernails were painted red. Daklin imagined her wrapping her fingers around his dick the way she held the wineglass stem. He imagined the feel of her nails, on his chest, on his back, as she arched into him while she came. "I arrived earlier this afternoon, a few hours before you, as it happens."

He waited to see if she'd mention seeing him at the airport. She didn't.

The woman who'd called them in to dinner served the first course, along with a young, clearly pregnant woman with downcast eyes. They entered and set down bowls of steaming shrimp chowder at each place.

River picked up her spoon. "Where are you from, Bishop Daklin?" She dipped her spoon into her soup, then brought it to her lips and opened her mouth. No delicate trial to see if she'd like it. She merely took the spoon into her mouth then chewed and swallowed before dipping it into the spicy dish again.

Daklin imagined those soft lips closing around his dick, and the feel of her silky hair fisted in his hands. As his dick hardened, and his blood pressure spiked, he reminded himself she'd be gone tomorrow. He just had to put up with her for one night. Hell, it was only because he hadn't had sex in so long; he'd be turned on by any clean, mildly attractive woman.

He'd been injured in the explosion in Ben Talha and then again attempting to save Josh. Between the injuries, he'd been drunk, semi-sober, and then mostly drunk. Since Josh died, he'd been in rehab for both the leg and the boozing. All told, for the better of eighteen months, his focus had been on things other than fucking, and right about now, fucking was the only thing he wanted to focus on, because he suddenly wanted one more fuck before he died.

"Salem, Mass, originally." That much was true; the rest was a skillfully crafted cover. "Seminary college in Jamaica Plains, then I earned my doctorate in theology from Boston University." The truth was, he'd gone to MIT and been four years behind her brother's graduating class. Same courses, same degrees.

She picked up her glass, brought it to her lips without drinking, and watched him with serious eyes over the rim. "And is Boston where you minister, Your Excellency?"

"I'm bishop in Portland, Maine. What is it you do, Miss Sullivan?"

Marcus used a white handkerchief to blot the perspiration on his forehead. Fine for him, he wore a short-sleeved black shirt. Daklin was decked out in multiple layers of fabric that defied the breeze and made his balls sweat. Watching River Sullivan look at him with hungry eyes made Daklin blistering hot under his clerical collar and robes.

"I'm a clothing designer." She took a sip of water, then licked a glistening drop from the corner of her mouth. Her eyes were smoky with skillfully applied makeup, but her mouth was bare. Daklin found the soft pink of her unadorned lips unbearably arousing. "Lingerie. I have my own company based out of Portland, Oregon, and New York."

"Your own company? That's impressive. Would I be familiar with your brand, Miss Sullivan? Something similar to Agent Provocateur or La Perla, perhaps?"

"Both are my competitors, actually." Her gray eyes gleamed with amusement as she set the glass down without looking where she placed it. It tilted on the edge of the thick place mat as she picked up her spoon. "How interesting that you're so familiar with luxe, high-end lingerie, Your Excellency. Your lady friends must eagerly await their birthdays. You have excellent taste."

"One does not have to bite into a peach to know it's juicy, Miss Sullivan."

Now all Daklin could think of was what River might be wearing under that modest *ladies-that-lunch* dress. Marcus cleared his throat, breaking the tension that seemed to tighten like a silk thread across the table between Daklin and River.

"Where are Deifilia and the boys tonight, Franco?" Looking at Xavier, Marcus spread a crisp white napkin on his lap. From his round physique, it was apparent he enjoyed his meals, and his lack of T-FLAC's physical discipline was marked.

"I dropped Liseo and Delly in Santa de Porres to do some shopping before I picked up Bishop Daklin from the airport this morning." Xavier offered wine. No one accepted, and he poured a half a glass for himself. "Trini isn't feeling well. He might join us later."

According to intel, twenty-five year old Trinidad Xavier was a cokehead. He was probably upstairs sleeping off an expensive binge.

Xavier and his long-suffering, absent, wife Maria, had a dozen kids. Half were saints: a couple of nuns and several priests. The others, like Trini, and Salvador, who was currently enjoying the hospitality of a Turkish prison for drug possession, were on the sinner side.

Twenty-three year old Deifilia did clerical work at the plant. She spent most of her spare time shopping in the capital city. Both of Xavier's oldest sons, Eliseo and Trinidad, worked at the plant as well. Eliseo was in charge of the mining operation; Trinidad, in charge of the plant. Eliseo de facto ran things when his father was away.

T-FLAC intel indicated that extensive and expensive vacations with his wife and children were really a cover for Xavier's dealings with terrorists worldwide. The two sons weren't the sharpest knives in the drawer, and yet, according to intel, his business was thriving. According to Marcus, Xavier had returned to Los Santos ninety days ago. Ram's father had given them the head's up about the unusual mine activity just over a week ago and they'd hit the ground running. Marcus was a reliable source of intel. He lived and worked here. He knew all the players and he'd help them figure out if there was indeed someone above Xavier, so they could eliminate that player, too.

"Franco." Daklin realized he was watching River's hands fidgeting with the stem of her water glass, and dragged his attention to Xavier. "I'd like to visit the plant tomorrow to say prayers for the dead."

River's head shot up. "Who died? What happened?"

"The accident at the plant." Xavier told her. "Unfortunately, several men died that day. God rest their souls."

Your product, your fault, and sure as shit not an accident, you hypocritical asshat.

Eyes intent on Xavier's face, River's voice was raw as she asked, "When was the accident?"

God, she was pretty. And so fucking out of her element. Daklin could smell her light tropical fragrance from across the table. He had the insane urge to bury his face in the curve where her slender throat met the slope of her shoulder.

For Christ's sake, in seventy-two hours she wouldn't matter. He only had to keep his hands off her for two and a half fucking days. Or less, if she took the hint and hightailed it back to the airport in the morning.

"Three weeks ago."

"What day?"

"The seventeenth."

Her entire body seemed to sag with relief and she sucked in a sharp breath. "Was Oliver involved? Shi—" She closed her eyes for a moment, her throat working. "I'm so sorry about the people

51

killed, but are you sure my brother wasn't hurt?"

"It was an explosion, but Dr. Sullivan was not injured, my dear." Xavier leaned across the table, his tone earnest as he tried to ease River's fear. "I saw him later that day. He was unharmed."

Sullivan's disappearance could possibly be attributed to guilt for causing the explosion. Daklin glanced briefly at a silent Ram standing beside the door. The five operatives in town were sure to have checked that possibility, but it was worth another look.

Just that morning, they'd discovered that five million US dollars had been moved from Sullivan's bank account in the Cayman's at about the same time as the explosion. It was something else they were looking into. Possibly, Sullivan had planned this disappearance and rerouted his money to start a new life somewhere else. Pretty goddamn cold to leave his sister wondering and worrying.

Not his problem.

If Josh had disappeared, Daklin would've left no stone unturned in order to find him. He wouldn't have given a flying fuck if his brother wanted to be found or not. Knowing how he would behave in similar circumstances made him very much aware of how River must be feeling and what she might be willing to do to find her brother.

He didn't have to know her for more than an hour to be aware of how tenacious she was. She'd flown halfway around the world, and driven, alone, through the jungle on what could barely be described as a road. And despite her dubious welcome, she'd ignored Xavier's suggestion that she leave.

Her hands were beneath the table out of sight, but Daklin got the impression her fingers were tightly clasped as she braced herself for bad news. Her lashes fluttered upward as she looked at Xavier. "Was Oliver responsible?"

He admired the unflinching way she asked. A less observant person wouldn't notice the muscle contraction around her eyes, how her entire body seemed to be clenched in anticipation of more bad news.

He'd loved Josh like that. Unconditional love for the brother he'd failed. Jesus, all this sturm und drang made him crave a fucking drink. Too bad, because drinking wasn't on his schedule until this situation was sewn up nice and tight.

Soon.

"He's our biochemist and deals with explosives, my dear, so it is, of course, possible. But I don't cast blame. It was an accident."

As one of the young women served some kind of meat and rice dish, Daklin observed Xavier's eyes slide over her, over her lightly swollen belly and heavy bosom. If she was seventeen years old, she'd just made it there. He wondered if the child was Xavier's. Intel painted him as the kind of man who had sex with women indiscriminately, and he doubted a young, under-educated household employee from the village would have the power or resources to reject him.

Dark brown eyes finished eye fucking the pregnant girl and found Daklin's. Despite the soul-sucking heat, Xavier was decked out in a suit, coupled with a freshly ironed, light blue open necked shirt. He gave no indication that he was as hot and uncomfortable as the rest of them. Tall, and well groomed, Francisco Xavier looked as benign as someone's favorite uncle, a favorite uncle who mined and manufactured perhaps the most deadly explosive in the world.

"Liseo will return in a couple of days and he can take you up to the plant and give you a tour of our facilities, Your Excellency." Xavier frowned at the maid as she adroitly avoided his groping hand.

"I would appreciate that." Daklin shifted so the women could set his meal before him. "But I don't think it should wait. I don't need Eliseo to come with me. If I may borrow a vehicle, I'll drive myself up there at first light while it's still cool."

"You're welcome to take one of the four-wheel drive vehicles, Your Excellency. But I will come with you to ensure you don't become lost."

"I'd welcome your company, Franco." *No, I sure as hell wouldn't.* Daklin had zero interest in the explosion. He wanted to go up there to get the lay of the land. As he picked up his fork, he felt someone's gaze on him. Glancing up through his lashes, he found River's soft gray eyes focused on his mouth.

Fuck me.

FOUR

River lost her appetite. *Damn it, Oliver, what have you done? Is that why you gave me all that money? Did you run away from the problem instead of facing it?* Because now she had confirmation that her brother was very much alive. He'd called her two days after the explosion.

Alive but gone. *Will you let me find you?*

Father Marcus and Franco discussed a recent terrorist threat in Cosio and the political climate in their country. Bishop Daklin ate his meal and drank two glasses of lemonade, contributing little.

The two serving women came and went. River declined the *bienmesabe*, a honey, egg yoke and ground almond Venezuelan dessert she'd read about on the incoming flight. The name translated to "tastes good to me" and it *did* look delicious. Too bad she didn't have the appetite for it. With a sharp pang, she thought that Oliver would've loved the decadent looking rich coconut cake with layers of cream and meringue.

"May I go with you to the plant in the morning?" She was careful to direct her question to Franco. Bishop Daklin had made it clear that he'd be glad to drive her to the closest airport or landfill. Unless she could find her brother there, or she had to catch a plane to his location, River had no intention of leaving.

"It's not a particularly pleasant trip, my dear. By necessity, the mines are high in the mountains, so the processing plant and offices are nearby. The road is narrow and steep. You're welcome to sleep in. Your car will be repaired whenever you're ready to leave."

Wow, he couldn't be any plainer than that. "Oliver told me the drive is beautiful. I love heights," she said cheerfully, "and I slept for hours on the plane. I'll be up bright and early, ready for an adventure. I'd like to see where my brother worked. Maybe I'll get a sense of where he might have gone. As for leaving tomorrow, thank you for having someone fix that tire, but I'd like to stay for a few more days. With any luck, Oliver will return while I'm here. I'd be more than happy to move into a hotel if my staying in your home isn't convenient."

River presumed Franco wouldn't want to look bad in front of his guests and waited to see if he'd direct her to a hotel, or extend his hospitality.

"We have no hotels in Los Santos, I'm afraid. But you're welcome to stay another night, my dear. And if Bishop Daklin has no objections, it would be acceptable for you to accompany us in the morning."

Done and done. River smiled at him. "Thank you. You're very kind." *You.* Not your other guest.

Bishop Daklin gave her a look she couldn't interpret. She didn't care. What he thought had nothing to do with her. Unless he blocked her from finding Oliver for some reason. Then the gloves would come off.

"It's a lovely night," Father Daklin said when they finished their meal. "Would anyone like a stroll in Franco's beautiful garden?" He indicated the dimly illuminated inner courtyard beyond the French doors.

Franco rose, throwing his napkin down on his plate. "Your Exccllency, I would be honored if you'd take my confession before retiring. I pray that my apparition appears tonight so that you can witness how I am being blessed."

"Apparition? As in a vision?" River glanced between Franco and the bishop.

"Yes, an angel comes to m—"

"The appearance of an angel is, as yet, unsubstantiated." The bishop lay his hand on Franco's arm. He had big, elegant hands. Strong. Not bishop-like at all. Not that River had ever met a bishop before, but maybe this one plowed the fields or did kickboxing in his spare time. His broad shoulders indicated he did *some* form of strenuous exercise.

She studied his wintery blue X-ray eyes, and his sensual mouth, made to whisper sweet nothings in a woman's ear. What a freaking waste. If this was what bishops looked like in the Catholic Church, she'd gladly sit through an hour of mass, in the first pew, so he could pray over her.

River wondered briefly if a lapsed Protestant would go to hell for having salacious thoughts about a man of God.

"The Church's approval does not come easily or quickly," Bishop Daklin said. "The Church never gives approval on an apparition without exhaustive and repeated investigation. It isn't unusual for the Church to grant approval *after* the apparitions cease and/or after the death of the visionary. Apparitions are private revelations. You are free to believe in them without Church approval, so long as the apparition contains nothing which contravenes with faith and morals."

Wow, wasn't he cheerful? Franco went pale, as he gave the bishop a hopeful look. "I have given much money to the Vatican, Your Excellency—"

"Are you suggesting the Church accepted a bribe?"

"No. No. No, Your Excellency. Not at all."

"Do not believe every spirit," Bishop Daklin said in a voice that would make angels weep. Deep, and sensuous and, damn it, forbidden. "But test the spirits to see whether they are from God, for many false prophets have gone out into the world. 1 John 4:1."

"Yes, Your Excellency," Franco, face flushed, said earnestly. "But you'll bear witness yourself—"

"A walk in the garden will be pleasant." The bishop rounded the end of the table, and for the first time, River noticed he had a slight limp, favoring his left leg. Kicked by some dreamy-eyed church member, no doubt. Franco gave him an anxious look. "But you'll come—"

"That's why I'm here, Franco. Let's go out and enjoy the air before we go upstairs."

Side by side, the bishop and Franco set off down a wide path. Small landscaping lights flickered on to illuminate the path. The entire courtyard was flooded with bright moonlight, which left puddles of darkness in the shadows. The high walls of the hacienda surrounded the expansive inner courtyard on three sides, with a church with a bell tower on the fourth. The air, heavy with the smell of damp earth, carried the fruity-sweet scent of flowers. "Is that honeysuckle?"

"Yes, *lonicera periclymenum*. I always imagine I hear beautiful music when I smell their fragrance." Smiling, Father Marcus glanced up at her. "Over in that corner is a particularly spectacular bougainvillea. You have to come out and see it in the sunlight. The brilliant purple-pink color is remarkable. It's been here for at least fifty years."

The flowering vine the priest pointed at covered a large section of the stone wall. "Are you a gardener, Miss Sullivan?"

"*River*. No, unfortunately I have a black thumb. Besides, I live in a condo with a tiny balcony, and do a lot of traveling. But I love flowers, and this courtyard is spectacular. I'm sure it's even more so in sunlight."

"That it is. The whitewash of moonlight is beautiful, too. The bricks are a bit uneven. Do you need to take my arm?"

"Thanks, but I'm pretty sure footed. I wear heels all the time, over all kinds of terrain. But I'll grab you if I start to fall."

He smiled. "Are you always this cheerful, Miss River?"

"No, Father, I can also be impatient, outspoken, cranky,

and a workaholic."

He laughed. "In other words, human."

A bright white half-moon illuminated banks of red flowers on either side of a well-tended brick path that meandered between tall shrubs and trees, and then opened to areas filled with what were probably brightly colored flowers that looked beige in the moonlight. "Did Franco really see an angel?" she asked, intrigued.

"So he says. That's why Bishop Daklin is here. He's an investigative bishop. He'll report his findings directly to the Pope."

"Does everyone who sees an angel get a visit from a bishop with a direct line of communication to the Pope?"

The priest chuckled. "Francisco Xavier is very persuasive, very pious, and very generous with the church."

Understood. Not everyone who saw Jesus in a potato chip got a visit from a bishop. But this man donated a lot of money to the church, so the Vatican paid attention when he claimed to have seen an angel. Whether this had anything to do with Oliver's disappearance was unlikely. The fact that Oliver worked for a man who was so wealthy that his sighting of an angel warranted a visit from a bishop was certainly interesting.

"Do you think he'd let me see it too?"

"You could ask. We're the only people who know about it—and now you, of course. He wants it kept quiet, and I'm encouraging him to remain silent on the issue. None of us want Los Santos to become a site of devotion unless Bishop Daklin authenticates the apparitions and the Miracle Commission accepts his findings."

"So he'll probably be here for a while." River noticed men standing in the shadows along the path. She lowered her voice. "Are those bodyguards?"

"Franco is used to big cities. I'm afraid he's forgotten what it's like here in Los Santos."

"Oh? There are so many pictures of his wife and children throughout the house, I thought he lived here."

The priest smiled again. "He spends a lot of time here. But Maria likes to travel, and he dotes on his family."

"How many children does he have?" She stepped over a crack in the brick. "From the photos, it looks like quite a few."

"Twelve now. He had a daughter who died in infancy, and a thirty-one year old son, Amadis, who has spina bifida. Tragic. Franco likes to keep them close. He and Maria travel all over the world in hopes of finding a cure. The family has homes in America and Europe."

"I wondered where his wife was."

"Maria and the youngest boy, Teodoro, are currently in Rome. Franco wants to give another child to the church. Teo is sixteen. He's their last. Do you come from a large family, River?"

"No, it's just Oliver and myself. Our parents owned a convenience store in Portland." She swallowed the lump in her throat. It never got easier talking about them. Oliver was all she had left, the only other person who remembered their family.

Oliver, where the hell are you? "They were killed twelve

years ago in an armed robbery."

"I'm sorry."

"Me too. They were great, and I miss them every day. I was fifteen when they died. Oliver stuck around until I was old enough to take care of myself, then paid for my schooling when I wanted to get into clothing design." He was easy to talk to. "I haven't heard from him in weeks. That's unlike him. I'm sure you're aware that he has mild Asperger's? He's a creature of habit and lives by his routines and schedules. This explosion, whether it was his fault or not, would throw him off. Since his ASD makes empathy problematic, being surrounded by grieving families would make him extremely uncomfortable.

"I was not aware of that diagnosis, but it explains a great deal. I just thought he was a brilliant young scientist who was extremely focused and serious."

River smiled. "Oliver's off the charts brilliant, but he doesn't have much of a sense of humor."

Father Marcus patted her arm. "Then it's a blessing that *you* have enough joy for two." He held aside a branch for her as they rounded a corner. Ahead, Bishop Daklin and Franco talked quietly and intently, but River couldn't hear their conversation.

"Your brother is a smart man, and one Franco trusts implicitly. I'm sure he's all right. You know how focused he gets. He probably went off to chase some bit of information he needed, and he'll return to find you here waiting for him."

Oliver would be *pissed* to find her in Los Santos, River

knew. He had done everything but send a skywriter to dissuade her from ever visiting him here, up to and including stressing what a perv and all around terrible person his boss was. This, as far as River could tell, was a complete fabrication.

Francisco Xavier appeared to be a loving, and devoted family man, and not the sexual deviant her brother had portrayed. Although some of Oliver's detail amused River, Carly was right: her brother didn't have much imagination. She'd have to check out some of her brother's reading material while she was here.

#

By the time River and Father Marcus returned to the dining room, the other two men had disappeared inside. Father Marcus walked her to the foot of the Gone-With-The-Wind style sweeping staircase, said goodnight to her, and left.

River went upstairs, hoping she'd see Franco so she could ask if she could join in the apparition hunt, which would be a good distraction from the worry. But she didn't see either man, nor did she hear their voices, so she let herself into her room.

As she went to her suitcase to grab the t-shirt she wore to bed, she noticed that her crimson Chantilly lace *el roce* bra and matching thong were missing. "What the hell?" River dumped everything out on the bed to be sure. No red lace. "That's damn rude," she muttered as she repacked the case.

Someone had been in her room, rifled through her personal belongings, and had taken her damned underwear.

One of the maids, she suspected. She had more lingerie

than any woman could wear. Plenty more where that came from. But not here. Who would be stupid enough to steal something so obvious? She really didn't care that a maid had spotted something pretty and helped herself. If she worked in this overheated, gloomy house and saw pretty red lace, she'd probably have swiped it too.

It wasn't a big deal, she thought as she went to wash her face and brush her teeth. Definitely not anything she'd report to Franco.

She did not look for the book Oliver had used for reference material, figuring she might find more than she could handle right now. He had to have based his vilification of Franco on something, after all. But tonight, that would be asking too much for her poor libido.

Do not, she told herself firmly as she climbed into the high bed and turned off the light, *under any circumstances dream of piercing blue eyes, a hard jaw line, and a sexy, unsmiling mouth,* which of course was exactly what she did.

#

"Get rid of her."

"Her timing is unfortunate." Franco gripped the phone, sweating, waiting for a reaction from the man who dominated him in every aspect of his life.

Told not to come, in no uncertain terms, River Sullivan had shown up anyway, like a bad penny, unannounced. The woman's inconvenient presence wasn't his fault, and he resented his partner's implication.

The phone line crackled ominously. Dear Lord, he *hated* these calls, when he went from being the feared *el jefe* to *discussing* things like a lowly peon. An assistant. A worm. If his partner hadn't had so much damned power, Franco would just screw the woman until she died, and be done with the problem. Now that his partner held the keys to the operation, he was walking on pins and needles, doing everything he could not to piss off the crazy man.

"Get. Rid. Of. Her."

Those words, and the calm, smooth voice that delivered them, made him feel as if fire ants were crawling along his skin. Most people would've hated the stinging sensation, but Franco perversely relished it. Truly, it was the only small blessing received from his association with his partner. The tickling of his nerves matched the thrill of a new hunt. Did his partner mean to sanction this kill? If so, this was an order he'd willingly take. And perhaps since his partner only wanted her dead, he'd be none too picky about the method. Maybe Franco would get to fuck her to death anyway.

"Things are moving fast now." The crackling on the line juxtaposed with the velvety voice sent shivers of revulsion and need across Franco's cold skin, causing his balls to curl up tighter against his body with anticipation. "In three days everything will be in place. Either get rid of her before she gets nosey and discovers things she has no business discovering, or she'll have to die."

That was easy for his partner to say when he was physically distant and out of harm's way. Franco had Father Marcus and a bishop sent by the Pope to deal with, as well as his other duties. "This one can't just disappear without anyone noticing. She has friends, business associates. People know where she is. They'll miss her and come looking."

"And in three days *we* won't be here. Let them come."

"The fact that she's here in the first place indicates she's a stubborn little bitch. What would you suggest I do with her?"

"If she doesn't leave by morning, dispose of her."

Franco's heart leapt with excitement. Kill a pale-skinned blonde? Christ, yes. After playing with her for a while, if he could find the time. "*Kill* her?"

He needed clarification. No wrong moves. His partner was a man without humor. His methods of retribution made Franco's games look like child's play. The student had surpassed the master, and his partner now had skills Franco had only imagined before they met. Franco got an erection just thinking about the other man's methods of persuasion and reward. He both scared the living shit out of him and excited him unbearably. There was nothing the other man wouldn't do, no depravity he shied away from, no punishment too extreme.

Catarina had seen to that. Franco had been encouraged to watch, to learn at the feet of a dominatrix who used blood like an engine used oil.

"Don't give me fucking details. I've got work to do. Just do it."

"In my play room?"

"*My* playroom. If you have time to 'play,' then by all means, do whatever the hell you want with her. Just make sure her body isn't found to lead anyone back to us."

"Don't worry," Franco assured him. "It will be done to your satisfaction."

"Don't take too long. We have a goal. She isn't part of it. End of story."

"Tonight?"

"With a bishop in the house, you fucking moron?"

"I can make it look like an accident."

There was an annoyed growl at the other end of the phone, underscoring just how incompetent his partner believed him to be. "Never mind. You're incapable of that kind of planning. You play rough, and the girls die. You've gotten away with it so far, but no one believes those were accidents. Let the woman go up to the mine. I'll instruct the men to dispose of her there."

#

After observing the *apparition*, Xavier had attempted, at length, to convince him to authenticate what he'd seen. Daklin left Xavier to his prayers at midnight, telling him he was going for a run. In his own room, Daklin stripped off the robes, changed into lightweight running pants, and then went out.

By order of Xavier——ironic that his host wanted to protect

the bishop on his run—-fellow T-FLAC operative, and Xavier's personal bodyguard, Ramse Ortiz accompanied Daklin.

"Call me Ram," the operative told him as they moved through the dark village at a fucking *excruciating* limp that wasn't even a pretense at a jog. Two thigh surgeries down, five to go. He'd pass, thanks.

"How many surgeries?" Ram indicated his bum leg.

Word was Ramse Ortiz had been a physician before switching to full time operative. There was a story there, but Daklin wasn't about to share his medical history with him. "A couple."

"We won't compensate for your speed when we get up there."

Or lack thereof. "It won't be an issue."

"If you say so." Ramse Ortiz had no trouble keeping pace with him on the uneven, wet cobbled streets. It was good to be out in, fresh air that smelled of wet earth and green foliage. It had rained earlier, and the musical score of water dripping from the eaves mingled with the occasional cry of a bird, and the gruff note of a boar calling to its mate from the jungle surrounding the small village.

Ram was six feet of solid muscle. Dark eyes, dark hair. Like Daklin, his sharp eyes saw everything.

A native Cosian, Ram's father Renán lived in the village. It was he who'd tripped over intel, which he'd passed on to his son, who'd alerted T-FLAC. They, in turn, had put Ram in touch with

Father Marcus.

Discovering the priest was a former T-FLAC operative had been a revelation to those sent to investigate Ortiz's intel. They'd had no idea. Through Father Marcus Cawcutt, they quickly discovered that it wasn't just *any* explosive compound being excavated in the played-out emerald mines in the mountains shadowing the village; it was E-1x.

Los Santos, Cosio, was the point source of rawE-1x. The discovery was *huge*. But close on the heels of that earth-shattering intel was chatter that something big was about to go down. Something so large, so spectacularly bad that T-FLAC's intel was lit up like the Fourth of July. A more literally earth-shattering event.

T-FLAC had little time, and a compelling need to discover what, who and where. Ramse and four men had been dispatched immediately to the mining town. But they'd needed someone inside the house who was a confidant of Francisco Xavier. The plot to give Xavier a religious apparition had been born. With Marcus's help, the application to the Pope had been fast tracked so that Bishop Daklin could show up immediately. In the real world, that process would've taken months, if not years.

The Pope, aware of the ramifications should this op go south, had reluctantly given, if not exactly his blessing, his okay to the ruse. All the ducks were now in a row.

"In here." Ortiz indicated a narrow staircase inside a small, rundown two-story apartment building on the other side of town.

Pitch dark, no sign of life.

The other four members of Daklin's A-team waited on the second floor in a dimly lit one-room apartment. The building, a hovel, was barely habitable by animals, let alone humans. It used to house miners and plant workers, but was occupied at the moment only by their T-FLAC special ops support team. Thick black fabric covered the windows, making the heat inside oppressive.

Ryan Gibbs and Travis Nyhuis occupied the two bottomed out lawn chairs. Daklin and Ortiz squeezed into the small space, then propped themselves up against the wall on either side of the falling-off-its-hinges bathroom door at the back of the room.

Kai Turley, and Angel Aiza, standing in front of the two large screen monitors, turned to greet them.

A jerry-rigged swamp cooler, going full blast, wheezed out muggy, mold-scented air. Unlike the crappy apartment, the tech was state-of-the-art, top-of-the-line. Black power cables snaked across the floor, connected to powerful back-up super batteries. One monitor showed night vision views of the mine building and surrounding area. A light strafed swaths of dark ground, illuminating the patrolling soldiers and long low building that fronted the mine entrance itself.

The other monitor sectioned off the image into twelve squares, each showing an infrared image of various rooms in the hacienda. Any movement and the computer would alert them to the activity and they'd zoom in.

Aiza turned away from his keyboard to address Daklin. Husky, but without an ounce of fat, five nine-ish, his features were unremarkable. He'd blend in anywhere without a second glance. "How far back you want me to go?" He was a fellow bodyguard for *el jefe* and would be on duty at the hacienda tomorrow. Of Basque origin, and based in San Francisco, he was frequently assigned ops in South America. He could apparently change his vocal inflections to mimic the locals of any Latin country.

"When we went up to his quarters," Daklin instructed. He didn't want to relive the hours spent at dinner with River Sullivan. She was distracting enough in real time.

Agonizing pain shot through Daklin's leg. He resisted clamping his hand on his thigh. The scars, both surgical and bomb produced, and the pain, were no one's business, and best kept to himself. Hell, even he didn't want to acknowledge just how fucking much pain he was in. It was a sign of weakness he refused to give in to.

His body had always been a dependable machine, trained and honed, kept in prime condition for the work he loved. He'd never given his own physical limitations a thought. Now he had to consider them just to fucking cross the street.

He'd hated living with the uncertainty that the leg might not ever be the way it had been before two encounters with E-1x. This op would remove that uncertainty. There was a simple beauty in that. Daklin hated this agony-ridden body. He, it, craved a drink to combat the pain.

Damn, the beer smelled good. He could practically taste the bitter hops, and swallowed against the phantom sensation of the snap, crackle, and pop of the effervescence trailing down his throat. His fingers flexed, itching for the play of a cold metal can in his hand. Resolutely, he helped himself to a bottle of water from the cooler, then returned to his position on the back wall and cracked the top.

He took a slug of flat, tepid water.

Not the same. Not nearly the same.

He sure as shit refused to end up like his father, a sloppy, belligerent drunk who couldn't hold a job. At some point, Daklin had felt confident that one day he'd get to the point where he didn't crave it. Confidence that failure wasn't an option came easy to him; because he could do anything he put his mind to.

He'd goddamn well wanted *that* life: a life where there were so many good things happening that drinking himself into oblivion on a regular basis wasn't the one and only thing for which he lived.

Now he was sober by necessity and fucking unhappy about it.

Soon he wouldn't be sober, and then he'd be dead.

Win fucking win.

A small black lizard scurried up the wall and wriggled through a crack near the ceiling. Daklin propped a shoulder on the filthy, rough-plastered wall and returned his focus to a recorded feed of earlier events at the hacienda.

"Just a head's up," Gibbs told him. He and Nyhuis worked security at the plant. Gibbs was skilled at explosives. Daklin had worked with him a couple of years ago in Spain. The guy was solid and knew his shit. "The connection could go at any minute. Xavier has a jammer scrambling signals. There's a system lockdown in play. The security protocol allows administrators to tightly control which users can execute."

"Is there a fingerprint list?" Daklin asked.

"We found an .exe output file. It blocks unapproved applications. HQ is trying some new shit with the satellite to see if we can't boost the signals from our end. Spotty at best. It's like we're in a giant Faraday cage."

Daklin had already gotten that memo. But they weren't in a Faraday cage, which was a hollow conductor built to shield its contents from static electric fields and electromagnetic radiation. One the size necessary to cover the valley was physically impossible. Still, a powerful electric force field *was* blocking and cancelling out electrical charges for miles around. And that was a problem, since it blocked all signals and communications with their other teams, their Control at HQ, and each other.

He rolled the bottle over his sweaty chest. "Let's see what you've got."

FIVE

The feed showed himself and Xavier entering Xavier's bedroom. He looked like the real deal in the pink cassock, white rochet, and black Chimere. All he needed was a pointy hat and a purer heart and he'd be ready for a goddamn visit to the Vatican.

A large stone fireplace in the bedroom, filled with wood, sat unlit. Thick burgundy velvet drapes with miles of braided gold cording and tassels were drawn tightly over the windows.

"Has Echo located the jammer?" Echo was their eyes in the sky and tech unit on this op. Daklin chugged half the water, eyes on the screen as Xavier proudly pointed out a Saint Mary Magdalene relic, holy water, and a bronze miniature of the crucifixion. Xavier claimed all pieces came from the Vatican as gifts after hours and hours of prayer and devotion. And a shitload of money, no doubt.

He'd offered, and Daklin had declined, a gift of one of his most prized possessions; a small, thirteenth century, Russian pre-Mongolian pectoral brass Encolpion Crucifix cross obtained—Daklin was sure illegally—in Russia. Xavier was out to impress, and, if necessary, bribe his way into the Church's good graces to authenticate his apparition.

"All they've told us is that our comms are manually blocked," Ram told him. "It's weirdly erratic. Sometimes, we have the capability. Mostly, we don't. My father says it's been this way for months. He's always complaining that he never has any bars on his phone."

"We're all working on finding the jamming device," Turley added. He was a slight, sinewy black guy with intelligent eyes and an upbeat, professional vibe. A pilot, he flew anything with wings or rotors. "None of us wants to go in blind."

Daklin swigged his water. "Thermals?" So far, Nyhuis had yet to contribute. Daklin glanced at the back of the guy's bald head. There were only six operatives in the valley. He couldn't afford any dead wood. "Anything to add, Nyhuis?"

"Nah, not right now." He went back to cleaning his nails with a pocketknife.

Ortiz shook his head. "Nada on the thermals. And nada to our ground penetrating radar. When our comms are down, we're completely blind."

Not being able to communicate with his team on the ground was a problem. Not having the capability to see inside the building that was near the mine, and the mineshaft itself, was a major setback. "We need to fix this ASAP," Daklin said, stating the obvious. Then he addressed Turley. "Find some old fashioned walkie-talkies." With luck, Control might be eavesdropping from his all-seeing, all-knowing, op oversight position from HQ in

Montana. They were keeping a special eye and ear on him, no doubt. They trusted Daklin's expertise to do the job, but had told him flat out they were profoundly worried he'd fuck up.

So much for the vote of confidence.

"Any updates on our intel?"

Daklin had been updated prior to landing, but hadn't been on comm since. When he'd inserted his earpiece before leaving the hacienda, all he'd gotten was dead air.

Turley shrugged. "Our communications are sporadic, so we have only been able to get shit in small windows since we've been boots on the ground. Whatever is going down is still scheduled for the twelfth, three days from now. But we got some new intel an hour ago. The numbers 333 started popping up in the chatter. Location? Time? Part of a coordinate? Control's working on it."

Gibbs turned. "We're checking every lead, every scrap of cyber chatter. Of more immediate interest is that they uncovered a highly encrypted black net cloud site about an hour ago. One of the 333 chatter sources, in an extremely roundabout way, might be linked to this new cloud." "Extremely sophisticated. Never-before-seen. Hopefully, whatever's stored there will give us all the answers we need. Control will clue us in as soon as they have something."

"Excellent. Meantime, we'd better figure out this jamming shit before they have relevant and actionable intel for us. We need to be able to receive any whatever they figure out. If we don't get it, we'll be flying blind."

Flying blind was par for the course. Operatives rarely had all the pieces necessary to thwart the bad guys, or prevent an act of terror. Yet they were still more than capable of doing the job. It was harder, but not impossible. Even so, it sure as hell would help to have the majority of the information that T-FLAC could develop.

Aiza dug out a beer from the cooler, then slid down the wall to sit on the dirty tiled floor, extending his legs as he pulled the ring top. The sound made Daklin lick his lips. Vodka was his drug of choice, but he'd drink pretty much anything.

Last chance, dickhead. Last fucking chance. For him, this was a booze free op by necessity. He'd pop the cap on the vodka soon enough. Until then, he'd stay clean and fucking sober. Even if it killed him. Daklin let out a hoarse laugh.

"You okay?" Ram shot him a puzzled glance.

"We have forty-eight hours to figure this out, people. Every minute counts." Daklin waved the plastic bottle to indicate everyone return their attention to the monitor.

"Fortunately, the feed is recorded on site as well, so we might not see shit in real time. But with Ram inside the hacienda, we at least have something," Gibbs offered, still nursing his first beer as he leaned back, legs extended, in one of the old webbed lawn chairs. "We had comms for six minutes yesterday, and ten minutes about half an hour ago. That's it."Daklin rubbed the bottle over his sweaty chest again, considering a hunch that seemed logical. "Someone on the ground must have needed to make contact outside the valley."

"The video feed from the house doesn't seem to be affected by the jam, so we're trying to feed off that signal for the rest of the comms. So far it hasn't worked, but we'll keep trying," Gibbs said. "We have sporadic eyes and ears on the majority of the rooms."

Daklin's gaze roamed Xavier's private quarters on the screen, picking out details he'd been too busy to notice at the time, like the dust-free spot on the altar next to Mary.

"Hold it right there," Daklin ordered. "Zoom in on the top of the altar on the left. See that? No dust. Something was there. A picture frame? See the mark of the easel? Same as the fancy silver frames on every flat surface in the house. That's prime real estate. His inner sanctum is where he keeps his most valued and prized religious relics. Go back to earlier feeds and see what sat there. Who was it a photograph of?" Daklin glanced at the others.

"His wife, maybe?" Ryan Gibbs suggested. "There's been nothing in that spot since we've been monitoring the house."

"Well, something was there. Who, and why was it removed? And when? Let's talk to whoever cleans his rooms."

"I'll talk to Juanita, the girl who served your dinner. She's my cousin," Ram offered, using the bottom of his shirt to wipe sweat off his forehead, exposing a jagged scar across his belly. "Man, I forgot how hot it gets in the valley. Temp doesn't even drop at night."

Turley, pilot, explosives engineer, and a veteran operative who'd been with T-FLAC about the same dozen years as Daklin, shook his head. His dark skin gleamed with perspiration in the flickering light from the screen. He kept watching the play by play from a few hours earlier. He balanced his open beer can precariously on his up-drawn knee, but had yet to drink. "No A/C at the hacienda. It was built in the 1800's and the wiring doesn't support it. Ceiling fans don't cut it."

Gibbs ran his hand over his short-cropped, light brown hair. "You're going up to the plant with him, right, Daklin?"

"Yeah." Xavier and Chirpy Barbie. Should be fun. *Not.* Daklin, watching Xavier's expressions and hand gestures as he talked on the screen, said, "Tomorrow, during the day, I'll check out the area with Xavier. Tomorrow night we'll recon. The night after that, we set the charges. Talk to me about security."

"He has an army up there," Aiza told him. "Private contractors. We guesstimate upwards of a hundred. Mostly Russian, military-trained."

"Ruskies don't fuckin' sleep," Nyhuis added before slugging back a mouthful of beer. "They're like robots."

Daklin rotated a kink out of his neck, wished for his icy vodka, and chugged warm water. "They've gotta sleep. Where and when?"

"Barracks off the mine road," Ram responded. "Eighty percent of the men on duty at all times. He keeps security outside. No one allowed inside either the mine or the building. Guard towers. Heavy muscle, well armed, well organized. Twelve man patrols. Doberman pinchers. LED stadium lights. Soldiers sleep on the property most nights. The bunks there beat this shithole, but not by much. We're given our assignments every night, and our locations are random until we report for duty on the property, then the guy in charge, Vadim, no other name, tells us where to patrol.

"Facial rec on this guy?"

"Nothing."

"Why aren't you guys in the barracks?" Daklin asked. It wasn't just curiosity. They had less than seventy-two hours to learn how everything ticked, how everything fit together. How everything could be broken apart. Getting that intel on the premises beat hanging out miles away.

"Yeah, that came as an unwelcome surprise," Ram admitted. "New hires aren't allowed to be up there at night. It takes six months to prove loyalty or some such. We're fortunate Xavier agreed to hire so many of us at one time. My dad's word was good, and he's worked for el jefe for thirty years. He's well trusted." Ram looked at each man in turn, his expression grim. "I'm trusting you guys to keep my village safe and not fucking get my father killed in the crossfire."

"We're blowing a mountain riddled with raw E-1x. There will be no controlling the blast. Zip. Zero. There will be collateral damage, and a shit ton of it. Charlie team will evacuate villagers starting tomorrow, well before the fireworks. Ram, make sure your dad gets the hell out." Daklin ran his hand around the back of his sweaty neck. "What else do we know?"

"Security has plenty of weapons, enough ammo to take down a decent sized army, and the skills to make good use of both," Gibbs answered. "They train daily. They're machines. They know what they're doing, and have orders to kill all intruders."

"Who are they expecting?" Daklin asked, not taking his eye off Xavier on screen as he expounded on a rosary he'd been given at St. Basil's Cathedral in Moscow. Each religious artifact had a story, and Xavier was determined to tell Bishop Daklin every one in an effort to cement his Godliness.

Not getting any answer, Daklin continued. "Both the ALNF and Escobar Maza's Sangre Y Puño were taken out by operative Riva Rimaldi last year. We didn't even know that he mined E-1x here until a week ago."

Daklin drank deeply, then went on. "This army of his was hired sometime in the last year, right? What precipitated the massive hire? The war between the ALNF and SYP's? Something else? We need answers, guys. Now. I repeat: who the fuck are they expecting? Do they anticipate tangos looking to score his emeralds after the guerillas are driven out?"

"He's sitting on an estimated twenty-trillion dollars in Nuts up there. Processed and ready to ship," Turley offered. "If anyone other than us figures out what he has, and how much, you can bet they'll crawl out of the woodwork and right up his ass."

"We'd better be quick and damned efficient," Daklin told his men. "If any tangos hear the same chatter we did, they'll know that he's planning Armageddon. They'll want in on the action. That's not gonna happen on our watch."

Aiza crossed himself. "Amen."

They all paused to listen as their comms went live with a sudden buzz. They had a date. Now they had the numbers 333.

What the numbers meant was anybody's guess.

"Why don't we just go up the fucking mountain right now and blow it to hell? Why the fuck wait?" Nyhuis demanded, shooting Turley a belligerent look as he rubbed both hands over his bald head. His smile brought to mind a serial killer. Records indicated the guy was a proponent of hand-to-hand combat, that he'd killed five heavily armed tangos one morning before breakfast with nothing but his bare hands. "We could get it done, go the fuck back home for our next assignment?"

His thick neck swiveled so he faced Daklin over his heavy shoulder. "You've been here one fucking *day*. We've been here almost a sodding week." Crossing his feet at the ankle, he rested his beer can on his chest.

"There's fuck-all to do in this Halcion-sucking hick village. No chicks worth porking, gotta drive all the way to hell-and-gone and into Abad to buy our booze. This could be over before anyone wakes up for fucking breakfast, right?" Nyhuis glanced from man to man.

"This isn't a tropical vacation, Nyhuis. No more booze, no

women. Recon tomorrow night. Evacuate villagers." Daklin checked his temper. "Set charges the night after. Anyone got a problem with that?"

Nobody voiced a problem.

"Anything on Dr. Sullivan?"

"No." Nyhuis shrugged. "People around here don't talk about him. Like at *all*."

"No one talked about him at MIT, either. He was ahead of me by several years. He's the epitome of an antisocial nerd. Kept his head down, barely communicated. See if you can find out where he went. His sister seems like she'll be a dog with a bone until she gets some answers."

"I'll ask around tomorrow," Ram told him.

"Do that. Let Control know we're looking." T-FLAC wanted the product, they wanted the buyers, they wanted Xavier, and they needed Sullivan to tell them how the raw material was manufactured into the Nuts for easy distribution. *And* they *had* to find out how to diffuse the bombs made from said product. Sullivan was the only person who could tell them how to defuse any future bombs.

In the meantime, they'd light up the fucking mountain and get rid of E-1x once and for all.

I'll have peace. Peace and redemption.

Daklin thought of Sullivan's sister. She'd had a long flight and a stressful day. He wondered how she slept. Curled in a ball, or sprawled out across the bed? Nude, or in some of the lingerie she designed? He could find out easily enough. There was a camera in her room, put there in anticipation of an appearance from Sullivan.

On the screen, he and Xavier circumvented his massive, carved mahogany bed, draped in dark blue velvet and mounded with shiny gold pillows that took center stage. "You see the apparition, not next door in the *church*, but here in your personal chapel?" Daklin was asking Franco.

He knew exactly where Xavier saw his apparition. The T-FLAC operatives had set up the state-of-the-art projection equipment to make it happen. Every night at eleven, they were projecting videos, produced in Montana through multi-media streaming into Xavier's private chapel off his bedroom.

A microscopic lens, hidden in the eye of the painting of the Virgin Mary hanging above the altar, relayed in real time footage to the operatives across town and also to HQ back in Montana, *when* the comms worked.

At HQ, Xavier's every word and micro expression were analyzed so that they could tailor the next apparition specifically to extract more precise and specific intel.

"The Madonna comes to me here, Your Excellency." The pious look on Xavier's face was more proud than humble. He was about bursting out of his suit, showing off to the bishop.

"Other than yourself and Father Marcus, has anyone else seen it?" Daklin asked.

Watching the replay, Angel Aiza laughed. "Yeah, only about fifty of us so far."

While they kept the apparitions going, Daklin's Alpha team--the crew with him in Los Santos--was to eliminate the only known source of the compound E-1x, eliminate Xavier, and capture Oliver Sullivan.

Bravo team had been tasked to chase down the location of a truck suspected to be carrying a payload containing the finished explosives on its way to fuck-knew-where. A couple of ounces of E-1x was enough to turn all of Manhattan into a desolate, burned out crater. HQ scientists had determined that with enough material, E-1x could blow a hole deep enough to fracture the earth's crust, or blow a small country off the map completely. Carrying a horrific amount of E-1x to unleash on the world in one go, Bravo had tracked the vehicle from Los Santos to half way over the mountain range, and then it had disappeared. Could've made it through Peru or Venezuela to the coast and be in a container on its way to Anywhereistan.

Charlie team had been tasked with evacuation. They were waiting over the pass to transport the villagers out of the valley before Daklin and his team blew the mountain. Delta team waitedat the pass for orders to back up the Alpha team.

"Fast forward to the apparition," Daklin ordered. The pain in his leg from sitting in a plane for hours, driving to the valley, and the half-assed attempt at jogging earlier was almost down to a dull roar. With any luck, he'd be able to get some shuteye and be ready for morning.

"Then let's go straight to dessert." Nyhuis smacked his lips as he rubbed his crotch

Daklin ignored him. The crew who'd put together the short film of the apparition had found a fresh-faced young woman who looked eerily like the two-foot high, carved and painted Madonna statue on Xavier's altar. "If I didn't know this was movie magic I would've bought into it myself." The images of the actress, dressed in identical blue robes, had been superimposed over the statue, and looked unnervingly authentic. He'd been standing a mere three feet away in the chapel, and still Daklin had found the hair on the back of his neck lifting as she silently reached out to Xavier.

Faux blood tears welled in her blue eyes as she soundlessly whispered Xavier's name. Then she disappeared, making it look as though she'd gone from statue to live woman and back to an inanimate figurine again.

He rubbed a hand around the back of his neck as he pushed away from the wall. "Damn good job. Ramp it up tomorrow night. Add 333 and twelfth to what she's saying. Hopefully we'll get some answers."

On the screen, the 'bishop' had just told Xavier it would take his witnessing more than one apparition to substantiate the claim. Xavier had had a fucking meltdown.

"Man, he did *not* like hearing that the good bishop wasn't going to put in a call to the High See Rome immediately." Turley sat forward, his teeth a flash of white in the dimness.

"Okay, that show's over, dickheads." Nyhuis grabbed the keyboard and clicked to another view of one of the rooms in the house. "I'm ready for some sweetness."

Daklin, having just tossed his empty bottle into an overflowing trash can, turned and got a full frontal view of River Sullivan strolling bare-assed naked out of her bathroom, her sleek body beaded with droplets of water.

"Now that's what I'm talking about," Nyhuis said.

"Fuck me," someone else said with real feeling.

"Holy shit, is that a-"

The others commented, too, but the melded voices muted to the faint buzz of bees.

Jesus H. Christ. Instantly rock hard, Daklin felt sucker punched. His tongue stuck to the roof of his dry mouth. She was all sleek curves and glistening skin. Slicked back wet hair exposed the oval perfection of her face. She was so pretty, she made his balls ache. Heartbeat tripping unevenly, his gaze travelled to her small, perky breasts and hard pale pink nipples. His gaze lingered on the smooth skin of her belly, then traveled slowly lower. A pale, bikini bottom outline indicated the lady not only tanned topless, but she was also a natural blonde. The pale fluff between her lightly tanned legs was trimmed into a neat heart shape.

Kill me now.

He wanted to taste her. Everywhere, but especially there at the apex where dewy, golden curls covered her mound. Dozens of ways to react to the visual feast filled his mind: lunge and lick the image on the monitor, get a cockstand, rein it in. Son of a *fucking* bitch. This op was already a test. Adding her to the mix was like throwing gasoline on the flame.

Hell. With any other op, he *would've* failed. Gladly, with a fucking-aye-hoorah to the genetic wonder of a natural blonde, her perky breasts, and drops of water sluicing slowly over skin calling for his touch.

"Turn it off," Daklin managed to say in a calm and authoritative tone he didn't feel, making the only correct choice. Correct, not for himself, but for T-FLAC. "Delete all the footage, and turn off the surveillance camera in the lady's bedroom. Immediately. She's not a tango, and we're not voyeurs. Turn. It. The. Fuck. *Off.* Permanently."

His racing heartbeat sounded like a drumbeat in his ears. The bigger, *much bigger*, problem was he was so fucking hard; he could pole vault back to the hacienda.

Dear God.

Behind him, Nyhuis grumbled. Daklin felt the exact same way. The screen returned to the room-by-room grid, with one black square. Good enough. "Let's take a look at that topographic map."

After a dose of the naked splendor that was River Sullivan, topographic maps weren't what he felt like looking at, but for this job, the stakes were too high to do anything but work. He couldn't fail. It wasn't an option. He'd seen maps, aerial surveillance footage, satellite infrared, and ground penetrating X-rays. Now that he was boots on the ground, he wanted to see everything for himself in real time.

A real time image of Miss Sullivan's naked body was now

imprinted on the back of his throbbing eyeballs. *Fuck.*

Turley retrieved a roll of maps and spread them out on the locked gun vault they were using as a coffee table. He punched a finger on the map as he spoke. "Here's the mine entrance. Excavated shafts go into the mountain, approximately fifteen thousand feet."

"How stable are the shafts?" Daklin asked. Three miles of dug out tunnel was a long way in, and gave them no room for fuck-ups if they had to haul ass to get out. Old, unstable mines could collapse before the first explosive blew if they didn't set the charge correctly. Worse, even if they did set them correctly, they could destabilize the mountain enough to cause cave-ins to happen before they ever got out.

Before the others got out.

He and a bottle of Tovaritch would have a front row seat.

"This one and this one are okay, I think." Gibbs leaned over to indicate which ones. "Judge for yourself when we go up tomorrow. These three," he said, pointing to the map, "We're on shaky ground, literally. No one has extracted product from themfor about a year or more. They're either played out or just too damned dangerous."

"We confirmed Sullivan *wasn't* one of the people killed or injured in the explosion last month," Aiza said.

"You went into the lab, saw the bodies?"

"New hires aren't allowed in the building," Ram told him. "Hell, *I'm* not allowed in the building and I'm practically a relative."

"But you saw where the explosion took place?"

"Nope." Turley shook his head. "The building is about a thousand feet directly in front of the main mine opening. We're talking high security fencing, titanium gates, and no entrance without authorization. No exceptions. They've done a damn good job of securing the facility." He nodded to Ortiz. "Tell Daklin about the explosion the day before we arrived."

Ram shifted his shoulder on the wall. "My father told me there was a small explosion behind the gates the previous morning."

"Yeah, I heard." And he'd seen the color drain from River's face when she'd thought her brother might've been involved. "*How* small?"

"Semtex? Quarter stick. E-1x? Quarter of a *gram* maybe?"

Daklin considered the possibilities. "Misdirect?"

Gibbs scratched his jaw. "We're thinking."

"Anyone know if Sullivan left before you guys got here?"

Turley shrugged. "Possible. No one's seen him in weeks. Not that unusual. Apparently, he comes down to town every couple of weeks, stays at the hacienda for one night, gets supplies, and goes back. Security does the driving. Sullivan doesn't drive. Sucker could'a *walked* out. But all you'd have to do is take a look at him, and you'd see that guy hasn't done a days' worth of anything physical in his life. He's a lab potato."

Turley grinned. "Apparently he chain smokes or chews

Nicorette gum incessantly. He was supposed to have the brains to chew on the gum when he was working in the lab. Guess he fucking forgot *that* rule three weeks ago when he lit up and everything went to shit with a big boom."

"Is the plant large enough for him to hide there, unnoticed?" Daklin asked.

Gibbs shrugged. "Sure, it's possible. It's a big place. But why hide, and from whom?"

"Good question." Daklin chugged his water. "Does Xavier know where he is? Does Eliseo?"

Nyhuis shrugged. "Maybe. Seems like one of them would have to. You're in the house. Maybe the bishop could ask?"

"Rest assured, I will."

"Xavier has an encrypted computer in his office at the hacienda." Aiza leaned back on his hands. "I've almost figured out the encryption. Once we're there, we can see what he has to hide."

Gibbs frowned. "Could Sullivan be somewhere else tweaking the formula for the bombs? How could he make that shit any worse?"

What they'd seen was as bad as any of them had ever witnessed, and they'd seen the worst, most lethal explosives worldwide. The impact of even the smallest amount of E-1x was a hundred times *worse* than that.

Daklin's leg sent piercing reminders shooting through his entire body that he wasn't ready to return to the hacienda yet. Hell, he wasn't ready to *stand* for any length of time yet.

River was a finely tuned Porsche of a woman, one who'd deserved to be treated with skill and precision. He wondered if his performance capabilities—-hindered by his leg injury—-would be up to par, then wondered what the fuck was wrong with his brain.

Yeah, she might have the conditioning of a sleek sports car. But she wasn't one he was going to be driving anytime soon. Or ever.

"How many people work at the plant? And how many in the mines?" Daklin asked.

"Forty some in the mines. In the office, eight, nine, once in a while, the daughter," Turley told him. "Doing what, we have no idea. All anyone sees or mentions is her talking on the phone mostly, when there's a signal, and doing her nails. Then there's the two sons. Trinidad is a cokehead, so he rarely shows. Liseo pretty much runs the place with his father. Or on his own, when Xavier's gone."

Daklin pushed away from the wall. His leg screamed in protest. He forced his expression to remain unchanged when he wanted to grunt, scream, pound out the pain on the stone wall. He couldn't prevent the perspiration from forming on his brow. "We're on a timer. Whether the other team finds that truck or not, we have less than seventy-two hours to set the charges, clear the village, and blow the fuck out of that mine."

Aiza gave him a mock salute. "See you at the party tomorrow night."

Daklin glanced at Ram who was getting ready to

accompany him back to the hacienda. "What party?"

"The villagers want to meet the bishop. It's a huge honor having you visit our humble village. Everyone will be attending."

Crap. He'd have to be on his most pious behavior. It would also delay going up to the mines after dark. "At the hacienda?"

Gibbs nodded. "You're an asset, man. The guy's got to show off, right?"

"Let's hit the road," Daklin told Ortiz. At least he could get a few hours shut-eye before he had to come face-to-face with his new, unwelcome fantasy.

He craved a taste of River Sullivan more than he craved a slug of vodka. If given an opportunity to taste her, he knew exactly what he'd do first on bended knee, and it had nothing to do with prayer. At least, not the kind he'd been studying for in his role as bishop.

That was an unexpected kick in the head. Because the pain in his balls and full-throttle longing in his dick were competing with the sharp agony in his leg. As he limped back to the hacienda, he realized which type of pain was winning.

Goddammit, he needed a drink. Or River. Or a river of fucking vodka. His body told him just River would do, while his brain told him he'd lost his fucking mind and he better get his shit together, pronto.

SIX

Heatless sunlight grazed the edges of the trees as Ram drove up the steep, winding mountain road at dawn the next day. Xavier was in the front passenger seat. Daklin, in back, was uselessly clamping his fingers around the pain in his thigh and gritting his teeth every time they hit a pothole in the road.

The blast at T-FLAC's Montana lab eighteen months ago had sent him airborne two hundred feet. He'd broken so many bones; they doubted he'd ever walk again. Yet, even with his femur protruding from his mangled left leg, which had already been injured from the previous op, he'd dragged, crawled, and cursed his way to the burning building to look for his little brother.

After the second corrective surgery sixteen months ago, the T-FLAC doctors gave him a prescription for Zohydro, a new opiate ten times more potent than Vicodin. Daklin was damn well going to take the doctors' word for the potency. If he started taking something that strong, he was worried he'd never stop. The proviso was that if he took the meds, he'd be benched until he didn't need them any longer. Bottom line: if he swallowed one of those fucking pills, he'd lose his job.

He'd crumpled the prescription and tossed it on the way out of the doc's office. Hell, yeah, he still needed pain meds. The stronger the better. Standing, sitting, walking, or remaining still. It didn't matter; it fucking hurt. The agony in his thigh was unrelenting and never-ending, but nothing compared to the bitter-to-the-fucking-core pain of losing Josh.

All he had to do was think of Josh's easy smile and laughing blue eyes, and, like a bite of teeth clamping on a bullet, he found the strength to make himself walk. Now he was working his way up to a run. On good days, he could even sprint a few yards at a time.

He'd managed to bullshit through his fitness exams. He'd always been trustworthy. No one doubted his ability to heal fast, and they'd sent him back into the field, where he'd used booze as a pain management tool one too many times.

Daklin was heeding the warnings. Fuck this one up, use booze to medicate, and he was out of T-FLAC. No more chances. He'd fallen a long, long, fucking long way down.

No booze, no chicks, no fuck-ups.

His life, and those of his men, would depend on his speed, mobility, and sober thinking. He'd work through the pain, just as he'd work through resisting booze.

Mind over matter.

The heavy-duty truck bounced and jolted over potholes and ridges left by pounding tropical rains followed by baking heat. Even though he'd left the dress robes and layers of fabric at the house, the black pants, black shirt, and white clerical collar weren't exactly tropical attire.

The road snaked up the side of the mountain. The Yungas, a sub-tropical montane comprising both deciduous and evergreen forest, flanked the eastern slopes. Daklin knew from the research he had done while en route from Montana that this area had hundreds of species of birds, mammals, and reptiles found nowhere else in the world. Banks of giant-size lush green ferns lined the road and underbrush, and thin waving branches of colorful orchids the size of dinner plates broke the miles of green with bright splashes of purple, pink, or orange.

He didn't care about what was pretty, but he'd have to watch for the poisonous and carnivorous. The vegetation obscured the steepness of this side of the mountain range, along with its caves, cliffs, ridges, and valleys. All of it hid various dangers just waiting to pluck out your eyeballs and eat them for breakfast. "We'll be there in ten minutes," Ram said, meeting Daklin's eyes in the rearview mirror.

There had been no hiding his pain when he and Ram had returned to the hacienda the previous night. Daklin had given the Ram a brief, unemotional overview of the event leading to his injury. The guy had been a doctor. He could fill in the blanks if he chose to do so. Daklin didn't mention Josh. He hadn't said his brother's name aloud in over a year.

Returning to his room in the early hours of the morning, Daklin had opened the window to let out some of the heat. He'd stripped, showered, and then, naked and wet, flung himself on the bed. Thank God he didn't need much sleep, because these days, he got precious little.

He'd only managed to fall down the rabbit hole after he'd conjured an explicit, detailed fantasy involving an iced bottle of Tovaritch, a hot and naked River Sullivan, and his fist.

"There is water in the cooler behind you, Your Excellency," Ram addressed Daklin, jolting his thoughts back to the present. The operative/bodyguard turned to Xavier. "Would you like some cold water, jefe?" he asked in the local dialect.

Daklin took a bottle from the small cooler in the other foot well and twisted off the cap. Right then, he'd give both his nuts for a handful of the opiates or a half dozen bottles of vodka to go with it. A few hours of blessed relief would do wonders for his disposition, which was hanging on by a fucking thread. He just wanted to say fuck it, kill Xavier, and blow the shit out of this mountain now instead of waiting one more day. That should be enough retribution for E-1x killing Josh and thousands of other people. Did he have to fucking avenge everyone in the whole goddamned world?

Yeah. Apparently so. Or so he'd think, if he was pain and guilt free. He had to go with what he would've done under optimal circumstances.

One thing he wasn't prepared to slap on his plate was spending any more time than was absolutely necessary with River. With any luck—-not that he believed in luck—-he'd encounter the mysteriously absent Oliver Sullivan and reunite the two. Then he'd send Sullivan, under armed guard, directly to Montana, and his sister to wherever the hell she wanted to go. Other than anywhere near *him*.

This morning, before their departure, Daklin had suggested they not wake her, but leave right away to avoid the heat. Since he didn't know her, he wasn't sure how well that decision would manifest when they returned. Tears? Fury? He anticipated all the emotions that followed when a beautiful woman used to getting her own way was thwarted.

Tough shit.

All he knew was he couldn't handle the pain and her at the same damned time. Something would have to give, and he couldn't afford for it to be his resolve.

#

"Okay, that's just freaking rude!" Hands on her hips, River walked outside at six a.m., just in time to watch the taillights of the big truck as it turned the corner at the bottom of the hill. Standing in the driveway of the hacienda, she looked down the empty road. "Did you leave this early so I wouldn't be able to go with you? Or did you forget I was here?" *Probably both.* She was perfectly aware she was here under sufferance. The bishop didn't like her, and though Franco had been polite about letting her stay, he hadn't seemed terribly enthusiastic about it.

She got it. But that didn't mean she liked it. It didn't mean she'd leave either. "Fine," she said aloud, walking back into the house through the massive, carved, teak double doors with sidelights of stained glass that looked as if they should be in a church somewhere. "I have plenty to do to amuse myself. Just bring Oliver back with you and all will be forgiven."

She'd dealt with plenty of opposition and stonewalling when she was starting her business. She'd bulldozed her way through, around, or over. All that was important here was the wellbeing of Oliver. The rest just...was.

Running up the curved stairs with its intricate, black, wrought iron railings, she returned to her room to change out of her jeans and T-shirt and into something suitable for a run around the quaint town. She could spend some time searching the room more thoroughly, but she decided she'd be better served talking to the villagers. If Oliver wasn't with the men when they returned, she'd look for clues in the room he occasionally occupied.

She'd ask some questions, get a feel for the place Oliver had made home, and find a shady spot to sit and sip a cold drink where she could talk to the locals.

Wearing black running shorts, a bright pink sports bra, and her favorite pink running shoes, River clipped a neoprene, pocketed belt to her hip. It carried her cell phone, passport, and a small water bottle, which she filled from the bottles on the table in her bedroom. There wasn't a soul around as she ran down the stairs and exited the house.

She set off down the driveway and onto what passed for the main road, passing a quaint little stone church attached to the end of the main house. Her red rental car was nowhere in sight. Hopefully someone was repairing the tire, although, as adventurous as she was, she wasn't looking forward to driving down those switchbacks for the return trip to the airport in the old vehicle. Now, if she'd had her Tesla and an open road, *that* would be a different story.

If Oliver *had* disappeared, who'd taken him? He didn't drive, so someone must know when and how he'd left.

After a few warm up stretches, she plugged her earbuds into her cellphone, realized she had no signal for calls or the live streaming station she typically used, and started out at an easy jog listening to a playlist of upbeat music that she'd designed for fast-paced runs. The street was empty of people or vehicles, the air cool and fresh with the crisp fragrance of green growing things. In a few hours, it would probably be as hot and steamy as it had been yesterday. This was a great time to get out and talk to people while burning off some of her frustration.

River had a bad feeling, one that just wouldn't go away. It was a sense of ominous, impending doom, so unlike anything she'd felt before, that it had taken her overnight to identify.

Inhale. Exhale. She picked up the pace.

God. Was Oliver involved in something *illegal*? *Unethical*? It didn't seem likely. She knew her brother. Well, she'd *known* her brother. But why else would he run away? River's steps faltered. She'd reluctantly considered the possibility that he was dead. But what if someone had *taken* him away?

What were the options? He'd run away, reason unknown. He'd been kidnapped. He was being held hostage. He was dead. He'd somehow been involved in the explosion the men had talked about at dinner the night before. Had he caused it? He was a chemist as well as a scientist, after all, and he *designed* explosives.

Having all these questions in her head was counterproductive. She couldn't answer any of them herself, but the giant question mark made her chest ache, and her heartbeat kick unevenly in a way that had nothing to do with her run. She adjusted her pace, slowing a little to accommodate the unsteady heartbeat caused by her anxiety and compounded by the altitude.

Breathe. Just breathe.

Focus.

Make a plan.

"I'm going to find you Oliver Michael Sullivan. Wherever the hell you are. Count on it."

The single-story, attached houses were painted in Mediterranean colors: warm golds, umbers, terracotta, and a few ocean blues. The village was as pretty and picturesque as a jewel, nestled in the vibrant greenery of the surrounding tropical forest. Running through the quiet streets was like stepping back in time. There were no vehicles, no frantically rushing pedestrians, no corner liquor stores. As the sun crested the mountain, it looked as though she was seeing the colorful houses through amber glasses.

A little sandy brown dog with a crooked tail and floppy ears intersected her as she rounded a corner. He ran beside her for a few minutes until he peeled off and disappeared.

It took River a little over an hour to run through the entire village, making a wide loop from one end to the other. The few people she did see gave her a wide berth. Mostly she encountered women and children. An old man on crutches hobbled across the street when he saw her approaching.

Franco had mentioned last night that forty people worked in the mine. Where did everyone else spend their days?

The steeple and bell tower of the chapel, attached to the hacienda, was the tallest building in town. As River rounded the corner at a fast walk to cool down, she saw Father Marcus standing outside the church, watering a giant pot of red geraniums that exploded in a wild profusion of crimson flowers and waxy, glossy green leaves.

The enormous, waist-high terracotta pots, painted a vivid royal blue, one on either side of the low wrought iron gate, were a riot of color. In the morning light, the cobbled walkway, flowers, and yes, maybe even the black clad priest tending the crimson flowers, would make a great setting for a lingerie shoot. River turned off the music, and pulled the earbuds from her ears, slowing down as she approached him. "Good morning, Father."

He turned with a smile. "Good morning, my dear, I saw you run off earlier. A little more difficult jogging at this altitude, isn't it?"

"A bit, but I like the challenge. I was up bright and early to accompany Franco and the bishop up to the plant, but I was a few minutes too late. They left without me." Intentionally, she had no doubt. Whoever had been driving was sure to have seen her in the rearview mirror as she stood on the street watching them leave.

"Do you have any idea where they might've taken my rental car? Hopefully, someone repaired the tire. I'll drive up there myself in a bit."

"I'm sorry, my dear. I doubt the car's fixed. Jorge Abano does minor repairs. He has your car, but probably hasn't gotten to it yet. We operate on Los Santos time here." He smiled. "Franco and Bishop Daklin will be back soon. If they have anything to report, I'm sure they'll come straight to you."

River was pretty damned sure they'd do no such thing. "I'd prefer not to wait. I'll find some other form of transportation if necessary, and drive myself up to the mine."

"Why not wait a few hours and see what they have to say?" He shook his head, his smile dimming a little. "From the set of your jaw, I see that idea doesn't appeal to you. Of course, you're a grown woman and have the option to go about as you please. But I'd be derelict in my duty if I didn't warn you that these mountains can be *extremely* dangerous. The road up to the mines is usually treacherously slick from the rains or overspray from the river and waterfalls along the way, and heavily armed rogue guerrillas are frequently encountered trying to gain access to the plant or the mines."

River smiled, though the idea of armed guerillas gave her pause. "I drove nine hours in the same conditions *with* a flat tire to get here. I'll be careful."

"I'll give you directions to Jorge's house. You can see if that pretty smile will encourage him to move a little faster."

"Thank you, Father." As much as River wanted to run over to Jorge and motivate him to hurry the hell up, she nodded at the geraniums. "You have a green thumb."

"I enjoy gardening. Franco allows me to putter in the courtyard we were in last night. It's peaceful, communing with nature. Once I finish watering these, would you like to come inside? I can make you breakfast."

"I'd love to, thank you." A few minutes of her time with the priest might give her some insight as to Oliver's whereabouts. It was worth the delay. "Should I run up and change first?"

"No need. You're fine as you are. You didn't eat much last night and I'm sure you're hungry after that run. While I water, why don't you snip those dead blooms?" He handed her a small pair of shears from his back pocket. "Just drop them in the bucket there."

"How long have you been in Los Santos, Father?" There weren't that many faded blooms, but River did a thorough search, snipping off those she found. The sunlight tipped over the steeple, turning the spray of the hose and the puddles of water around their feet to sheets of copper.

"Just over four years. It's a good parish with good people. I'm content here." He turned the hose off at the nozzle, then started coiling it hand-over-hand, not seeming to care that his pants and shoes were being splattered. "Let me put this away, and we can go inside."

Hose over his arm, he opened the gate for her, following her into a narrow stone-paved area. The church steps were made from the same smooth terracotta-colored stone and led up to massive double doors of dark carved wood, similar to those in the hacienda next door. A smaller, plain wood door painted black was tucked to the side of the grand steps.

"This way." After dropping the coiled hose, Father Marcus led the way down to the open door of the rectory and walked inside, leading her through the small house to the tiny, 1950's style kitchen in back. A large window showed a corner of the inner courtyard, and a spectacular view of the mountains. Turning on a huge radio near the window, he indicated a small, yellow Formica topped table and chairs off to the side beside the window, then lowered the volume when it blasted out. Oldies.

Creedence Clearwater Revival belted out *Bad Moon Rising* just loudly enough to hear the lyrics. "Too loud?"

"No, it's perfect." River smiled. Even at the decibels he'd clearly been listening to, it wouldn't be too loud, but it would make conversation difficult. "It reminds me of my mom. She used to sing with the Petals, a not-very-successful girl band in the sixties. We both loved the music and my parents played oldies day and night in the convenience store they owned. Good memories."

"Please, sit down." He turned on the tap and washed his hands. "Do you have her voice?"

"Not really, but I sing anyway."

He looked over his shoulder. "Would you like tea or coffee? Scrambled eggs and burnt toast are my specialty. How hungry are you?"

Charmed, River's smile widened. "A few drops of coffee in a cup of sugar would be perfect." A floating shelf held a collection of whimsical salt and pepper shakers and a thriving pathos plant. "I love scrambled eggs, and I'm starving. What can I do to help?"

He brought the steaming pot from the two-burner gas stove over to the table, then went to get a mug and spoon. "Sit and enjoy your sugar. You can talk to me while I cook. The kitchen isn't big enough for two cooks, and I don't want you to show me up."

"Trust me, I couldn't." She poured coffee into both mugs, taking his over to him and placing it beside the stove as he pulled out a pan. "I'm the worst cook. I go out or order in most of the time." She returned to the table to doctor her coffee.

"Sofia Martinez brings me a loaf of her freshly baked bread every two days. She delivered this loaf about a half hour ago." He cut four thick slices of the dense white bread, then lay them on a pan and slid it under the broiler. "I hope that your husband or boyfriend knows how to cook. It's a good skill; one I wish I'd mastered earlier instead of later."

"I'm not married, and my boyfriends are happy to feed me when necessary."

He held up an egg for her to see. "Camilla Ruis's fine chickens." He broke the eggs directly into a buttered pan and stirred them with a fork. ""Boyfriends? Plural?"

She shrugged as she took a sip of scalding coffee. Strong, sweet, and perfect. The eggs started to burn, but she didn't say anything. "Nobody serious."

"I've been to Portland, Oregon. Pretty place. Nice people." Turning down the flame under the pan, he scowled at the eggs. "What do you do there with all the time you save by not cooking?"

River laughed. "I'm a clothing designer. Lingerie to be precise. I have a company called *El Beso*, based in Portland and New York."

"Hmm, so you mentioned last night. Sorry, I was striving not to melt in the heat inside the house and wasn't listening with both ears. The Kiss?" Taking out the pan, he used his knee to close the oven door, sliding the bread onto two plates. The slices were as thick as a doorstep and toasted a golden brown. "Why Spanish and not French or Italian?"

"Because it's an American company for American woman. And I liked the sound of it."

"And are you successful, River Sullivan?"

"I am. Yes." She smiled back at him. "My lingerie sells in the best department stores. People know and trust my brand. It's functional, pretty, and affordable. Classy sexy is extremely lucrative, but perhaps I shouldn't tell you that."

Father Marcus brought over a saucer holding a massive block of butter and gave her a slight smile. "People say all manner of things to a priest. Jimena Cortez churns this with her own two hands." His brown eyes twinkled. "Why both Portland *and* New

York?"

"My ex-husband is my business partner, and that's where we met and I went to school. It's where he now lives with his new wife and daughter."

He raised a dark brow as he set their plates down on the bare table. "Sounds amicable."

"It is. We weren't right for each other romantically." She waved a vague hand, "No--magic I guess. We're much better friends. He found the magic with Beth about a year after our divorce. I'm godmother to their daughter, Arabella."

"And what about a husband and children for you?" he asked, sitting opposite her as she buttered a piece of the toast.

"One day. I'm not in a hurry. When the right man comes along, I'll know." The priest was easy to talk to, enjoyable enough that River forged on to eat every scrap of rubbery eggs and heavy bread. "What about you, Father? What led you to Cosio and Los Santos?"

"I have a somewhat checkered past, I'm afraid. A lot of violence, a lot of death. I had the kind of job where I never knew from one day, no, one *hour* to the next, if it would be my last. I lived fast and hard with no thought of tomorrow. Then twelve years ago, I was in Portugal, barricaded behind a shipping crate on the docks, with people shooting at me."

He salted his eggs. "Suddenly, I seemed to go outside myself, and I felt this incredible warmth as I was engulfed in light. I heard a voice, a pure, gentle feminine voice that was both inside me, and outside. I felt liquid light pour over me and a profound feeling of pure maternal love."

River leaned forward. "Like Franco's apparition?"

For a moment, the bliss left Father Marcus's eyes, and his lips tightened. It was almost too quickly for anyone to notice, but River didn't miss it. She was intrigued by his story, and they were sitting so close, his expressions were hard to miss. "No, nothing like Franco's apparitions."

His features smoothed out. "The voice said, 'Markie, this isn't the life for you.' Markie was what my mother used to call me. With things blowing up, bullets flying, and people yelling around me, I'd never felt so peaceful. It was as though my mother held me in her arms. I fell asleep there, on the filthy ground behind the dockside container. Just fell into a deep restful sleep."

He got up to return with the coffeepot, then sat down again. "The phenomenon I experienced is called *locution cordis,* interior locution, the mystical grace of hearing a spiritual presence——in my case, Our Lady. I flew home the next day, quit my job, and went to study at the Franciscan University in Steubenville, Ohio, earning my B.A. in theology and philosophy."

"No people shooting at you here, at least. But there was an explosion at the plant a few weeks ago, right?" She took a mouthful of her eggs, and despite the burned bits, which she tried to convince herself looked like pepper, they tasted half-decent. Okay, better than she could have made.

He took a bite of his toast and swallowed hard. "An

accident. A hideous, unfortunate accident. So that's my life in a nutshell. That happened twelve years ago, and now I feel as though I've come home."

"That's fascinating. It's good to belong. Even though I haven't seen him in years, Oliver is all the family I have. I didn't realize how much I depended on his regular phone calls."

"I'm sure he'll contact you when he can."

She gave him a curious look. "When he *can*? Do you know something you're not telling me, Father?"

He smiled with his lips, but his kind, brown eyes were somber. "There are more things in heaven and earth, Horatio."

River pretended to be content with that. A priest with a shady past, who also quoted Shakespeare? Father Marcus was an interesting man. But that only made her wonder what he *hadn't* told her.

SEVEN

Daklin gritted his teeth, silently enduring the bone-jarring ride up the mountain as the vehicle rooster-tailed through one of several streams washing across the narrow winding road. They'd passed a large, water-filled, open mining pit two clicks back on the left. Thick vines overgrew a single story building and covered several large pieces of unused mining equipment, indicating the water-filled pit was no longer in play.

Around the next bend, vegetation had been cut back ruthlessly, the trees felled and removed. Not a tree, shrub, or blade of grass remained. Just rocks, sand, and gravel. He noted that Xavier had men hidden in ghillie suits, sniper rifles trained on the vehicle as it passed.

The barren mountainside, surrounded by lush vegetation and scattered Brazil nut, chinaberry, Cuban cedar, and sixty-foot tall Ecuadorian walnut trees, resembled a monk's tonsure.

They approached a sentried gate on the fenced property.

Cement guard towers two stories tall flanked the wide front gate. Vine-like razor wire, from top to bottom, wrapped the towers and the gate. The twin towers had three-hundred sixty degree visibility. There were six sentries, as well as snipers, stationed on various levels on each. There was one tower positioned on the eastern side of the fence, the other on the western side. The dark bulk of the sheared off mountain behind the compound was an unscaleable, impenetrable fourth wall.

Getting inside undetected tonight should be fun.

Daklin's intel had given him the stats on the top-track, galvanized speed gate. The open-close cycle took less than seven seconds. It was electrified, with motion sensors.

"Is there a reason the trees and vegetation have been cut back here? Is there danger of fire?" Smart move. No one could approach the mine without being seen. "Clearing the land surrounding the mines is standard operating procedure, Your Excellency," Xavier told him. "We sell the lumber, or allow villagers to take what they need. The cleared land, stripped to bare earth, makes blasting more efficient, and of course, dissuades thieves from entering the area."

Yeah. *That.*

On the grounds, guards accompanied by sleek Doberman pinschers patrolled the high, electrified perimeter fence. There wasn't a shrub or tree inside the fence either. Nowhere to hide. He'd seen less security at nuclear power plants and maximum-security prisons.

"Of course. That makes perfect sense." Daklin added a touch of admiration to his tone. His men had told him that half a dozen patrols, each two dozen men strong, crisscrossed the compound, twenty-four seven. A patrol passed on the other side of the gate as they approached.

Wearing camo military fatigues, an expressionless Kai Turley, with an Enfield LSSAI assault rifle slung on his back, and holding a Berretta 92FS pistol, peered into the car. He turned to activate the ten-foot tall, electrified gate. It slid aside and Ortiz drove through. The gate almost clipped their rear bumper as it closed.

"Is there an issue that requires such armed force?" Daklin looked at Xavier. "The Church does not support the use of guns. Perhaps the apparition of our lady is cautioning you against such potential violence?"

"That is, of course, for you to determine, Your Excellency. But I don't believe that's the message she is conveying." Xavier's skin flushed. "The emeralds we process are invaluable, and I use them, of course, for profit. Those profits enable me to be very generous to the Holy Church. Such valuable assets must be protected," he informed Daklin as two of four guards ran up to open the vehicle's doors. Each had an assault rifle and the same type of pistol that Turley carried.

"The guns are an unfortunate necessity, Your Excellency. We merely use them to defend ourselves if, and when necessary."

Bullshit, fucker. You kill people on a grand scale every time you sell E-1x to a terrorist.

Bringing his prayer book with him, Daklin swung his legs from the car and rose to his full height, trying not to wince as he stretched and stood on his injured leg. The guard on his side of the vehicle--not an undercover T-FLAC operative--stepped back.

Daklin waited for Xavier to round the front of the truck. "To one who strikes you on the cheek, offer the other also, and from one who takes away your cloak, do not withhold your tunic either. Luke 6:29."

"Indeed, Your Excellency." Xavier indicated that they should cross the graveled parking area toward the front of the building. Daklin fell into step with him. Ortiz followed. "If only everyone followed the scriptures," Xavier said piously, absolutely no irony in his tone. "Unfortunately, we live in a world where others want to steal the fruits of our labors. When they come, we deter them, as we must. And the Church is happy to accept my checks, which I could not provide if people robbed my mines."

The mountain, dark, craggy, and devoid of vegetation, rose as a backdrop directly behind the low building. "Cosio has been a country divided and war-torn for many years. The ALNF and SYP guerilla groups, right-wing paramilitary groups, and various drug cartels frequently make raids in an attempt to steal our product."

Daklin called bullshit again. There was no current threat. Six months earlier, T-FLAC had taken out the heads of both the ALNF and the SYP. Both terror groups were out of the picture. It was ironic that he was supposedly arming himself against terrorists, when terrorists worldwide were clamoring for Xavier's "product." The demand exceeded the supply Xavier dribbled onto the market. He kept his customer base eager, and the price sky high. Los Santos was the only place in the world where the raw material was found and mined. It was highly unlikely tangos were aware, or gave a flying fuck, where their product originated. But even if the bad guys discovered where E-1x was mined, they were shit out of luck unless they knew how to process the ore from here, and how to turn the raw material into the powerful explosive. Either they paid the fortune Xavier demanded, or they came and helped themselves, by whatever means possible, to the finished product at the plant.

As far as T-FLAC knew, Xavier and his biochemical engineer, Oliver Sullivan, were the only ones who knew how to convert the mined material into E-1x. The only way for two people to keep a secret was if one of them was dead. Could it be that Oliver Sullivan was out of the picture? Had Xavier used him for his expertise, and then killed him? Xavier was screwed. He desperately wanted to share the miracle of his apparition with the world, and at the same time, he couldn't afford to draw undue attention to Los Santos.

The sun crested the mountain behind the long, low, one-story cement building, shading the gravel in the front parking area. According to his men, the plant itself comprised thirty thousand square feet. Damned big for an emerald mining operation. But not too big if they were processing the E-1x here on the premises, which is what Turley and the others suspected. Only *suspected* because the operatives, being that they were new hires, had not yet been inside the building or the secure yard behind it.

According to Turley, who'd guesstimated the activity inside

using heat sensors and infrared scanning equipment on his night patrols, the lab and E-1x processing operations took up fully three quarters of the structure. The rest was for the sorting, and processing of the emeralds. Eight people worked in the emerald side of the building. Two in the lab area. Thirty in the mines. Now that he was up close and personal, Daklin knew there were at least one-hundred-forty-four guards with twenty, equally well trained, Dobermans.

The cinderblock building had one door in front, no windows and, according to Ram, via his father, one hell of a ventilation system, more suited to an industrial laboratory than a mining plant. Off to the left, partially hidden by the eastern corner of the building, an enormous, round vibrating screen stood silent beside a muddy Cat Track Drill.

The drill indicated they were digging down. Emeralds or E-1x? They sure as hell wouldn't be loading schist with the highly volatile E-1x into the vibrating screen for sorting. The action would take out half the mountain range. It was an excellent plan, but somewhat premature.

Several enormous earth-moving machines, clearly not in use, threw deep shadows off to the side of the building. Daklin made a mental note of their locations, and how much open space lay between them and potential entry points. They'd provide cover later.

"This way, Your Excellency." Xavier placed his hand on a biometric pad beside the Tungsten steel door, leaning closer for an iris scan. After a moment, the door swung open. "Wait here," he instructed Ram in Spanish, then indicated Daklin should precede him inside where another door led into a large, brightly lit room.

A dozen people worked inside gray office cubicles, heads down with no eye contact. No sign of emerald processing, or the scent of honey to indicate the presence of E-1x. An animated conversation between two men and a woman abruptly ended when they saw Xavier. All three scurried back to their desks.

A tube light, flickering overhead, wasn't doing any favors to the stark bare cement gray walls and open ceiling with exposed ductwork and electrical pipes. The place smelled of mold and body odor.

A phone rang somewhere, and was answered in soft tones. Daklin hoped Ortiz, stationed directly outside the door, was aware of the brief reprise in the jamming signal, and had contacted Control for updates. Just another day at the office, taking orders for explosives from terrorists all over the world. There were no direct lines into or out of the building. An elaborate routing system pinged the calls and internet connections to the far corners of the earth and back again in a spaghetti of misdirection and fail-safes.

As of this morning, Echo team, working around the clock, was nofuckingwhere close to breaking the encryption, locating the source of the jamming, and giving the T-FLAC teams dependable comm ability. Daklin glanced around. Gray cubicle walls could be any office pit, anywhere in the world. A closed door to the left, and another, this one solid steel and secure, to the right. The lab, he suspected. Closed circuit cameras provided more surveillance and covered most of the room. Daklin made a mental note of the blind spots; might come in handy later. Other than the click of the neon light overhead, and indistinguishable phone conversation, it was eerily quiet as everyone pretty much stopped what they were doing and seemed to be holding their breath as Xavier and Daklin walked in.

Xavier indicated their route with a broad gesture of his hand. "This way, Your Excellency."

Daklin stopped walking. "Before we go to the scene of the tragedy, I wonder if I might see Dr. Sullivan's workspace so I can report back to his sister? Perhaps I can put her concerns to rest and give her an explanation as to where her brother might be?"

He wanted a look at Sullivan's lab. Preferably with Sullivan in it. Then he'd haul the guy's ass back to the hacienda so his sister could see he was alive and well. His men could then take the scientist to Montana. Unfortunately, Daklin suspected they weren't going anywhere near the lab or Sullivan today. He was there to say a prayer for the dead, not take a tour.

"I don't *know* where Dr. Sullivan went, Your Excellency," Xavier said with some irritation. "I don't know how many ways I can tell Miss Sullivan her brother simply left in the middle of the night without explanation. Surely if he was in his lab, I'd know it."

"But as far as you know, he's alive and well?"

"He was when he was last seen here. This way, Your Excellency."

"The explosion was in his lab?"

"No, in a small storage building in back, outside the mine entrance." Other than a few closed doors, which didn't indicate what was behind them, the gray cement walls of the corridor were blank.

"You were fortunate to escape with your life, Franco. An explosion powerful enough to kill *five* people was possibly strong enough to kill even more if they'd been in the building that day."

Judging by the difference between the outside structure and the inside, the walls were nearly five-foot thick concrete and probably reinforced with a web of rebar. Strong enough to take a direct hit from something as big as a 747 and be left with nothing more than a dark smudge and maybe a nick or two on the exterior walls. "I was not here at the time, Your Excellency."

Convenient.

"We have to go outside, and unfortunately the area is quite wet." He arched a brow.

Daklin smiled. "I'm not afraid of getting my feet wet, Franco. Lead on."

Each door they passed had a card reader outside for secure entry. Xavier indicated one of them. "This is where we size and polish emeralds for shipping."

"I'd be interested in seeing the process if we have time." Not. Unless the room contained some part of the process for E-1x, Daklin didn't give a shit about what they were doing.

"I'll have Liseo show you when he returns. He's very

knowledgeable about the process."

Another biometric door. Franco did the hand and iris scan, and the foot-thick door opened onto an enormous gravel courtyard with fifteen-foot high metal gates at each end, presumably for trucks to enter and exit. On the other side of what was a twenty-thousand square foot parking lot, stood double tungsten steel doors that sealed the mine entrance.

Deep indentations of tire treads, filled with water, indicated the passage of heavy trucks to and from the mine to processing machines inside the secure compound, and continuing outside the electrical fences, passing security, to dump useless rock and by-product.

To the right of the mine entrance stood what remained of a small building, perhaps originally thirty feet by thirty feet. One story. Roof gone, walls blackened and crumbled. Blown to hell.

"I don't recommend going any closer, Your Excellency. The walls are precarious. My men will tear down the ruins when they have time."

Daklin's heavy black shoes crunched over soggy gravel. "Where lives have perished, I like to spend time alone to walk where they had their last moments on earth. Then I'll pray for them and give them the final blessing they weren't able to receive before God took them home." In other words, he wanted a closer look at the steel door blocking the mine entrance.

Daklin opened his prayer book and removed the handwritten list of names Xavier had someone prepare for him earlier. "I'll pray over each name."

"Of course, Your Excellency."

Remembering to pull the heavy cross and chain from his pocket, Daklin walked the perimeter, his head bowed, his gaze strafing the area. Speeding up his pace, he circled to the back of the small structure.

Crouching, he found the point of origin at the inside, back corner, then started a down and dirty search from the V shape outside of the fire's burn path. There was no need to conduct a chemical analysis. The V pattern indicated a small amount of E-1x had been detonated close to the ground. The six-foot deep crater formed by the explosion indicated a fraction of a gram of material had been used. E-1x was *that* powerful.

Rounding the corner, back into Xavier's view, Daklin withdrew from his pocket the small, plastic bottle of "Holy Water" he'd filled from the water bottle in his room earlier. He opened it and started to sprinkle the water on the ground. At the same time, analyzing and processing the visual evidence, he concluded this was not the explosion that killed the men. That had probably occurred *inside* the mine itself, not out here.

That, however, wasn't the point of this morning's exercise.

Now he had a firsthand view of the lay of the land and the scope of Xavier's security. As intel had indicated, this operation was pretty damn impenetrable.

#

After breakfast with Father Marcus, River returned to the

hacienda. The squat security guy with no neck gave her a silent nod when she came in, watching as she climbed the stairs. Did he think she was there to steal the silver or that dark and terrifying painting of a woman breastfeeding a rather demonic looking baby? She felt much better after she closed and locked the heavy bedroom door behind her.

After a shower, she changed into a simple red and white striped maxi sundress, fixed her hair and makeup, and went to sit on the bench at the foot of her bed to check for phone messages.

No messages. No signal.

With a successful business to run, she was always busy. It wasn't in her makeup to sit around doing nothing. There were always designs for the new collection to work on, spreadsheets to study, and sales calls to make. If she wasn't on her phone, iPad, or computer, she was at her drawing board. She hadn't taken a vacation in over five years, and she liked it that way. Now she couldn't even speak to her assistant thanks to the lack of cell signal. Lord, what she wouldn't give for a hot spot. Los Santos sorely needed a Starbucks.

This enforced pause away from work to find Oliver was frustrating. She hated feeling powerless. She needed a plan, needed to take freaking *action* instead of waiting around, twiddling her thumbs. She slipped her feet into flat sandals, then going in search of Jorge the mechanic, and her missing rental car.

The church and hacienda stood sentinel atop a small hill overlooking the long, straight road running through the narrow valley. The cobbled street wound through the town, like an artery flowing to the town's heart.

Taking measured steps on the uneven road, she headed toward the square in the village center. From a distance, clusters of small homes looked colorful and picturesque, but the closer she got, she noticed disrepair and peeling paint she hadn't observed on her run earlier. The over-decorated hacienda didn't reflect that Cosio was a dirt poor, third world country, but the outer streets did.

A large, two-tier stone fountain anchored the picturesque square, with side streets, like spokes of a wheel, leading off the central plaza. Houses were attached in a long row of colorful squares like beads on a thread. Painted warm, happy colors, many homes sported flowering plants in containers beside their front doors, or hanging from window ledges. Bright profusions of fiery red, vibrant pink, and sunny yellow blooms showed that Father Marcus wasn't the only one in town with a green thumb. The air was thick with the scent of the flowers lingering in the mid-morning air. Large flowering trees separated the blocks, casting shade and a dusting of orange petals onto the streets. Several elderly men sat on stone benches placed in the deep shade. To say that the people of Los Santos worked on a different time clock than the rest of the world was an understatement. It was Wednesday and barely nine in the morning. Were all the younger villagers at work? And where did they work? At the plant and mine? The closest town was hours away, and so far, the only vehicle she'd seen was the one the bishop and Franco had been in earlier. Despite the absence of traffic, the square was a hive of activity, a hive in slow motion, River observed, amused.

Taking her phone out of her bra, she scrolled to a picture of Oliver taken several years ago. Like herself, Oliver was fair-haired, and pale-skinned. Among the locals, with their glossy black hair and milk-coffee-colored skin, he'd stand out like a beacon.

Two dozen black-clad women and a handful of older men were setting up tables and chairs around the fountain. Several women threw colorful tablecloths on tables, while others centered fat, honey-colored wax candles amid cut boughs of leaves and flowers. They all paused to watch River's progress. Several gave shy greetings.

It looked pretty and festive, and even with everyone's slow pace, a feeling of excitement hummed in the air. After stopping here and there to admire someone's handiwork--beautifully stitched tablecloths or artfully arranged flowers--River showed them her brother's picture. She got no recognition from anyone. Chatting women, filling containers at the fountain, glanced up as she approached.

"What's the occasion?" River asked the three women, in Spanish. "*La fiesta.*" The youngest, sixty-ish, responded shyly as water dripped down her arm and splashed her black dress. "*Para dar la bienvenida el Obispo.*"

"Everyone is very excited and honored to meet such a great man." An older woman, the map of her life carved into the deep wrinkles on her face, gave River a gap-toothed smile. "Many hope the bishop will bless us, our village, and our families. To shake hands with a religious man who has touched the Pope would be like shaking hands with *el Papa* himself." Her snapping black eyes belied her age.

"I'm sure His Excellency will bless everyone." River presumed he would. Not that she had any clue what a bishop should do, but since he was here, why *wouldn't* he bless these people? He couldn't possibly be as surly and sarcastic to the villagers as he'd been with her.

After introducing herself to Maria, Magda, and Ines, River told them she was there to visit her brother. Like the others she'd spoken to, they didn't recognize Oliver by name. She showed them his photo on her phone. "Do you recognize him?"

They hadn't seen him.

They hailed several people working nearby, but everyone shook their heads after inspecting the photo. They were more fascinated by the phone itself than by Oliver's picture.

With a sigh, River asked directions to Jorge's garage. As she walked, she stopped more people on the street to show them Oliver's picture. All she got were consistent headshakes, and "No, señorita."

The sun beat down on her head and bare shoulders as she wandered through the narrow, picturesque streets. A young woman sweeping the sidewalk in front of her house smiled shyly, a little girl clinging to her legs. She didn't recognize Oliver when River showed her the picture either.

How could Oliver live in a place for *five years* and not have a single person recognize him? Yes, he was private and reclusive, but surely he came to town sometimes? At least for a goddamn walk! Franco said she was staying in the room Oliver used. He must've left the hacienda on occasion.

"Oliver, you have some explaining to do," River whispered as she walked further down the hill. She had such a heavy feeling of dread that she rubbed the goosebumps on her arms despite the heat of the sun.

It seemed farfetched and alarming, but maybe he *was* being held hostage. Oh, God. Had he suspected what was about to happen and sent her the money so she could pay a ransom? No one had contacted her to demand payment. And who was holding him prisoner? Franco? And if so, why?

That train of thought didn't make sense. But what else would explain Oliver's disappearance and the huge chunk of money he'd deposited in her account, with no explanation or warning?

If he *was* being held hostage, then the last person she could ask would be the very person holding him. "Damn it to hell, Oliver! Call me." At least then she'd know he was alive.

Who could she ask for help? Bishop Daklin? He wasn't warm and fuzzy, but maybe there was some goodness in his heart. He was a bishop, after all, and he could make discreet inquiries. She'd ask him when he returned. A sliver of optimism crept inside her. Maybe her concern would be all for nothing when they came back with Oliver.

Turning the corner, she encountered two men heading up the hill. She showed them Oliver's picture. They shook their heads. She thanked them and, as she was picking up her phone, saw that she had service! Hot damn! She hit speed dial. Oliver's phone just rang and rang. She would have left another message, but the recorded voice told her his message box was full. Shit. Of course it was. Ignoring his messages was par for the course for her brother. She tucked the phone back between her breasts.

Did the villagers know why Bishop Daklin was gracing their little town? Did they know about Franco's apparition? Had anyone else seen it? River was willing to bet they hadn't. Xavier didn't strike her as a gullible man, nor one with any imagination, so she had no idea what he'd *really* seen. Whatever it was, or wasn't, River wasn't a big believer in woowoo of any kind, whether from another dimension, or straight from heaven. But if a bishop had come all this way, sent by the Pope no less, then this might be a once in a lifetime event she shouldn't miss.

An apparition. A vision. Ephemeral. More than a dream, but not quite real.

What did an apparition *look* like? River wanted to know. She'd do a Zag search and find out.

Visions. Apparitions. Fantasy.

It could be the name of a new product line, inspired by the elusive and ephemeral, and the unsmiling bishop, his serious blue eyes and the impossibly hard set of his jaw. Sexy and tough. Hard and soft... She liked the juxtaposition.

What, exactly, would it take to make a man like that relax?

He might be a bishop, but he was still a man. Maybe all his testosterone was backed up?

She shook herself, immediately feeling as guilty as a Catholic schoolgirl, then chuckled when she reminded herself she had no clue how that was supposed to feel.

Just thinking about the bishop though, so quickly after thinking about decadent lingerie, made her realize how fast her thoughts could become really wrong.

Straight-out, flat-out wrong.

Seriously, deliciously, wrong.

Dear God, I'm going nuts, because I'm lusting after a freaking bishop, and I'm not that kind of person. I might not be a Catholic, but surely lusting after a bishop is a mortal sin even for non-Catholics. I might design lingerie for a living, but I'm not a mortal sin kind of woman. I'm just not.

Oliver, would you please let me know where you are so I can get the hell out of here?

She glanced down the road, almost expecting to see the vehicle from Xavier's compound returning. No such luck. *Great.*

River walked to the corner and headed for Jorge Abano's house on the next street over. When she arrived at the one that Ines had said was baby-poop-colored, she knew she was at the right place.

She guessed Jorge was at least a hundred and sixty-three

years old. His thinning hair was dyed jet black. But the dye hadn't taken as well to his bushy eyebrows, which were an interesting shade of muddy green. He was barely five feet tall, stooped, toothless, and so cheerful she couldn't help but smile back whenever he glanced up to give her a gummy grin.

River couldn't fathom why he'd removed all four tires from the car, which was in his crowded garage and up on blocks.

Noisily and often, he paused to suck Coke from a bottle through a straw. Eyes twinkling, he offered the bottle and straw for her to share. She politely declined.

The little red convertible wasn't ready. In fact, it was far from ready. The hood was up, all four tires were off, but Jorge insisted she wait. He directed her to a narrow retaining wall right outside the garage.

It was barely ten in the morning and already blistering hot. Sitting on the low wall in a miserly patch of shade outside Jorge's garage, River watched him "work" on the car for a while. It was as exciting as watching paint dry, but she was in no hurry. The drive up to the plant and mine would take, according to Father Marcus, less than thirty minutes.

With surprisingly good service, she was able to respond to a dozen e-mails, took two business calls, and spoke to her assistant in New York. Music started up in the square as musicians tuned up and rehearsed for later that night. They were only a few blocks away, but sounded as if they were standing practically at her hip. No more phone calls for a while.

Instead, River Zagged Bishop Daklin. Good grief, the man had a Wikipedia page! A small picture showed a non-smiling Bishop Daklin in his black robes with the pink sash and heavy gold cross, hands piously crossed. Clearly, surly was his resting face.

"*Señorita*?" Jorge held up the half-empty bottle of Coke with a straw in it.

"No, *gracias*, Jorge." With a smile, River declined his generous, but germy offer for the second time, then returned her attention to her phone and the delicious, forbidden Bishop Daklin.

The Most Reverend Asher Daklin had been born in Salem, Mass. Asher. The name suited him. River scanned the short entry. Like the bishop himself, the facts were cold and dry, short and to the point.

Pretty much all she learned was that he was a Virgo.

She tried Oliver's number again with the same results. She got up to walk over to show Jorge his picture. He shook his head and told her he'd never seen the man before.

They talked about Jorge's years working the emerald mines. The dark and wet. The constant cold deep inside the mountain. He didn't miss it.

Apparently *el Jefe's* sons, Eliseo and Trinidad, worked there. Eliseo in the mine itself, Trinidad in the plant, sorting. Jorge liked Eliseo, but had little time for Trinidad.

"In the old days, when *el Jefe* was a younger man, he'd allowed *garimpeiros*. You know what?" he asked in English.

River shook her head.

130

"Independent miners." He mimicked her headshake as he picked up a wrench. "No more. Either we work in the mine, or we have no job." He applied the wrench like a hammer to the tire rim. "We aren't greedy. We're all happy to dig in the smaller veins for emeralds. Main shaft go down a hundred and thirty meters. He say no. Too dangerous. Big trucks inside the mine now. Not before. Liseo say not so many emeralds no more."

River did some quick math. "The shaft goes down over four hundred feet?" She could just imagine the conditions. Give her fresh air and sunshine any day.

"Sí, with many branches deep into the mountain. When I worked there a year ago, we found a new vein with nice dark schist with how you say? Folded?" He made a motion, as if he were folding a sheet. "Good stringers of quartz. The emeralds like to hide where the quartz meets the schist. We drove a new horizontal tunnel out into the schist, maybe forty-meters. We no sure if it's one vein or the same one folding back on itself many times." He switched to Spanish. "Then Liseo say stop. No more work. Go home, not safe. Some people, maybe twenty, still go to work every day. But no more emeralds."

River tried to follow along as Jorge noisily slammed the wrench on some metal part of the undercarriage of the car as he talked. From the square, the mariachi band played with enthusiasm. She raised her voice, "The emeralds are played out?"

"No," he assured her. "Mining *ore* now."

She had no idea what he was talking about, but clearly he

was thrilled to have a captive audience. When he stopped talking to concentrate on beating the rental car to death, she said in Spanish, "I'll come back later, okay, Jorge?"

He beamed. "I will be here, señorita."

River grinned back. No doubt he would. "Is there somewhere I could rent a car? Or borrow a car?" Because it appeared unlikely that he'd get the tires back on her vehicle in the next decade.

"Abad?"

"That's three *hours* away."

He shrugged and went back to hitting the rim of the front wheel with a wrench.

EIGHT

Franco was aware, every second of every day, that his partner watched him from hidden cameras positioned strategically around the hacienda. As far as he knew, there was no audio, but someone like his partner would be adept at lip reading. Franco had nothing to hide. They often shared toys and playthings. He had no secrets. He knew where each camera was, having positioned the ones in the playroom himself. They often played back the recordings and shared those moments together as foreplay for their activities.

It amused him that hidden cameras watched her every move. Too bad there was no sound, but with the jammers intermittently, at his convenience, blocking all audio and cellular calls, he was lucky to maintain a visual on the camera feeds.

"I told you to get rid of her," his partner ordered. "Use whatever means necessary, and I mean it. Do so now, before we move."

"She'll be gone in the morning." *Best ask permission.* With rising excitement in anticipation of an affirmative answer, Franco fastened the top button of the crisp white shirt. "May I --?"

"Do whatever the hell you want with her. As long as she's gone before we leave."

Permission granted. Franco's cock leapt, and his heart

raced. Even though he couldn't be seen, he bowed his head in gratitude. "Thank you, Master."

#

Velvety dusk dropped like a soft blanket over the valley, leaving a sliver of orange rimming the highest black peaks of the mountains.

Standing between Xavier and Father Marcus in front of a table prepared for them on a raised dais, Daklin ran a finger beneath his cleric's collar. Tonight, he was full out bishop, with all the trappings. He'd like to strip off the layers of cloth and the restrictive collar and cool off in the fountain, but an orderly and somber line of people waited to speak to him and receive his blessing.

The townspeople had gone all out, with colorful Christmas tree lights strung in the trees, and flickering candles on tables. The potluck was in full swing, with women of every age bringing Daklin loaded plates of food to sample. Spicy fragrances of roasting meat and a tantalizing bouquet of spices drifted on the warm evening air, mingling with the scent of candles and humid vegetation that pressed in on all sides of the town.

Small lanterns placed beneath the fall of water surrounding the fountain's top tier turned the pouring water into liquid gold. Across the square, a group of musicians in colorful Cosian dress played enthusiastically, much to the appreciation of their toe-tapping, clapping–with-the-beat, audience.

The music was a combination of Andean and Spanish with

African roots. The sweet sounds of the *charango*, a flutelike instrument, the driving rhythms of Spanish guitars, and the pounding beat of the *cajón,* a six-sided box-shaped percussion instrument from Africa, underscored the sound of hundreds of people talking quietly. The low tones were an indication, Daklin, knew, of deference to the honor the bishop was bestowing on them.

It didn't matter who Daklin talked to, or where he looked, his vision was filled with River Sullivan. Most of the women wore black and most were well into middle age. The young people had left long ago to go to the bright lights and sophistication of big cities like Abad and Santa de Porres.

River was also dressed in black. But on her, it was sexy.

Who the fuck am I kidding?

He wanted her with a dangerous intensity that he had to fight to control. Hard. His mouth watered for a taste of her. Fuck, for a sip, just one goddamned fucking sip of Tovaritch. He wiped a rough hand across his mouth. She was sex personified with touchable creamy skin, and pale hair that made his fingers flex at his sides as he imagined his hands fisted in the sunny strands. It didn't help that he knew what she looked like under those clothes. Every dip and curve, every silken inch, every pale hair between her thighs was imprinted on his fucking synapses.

Heart-shaped pubes.

Shit, he was glad he was wearing this bishop's dress or the good people of Los Santos would know exactly what he was thinking.

"This is *Señora* Martinez." Father Marcus drew the elderly woman forward with a gentle hand on her stooped shoulder. "Sofia here bakes the best bread this side of the mountain."

The lady blushed like a girl and ducked her head. Daklin smiled and said the required blessing. His mind wasn't on the blessing, the woman, or her bread. He observed River in his peripheral vision as she moved around the party guests, talking, laughing.

She was as at ease, as if she'd known these people for years. It was a special talent. Josh had had it too: the ability to make friends wherever he went. Everyone had loved his brother. And, apparently everyone here was falling in love with River. Damn, she was so fucking pretty it was hard to drag his attention away from her and back to the people patiently waiting to speak with him.

Every now and then, she'd hold up her smart phone, showing people pictures of her brother. Marcus had told him this afternoon that she'd been busy in his absence. Running before having breakfast with Marcus, then spending time doing a Zag search before landing on Bishop Daklin's Wikipedia page. She'd spent seven minutes and eleven seconds reading about a man who didn't exist, then did two more searches with Daklin's name in an attempt to find out more about him. Headquarters had a trace on all people who were investigating Daklin's well-crafted cover.

Unfortunately, her damned rental car wasn't ready. A tire

and rim had to be brought in from Abad. Unacceptable. He needed her gone. Preferably yesterday. The day before he'd seen her naked in her room would have been even better.

He turned to Franco on his left. "Since Miss Sullivan's brother is no longer here, and her rental car is still out of commission, I wonder if you could spare a car and driver and have someone take her to Santa de Porres airport in the morning?"

"That's a good idea, Your Excellency. I'll have one of my men do that after breakfast."

"I'm sure she'll appreciate it," Daklin said smoothly as Marcus introduced him to an elderly couple. *I'm sure she'll be pissed as hell.* But she wasn't his concern.

The couple withdrew, and Marcus patted the back of a middle-aged man with a luxurious mustache. "And this is Cristopher Guispe. He is fourth generation in Los Santos. His great-grandfather, grandfather, father, and now he and his son, all worked in the mines."

"Sandro and I no longer work the emeralds, Your Excellency." Guispe met Daklin's gaze with steady black eyes. "There is no longer work for us here. Our families are hungry. We want to work."

"Bishop Daklin has many people who wish to speak with him," Xavier said sharply in the local dialect, cutting the man off. "Be on your way."

Daklin lifted a hand. "No," he said in Spanish. "I want to hear."

"We used to have open pit mining, many people working." Guispe spoke rapidly, as if afraid Xavier would cut him short again. "Working hard. Life was difficult but good. We fed our families and tithed to the church. But now," He cast a nervous glance at Xavier. "with underground operations, vertical shafts, Liseo says the emeralds are played out. Then, no need so many workers in the shafts. Big trucks do the work of twenty men moving the schist."

"That's progress." Xavier spoke directly to Daklin. "There's no need for a hundred men to toil all day when we have machinery to do most of the work. The shafts have had to be made deeper and deeper to locate the ore holding the emeralds. Soon the mines will near the end of their economic life. But for now, we still employ people to wash the ore on the sluices, and have workers at the sorting tables."

For show. They had to demonstrate some emerald production, if they didn't want the locals to pack up and move to the bigger towns, spreading word of what they were really mining.

"We are *garimpeiros*." Guispe raised an inquiring eyebrow, then explained. "Small, independent miners. We work only for ourselves. Yes? We go downriver for tailings."

Tailings, or mine dumps, were the materials left over after separating the valuable fraction from the uneconomic ore. They'd take the emeralds they found and sell them where they could.

Daklin talked with the man for several minutes, prayed briefly with him, and subtly looked for River before the next man

138

was introduced. His eyes found her, briefly, standing talking to three women, then he shifted his attention to Renán Ortiz.

Renán, Ramse's father, was the man who'd blown the whistle on the production of E-1x. They'd decided that Ortiz's father was not to know of Bishop Daklin's involvement. It was enough that he was aware that his son and T-FLAC were here.

In a brief lull between people, Daklin turned to Father Marcus. "After the explosion last month, have provisions been made to protect the miners and villagers if there is another such accident? Some way to warn the townspeople to evacuate the valley?"

"The church bells will ring five times. It instructs them to go to safety, to leave the valley."

In the next few hours, the Charlie team would send in transport trucks to get the villagers out of danger. "That's good," Daklin said piously. "I pray that there are no further accidents." Tomorrow it would be Father Marcus's job to evacuate the rest of village before Daklin and his team rained hell down on Xavier and his mining production.

He spoke to dozens of people, giving them a blessing and special silver medals with the image of the Pope on them. The medals were genuinely from the Vatican. Daklin was only prepared to go so far with this masquerade. Their perception of him was their reality. Knowing people, Daklin knew their moments talking to the Bishop would be the high point of their lives, a story to tell their children and grandchildren. He wasn't the real deal, but the medals were. That would have to be enough. This fiesta seemed to go on and on, his leg hurt like hell, and he'd handed out most of the medals in little black velvet sacks. Still, it didn't look as if it would end anytime soon. Four hundred and eighty-two souls lived in the town, and every one of them wanted a moment with the Bishop. They brought their children, and little old ladies brought their pets, two with their Chihuahuas, and three with their chickens, for a blessing. They all brought him food, and small gifts. No one knew of Xavier's vision, so they were curious, but too polite to ask, why he was there.

Daklin was used to being invisible; his job necessitated it. Since his field of expertise was explosives, it didn't require deep undercover, and in fact, he seldom had to endure large crowds of cheerful people in a social setting. And it wasn't even an option in his private life, not that there was much of that. He worked, returned home for the mandatory breaks between ops, then returned to work.

He dated on the rare occasions he could be bothered, usually women from inside T-FLAC. Those were few and far between. He had a high sex drive, but it didn't mean he stuck his dick just anywhere, and now that he'd gotten a visual on what River looked like wearing only diamond earrings, he realized he hadn't indulged enough lately. His fist was only going to get him so far.

Swarmed by the people of Los Santos, he stood between Father Marcus and a beaming Franco, nursing a watered-down, now lukewarm lemonade. In another time and place, he'd have just poured more vodka into the drink and splashed an ice cube or two into it. Now, though, nothing would make the liquid taste better, and if that wasn't bad enough, it pissed him off that he was failing in his attempt to avoid watching River Sullivan. If he had vodka to pour down his throat, he'd be able to forget about her, but no. The new world order meant no liquid-induced strength, so he had to suffer through the evening with nothing but sour, warm lemonade.

For fuck's sake, every nerve in his body vibrated as she headed in his direction. Candlelight made her skin look like satin. A hint of black lace drew his gaze to the softly rounded neckline.

Cleavage and lace. Fucking kill me now.

Steeling himself, he could smell the warm, tropical scent of her perfume as she approached. A modest neckline and wide straps exposed her throat and a hint of velvety cleavage. The dress fit like a lover's hands over her breasts, then flared from her hips to swirl around her thighs. Not too short, but short enough to show off long, bare legs. He bet the lace that covered her silky ass matched the black lace that peaked at him from her cleavage. He'd pull that lace off her with his teeth. The dress could stay on while he did her. The first time.

Jesus H. Christ. He ground his teeth imagining pushing the dress up above her hips and slipping into her wet heat. He shook his head, and refocused on the two heavy-set elderly women who stood in front of him. Thank God one of them had a faint moustache. The other had a large mole on her cheek with gray whiskers growing out of it.

Instant buzzkill.

River waited as he spoke to the two elderly sisters. When they reluctantly backed away, she stepped in front of him with a smile. The light from her phone gleamed through the fabric of her pocket. "Franco. Father Marcus," she said by way of a cheerful greeting. Big gray eyes, clear as water, returned to Daklin. "Are you having fun, Bishop Daklin?"

"Fun?"

"You know, that emotion you sometimes experience when you're relaxed and enjoying yourself?"

He gave her a disapproving look. "Aren't you afraid to walk on these uneven cobbles in those inappropriate shoes, Miss Sullivan?"

She extended a slender foot and the crisscrossed, strappy sandals with five-inch heels. "These are perfectly *appropriate* party shoes, Your Excellency. There might be dancing later." She gave him a cheerful look. "Can you dance, Bishop Daklin?"

"Can I or do I?"

"Either." She smiled. Her right eyetooth was slightly crooked. Daklin's heart did a double gainer and his blood pressure throbbed behind his eyeballs.

Xavier's man could take her to the airport *before* breakfast. He did *not* fucking want to be *charmed* by her. He was already wound tighter than a detonator cord with lust. Being charmed was taking it too goddamned far.

Her smile slipped, and hope made her eyes large and serious. "I take it Oliver wasn't at the plant." Stress lifted her slender shoulders, and a heavy pulse throbbed at the base of her throat. Daklin wanted to put his mouth there.

"I'm afraid not." He hated giving her the answer that her disappointed eyes told him she already knew.

She sighed. "I was hoping he was just avoiding me."

Xavier and Marcus were privy to the conversation, and while nothing earth shattering was being discussed, Daklin suddenly wanted them both a thousand miles away. Her hurt was raw and palpable, and he had to fight off the urge to do something about it. Something to make them both forget.

"Did you have a fight?" Daklin asked.

River shook her head, making pale silky strands of hair swing against her jaw. "We never fight. I talk, Oliver retreats. Silence is his default." Her eyes met his. "I'm not complaining. It's just that often he's...not there. Even when he is, if you know what I mean."

Yeah. Pretty much like himself. Josh was—-had been-— just the opposite. His brother had been the life of every party, the center around which the earth spun. Everyone had loved Josh.

"Has anyone recognized your brother, Miss Sullivan?"

She took the change of subject like a trooper. "Not yet." She set her jaw for a second, and a determined gleam flashed in her eyes. "But then, I haven't spoken to everyone here."

"And you don't find that odd, considering he worked at the

143

mine just up that hill for more than five years?"

"Yes. And yes," she said with a frown. He wanted to kiss the furrows between her eyes. Instead, he tightened his fingers around his glass. "It's *more* than odd."

"Well I'm sure he'll contact you once you're home. He probably met a pretty girl and he's off having a romantic interlude."

River's laugh sent a jolt of unadulterated lust shooting from the top of Daklin's head directly into his balls.

"Not in a million years. Neither the girl, pretty or otherwise, nor the romantic interlude. That's not who Oliver is. Not when he has work to do. Now, challenge him with a lengthy mathematical problem, or offer him a difficult chemical compound to produce, and he'll disappear for months on end."

"There you have it then," Daklin told her. "He's found a challenge. He'll appear when he's solved the problem. I suggest you return to Portland and wait for his call."

"I'll have my man take you to the airport in the morning, my dear," Xavier told her. He wasn't offering. Daklin had almost been oblivious to Xavier's presence from the second River had joined them. Not good. Not good at all. That kind of inattention could get him killed.

Hell. He needed to wrap this up. Xavier had already insisted he come to his rooms to wait for tonight's apparition. Daklin would give it an hour, then plead exhaustion, and retire to his own room. As soon as the household was asleep, he and his men would return to the mine and plant to reconnoiter where the charges would be set.

It was going to be a long night.

"Would you like a blessing for your journey home?" he asked River pointedly. He had to know if she would indeed leave.

She hesitated. "Sure."

Daklin pressed the Pope's medal in her hand, then placed his palm on her head, fighting the urge to run his fingers through her silky hair. He gave up and did it anyway--slightly. Just the tips of his fingers, sliding through an inch or two of those gold-spun strands. He almost groaned aloud as he bowed his head a moment, pretending to say a silent prayer, then lifted his chin and glanced at her, prematurely. Well, before any meaningful prayer could possibly be over.

Wide, gray eyes met his. Long lashes fluttered as she blinked, then she held his gaze again. For a second, her eyes narrowed in puzzlement, then her cheeks became pink with a slight flush.

If he had a prayer in him, he'd forgotten it. She obviously had no clue how to accept a blessing and, hell, they were a perfect pair, because he sure as fuck didn't know how to give one.

He may have just fooled a whole village of people who wanted to believe he was what he purported to be, but River's eyes widened as he returned her stare with a hunger he couldn't conceal. *Dumbshit.*

Easing the weight off his bum leg, Daklin stuffed his hands

in his pockets. "Have a safe trip home, Miss Sullivan."

#

Unable to sleep, River searched her room thoroughly for any clues as to her brother's mysterious disappearance. There was absolutely no sign he'd ever been there.

The fiesta had come to a close the minute the delectable Bishop Daklin left. He'd been a big hit. And she hadn't been the only woman there to notice his broad shoulders and sexy half-smile. She'd have good company when she went to hell.

That damned smile had thrown her off completely. It was easier dealing with her lustful thoughts when she'd merely seen him as a surly man she didn't stand a hope in hell of attracting. But that small smile, the way his gaze connected with each person he'd spoken to, made each individual feel as if they were the only person in the world to him, and sent her pulse and hormones into freaking overdrive. She'd watched him praying with each woman, old or young, each man, each child with that gentle smile.

Hell, he even gazed into the eyes of the dogs with freaking sincerity, as though imparting a message that they mattered in the grand scheme of things. When it came time for her blessing, he studied her with something else. There was no divine inspiration in his expression. For a fleeting second, with his fingertips brushing her hair, he'd given her a look of pure, unadulterated lust, as if she were the only woman in the world. Evil incarnate. It was heady.

"I'm downright freaking delusional! Get a grip!" she told herself for the fifteenth time.

Climbing down from a chair, she dusted off her hands. Nothing on top of, or inside, the high wardrobe, nothing on the bookshelf, or the bedside tables, nothing under the mattress, or hell, even under the mattress.

"Ever think you're here on a fool's errand?" she asked herself as she slithered backwards from under the bed. Yeah. She figured she was. Hating to admit she'd failed in her quest, River figured she at least had tonight to make sure she'd done as thorough a search as possible.

She had a sick feeling in her stomach, knowing that she'd go home, and would have to wait, possibly forfreakingever, for Oliver to contact her, not knowing if he was dead or alive.

Maybe he'd left some personal item, a book, a notebook, a pack of his ubiquitous cigarettes, somewhere in the house. It would be just like him to leave his things around. He wasn't the tidiest man.

In fact, Oliver tended to write notes on anything close to hand, and since his cigarettes were always nearby, he frequently jotted formulas on the pack. Maybe he'd left a note somewhere in this vast hacienda. It was unlikely as hell, but worth pursuing as a last shot.

The house was dead quiet. Franco and the Bishop had spent some time in their host's room communing with the spirits. The door at the end of the hall had opened and closed, and River had listened to Bishop Daklin's slightly uneven footfall as he returned to his own room, which was across the corridor from her own.

She'd heard his door open, then close, two hours earlier.

"Do not stand here imagining what he wears to bed," she whispered, amused at where her imagination was taking her. The problem was, she had an excellent imagination, and she could quite easily picture Asher Daklin bare ass naked.

"Asher." His name tasted delicious on her tongue. "Ash."

She was like an enthusiastic dog chasing a car. It wasn't as if he was seducible, though the look he'd given her at the party made her have doubts in that regard. She wouldn't feel good tempting him, though. She'd just keep her salacious imagination to herself. Fortunately, if he was at breakfast in the morning, it would be the last time their paths would ever cross.

Wearing black leggings and a long sleeved black silk T-shirt, handily packed for layering, depending on the weather, River sat on the padded bench at the foot of the bed to put on her black sneakers. She was ready to skulk.

Her heart pounded as she unlocked her door and opened it very, very slowly. No creaking. Good.

Stepping into the dimly lit corridor, she carefully pulled her door closed behind her. She didn't need the tiny penlight she'd brought with her. Wrought iron wall sconces lit the long corridor with faux flickering candlelight. Heavy wood paneling and thick carpet absorbed most of the light and all of the sound, but she could see easily enough. It was a good thing she didn't spook easily, because there were dark pools of shadow from alcoves, life-size statues, and ominous looking people depicted in scary religious oil paintings all along the way. The Crusades had been bloody, and these paintings showcasing gory, tangled bodies of men and horses were not exactly inspirational.

The thickly carpeted mahogany stairs didn't creak as she stepped cautiously onto each tread. So far, so good. If anyone discovered her downstairs, she'd say she was hungry and in search of the kitchen.

She checked the living room, dining room, kitchen——where she made herself a quick peanut butter sandwich—-and ended up in a study. Either Franco's or one of his son's, she presumed. Heavy Colonial furniture dominated the large room, with ceiling-to-floor, wall-to-wall bookcases, and a giant fireplace. Franco did love his fireplaces. The sweet fragrance of white roses in a silver vase on the desk mingled with the dusty smell of old paper and leather.

Desk first. With her lit penlight held between her teeth, River rifled through the drawers. None were locked. She found several photographs shoved to the back of a drawer. Curious, she aimed the beam of the light on the top one. A redheaded little girl of about three, sitting on the lap of a woman whose head and shoulders had been cut off from the top of the photograph, leaving just the child, and the woman's arm around her.

With one finger, River slid the photograph to the side to see the ones beneath it. Same child, she presumed, quite a bit older. This time, the girl looked to be in her early teens. Her hair was in a braid over one shoulder. High cheekbones, narrowed eyes, and long red hair should've made her pretty, but she had a sulky mouth, and an underlying look of anger in her eyes. Not a happy camper.

The next picture showed her as a woman, in her twenties. She was even more attractive, and even angrier. She clearly hadn't enjoyed having her picture taken.

River put them back as she'd found them and closed the drawer. Who was the woman? A relative? Hardly likely, as it seemed Franco had photographs of his enormous family all over the house. If she was a relative, she'd be in other photos, and River hadn't noticed her. Or, she theorized as she searched through pens, and rubber bands, and other flotsam and jetsam normally found in desk drawers, maybe the girl's mother had meant something to Franco?

If she had, the fact that he, or someone, had decapitated her in the picture was pretty telling. Maybe the redhead was his illegitimate daughter. Hell, maybe it was unimportant and none of her business, since it sure as hell didn't seem to have anything to do with where Oliver might be.

Come on, Oliver. A clue. Just one freaking clue.

The quietness of the house weighed on her. The silence allowed her to hear her own pulse throbbing in her ears. She lived alone and spent a good deal of time in her own company, but the almost ominous silence, and the faint, uneasy feeling of foreboding, gave River the creeps. She tried to shake it off. Almost done. She found another small photograph of the redhead in the back of the middle drawer of the desk amid the paperclips.

Whoever she was, she was important enough to keep photographs of her throughout the years, yet not important enough to frame and put up with the rest of his family.

River would never know. She closed that drawer, too. No secretly coded letter from her brother, who was definitely on her shit list. If he wasn't dead. Crap. No. She couldn't think that. She could think about how she'd chew his ass out when she found him. But no to that, too. Reality was, no matter how irritating and annoying her brother had been over the years, River always reined in her natural inclination to ream him out. It wasn't his fault he had Asperger's. Displaying her emotions with him was counterproductive, and just ended up making her feel bad.

Looking around, she tried to decide where to search next. The bookcase was more of a tchotchke case than a place for books. The religious relics and saint statues looked expensive and each item had its own shelf and display light above. Not that she had the lights on at the moment.

Every few feet, there was a shelf of books. How many Bibles did a man need? Not this many, she was sure. Flipping pages in a few, she gave up searching inside books, and picked up some of the religious artifacts and turned them over to look at their bases.

She'd lost her damned mind. What the hell did she hope to find? It wasn't in her brother's secretive nature to tell her, or anyone else for that matter, what he was doing. And it would never occur to him to leave a meaningful note for her where she couldn't possibly find it.

She was searching because it made her feel as though she was doing *something*. But the reality was, she was just going through Nancy Drew-type motions, and she was goddamned tired of being an amateur sleuth. Her stubborn, take-action streak had left her in the middle of a goddamned jungle, while her mind told her she should've known better than to leap before looking. She'd go home, hire a private investigator, and let him piece it together, because there sure as hell wasn't anything to find here. With a sweep of the narrow beam of her flashlight, River made sure she hadn't left anything out of place in the study, then headed back upstairs, her heart heavy. She'd given it her best shot.

Disappointment aside, tomorrow she'd insist on going up to the plant on the way to the airport. At least that way, she could tell herself she'd left no stone unturned and she could give the private investigator enough information to get started.

She moved toward the north corridor, where she believed the family had bedrooms. As she reached the upstairs landing, River noticed a door ajar down that side of the hallway. She hesitated, about to head in the other direction to her room. Then she stopped. It wasn't breaking and entering if it was already partly open.

After pushing open the heavy mahogany door, she closed it behind her, flicking on the penlight. Wrinkling her nose at the smell of musk, cheap perfume, and leather, she hoped she wasn't walking in on someone sleeping. Expecting to see another lavishly appointed bedroom, she frowned as she played the beam over various objects around her. It took River a few jaw-dropping moments to wrap her brain around what she was looking at. Not a set for a naughty lingerie shoot, but the real deal. No. Freaking. Way!

Unable to resist her curiosity, she flicked on the lights. Red bulbs revealed a mirrored BDSM room. "Dear God, what the hell is all this?" Benches, and what looked like a hospital bed—all with leather restraints were among the larger pieces of furniture. She couldn't even begin to imagine how some of the equipment was used. A few pieces looked like something she'd use at the gym, but she was willing to bet they weren't there so someone could work on defining their six-pack.

Avoiding looking at her horrified, but fascinated, self in the mirrors, she wondered between the strange contraptions, making sure not to touch anything. Repelled but intrigued, River couldn't help trying to figure out what the use could possibly be for some of the things she saw. She didn't have that good an imagination. Nor did she want to go there. Eyeing something that looked like it was made for binding ankles and arms while someone was bent over a waist-high, red-carpeted rail, she shivered. If a man ever tried to tie her up like that, he'd have to make sure she was unconscious first. If she wasn't, she'd hit him where it hurt the most.

When she got back to her room, she was going to take a long hot shower, and use lots of antibacterial soap.

Was this a *cage*? A *human-sized* cage with restraints?

Along both walls were various pulleys and more restraints, leather and metal cuffs for wrists and ankles, bars with toggles and straps with spikes neatly arranged. A shelf held God only knew what kind of sex toys. A muzzle? Blindfolds? A spiked dog collar? A hard rubber dog bone? What the hell?

River had had enough. The room, and the vibe it held, creeped her out. As to whether it was used by Franco's sons or someone else, she had no idea. It certainly could not belong to pious, overly religious, apparition-seeing Franco Xavier.

She smiled. She bet pious, surly, Bishop Daklin hadn't been given the tour of *this* room.

Two things caught her eye almost simultaneously as she was about to flick off the lights. Veering to the left, River shone the flashlight on a streak of red on the mirrored wall.

Blood. A lot of blood.

It couldn't be anything else.

The whips, tipped in sharp silver metal and hanging neatly nearby, told a story River didn't want to explore. Sick to her stomach, she backed away, bumping into some sort of metal restraint with straps behind her. Pivoting as if the bogeyman was waiting to pounce on her, her mouth went dry. "Oh, crap, seriously?"

With ice-cold fingers, she touched the scrap of familiar red lace tied to a metal bar. Her blood went hot, then freezing cold. Dear God, this was her missing crimson lace el roce bra. The matching Chantilly lace thong was knotted on the other end of the bar. The lingerie had been in her suitcase yesterday, and gone last night after dinner. A cold chill raced up her spine, and her heart pounded so hard, she thought she'd pass out.

"This isn't a playroom for one, Miss Sullivan. Are you expecting company?"

NINE

H oly shit!" Hand over her heart, River spun around. Bishop Daklin stood inside the room, the closed door behind him as if he'd materialized out of thin air. The red glow of the lights on his stern features made him look demonic. "You scared the crap out of me."

"Did Franco invite you into his BDSM dungeon?"

BDSM dungeon? Lovely. "This is *Franco's* room?" Icy shivers vibrated through her bones.

Lips twitching, or a sly trick of the light, the bishop nodded.

"He has Bibles and crosses and crucifixes, and religious...*things*. All over the house." She waved a hand for emphasis. River couldn't pull her gaze away from him. He was her anchor in this bondage torture storm. "*You're* here!"

"And you shouldn't be. Come along, I'll walk you to your room."

She started wending her way to the door, then it suddenly registered what he wore, or didn't wear. Gone was the clerical garb, the collar and robes. Instead he wore black pants and a long-sleeved black T-shirt that hugged his body as faithfully as a layer of paint. His dark hair, slicked off his face, was tied in a stubby ponytail. He looked hard, sexy, and perfectly at ease in this room built for sin.

"If you've looked your fill, I suggest we return to our rooms before our host finds you snooping, or invites you to stay."

"God, no." She jerked her chin, indicating her awareness of his change of clothing, "Aren't you snooping, too?" Curious. Interesting. Out of left field.

"I went for a run. Vestments aren't designed for running."

"Unless it's down the corridors of the hacienda? At this time of morning?" *Liar, liar, pants on fire.*

His shoulders were even wider than she'd thought. His biceps flexed as he folded his arms over his broad chest. The shirt showed the ridges of his abs, and the slab of hard muscle of his chest. After the formal robes, and heavy chain and cross, seeing him dressed this way was almost like seeing him naked. And since she'd already imagined him that way, the black cloth merely hid what she was painfully aware was underneath his clothes.

"Outside. The streets were quiet and it's cooler. And what are you doing up at this hour?"

River swallowed to moisten her dry mouth. "Looking for any indication that my brother has been here." She stared up at him. "And before you ask, I didn't find anything."

His black pants, tucked into black—*not* running—boots, showed how long his legs were. Nothing made sense any longer. A bishop looked like a spy, he was lying about going for a run, her brother was missing, her stolen lingerie was in a BDSM room, there was blood on the wall, and dear God, what the hell was she *doing* here?

River felt a constriction in her chest and her eyelids burned. *Oh, shit.* Don't go all girly and *cry*! She was tired, scared, the room was overtly sexual and clearly had seen violence. Worse, Bishop Daklin was practically naked, but just as unobtainable as he'd been earlier at the fiesta. A good cry would wash away some of the tension and stress. But this man,

whoever or whatever he was, wasn't going to witness her moment of weakness.

Straightening her spine, she squared her shoulders and locked her knees. Tears deferred. "Seriously? Running? At four in the morning, in boots, in the dark?"

"Boots protect my ankles, and I have eyes like a wolf, Miss Sullivan."

The eyes like a wolf she believed. "Protect your *ankles*?" He shrugged. Which damn well didn't answer any of her questions.

His gaze flicked to the red of her bra and panties on display.

Her gaze followed his. "None of this is making sense."

"How so?"

"Those are mine. I don't know how they ended up here, and you certainly don't look like a bishop. Or a runner."

He focused on the red underwear, ignoring the other things she'd said. "Are they now?"

"Taken out of my suitcase last night." A shudder rippled through her. "Now I guess I know why. But by whom?" She edged her way toward the door.

The bishop frowned. "Aren't you going to take your lingerie?"

"Not just no, but hell, no." Like a child warned not to touch a hot stove, River put her hands behind her back. "The el roce were my favs, but I'd never wear them again after--" She shuddered. "--this. Can we *please* get out of here?" She desperately *wanted* to, but he wasn't moving, so she didn't either.

Their eyes locked.

"After you, Miss Sullivan."

"For God's sake, open the damn door," she snapped, walking right up to him. The heat of his body penetrated her clothes. The smell of him—-male, fresh air, testosterone—-filled her senses. Her heartbeat tripped, her mouth went dry, and prickly heat flooded her body. She was close enough to see a darker rim of blue around his irises, and the stubble on his jaw. He looked even more forbidding and too damned sexy. "And after being in this room together, discussing my underwear, for goodness sake, the least you can do is call me River."

#

Daklin ushered River down the long, dimly lit corridor to her room. He'd been about to go meet his men when he'd heard her leave her room. He'd taken the time to watch her sneak downstairs, following her movements on the live feed on his phone as she searched. He'd timed his departure to intersect with her visit to the BDSM room.

He knew what was in there. He also knew Xavier was in his bedroom now, having spent an hour in the BDSM room earlier with the maid. Xavier slept in his suite at the other end of the corridor in the family wing, the still bleeding Juanita wide-awake beside him biding her time to flee.

Daklin could watch the video feed from each room on his smarter-than-most phone. He'd spent an entertaining few minutes watching River move about the BDSM room. Her expression had gone from fascination, to adorable confusion, and then to horror when she'd seen the underwear and the blood. The look of wild-eyed fear in her eyes told him she'd had enough. That's when he'd decided to go to her side, telling himself all he was doing was making sure Xavier didn't find her snooping while she was alone, vulnerable, and in that damn room.

She'd taken a hell of a risk being nosy. Xavier, he of the BDSM room and torture devices, loved his sick games, and if he thought, for even a second, that River had any interest...

Fucking hell. The thought of that psychopath putting his hands on her twisted Daklin's gut. Her departure tomorrow couldn't come soon enough.

When she fumbled, attempting to get the key into the antiquated lock, Daklin silently plucked the small wrought iron key from her fingers and opened her door. Placing his palm on the small of her back, he, none too gently, shoved her ahead of him into the room. Her skin heated beneath the thin silk, and her breathing felt, more than sounded, erratic.

Fuck it! He shouldn't have touched her. The physical contact sent a maelstrom of sensations through his body, and aroused him to a degree he'd never experienced before simply by touching a woman when they were both fully dressed.

She turned to face him.

Time to go.

He who hesitates is lost.

Eyes not leaving her face, he nudged the door shut behind him with his foot. She didn't move back, and they were just inches apart. Far too close for strangers, far too fucking close for his libido, and far too damned close for a celibate bishop.

Her breath smelled of the peanut butter she'd raided from the kitchen as she snooped. "Do you enjoy playing with fire? *River*?"

Don't touch her again, dickwad. Keep your hands and other body parts to yourself. Open the door, close it between you, cross the corridor, repeat.

"I know guys hate seeing a woman cry." Her jaw trembled and her soft gray eyes welled. She didn't need to answer the question. He already knew she was bold and fearless, and would take risks she shouldn't take. Would he do any less if their roles were reversed, and it was *his* brother who had gone missing?

Fuck no. If anything, he would have been worse. If he still had the chance to keep his brother alive, he would have done anything. But that ship had sailed on a tide of Tovaritch Premium Russian Vodka.

161

"Fair w-warning." Her soft voice shook slightly and her chin lifted. "I'm about to cry now. You'd better make a run for it, Y-your Excellency."

Aw, shit. He admired her candor. The warning was unnecessary, since a glisten of tears already tracked down her cheeks. She didn't duck her chin, but merely used the flat of her hand to wipe them away as she maintained eye contact. It was both endearing and disturbing. Those liquid, gray eyes seemed to see directly into his blackened soul.

Daklin cupped her wobbly chin. Her skin felt warm and vibrantly alive beneath his fingers. "Ugly or pretty?" he murmured, indulging a greater need by allowing his thumb to brush across her full lower lip. Soft. Damp. Kissable.

"Oh, *ugly* tonight," she said with endearing honesty. "I haven't c-cried for a while, and I'm due, so this deluge will be epically hideous, I'm sure."

Daklin drank her in. Flushed cheeks, shiny, quicksilver eyes, and soft pink lips. Hot tears seeped beneath his palm, but he didn't help her when she wiped them away. As she did so, her fingers brushed his. Sparks instantly shot from the secondary contact directly to his groin.

"Why are you sad?" he asked, his voice unusually gruff.

Her jaw flexed. "I'm not *sad*. I-I'm frustrated. Scared. Angry. *Helpless.* Oliver's disappearance is getting to me. He deposited millions of dollars in my bank account without telli-- What?"

162

"He gave you millions?" That answered the question of where the money had gone.

"Five to be exact. I've been trying to figure out why. To pay a ransom? If so, I haven't had any demands. And who would kidnap him? He's mega smart, and apparently his skills are in great demand. He's been fending off job offers from corporations all over the world for years. Do you think maybe someone made him an offer he refused and they just *took* him?"

She was on a roll. Daklin merely shrugged in response, kept his mouth shut, and just enjoyed the view.

"And here's the other weird part of all this. No one in town seems to know him and he's lived here for *years*. *And* I discovered tonight that what Oliver told me about Franco being a sick puppy is true. And *you*."

"Me?"

"You jangle my nerves, Ash Daklin."

He craved the taste of her as badly as he'd ever craved Russian vodka. "Say that again."

"You jangle my nerves?"

He smiled. "My name." No one called him by his first name other than his mother. And Josh.

"Ash. Asher," she whispered.

Daklin didn't realize he'd lowered his head until her swimming eyes widened and she sucked in a small gasp. Warm, moist, peanut butter-scented breath flavored his lips. Long dark lashes lowered as she lifted her face for his kiss.

Using every ounce of discipline he could muster, Daklin pulled away, cupped her shoulders, and stepped back. Not far enough, because they stood right inside the door.

"No more exploring, Miss Sullivan. You're treading into places far more dangerous than you realize." He reached back for the door handle, and when his fingers closed around the cold metal, he gripped it so tightly, he felt the bones in his hands twist.

Dazed gray eyes snapped open.

"Lock your door. Have a safe return home. I probably won't see you before you leave." Opening the door just wide enough to slip through it, Daklin shut it softly in her astonished face.

For several seconds he stood in the dim corridor, struggling to regulate his heartbeat, which was in fight or flight mode. *Run.*

Straightening, he was about to do just do that when he heard her muffled response to his hasty exit. "And fuck you, too, Ash Daklin!"

Daklin had to wait until he was outside, and well away from the hacienda before he cracked up laughing. It hurt like hell, and he stopped abruptly. It wasn't funny. River Sullivan was more addictive than Tovaritch, and a hell of a lot more dangerous to his peace of mind than E-1x.

#

"Check out your bishop's face when he looks at her."

"Whatever you think you're seeing is your imagination. He's a man of God."

"He's a *man*. He wants to fuck her. Trust me."

"*I* want to fuck her."

"Fucking clouds your brain, Franco. Thinking with your cock makes you more stupid than usual. I don't like your bishop. He's too nosy, asks too many questions that have nothing to do with your apparition. I won't tell you again. Kill them both."

Distance made him bold. If the other man had been in striking distance, Franco would have remained mute until given permission to speak. "First of all," Franco said, his voice flat and dead, "Don't you *dare* tell me what to do in my own home, nor how to do it. I refuse to kill a man of God, a man sent by the Pope himself."

Refusing his partner's requests would have repercussions. Refusing brought terrifying retribution. Not their normal dominator subservient style retribution, but consequences Franco could only imagine. Which was why Franco had forced his sons and daughter to leave the valley days ago.

"Jesus, did you suddenly grow a pair, Francisco? Apparently we've been apart far too long. When we get off the line, use the flogger with the metal tips. Five hundred lashes. Put some muscle into it. I'll be watching."

Franco bit his lip. *Fuck him.*

"Answer me."

It was impossible not to. 'Yes' was always the correct response. He was like Pavlov's dog. "Yes, Master." His skin felt too tight, too hot. With only two days until their shared mission came to fruition, they were both walking on pins and needles.

"You made a fatal mistake inviting anyone, *particularly* a bishop here, now of all times. *You* made this problem. *You'd* better solve it.

Franco would get rid of the girl. Bishop Daklin, though, was another matter. If only the bishop would write that letter authenticating his apparition to Rome. Franco could go to his Maker in peace.

#

Daklin needed a drink.

A bottle.

Instead, the sky opened up about a mile from town and in seconds, the deluge soaked him to the skin as he trudged up the mountain on foot. "Great, just fucking great." It didn't cool him off any. If anything, it intensified the itch beneath his skin. Still mind-fucked from the exchange with the delectable, enticing, forbidden River Sullivan a few minutes earlier, he knew damn well that if he'd kissed her, he wouldn't have stopped.

While he empathized with her desire to find her brother, he wasn't prepared to indulge her need to try to find him in Los Santos. She'd most certainly hate him if, and when, they captured him. Knowing unequivocally how she'd feel about his part in it, Daklin didn't need to be present to witness it.

River couldn't be allowed in any way to compromise the op. And she wouldn't, thank God. In a few hours, she'd be gone. Out of sight, out of mind. She was a fever in his blood, and *almost* made him forget what he was there to do.

Redeem himself. Do an exemplary job blowing the shit out of the target, apprehend Xavier, capture, if he was still alive, the brilliant and elusive chemical engineer who'd almost certainly invented E-1x, and kill as few civilians as humanly possible.

Daklin shook his head, his hair spraying water as he half-ran, half-lurched his way up the steep hill. In the equation, he was expendable. He didn't particularly want to die. But he didn't particularly care if he lived either.

Before his leg injuries, he'd been capable of running ten miles with a loaded pack on his back. No sweat. Now, a couple of miles up a steep grade had him sweating and gritting his teeth from the agony in his thigh. Because of the injury to his left leg, his gait changed as he walked/ran/hobbled, throwing his body out of sync, torqueing different muscles and tendons.

The only reason he was making it one more step, and then another, was that he'd faked himself out, promising himself a slug of Tovaritch when he reached the others.

Too bad it was a lie, because by the time he reached the bend before the river where he'd arranged to meet his men, he was in too much pain to walk. Hobbling, every step was white-hot agony.

He walked the last half-mile so when he rounded the bend and saw the truck, his breathing was normal, and his gait steadier. His men didn't need to know his physical limitations until it was essential for them to have that knowledge.

A full moon flooded the narrow, jungle-lined road with

white light that even the dense overhang and torrential rain couldn't completely block. If it wasn't raining tomorrow night at this time, the moon would be an even brighter spotlight. With any luck, it wouldn't affect what they were here to do.

Turley and Gibbs were on duty at the mine. Nyhuis, Ram, and Aiza, leaning against the side of a dusty black four by four, straightened as Daklin approached.

"You're late," Aiza said as Daklin joined the men where they waited under the heavy foliage of a twisted rubber tree. "We thought Xavier might be insisting you stay once 'Mary' mentioned the twelfth."

Tonight's apparition had been masterful. "Nicely done weaving in those numbers to see if he would bite." Daklin stood still, allowing the pain to wash through him. "As you saw, he wouldn't be dissuaded from his course of action, but he did confirm that the numbers were a time. 3:33 in the afternoon."

"Now all we need is the location." Ortiz directed them toward the truck. "Let's pray our tech people are making inroads into that cloud site. The sooner the better."

"That's one mean limp, Daklin. I'm surprised Control cleared you to be in the field." Nyhuis smirked, his bald head catching the light like a white skullcap.

"It's fine." Daklin bit back the urge to tell the man to fuck off.

"An explosives engineer who can't run when the need arises is a dead man." Travis Nyhuis was not only good at getting under his skin, he was an all-around dick, and dangerously unpredictable. Commonly referred to as a meat eater, he was an operative whose method in combat was to fight tangos using the most violent methods possible. There was a time and place for that, but this wasn't that time. This was merely a reconnoitering exercise so they knew where to set the charges when they were ready. Daklin didn't like Nyhuis, and he knew the feeling was mutual.

But the dickhead had a point. There were no ifs, ands, or buts: he was fucked, because an explosives expert who couldn't run was going to die. But then Daklin had known that from day one. As long as his men got out, he accepted the cards he'd been dealt.

"Let Gibbs know we're on our way," he instructed Ortiz as he opened the passenger side door. They were continually testing the range of their comms and their satellite communications. The comms, when they weren't jammed, ranged about a mile, give or take. Satellite connection remained spotty and annoyingly erratic. The mountains would normally not have any impact on the powerful T-FLAC toys in the sky. But here, the signals were jammed surrounding the plant, the mine, and also Xavier's home. The jam was periodically lifted, presumably when Xavier needed to communicate, probably with his buyers. Then it slammed off again like a bolted door.

During several of the lulls, Control had procured the schematics for the mine. The two operatives working security had filled in many of the gaps. None of them had been inside the tunnels, however, and that was where they'd set their explosives.

Gibbs and Turley, on duty in their positions as security at the mine, would make sure a side gate was unlocked for them.

Ortiz spoke into his lip mic. "ETA fourteen minutes."

"Roger that." Gibbs' voice came through the earpiece clearly as Daklin climbed into the truck with the others. Ram started the vehicle, easing out of the shadows. There was no need for headlights, it was as bright as day. The engine, as any T-FLAC sanctioned vehicle always was, was almost silent as they drove on the narrow winding road filled with potholes, and rocks of various sizes that had come loose from mountainside.

"Sit-rep?" Daklin asked Ram, over the thump-thonk-thump of the windshield wipers as they fought with the water sluicing over the car. Moonlight shone through the glittering curtain in a surreal silver sheet in front of them. On either side of the one-lane road, the trees bowed with the weight of the deluge.

"My Dad, Marcus, and Charlie team started quietly evacuating as soon as you and Xavier left the party," Ram confirmed. "Father Marcus didn't want to wait until the last minute to get his people out."

As planned, half an hour after the fiesta shut down, two transport trucks had been waiting out of sight on the winding road going north. "How many?"

"Almost three hundred," Ram confirmed. "They'll go back for another fifty and be ready to transport the others at full dark tomorrow night. Or whenever you say the word."

Half the village evacuated and transported to Abad. T-FLAC was buying their silence with premium hotel rooms, meals, and the promise of more to come, all under the guise of the Cosio Government's concern for instability in the mine. Partially true. Blowing the shit out of a mine filled with unstable E-E-1x was going to make a big fucking bang, and a crater of a size none of them could predict. It didn't matter how good Daklin and his team were, or how carefully their charges were set, the danger was off the charts. Daklin didn't want more collateral damage than necessary.

He watched the road ahead, a snake-thin sliver bisecting the lush foliage. "Xavier didn't know who ninety percent of the people were tonight at the fiesta, so he probably won't even notice they're missing." The eyes of a prowling jaguar glowed red on the verge, then disappeared. "Talk to Marcus at first light. I want Juanita Perez out of town before he fucking kills her."

"My cousin?" Ram's Adam's apple bobbed and he nodded, his knuckles white on the steering wheel. "Her oldest sister lives in Santa de Porres."

"Get her out first thing. Were you aware Xavier's using her as a sex toy?"

"No fucking idea."

"Have our people connect her there." Control would arrange medics, psych eval, and counseling. SOP for operatives and/or their immediate families in a similar situation. Ram was T-FLAC, and his cousin was family.

"Yeah." Ram breathed out. "I will, thanks. This sick fucker has to be annihilated."

Ram had been with his father and Marcus. Daklin knew he hadn't seen what he'd seen, and for once, Nyhuis kept his mouth shut.

River had missed tonight's show by less than ten minutes.

Xavier's sex play with the young woman had been brutal, turning Daklin's stomach. First he'd made the girl whip him until she sobbed and begged him to let her stop as she sliced open his back, the blur of the sharp silver tips of the multiple strand whip slicing through his skin. When she'd collapsed because she couldn't wield the whip any longer, he'd buckled a spiked choke collar around her throat and strung her up so she hung from a bar, her feet swinging above the floor while he masturbated on her feet.

"The devil will be waiting for that one," Aiza said. "The cruelty we know of, I'm sure, is only the tip of the iceberg."
"Yeah. He's one sick fuck," Nyhuis said from the back seat. "I like a few of the toys he's got in there, but some of that crap. Man, we're talking mega fucked-up pain there." Apparently, there was a line even he wouldn't cross.

"We have Eliseo and the daughter, right?" It was frustrating for Daklin not to have 24/7 comm with Control.

"Yeah," Aiza told him, from the back seat. "Picked them up a couple of hours ago at their hotel. An unexpected bonus was that Trinidad was with them."

Trinidad was the plant supervisor and Xavier's younger

son. Daklin twisted in his seat. "So, he wasn't sleeping off a high at the hacienda?"

"Apparently not."

Hell, was Xavier not aware of anything happening under his nose? "Now all we need is for our people to find that damned truck and Oliver Sullivan. Then we can start the party." And they could get Sullivan's sister on her way home. She needed to be out of danger and away from the valley before her brother was hauled into custody.

They drove over the narrow bridge, where rainwater flooded the road. Two miles further, Turley hid the truck near the old strip mine—-now practically a lake—-in the weeds and shrubs off an unused side road.

They walked the rest of the way, sticking to the dense shadows beneath the dripping trees. The secured area surrounding the plant and mine entrance was lit up with massive, powerful four-hundred-watt stadium lights. They didn't need moonlight. The area was as bright as fucking day. Every leaf and blade of grass stood out in sharp relief. Between the tree line and the perimeter fence was nothing but scorched earth.

"Told you this place was as bare as a hooker's snatch," Nyhuis reminded them unnecessarily, speaking just loudly enough for their comms to pick up. "What'cha wanna do?"

"Crawl." Daklin dropped to his belly on the muddy ground. "Drop, and haul ass, ladies

TEN

Entry into the secured area, facilitated by Turley and Gibbs, had gone smoothly, with no one the wiser. The two operatives, still on security duty, remained outside to cover their asses. Not that Daklin and the others would know if there was a problem. As soon as the giant, titanium door blocking the entrance to the mine shut behind them and plunged them into stygian darkness deep inside the mountain, their comms wouldn't work.

The closed up space, with no circulation, smelled of body odor, diesel oil, and the familiar, underlying sickly, cheap perfumey smell of raw E-1x.

Heavy-duty tire tracks, filled with dirty water, sliced down the middle of a muddy road behind the huge steel door. The tunnel was big enough to drive a truck through. It was obvious trucks and large equipment had gone in and out, removing schist and ore for sorting, but also transporting miners and tools.

In the strong beams of their Mag lights, they saw a row of hard hats with embedded comms hanging near the entrance, ready for the miners first shift in a couple of hours. Daklin handed one to each man, then put one on himself.

Thanks to the value of the emeralds mined here, and now the absolute secrecy of the E-1x, T-FLAC already knew that

Xavier didn't allow anything extraneous on the premises other than the clothes worn by employees as they walked in. No shoes, jackets, bags, or anything carried in their pockets. Employees parked outside the perimeter fence, and were searched coming and going every shift.

Hardhat adjusted, comm on, Daklin turned his back to the others, and said softly, "Copy?" He already knew where the last explosive would be set: beside the enormous titanium doors, sealing off the mine for good.

Through the hardhat comm system, Nyhuis, Ortiz, and Aiza gave the affirmative. Although Daklin was the one who'd set the charges when the time came, the others were more than troubleshooters and muscle. They too had extensive explosives skills. It was just as important for their eyes to be on this preliminary run as Daklin's, because if the mission turned to shit, it would be their job to finish it.

The man he really wanted to have watching his back was his friend, Rafe Navarro, whose skill and experience matched Daklin's, but Navarro was about to become a first-time father, and Daklin had insisted he stay behind in Montana.

He motioned for them to move out, then glanced at his watch and set the timer. Half their allotted time would be for going as deep into the vast tunnel as they could, half the time getting back out.

Daklin counted on minimizing any collateral damage by blowing the mine and mountain sky high between shifts. By that time, the villagers would've been cleared out of town.

"We have less than two hours before Turley and Gibbs go off duty," he reminded them, over the crackle of feedback from the small speaker beside his ear. "And the Bishop needs to be back at the hacienda for breakfast with his host. Which gives us less than ninety minutes to reconnoiter and ten minutes to exit the perimeter." He gave them a hurry up hand signal, and they increased their pace. "Let's make the most of it."

"Smells like shit in here," Nyhuis bitched as they splashed through muddy stagnant water. Their footsteps echoed in the cavernous space.

"It's a mine, Nyhuis, what did you expect?" Ram asked rhetorically.

Satellite images had showed them the breadth and scope of the shaft. It went a good five miles straight into the heart of the mountain. A dozen shafts dropped periodically as the miners searched for a new vein of ore. Emeralds or E-1x. Daklin doubted Xavier wasted much time with emeralds anymore. E-1x was by far the most lucrative product mined here.

As he increased speed, grinding his teeth against the pain shooting down his leg, Daklin gauged the distance. Time in, time out, *where* to set the charges the next time he was here, how long each set up would take. In his brain, he calculated. Tallied. Weighed odds and variables.

If he screwed up his timing by so much as a second or two, he'd become part of the big bang. A footnote in the lore of T-

FLAC.

One of their fallen agents who was never resurrected.

That alcoholic Daklin guy who'd killed his brother, then fucked up an op and died himself. Too bad. So sad. The end.

Hell of a thing to leave as his legacy.

Legacy to whom? Josh was dead. Dear old wife-beating, alcoholic dad was long gone. His stepmother, who he'd always had a contentious relationship with, hated his guts for killing her golden boy.

So, no one.

No one to give a flying fuck if he lived or died.

He had his reputation, tarnished as it was; that was fucking *it*.

He'd do this job right, even if it killed him. Which it very well might.

He came across another side tunnel, which indicated a vertical shaft. Personally climbing down any of the shafts was a job for an able-bodied man with the use of both legs, and the ability to run like hell if things went sideways. Daklin discounted going down. He'd place the explosives along the walls lining the main tunnel, working back to front.

Timing was everything.

Poetic justice. E-1x to blow the shit out of E-1x.

"Five-ton dump truck?" Aiza jerked his chin at a secondary tire track slightly off center from the larger imprint. "Light in, heavy out?"

Miners had to remove the ore and schist. "Looks like." Daklin crouched down on his hunches, owning the pain that sluiced up his right thigh, into his hip, and sucking it up to shine his Mag light at an angle across the second set of treads.

He whistled. "Check this out. *Not* a tractor and semi-trailer. Look at these treads. This looks like a Bridgestone tire track. I guesstimate the transport vehicle is only a three and a half ton. Probably panel van. We've been looking for big. We *should* have been looking for *small*. Small and heavy."

"Or the E-1x could be removed from here in the panel van containing tons of E-1x, then driven into the back of that semi my dad saw," Ram suggested, adding the beam of his powerful light to the others as Daklin got to his feet. "Bringing us back to square one."

"It's a long-haul to the coast. Mountains, insurgents, rebels." Daklin's hand signal urged them to continue walking at a faster pace. They'd set some charges at the entrance, but to get the biggest bang for their buck, he wanted to get as deep inside the mountain as possible. That meant another five miles of walking on uneven ground. Without limping. Or crying like a little girl. Or fucking passing out.

A flash of River's sweet face crumpled with stress tears caused a hard pang in his chest. He'd been dangerously close to saying fuck it all, and crushing her mouth under his. He wanted her so bad, even his teeth ached with need. Thank God she'd be gone in the morning. She was a dangerous distraction on an op where his leg was dangerously distracting already.

Fuck, a drink would hit the spot right now.

Focus. Block everything but the job at hand.

At a fast clip, it should take them, give or take, an hour fifteen to travel the length of the tunnel, an hour fifteen back. They had two hours max. In those two hours, Daklin had to figure out where he'd lay the explosives when he came back. It didn't have to be neat. All he needed was to follow the pale vein of E-1x when he found it. A timed blast, beginning, middle, and end would blow the whole mountain. He just had to figure out how to do a two-and-a-half-hour job in under two hours.

"Pick up the pace." He increased his speed at a hell of a cost. The uneven ground wasn't helping any. The pain was gripping and unrelenting. Sweat popped up on his brow despite the still, cool air.

He gritted his teeth. "Airports have all been staked out. My vote is still that they're taking the load to a ship. And if they went through a broker for the tractor and semi, the broker probably doesn't have any idea what they're transporting.

"Find the broker, and they'll probably have an EOBR." The electronic-on-board recorder would track the semi with a GPS. No truck owner wanted his truck, or his customer's cargo, to go missing. Unless the broker was in on it, and/or there *was* no EOBR. Or unless Xavier's people had their own semi and tractor, which made more sense.

That was a fuck-load of ifs.

"We track it that way," he told them, able to talk at a normal volume only because of the helmet mics. The cavernous space smelled of gym socks. The space echoed and gave false direction sounds. "As soon as we have a comm link, contact Control. I want every single shipping company between here and the coast contacted. Cosio, Peru, Columbia, and Ecuador, hell, throw in Brazil as well. Anything and everything shipped out of Cosio in the past forty-five days. Also outgoing cargo on *every* ship stopped. It's there, we just have to find it."

"That's a fucking tall order." Aiza's voice echoed slightly. "Unless they don't give a shit if they blow up everything en route, *and* lose their big payday, I think they'd make sure that the semi has hazmat signs all over it. We can start there."

"Have them do a search on any semi and tractor purchased for delivery to Cosio." Daklin mentally marked a place low on the rock wall for one of his charges and kept moving. Faster now as time ticked away and they weren't deep enough yet. "Nyhuis." Daklin had misgivings about sending Nyhuis outside on his own. No one had been killed so far. He'd like to keep it that way until it became completely necessary. Daklin changed his order. "No. Ram, go outside, see if we lucked out and have a sat link. Call this in. Meet us back at the truck. We're not waiting for anything. If they find the shipment, great, but we're lighting up the mountain tomorrow night."

"What about Dr. Sullivan?" Angel Aiza asked, catching up with him.

Yeah, what the fuck about Oliver Sullivan? Where was he? Dead? Incapacitated? Didn't want to be found? "If he's able to be found, we'll find him. If not, hopefully that cloud site will give us what we need to know. Either way, we have to learn how to defuse E-1x safely."

"This time tomorrow then," Nyhuis said with relish.

Daklin figured if this was his time to die, he'd rather it came sooner than later. As long as River was far away, he'd only have himself and his men to be concerned about. Taking himself out of that equation, he just had to set the charges, and make sure he didn't kill his men or have massive, unexpected collateral damage.

Fortunately, the last of the villagers would be whisked away to safety by afternoon. River would be winging her way back to Portland, and Xavier would be trapped here to see the end of his lucrative enterprise.

A win-win.

As he walked, Daklin mentally heard the pulsing beat of a detonator echoing with his rapid footsteps.

#

A good cry was always cathartic. River didn't do it often, but when she did, like in the early hours of the morning, she gave it her all. It was both exhausting and therapeutic. This morning she felt positive and, barring seeing Bishop Daklin again, ready for anything. A few splashes of cold water, judiciously applied concealer under her makeup, and a deep breath, and she was good as new.

It was barely light, the sky still colorless and milky, the sleeping village painted in shades of hazy gray. A glance out of her window showed the dim streets empty except for a scrawny black cat, wandering down the middle of the road, presumably looking for breakfast.

Dressed in jeans, a sleeveless blue and white striped cotton top, and gray hiking shoes, River grabbed a lightweight jacket and left her room. A shiver of revulsion made her speed up her steps as she passed the closed door of the kink room. The house was quiet as she tiptoed down the stairs. Thank God she was leaving, because she'd never be able to look Franco Xavier in the eye knowing what he did in that room.

Before he packed her off to the airport, she was going up to the plant where Oliver had worked. Her last hurrah.

She knew he wasn't there. But perhaps he'd left something behind. No, that wasn't Oliver. He never even said goodbye when he disconnected a phone call. One moment he was talking, sure, in monosyllables, but still, talking; then next, there'd be dead air.

River wanted to see where he'd worked, where he'd spent the past mysterious five years. Hell, she just wanted to know she'd tried every which way to get answers before she got on that plane. When she got home, she was going to hire the best P.I. Oliver's money could buy.

As she reached the entry hall, she heard faint sounds from the kitchen, but didn't see anyone as she went through the front door, and down the curved front steps framed by massive stone columns. She'd walk up the damn mountain if she had to, but she'd much rather have wheels. There was a slight hope the rental car actually had four tires on it by now.

If not, she'd borrow a car from someone. If not that, hell, she'd steal a car. Oliver had taught her how to a hotwire a car on her thirteenth birthday as a lark. River hoped it wouldn't come to that.

The sky was just tinged with color, and the dawn air smelled fresh and invigorating as she headed to Jorge's house through the empty streets. The town was so quiet it was almost like walking onto the set of some apocalyptic movie. She pulled on the lime green windbreaker, as if it would stop a zombie attack.

Jorge was in his garage when River walked up to his house.

"Good morning, señorita." He waved a steaming coffee cup in the direction of the car, where a fat speckled hen perched on the steering wheel. "She is ready for you, and as good as new."

As new as it had been twenty years ago anyway, but at least the little convertible would make it back to the airport. The chicken gave River a disinterested look, then tucked her beak under her wing. "That's terrific news, Jorge, thank you."

She always carried her passport and money on her when she traveled, but now River considered, for a moment, going back to the hacienda to pick up her suitcase. She had the car. She could drive up to the plant, heading directly after to the airport. But no matter how creepy her host was, he'd been gracious enough to allow her to stay. She owed him a thank you, at least.

River knew damned well it wasn't Franco Xavier she wanted to see one last time. To be absolutely honest, she wanted one more chance to see the surly, but oh so tempting Bishop Ash Daklin to give him a last look at the temptation he was allowing to walk away.

So, up the mountain, back to say adios, and she'd be on her way home.

Reaching into the pack clipped to her waistband, River took out her wallet. "How much do I owe you?"

"No, no." He waved a gnarled hand. "The bishop he come. His Excellency. He pay."

"Seriously? When was that?"

"Yesterday afternoon. Before the fiesta. He is a good man, yes?"

"That was very...kind of him, yes." Wow. So, he'd wanted her gone long before last night. Then why had he almost kissed her? Why give her those hungry looks? River paused her mental musings. Was it precisely because he was tempted that he wanted to get rid of her? Of course it was. It was cruel of her to flex her femme fatale muscles on a man who, whether he wanted her or not, couldn't have her.

It was a good thing she was leaving. She'd remove temptation for both of them.

Walking over to a pegboard holding hundreds of bunches of dusty keys and two, very much alive, green lizards, Jorge took down the key with the rental tag on it and shuffled over to her, dropping it in River's hand. "My wife's third brother's son, Ramse, come help me last night. He's a good boy. You know him? He work for *el Jefe*."

She vaguely remembered the tall, swarthy, serious-looking guy from when she arrived. "He's Franco's bodyguard, right?"

Yes, he was. Jorge was delighted to talk about his nephew for as long as she was willing to stand there. Ram had been a doctor. Very rich. Something bad had happened, and now he was home for a while. Glad for the job as bodyguard to *el Jefe.*

The guy didn't look like a doctor, but that was none of her business. She was sure he was a lovely man who was happy to have a job.

River zipped the windbreaker against the morning chill, sticking her hands in her pockets as he talked. After a few minutes and having waited for a pause, she thanked him profusely, asked him politely to remove his chicken from the car, waited as he apologetically cleaned the chicken shit off the white, genuine, artificial imitation leather seat, then finally got behind the wheel.

"You go to Santa de Porres today, yes?"

"A little later, yes." She started the car. It smelled a little like a chicken coop, and sounded asthmatic, but at least it started. "Would you like to go with me?"

He ducked his head. "I would ask that you take my youngest sister's girl, Juanita, with you. She has a married sister who lives there."

"I'd be happy to take her. Can you let her know I'll be leaving at about ten? Where does she live? I can pick her up when I'm on my way."

The old man's eyes met hers as he said carefully in English, "She lives at the hacienda, señorita. I will tell her to be ready at ten."

Juanita, the pregnant maid who River suspected had taken her lingerie and who'd participated in Franco's sick game in that kink room? River might, briefly, have wondered if the young woman had participated willingly, but hearing the urgency in Jorge's voice, she realized there'd been nothing willing about it. She felt sick to her stomach when she realized some of the things her brother had told her about Franco's proclivities were true.

River hadn't believed him at the time, but after last night, she did.

She thanked Jorge again, and with a wave, was on her way out of town. Thank God she was leaving. She couldn't have spent another night in that house.

"Ugh." She shuddered. She was glad for the windbreaker. The convertible's top couldn't go up, and the early morning air was chilly. As soon as the sun crested the mountain, the temperature would soar, but for now, she enjoyed the cool wind blowing in her face.

"Where is everybody?" Surely, people were going to work, or returning from work? There wasn't a single soul outside. River drove through the square, and around the splashing fountain, then headed north out of town. Straight ahead was the winding road back to the towns along the route to the capital city, Santa de Porres, and the airport.

She presumed there was a road nearby that would take her up to the plant, and then almost passed it. There was no sign, but she saw it just in time and made a hard right onto a much narrower road. Jungle vegetation crowded the path on either side, forming a dim green tunnel. The air smelled fresh. Rain from earlier dripped off the trees overhead and sheened the road.

On either side of the narrow road, giant trees and tall palms blocked most of the light, and River turned on her high beams, even though it would be light soon enough. Her hair whipped across her face as she reached out to turn on the radio. She fiddled with the buttons. Nada. Not even a crackle. That wasn't unexpected, though. She was in between folds of the mountain.

The digital clock had displayed 1:14 since she'd picked the car up at the airport.

She didn't care what time it was. She'd take whatever flight she made. She started to sing Waterloo. She wasn't Abba, but she could hold a tune, and it reminded her of her mom and seemed appropriate for the moment.

Singing while driving along a winding mountain road, the wind in her hair, was almost as good as singing in the shower. She sang at full volume.

Her fate had nothing to do with Bishop Ash Daklin, and she knew it. The road was twisty, and the elevation so steep the little car labored instead of zipping.

Glancing at the speedometer, it read forty, she stopped singing mid-phrase. "Want me to push you, little car? We'd go a damn sight faster." At least the return trip would be downhill all the way. She resumed tapping her foot in time with the tune. Slowing as she came to a water-covered bridge spanning a swiftly moving river, she cast a wary eye at the rippling water reflecting the pale whitish blue of the sky. The reflection made it hard to see the edge and there were no railings. Oh man, this was a little terrifying.

"Oliver, if you had to drive this commute every day, I see why you never went into town. This is freaking nerve-wracking."

Going at a snail's pace down the center, she concentrated so hard her eyes burned from not blinking the whole way. On the other side of the bridge, she huffed out a big breath, resuming her singing. Her singing abruptly stopped and changed to a scream as the blurred, dark shape of a man appeared out of nowhere beside the car.

He vaulted over the door to land in the passenger seat with a thump and a curse. River automatically slammed her foot down on the brake. The car slowed to a stop, nose-deep in a dense clump of ferns on the side of the road. A cloud of tiny green butterflies drifted off a shrub and floated in the air like smoke.

Twisting in her seat she punched Bishop Daklin in the chest. "You scared the shit out of me! What are you doing up here?"

He scowled. "What are *you* doing here?"

"I asked first." He wore the same clothes as earlier. Black on black on black, though now with the added sartorial accessory of semi-dried mud all over his clothes and face. It looked as though he'd rolled in the dirt after a bank heist. Is that what he'd done since leaving her unfulfilled five hours ago? Gone mud wrestling?

He stared at her without responding. She waited. He remained silent. After a few more seconds, River huffed out a sigh. *Exasperating man.* "I want to see where my brother worked."

She returned his scowl as she eased her foot off the brake and angled back on the road. She needed more distance time-wise than the few hours since she'd seen him last. In fact, since she hadn't expected to see him at all, having him drop into the car unexpectedly rattled her.

She shot him a sideways glance, distracted by a teeny, jade colored butterfly on his dark hair. She resisted the urge to brush it away, giving her a reason to touch him in the process. She resisted harder. After a moment, it fluttered off on its own.

"Did you walk all the way up here to play in the mud, Pigpen?"

"The plant has top-notch, armed guards." Adjusting the seat, he angled his long legs in the small foot-well to find more, nonexistent, space. The deep red-brown mud on his face didn't seem to bother him, but the way the dark dirt accentuated his piercing blue eyes bothered *her*. A lot. It annoyed the hell out of her that even as annoyed as she was, there was still something so compelling about him. Her heart raced, and her skin felt overly sensitized. Crazy. Foolish.

"They won't let you in." His voice was curt to the point of rudeness. "This place isn't a lingerie factory, River. We're not talking sewing machines and swatches of silk."

"I know," Yeah, she really did, and once again he'd adroitly managed to not answer a question. No wonder he was crankier than usual. She noticed how hard he was gripping his left thigh with his fingers. The man was in pain. What on earth induced him to walk all the way up the mountainside? Then catapult into the car?

"Your brother isn't there. Turn around, and head back."

His words, phrased as an order, mitigated some of River's sympathy. "You're welcome to hop back *out* of the car right here if you like. Flag down a ride from those guys." She indicated a beat-up gray pickup truck traveling in the opposite direction. "I'm on a mission."

"A mission impossible, Miss Sullivan. We both know you're wasting your time. Go back to Portland and your life. Your brother's an adult. If he's alive, he'll eventually contact you. If not. Not."

She stared at him. "Wow. Is that what they teach you about empathy at the seminary, Bishop?"

His eyes glinted and his lips might've twitched. It was hard to tell on his dirt-covered face, and the mottled light shining through the trees surrounding them. "Want me to lie? That's a sin you know."

Good thing he couldn't read her mind then.

As they rounded a sharp bend into the pale rose-gold rays of early morning, the thick vegetation abruptly stopped. It was as though a giant's razor had scraped the ground leaving nothing but dirt and mud behind.

River didn't need the distraction of him up close and personal. Even smeared with mud, he was...*too*. Too big. Too sexy. Too rude. Too damned well *here*. "All I want you to do is drive, and enjoy the scenery. And respectfully? Shut the hell up unless you have something positive and affirming to say."

He made a choking sound, but when she shot him a fulminating glance, he was looking straight ahead, his expression somber.

"I don't know why I think my brother would leave a clue behind. I know that's not at all who Oliver is." She didn't know why she felt the need to talk to him since he was clearly unsympathetic, and impatient to get back to the hacienda. Well, too damn bad.

"Because you need a way to make sense of his disappearance." His tone softened slightly. But the sympathy was short-lived. "You're wasting your time. Trust me on this."

He was right about the security at the plant. The low building, surrounded by a high fence complete with two tall guard towers, was backed by the dark bulk of the mountain. "It's my time to waste," she added, slowing as she approached the front gate and a parking lot-sized area of gravel. It crackled and crunched like breakfast cereal under the tires.

"I'll never come back here, so this is my last shot, and armed guards, or not, I'm *going* to see Oliver's la—"

"Turn around, River." Tone implacable, he wrapped strong, muddy fingers over hers and took control of the steering wheel. With his other hand, he withdrew a large black gun from the small of his back. "*Now!*"

Holy crap. Was he going to *shoot* her?

Just as she yelled an indignant, "Hey!" something slammed into the dash, splintering the clock. It took a second or two to compute what had just happened as she stared with incomprehension at the small black hole where the numbers had been frozen at 1:14. "What the hell?"

Then it clicked. Someone was shooting at *them.* Her heart raced and her palms grew sweaty as she tried to twist around to see who was taking pot shots.

"Don't look. *Drive.*" Aiming the gun over her head, Bishop Daklin fired off half a dozen shots. River's ears rang as her brain tried to catch up with what the hell was happening.

"Let go, damn it." A surge of adrenaline had her heart catapulted into her throat. Ineffectually, she slapped at his hand. "Do you want to kill us both?"

Fighting him for control of the steering wheel, she yelped as the side mirror, inches from her propped elbow, exploded, showering her with shards of glass.

ELEVEN

H oly shit!" Her voice went high with shock as the mirror, inches from her arm, shattered. Daklin wrenched the wheel hard left. Twisting in the passenger seat, he squeezed off several shots of his own.

Fuck!

The piece of crap car skittered on the gravel as he spun the wheel away from the gunfire and pointed back the way they'd come. The small car slewed across the road three hundred yards in front of the gate, spewing hail-like pea gravel. The men in the twin guard towers fired again.

For fucksake, did they really think a blonde in an ancient red sports car was going to break in? Clearly Xavier's men didn't recognize him as the Bishop with his face covered in mud, and his non-traditional clothing. Xavier would have their asses if his bishop died before his apparition was authenticated.

These guys hadn't had anyone to shoot at for weeks. Daklin already knew from his men that they were itching for some action. River had sure as shit just given it to them.

He gave her credit for not freezing as she stomped on the gas, propelling them forward as he squeezed off several more shots. This time, the bullets came fast and dangerously close. M4, rotating bolt, five hundred and fifty yard range, muzzle velocity three thousand feet, gas-operating assault rifles were spitting out close to a thousand rounds a minute.

It was fucking divine providence they weren't already filled with holes. The M4 had the capability to mount the M203 grenade launcher, but he doubted they'd bring out the big guns without ascertaining a credible threat. But what the fuck did he know? Maybe any threat was credible to them.

The scare tactics were effective, but if that didn't work, Daklin knew the order was to kill. They were in a fatal funnel. No fucking cover for three miles. He was eager as hell to get the fuck out of range before that happened.

Gravel jumped and pinged against the sides and undercarriage of the car as they gathered speed going downhill.

"You hurt?" Cutting her a quick glance, he checked for any signs of blood.

"That's the freaking *least* of my problems right now!" River flinched as a bullet ripped through the headrest on the back seat in a burst of foam and faux leather. *Thwap.* Daklin felt the zap as it pierced the floorboard behind the passenger seat, inches from his ass.

"Never mind," she shouted, brow furrowed in concentration, as she focused on where they were headed, not where they'd been.

Another slug ricocheted off the passenger door with a high-pitched screech. She flinched reflexively. No screaming, no theatrics.

"Floor it," he ordered, tightening his fingers over hers as she slowed instinctively to avoid something small and fury scurrying across the narrow road.

River flinched again as something hit her cheek——a bit of upholstery, he deduced, since it left a red mark but no blood. "You can't——"

"Fucking *punch* it, River. These guys aren't dicking around. They're using us as target practice." His Glock was now out of range, their M4's were not. Xavier's security guys would stop dicking around *trying* to miss them soon. Then all bets were off.

He spoke into his comm. "Taking fire. What the hell's going on?"

Having just passed them going the opposite way, they weren't out of comm range yet. Gibbs responded immediately. "Turley and I are halfway back. Want us to——"

"No, stay put. I got this." No way to get his foot on the accelerator, but his grip over her hands was enough to adroitly steer the car once she stopped fighting him.

"Don't freak out," he told her calmly, seeing the stark fear on her face as a bullet passed between their heads to shatter the windshield a mere arm's-length in front of their faces. Instantly the safety glass exploded, rendering visibility zero.

"Who are you talking to? God or me? Oh, shit!" she cried as he levered himself out of the passenger seat and extricated his good leg. "What the hell are you doing?"

Fingers still clamped tightly over hers, his bum leg

screaming for mercy, Daklin kicked out the frame of the windshield. The fragmented panel of glass didn't break off cleanly. Instead, it stayed hinged at the bottom and bounced on the hood of the car, but at least he had a clear view of the road ahead.

"What are you? Some kind of ninja priest?"

Daklin maneuvered his body back into the small bucket seat as fast as he could, given the confined space and the agony in his leg. It was sheer luck the guards on the gates *hadn't* hit them. Bullets came so close to his head, he felt them pass and heard their whine.

"Hands off the wheel," he yelled as a barrage of bullets struck various parts of the car.

His men hadn't been kidding when they said the mine's security team was top notch. They were hitting everything *but* the two people inside the moving vehicle. "I've got it," he yelled over the loud bangs, screeches, and percussion of bullets hitting metal. "Go! Go! Go!"

Sliding her hands from beneath his one at a time, River gripped them together in her lap. Her foot on the gas, his hands steering. "She won't go any faster!"

A hail of bullets hit the trunk. Loud and dramatic. She recoiled, then hunching her shoulders.

Her pale, whipping hair was a perfect target. He took one hand off the wheel to push down on the top of her head. "Slouch down as low as you can."

River wriggled to reposition herself, in the process

inadvertently rubbing her breasts against his arm. Daklin laughed.

"You're *enjoying* this?!"

"It has its perks," he said, voice dry. No way for her to crouch completely out of sight. No room. "Duck and come up between my arms." It was tricky in a fast moving little convertible, but after a couple of heartbeats, she maneuvered between his outstretched arms until her head was tucked beneath his chin. "Good girl, almost out of range."

"Why—?" Her breath felt hot through his damp T-shirt, right over his heart. "Who—-? Never mind."

Strands of silky, sunny hair lashed his jaw. It smelled like summer rain and flowers. "Two more turns. We'll be out of range. They won't be able to see us." Unless they were in a vehicle chasing them down. "Another mile and a half to the tree line. What's protocol?" he asked into his comm. "Give chase or repel?" He was met with dead air. The others were out of range.

A mile and a half with targets painted on their backs.

Another hail of bullets struck the back of car as they approached the bend leading to the bridge. The trunk, the side panel, the back seat, his side mirror. Chunks of metal, glass, rubber, and leather flew. Eyes narrowed against the wind, he kept going, protecting River with his body as they drove as fast as the car was capable of going.

His death would be premature and inglorious. *River's* death was unacceptable.

"Should I—-?"

"No." Whatever it was she was asking they couldn't stop. Couldn't slow down. She couldn't sit up. He didn't need her help.

Almost home free... The convertible skittered sideways as the left rear tire blew out. "*Fuck*." Daklin fought for control of the car from his position in the passenger seat as she automatically took her foot off the pedal. "No! Foot back on the accelerator, don't slow down."

Returning her foot to the gas immediately, the car jerked back to full speed. "Good girl."

The sky opened, and it started to rain. Fat drops poured over them in a hard shower. The strength of the deluge was powerful enough to bend branches almost to the ground, and whip leaves and flowers as if they were in a dishwasher. Daklin blinked muddy water out of his eyes, and peered down the road through a thick gray curtain.

"Murphy's Law in full effect!" River shouted against the drumming sound of water pounding them, the vehicle, and the road. "Can you see to drive?"

Barely. The road itself was a shade darker than the pounding deluge. "Want me to pull over until it stops?" he yelled, being facetious. The tires slithered in a pool of water sheeting the tarmac, and he adjusted his grip on the steering wheel.

"Sure, if you see a gas station."

Because she sounded so damned pithy, Daklin smiled despite his fear that she'd be the one hurt if this turned to even more shit.

A stash of weapons and ammo, explosives, and comms, ready for tonight, was hidden where he and his men had parked earlier. He could hold off an army from there if necessary. The arterial dirt road, which led to the strip mine where they'd hidden the truck earlier, was coming up fast on the left. It was veer off now, or limp back into town possibly with the bad guys hot on their asses.

Now. Wrenching the steering wheel a hard left, Daklin drove the car straight for the bushes. Branches and leaves slapped at his head and shoulders, wet leaves rained down on them as they bumped and lurched through the heavy underbrush. They'd covered their tracks coming and going in the truck earlier, and Daklin forged the same path over logs, rocks, and slick mud, deeper into the jungle. Thick vegetation closed behind them. A visually impenetrable green wall closed them off from the road.

Sounding like sharp nails on a blackboard, small branches raked the paintwork. The sound blended in a discordant chorus with indignant cries of two roosting green yellow crown parrots, which swooped inches from their heads to fly, squawking, higher into the trees.

Daklin held up his arm to protect River's head as the car swept aside dense foliage in its plunge deeper into the undergrowth. A small troop of red howler monkeys launched themselves to a higher, safer perch, screeching as they hurled themselves from branch to branch.

"Foot off the pedal!" he shouted.

Listing, the small car came to a shuddering stop with the front end buried deep inside a dense, small-leafed, acid-green shrub. The thick vegetation surrounding them blocked some of the rain, leaving them in a dim, green cavernous thicket.

Daklin turned off the engine. It pinged and popped as River's warm, moist breath penetrated his T-shirt. The hot, sweaty, summer rain scent of her fogged his brain. His erection was instantaneous. Or hell, perhaps it hadn't subsided in the past twenty-four hours.

For someone usually animated and opinionated, she sat as if frozen. Being shot at would scare anyone not used to that kind of violence. He brushed a tender kiss over the crown of her bowed head, still nestled on his chest. "It's okay. No one can see us here."

"There's a snake in my lap," she said quietly, barely breathing.

He went hot, cold, then hot as he looked down. Indeed, beside a small broken branch from the trees they just crashed through, a two and a half foot long green tree viper, with its distinct orange ventrolateral stripe, lay draped over her jean-clad thigh.

Fucking hell.

Grabbing the snake around its middle, Daklin flung its writhing coils back into the underbrush.

Holy Christ. Several years ago, he'd been bitten by a viper while on an op in Burma. Its potent hemotoxin had felt like a branding iron burning into his upper back. It had hurt like the fires of hell. Aside from his assorted dings and dents, he had a divot in his back where one of his men had dug out the necrosis and saved his life.

Dropping his hand from the wheel, he ran his fingers over her thigh as he did a visual inspection of her leg. No puncture marks that he could see. No blood. Not breathing, he pressed two fingers hard into the taut muscles, then walked them up her leg almost to the juncture of her thighs. He felt the heat of her there, and was furious with himself for being horny, and wanting her this badly when she might be fatally wounded.

"Does this hurt?"

River had turned to watch the snake's trajectory as she responded, "Uh-uh." She waited until it had landed soundlessly out of sight before she twisted her head to look up at him. "Not poisonous, right?"

There wasn't a damn thing, flora, fauna, or man, in the Cosian jungles that couldn't kill. Daklin found his heart in his throat, a fear he'd never felt for himself while on an op.

Her tilted face made it almost impossible not to close the few inches' gap to kiss her. As he looked in her clear, brave eyes, he had the sudden feeling that all truths needed to be told.

Unnecessary. She'd be gone in an hour.

"Did it bite you?" He found he had to push the words out of his restricted throat. The last time he'd felt fear like this was the fateful night Josh called.

Wide-eyed, she stayed silent. "River? Did you feel a sharp

sting? Pressure? *Pain.* Heat? Anything at all?" Symptoms would appear within minutes of a bite. The pain would come first, intense enough that he wouldn't need to ask.

"No."

He could feel her heartbeat as she leaned against him. Rapid with fear. "Then it wasn't poisonous."

"Meaning if it *had* bitten me..."

Lightheaded, he rested his cheek on her hair. "Lethal."

Letting out a shaky breath, she ran her fingers over her thigh where he'd touched her. When she was done with her own inspection, she turned her head. Their faces were inches apart. Close enough for Daklin to notice the intriguing flecks of dark blue in the gray smoke of her eyes. They shone, not with fear, but with high adrenaline.

He got it. His own heart was pumping at double speed, and he was wired with a flood of adrenalin that had fuck-all to do with being shot at. *That* he was used to.

"No holes," she assured him, her voice husky. She didn't look around to see where they were, just sat upright inside the circle of his arms, her spikey-lashed gaze fixed on his face. Water sluiced her skin, making it look as delicate and glowing as pink pearl. With her pale hair plastered to her head, the pure oval of her face gave her a delicate appearance at odds with the fierce, determined woman he knew her to be. "Are we safe here?"

Daklin's gaze dropped to her slightly parted lips. "From the men who were shooting at us, yeah." The insidious, gnawing hunger that had been building inside him since he'd first laid eyes on her surged through him. "What the fuck am I going to do about you?" His voice was low, nothing but gravel and greed.

"That depends on how much instruction you might need. Have you always been celibate, Bishop Daklin?"

"Are you asking if I want you, or if I know how to do what I want to do to you, Miss Sullivan?"

Twisting in her seat to face him fully, River's eyes remained steady on his face. "Either. Both. Do you?"

He took her hand, pulling it to his lap and placing it on his throbbing erection. "Does this answer the question?

"One of them. For the other, I'm willing to provide a tutorial, if necessary." The hunger in her eyes matched his own, while the teasing tone of her voice captivated him. "Are you going to remember you're Bishop Daklin and make a hasty retreat again?"

"I know exactly who I am, and who I'm not."

"You're no bishop." Not quite a question.

"If I was, I'd be in deep trouble with you around. I wouldn't allow myself to fall into this...situation."

"Thank God," she said with feeling. "I was afraid if I seduced you, I'd be smote."

Daklin grinned. "Smote?"

"Sent to hell in a handbasket," she whispered breathlessly. "But *so* worth—"

Daklin kissed her. Hard.

#

Breathless, every hair follicle on her body quivering with need, River barely had time to drag in a sip of air before he ravished her mouth. Goosebumps raced across her skin as Ash's hot, slick tongue swept hungrily inside to tangle with hers.

Calling the abrupt assault a kiss was too tame. Too civilized. This was thunder. Cymbals. Drums. She went deaf and blind. A surge of intense heat swept through her as their mouths joined, the locking of lips shocking in its intensity. The glide of his tongue, the sharp nip of his teeth, resonated through every fiber of her body as if he were electrically charged and her body could do nothing but let his unleashed energy surge through her every cell.

Wrapping her arms around his neck dislodged his hands from her face, but he put them to better use as he attempted to get her out of her jacket and T-shirt at the same time. Mouths still locked, she tried to help him get one jacket sleeve off her shoulder, and tug it over her hand.

Asher came up for air, his eyes glazed. "Jesus."

Jacket off, T-shirt shoved up under her chin, she wiggled up on her knees, thigh pressed against the center console and the hard gearshift. "*More*," she demanded, pulling his mouth back to hers.

She wanted his hands. On her bare skin. On her. In her. Not willing to break the lip lock, she gripped his strong nape to pull his mouth back to hers.

River imagined the pounding rain of the early morning

204

shower was turning to steam as it hit their overheated bodies. The sluicing water on her skin added to the entire sensory experience and she reveled in the juxtaposition of hot and cold, silky liquid and calloused fingers, fighting her own need and fulfilling his.

Fire and longing licked along her nerve endings, spreading like wildfire through her body. When he slid a large, calloused hand beneath her T-shirt to close over her breast, her entire body shuddered. Dear God, she'd never felt anything this intense in her life.

River arched into the hard cup of his fingers. He skimmed a fingertip under the Chantilly lace edge of her demi-bra. "*El soplo.*" She whispered the name of the bra brokenly against his mouth when she had to break away to suck air into her burning lungs. Breathing was overrated. She combed her fingers through his wet hair at his nape.

"A breath? God, I can't catch mine. What is this made of? Fairy wings?" His blue eyes were all pupil as he took in the stretchy georgette silk and lace barely covering the swells of her breasts. The deep pink of her erect nipples wasn't hidden at all behind the sheer, misty pale blue fabric of her rain-soaked bra. With a groan, he lowered his head to draw one tight bud into the heated cavern of his mouth.

Throwing back her head, River raked her fingernails down his nape, reveling when he shuddered. She did it again.

Dragging her other hand down his chest, she felt the furnace of his skin through the damp, muddy fabric of his T-shirt, and the rapid thud of his heartbeat beneath her fingers.

Rain spiked his lashes, caught in the stubble on his jaw, glued his clothes to his body, but did nothing to cool her down.

The small bucket seats, hell, the size of the interior of the convertible, weren't exactly conducive to any of this, but she didn't give a damn as she shoved up his shirt to get it out of the way. His skin was hot, silky, vibrantly alive. A happy trail of crisp dark hair arrowed down to disappear beneath his black pants.

She wanted to taste him, consume him. Wanted to feel skin on naked skin. Feel his roughness against her smoothness, feel his heat against her own burning flesh.

Through the wet fabric, he pinched her nipple. It was so sharp, so exquisite that River almost came out of her seat. She almost *came*, period. Dropping her head to his shoulder, she buried her face against his wet neck, her lungs laboring for air and heavy raindrops blurred her vision. He found the delicate bra clasp in back.

Her freed breasts cooled with the kiss of the rain and she arched back like a pagan jungle goddess, face and breasts upturned to welcome the warm drumbeat of the tropical shower.

Ash bent his head, and River shuddered at the sharp nip as he closed his teeth around an erect nipple. The sensation drove straight to her womb.

"Stop." To her own ears, her voice sounded faint, weak, tremulous. Not lifting his head, nor unclasping the delicate nip of his strong white teeth, Ash looked up at her through spiky, black lashes. Eyes unfocused, he mumbled, "Huh?"

River leaned back, out of reach, and he lifted his head, narrow eyes glittering. "Too far! Get your pants off, down, out of my way," she instructed without losing eye contact. "*Hurry.*"

Her fingers felt thick, clumsy, and damned uncooperative as she fumbled with the recalcitrant damp drawstring at her waist, all the while watching his every move like a mongoose watching a snake. "Faster!"

Lifting his butt, Ash unzipped his pants, shoved them down his legs. His penis, thick and long, pulsed with life. She gave a little scream as she reached for the prize with an eager hand. The muscles in his arms flexed when he yanked her from her knees to hoist her over the center gearshift so her knees bracketed his hips and her crotch straddled his.

A flash of the mangled flesh on his thigh caught her eye. Gnarled and pink, an old scar, the injury too horrific to contemplate. Then she was open and astride his lap, her own thigh covering his. Bare flesh to bare flesh, their legs constricted by the confined foot well, and the binding of their pants.

Heat. Hardness. Their eyes locked. Nothing else in the world existed for them but this moment.

Strong hands on her hips, Ash plunged her onto the hard spear of his penis, seating himself in her balls deep. She gasped with the sudden, overwhelming sensation of complete fullness.

With each surge and thrust, she forgot to breathe as the intensity built and built. Each slick stroke made her hotter. Sweat mingled with a drop of rain and trickled down her temple. Her shallow breath hitched. "Dear God."

Digging nails into the soaking wet fabric of his T-shirt, River's back arched and the muscles in her throat strained as he pumped his hips, and she met each hard thrust. She was one giant nerve ending trembling on a precipice. It was terrifyingly thrilling. Unprecedented. The biggest, most thrilling roller coaster ride of her life.

He swiveled his hips and she writhed, moaning, frantic for relief. But not wanting it to end.

Groaning, he looked at her, eyes heavy-lidded with lust. "Okay?" His arms tightened around her, and he fanned a large hand on the small of her back, his smile gentle but strained. She realized he was gritting his teeth as he waited.

She managed a nod. Internal muscles torqued tighter and tighter as he raised her slightly, then brought her down as she clenched around him. Her toes curled. "Better than okay. D-don't stop."

Jerking his hips to meet her, he said, "Never," his voice thick, his eyes dark and feral as he watched her face intently. He drove into her, again and again. Her entire body shook as his fingers dug into her hips, helping her maintain some sort of rhythm instead of exploding into a million pieces.

Waves of pleasure crashed over her, leaving her deaf and mute. Every nerve, every atom in her body, surged and pulsed, tightening unbearably, then releasing in a succession of tidal waves. The climax seemed to go on for an eternity.

Panting as if she'd run a marathon, River fell against his chest, burying her sweaty face against his damp throat. "Sorry." Breathing ragged, her body spent, she tried to formulate a response to the cataclysmic event, which, apparently, had only been explosive for her. He was still rock hard and in relative control of his senses. She'd fix that. In a minute, when she could gather her thoughts enough to forget her own response to him, and focus on his needs.

Maybe in two minutes, since her breath seemed to be on a runaway train and her heartbeat still pounded like mad. "I've wanted to do that from the second I met you. Inappropriate as I thought it was. Give me a minute."

His skin tasted salty against her tongue as her internal muscles flexed against his still-rampant erection and her lungs labored to draw in enough air. Trying to lift her hand to touch his face was impossible, so she licked his throat instead. His large body shuddered, and she realized that he was waiting for a sign that she was ready to go again.

Her throat ached with a well of emotion as his chest rose and fell—waiting.

"Minute's up." His voice sounded raw as he cupped the back of her head and tilted her face up so he could kiss her.

"Hmm." It was the only encouragement he needed. Blood thrummed through her veins as he tightened his hands around the globes of her butt, plunging her down, guiding her to ride him to a shared orgasm. His body bucked, shuddering as he slammed home, his body locking with hers with each downward pull on her hips, each upward thrust of his own. After a long minute, he held her still and arched into her. Taking her mouth in another mind-drugging kiss, their joined bodies pulsed as he kissed her.

Finally, breathless, flushed, and sweaty, they broke apart.

With a gentle finger, he stroked a damp strand of hair off her cheek. "That has to go in the Guinness Book of Records as the longest fucking foreplay *ever*."

A day and a half. It seemed she'd wanted him for a lot longer than that. Limp as an over-cooked noodle, it took great effort for her to murmur, "Hmm." Her mind was still too hazed and drugged with Ash's mind-blowing touch to be coherent.

"Don't look now, but we're being watched."

He laughed as she shot upright, one arm covering her breasts as she frantically looked around. "Him." He indicated a small, brown, big-eyed monkey, staring at them from the hood of the car.

Heart racing, River punched Ash in the arm. "You gave me a freaking heart attack!"

He smiled. "I like to look at you, too." Looping his finger around a strand of her wet hair, he tugged her face in for a lingering kiss.

River forgot where they were for a few more blissful minutes. God, the man could kiss. "I hate to spoil the moment, and I love having you inside me… But my underwear is like a tourniquet around my legs and is cutting off all feeling to my extremities."

"Hell, I should've done this before."

The spider monkey leapt off the car as Ash tore the delicate silk and lace apart. River shook her head. "There goes a hundred bucks."

"Jesus. Don't you get a discount?"

"That *is* my discount."

"Money well spent. Send me a bill. "

Since she had no idea what his real name was, nor did she have any idea where he lived, that would be tricky. Pulling her tank top down over her bare breasts—-she had no idea where her bra had ended up—-River eased off him.

Still erect, he gave her a frown of regret, holding her hips in place. She ignored the overwhelming temptation to stay there, with him warm and snug inside her. "The rain's stopped. Shouldn't you be getting back to town?"

He glanced at the black-faced watch on his wrist. "This car isn't going anywhere."

"Your watch just told you that?"

"Missing one tire and all these bullet holes tells me the car's almost certainly incapacitated. I'll call for pickup in thirteen minutes."

Thirteen minutes was pretty precise. River suppressed a smile. "You have a phone that works? Mine doesn't. Who're you going to call? Uber?"

"My men in town. But we have to wait for the satellite to position overhead for me to get a signal again."

River slid, bottom first, over the gearshift and into the small puddle on the wet leatherette seat on the driver's side. It felt cold and clammy against her bare heated skin. "Ew."

Cuffing her ankles with his warm hand convinced her to leave her feet where they were. In his warm, naked, lap.

They stared at each other as the leaves dripped, and the sound of rushing water indicated the nearby river. Birds started cheeping again now the rain had stopped, and their friendly voyeur was now perched with half a dozen of his friends on a nearby branch.

River indicated her linen pants, which were around her ankles. "Would you—-?"

"Nah. Like I said. We have thirteen minutes." Like a heated physical touch, he dragged his gaze along her thighs, and at what lay between. His voice turned hoarse. "Eleven and a half now."

She shook her head at the look of pure lust that still filled his eyes. Reaching for her pants, she lifted her butt to drag the wet fabric up over her naked parts. "Before we do that again, I think you'd better tell me who you really are, and what you and 'your men' are doing here."

TWELVE

Lust quickly faded to something else. Professionalism? Respect? A man of honor, getting ready to live up to it? Whatever it was, she took it as an encouraging sign that he wasn't going to keep her in the dark.

As she put herself back together, Ash also dressed. Pulling his pants up, arching to zip them, he then settled sideways in the seat to face her. "I work for T-FLAC. It's a private counterterrorist organization. We go after the biggest and baddest tangos around the world."

"Sounds like a non-stick frying pan."

He smiled. "Terrorist Force Logistical Assault Command.

A counterterrorist operative. That made more sense than his being a bishop. "Is your name really Ash Daklin, or is that an alias?"

"When I build a legend, I stick as close to the truth as I can. That's my real name. Everyone calls me Daklin."

His name suited him. "What are you really doing in Los Santos, Ash?" *God, please don't tell me he thinks Oliver's a terrorist.* Was he there expressly to arrest her brother for the explosion a couple of weeks ago? But no. Oliver was anything but a terrorist. *Damn it, Oliver, where the hell are you?*

"Francisco Xavier is a terrorist. He was relatively unknown until he discovered a vein of a highly explosive substance in his emerald mines a couple of years ago."

River let out the breath she'd been holding. "Five years ago?"

He raised a dark brow. "Probably, why?"

"That's when my brother was offered a lucrative job for which he was paid a stupid amount of money. He didn't tell me where he was, but he described Franco to a T. Oliver's a chemical engineer, specializing in explosives. But you already know that." Of course he did.

"We keep track of people like your brother," he said gently. "It's our job to keep a close watch on anyone that adept at bomb making. We think Dr. Sullivan——"

"He's not Dr. Sullivan to me." River looked around for her jacket. She wanted to cover herself, hide herself from the intensity of Asher's pale eyes but she couldn't look away. "He's just Oliver, my brother." Her voice broke, which annoyed her.

His expression softened as he ran his fingers up her arm, tethering her with his light touch. "I get it. Trust me. I know all about family bonds, but I'm not going to lie to you. We think your brother's responsible for manufacturing the most powerful explosive ever made. It's lethal and it's now being used worldwide, thanks to your brother and Francisco Xavier. We're here to shut the operation down, and as much as you're looking for your brother, I'm damn well looking for him, too. He isn't just your brother, River. He's the engineering genius who knows the chemical components of E-1x, how to manufacture it, and more importantly, how to safely defuse it."

Hope beat an unsteady drum roll in her chest. "That means if and when you find him, you'll want him alive."

"We do."

She was afraid to breathe. "And once he tells you what you need to know?"

His eyes darkened. River's heart sank. Oliver was in big, big trouble and Ash wasn't going to sugarcoat it. Now, instead of hoping she'd find Oliver here in Los Santos, River wished him far, far away.

"He's part of a criminal enterprise. A shit-load of people have died. He's an American citizen. If convicted, he'll be tried as a terrorist for murder."

Panic and fear beat inside her chest like a trapped bird. She didn't know how to contain all the emotions rattling around inside her. Fear for her brother. Anger. At Ash, at Oliver. At Franco Xavier.

River observed Ash's tightened features and laser-like focus as he stared out into the trees. He wasn't seeing the golden rays of sunlight piercing the canopy, or the way droplets of water shimmered on the edges of the leaves like silver sequins.

T-FLAC operative Ash Daklin didn't see the beauty.

He saw danger.

Man. Animals. Poisonous flora and fauna.

She reached out to grab his upper arm. "Look at me." When he looked into her eyes, she didn't see anything that told her that he'd believe what she had to say. "I know my brother." Her voice was thick with emotion because she *didn't* know her brother.

She hadn't a freaking clue what he thought or even what his values were. "Oliver would never intend to kill anyone. Never. He just doesn't think that way. If that was the end result," she paused to control her erratic breathing, "then he was duped into believing he was doing something noble." She didn't know that for certain. It was just what she had to believe. Anything else was unimaginable.

"Whether his intentions were altruistic or not, he did manufacture E-1x. It has killed thousands of people, and if allowed to continue, it will kill possibly millions more. He must be stopped, River. The courts won't give a damn why he did what he did. They'll throw the damned book at him."

Dropping her hand from his arm, she pressed it to her churning stomach. "Oliver has a mild form of Asperger's. He won't do well in prison."

"One step at a time. First we have to find him, then we see where the information he gives us leads."

"I know he suspected something bad was going to happen. That's got to be why he deposited millions into my bank account without explanation just before he disappeared."

"We knew he moved money, we just didn't know where."

"He sent it to me. What gave me chills was the amount. Five million dollars! And he deposited the money without saying a word, then immediately dropped off the face of the Earth. That was when he stopped calling. From then on, my calls went directly to his voicemail."

"If he's alive, we'll find him. I swear to you, as soon as we do, I'll contact you so you know. One way or another."

"Can you promise me that if and when you find him, you won't hurt him?"

His expression gentled. "We don't want to hurt him. We need him. A half ounce Nut can bring down a twenty story building."

She frowned. "Nut?"

"The E-1x is treated with a hard substance to prevent premature detonation. Since it's a dark brown, almost black coating, it has the appearance of a Hawaiian kukui nut. We believe Dr. Sullivan was the one who took E-1x and encased it in a hard protective coating to make it safer to transport and ship."

Ash used his finger to slide back the hank of damp hair that kept falling into her eyes. His touch made her shiver with pleasure. She wanted to cradle his palm to her face, wanted to bury her face in his neck and have him hold her so tightly her ribs protested. She leaned back against the door instead.

"This is the most powerful explosive we've ever encountered," he told her, his steady eyes indicating he'd done this before. How far was he willing to go to get the person he was really after?

"We have no idea how to defuse E-1x in its whole state. It takes a sniper's bullet or remote control to detonate it. We don't know how to neutralize it once the casing is shattered."

It didn't surprise River that the explosive casing Oliver had made resembled something from Hawaii. The trip they'd taken to Maui with their parents when they were young had been a happy one. The thought that her brother had used that memory to make an explosive made her want to cry. Damn it, Oliver. She swallowed the lump of fear in her throat. "Did you injure your leg in one of these explosions?"

"Twice. My lower leg the first time on an op in Algeria, then my thigh eighteen months ago when my brother, also an operative, tried to help me out and went to our lab to work on disarming it on his own. I was too late. He was killed in the blast."

Instinctively, she reached out her hand in sympathy, twining her fingers with Ash's, while her heart pounded with mounting fear for her own brother's safety. Now she prayed she wouldn't find him.

"I'm sorry." Acid rose in the back of her throat as she read pain and determination in Asher's intense blue eyes.

Oh, God. An eye for an eye? Oliver wasn't destined for prison, River knew with utmost certainty; Ash was here for revenge. Those hard blue eyes told her with certainty that if Oliver crossed Ash Daklin's path, her brother wouldn't survive.

"Part of the job." His expression sober, he stroked the back of her hand with his thumb almost absently. "All operatives know that. But Josh shouldn't have been killed on my watch. Not in our own backyard."

He wanted retaliation against the man he believed responsible for manufacturing the explosive that had killed his brother.

Not an eye for an eye.

River's blood froze, moving sluggishly through her body as her heart clenched. A brother for a brother.

Her constricted throat felt as raw as if she'd been screaming. Her mind darted back and forth like a hamster in a cage, as around them, the jungle came back to life. Water dripped musically from the leaves, and a fine fog surrounded them as the sunlight heated the rain-wet leaves and evaporated. Her throat was so constricted, it was hard to draw a real breath.

"You pretended to be a bishop because Franco is such a staunch Catholic and you wanted to get close to him."

He nodded. "That, and he's so paranoid he won't allow strangers into the village, and certainly nowhere near the mines. One of my men, Ramse Ortiz, the tall bodyguard up at the hacienda, has a father who's lived here all his life, and alerted us to unusual activity at the mine, as well as an increase in highly skilled security. T-FLAC sent in an advance team as "friends." They all got jobs here, either as security at the plant and mine, or as Xavier's bodyguards."

"Nice." Her voice was dry. "Were those the guys shooting at us?"

"No. My guys went off duty as we were driving up. That truck we passed earlier was them headed back to town. Because Ram couldn't realistically bring any more of his "out of work" friends in, we set up an apparition. Father Marcus encouraged Xavier to ask the Pope to send someone to validate his claim."

"Aw, really?" She gave him a mock amazed face. "The apparition is fake?"

He smiled. "Xavier believes it one hundred percent. It also is one way to keep him right where we want him."

"If he doesn't want strangers in Los Santos, wouldn't having an apparition make everyone in the world want to see it?" As long as the subject wasn't her brother, River was able to pretend, just for a few moments, that she wasn't waiting for the other shoe to drop.

"Yeah. He's constantly wrestling on the horns of that dilemma."

"Is that why you're here? To arrest Franco and find Oliver so he can tell you how to defuse this bomb?"

"That and because E-1x is found in only one place on Earth that we know of."

Something tickled her neck. With a start, River slapped a hand there, squashing a big blue butterfly against her damp, sweaty skin. Sad that she'd killed something so beautiful, she wiped her hand on her pants, and fought back the tears that were so close she could taste them on her tongue. "If it's found in this emerald mine, it's probably in all the emerald mines in South America. In fact wherever they mine emeralds, right?"

"E-1x has nothing to do with emeralds. We've checked worldwide. The Los Santos mine is the only area where it's found."

"How will you get rid of it?"

"Blow the mine to hell."

"That's pretty extreme isn't it? Doesn't it go deep into the mountain?" The situation was grave. Disastrous for the innocent lives in the valley, terrible for the animals in the jungle, and cataclysmic for Oliver, if he was still here.

"Five miles at least. The whole mountain will blow like a volcano."

Skin prickling with nervous sweat, her stomach tight, she rubbed her upper arms as she hugged herself. "You're going to blow up a whole mountain? Dear God, what about everyone living and working in the valley?"

"We already moved most of them last night. The rest will be removed discreetly today."

"That explains why the streets looked so empty when I left earlier. When exactly is this going to happen?" She could hire a private investigator locally. Not Los Santos, but a big city like Santa de Porres must have private detectives. She'd pay whatever they asked for them to find Oliver discreetly. She'd find out which country didn't have extradition. God. What was she thinking? Oliver wasn't guilty. A conversation with him would prove that to Ash.

"Tonight."

"Tonight?"

"I don't want you going back to town. Head straight to the airport. My people will make sure you get there safely."

"No argument from me, believe me." This would work. She'd go to the city. Hire...people...and then stay in Cosio until she had definitive proof that Oliver was somewhere safe. "Just promise that you'll have someone contact me when you find Oliver or when you have information on Oliver. Good news or bad. I have to know."

Taking her hand, he squeezed it, his fingers warm, comforting, strong. "I promise. Stay put safely back in Portland." He leaned closer to her. "We'll call you."

We'll call you wasn't *I'll* call you. But then River didn't expect anything else. She would have protested. The words were actually on her lips, but then his lips were there before she managed to say anything.

Lifting his head, he murmured, "I sure as hell hope we talked enough." He cocked a brow.

God, he was irresistible. "Yes, damn it!"

With a smile, he lifted her over the console. He was a master at stripping her naked. In seconds, he'd undone the drawstring on her pants, and in another, he was gripping her hips and plunging inside her, giving her a fast, hard repeat of the mind-blowing performance he'd given her earlier.

#

Basking in the afterglow, River's body wasn't in any hurry to go anywhere. Sweaty, sticky, and blissfully in-the-moment happy, she was well aware the moment wasn't going to last. Seeing Ash subtly check his watch every five minutes when he thought she wouldn't notice, didn't help.

He protested when she peeled herself off his chest. Literally *peeled*. They were stuck together. Untangling their limbs proved a little more complicated when they both shifted and twisted in counterpoint. River put her hands on his shoulders. "You stay still, let me do the work."

Cupping her bottom, he helped her lift off him. "My pleasure."

"That's not letting *me* do it."

"It worked, didn't it?"

It did, and he gave her bare butt a little pat as she moved from him into the driver's seat, although that was easier said than done. Having sex in a convertible, while exhilarating, wasn't exactly graceful. The dismount left a lot to be desired.

"Don't you dare laugh at me, Ash Daklin. You're the one who turned me into a pretzel! If I'd wanted to be a contortionist, I would've joined Cirque du Soleil."

His smile widened. "You still can." Easy for him to say. His zipper was up, his shirt untwisted, and he wore the look of a man well satisfied. Most of the mud had washed off his face, and River feasted her eyes, committing his features to memory. She loved the way his pale eyes danced with amusement, and the possessive way he kept touching her: her arm, her shoulder as she pulled up her bra strap, the gentle way he combed his fingers through her wet hair to get the strands off her face. As if he couldn't *not* touch her.

"Don't look so smug," she said tartly, leaning over to brush her mouth over his in a fleeting kiss before finally unfolding her legs under the steering wheel.

"It's been over half an hour." She struggled to get her crumpled linen pants up her wet legs with great difficulty in the confined space. "It doesn't look as though your satellite is doing its satellite thing."

Smile gone, he shook his head. "If we don't have comms now, it's unlikely we will any time in the foreseeable future. We can't wait for reinforcements."

There was no way to communicate with his men to alert them to their predicament. It was up to them to get down the mountain by whatever means possible if they wanted to stay alive. River worried about his leg. If it felt half as bad as it looked, he must be in constant pain. "How far is it to the valley?"

"Twenty-three miles, give or take."

"I can't walk back to the hacienda to ask for a ride to the airport. Not in this rain." Not true. She'd run marathons in considerably worse weather. Portland had over a hundred and sixty rainy days a year. If one waited for a clear day there, nothing would ever get done.

It was barely past eight in the morning and still relatively cool. It would be a downhill walk. It was doable. For her. "We'll just have to drive without that back tire. Is that possible?"

"Yeah. Not good for the car, but since it's a piece of shit and the leasing company should be sued for renting it to you in the first place, they can add it to the bill if, and when, they get it back."

"Filled with holes?" River added dryly, wiping a drop of water off her face. It was now sprinkling instead of pouring, the drips and plops lending their musical accompaniment to the small birds singing nearby and the skittering of toucans' claws on a nearby leafy branch. "I have a feeling I just bought myself an aerated convertible with three tires. Won't Franco be wondering where his bishop is?"

"He's a late riser. Chances are he won't know I'm not sleeping the sleep of the pure in heart upstairs in my celibate bed. And if he does notice my absence, I'll just say I went for a run."

Not if he sees you limping, River thought, biting her tongue.

"Stay where you are. I'll push us out of this dip. You steer." Ash hopped over the door into waist-high shrubbery, and waded his way to the back of the car. "Put her in neutral."

River rearranged herself behind the wheel, and shifted gears. The car slowly inched through the wet, drippy, slimy and bug-infested foliage until finally, the front tires bit into the tarred road a few minutes later.

When he started rearranging the broken tree limbs, River got out to help, even though the memory of that snake freaked her out. Together they arranged the branches to cover and hide the makeshift road they'd cut into the understory.

"That's good." Wrapping an arm around her shoulders, they inspected their handiwork just as the rain stopped. The sun broke through the clouds, causing the water on the vegetation to steam. "Just in case anyone looks this way in the next few hours. After that, it won't matter."

Oliver, I hope to hell you're sipping an umbrella drink in some tropical location without extradition right now.

She loved the warm weight of Ash's muscular arm across her back, and the fact that he pulled her tightly against his side. She loved the smell of his skin, and the feel of his hard abs flexing when he hugged her. Turning River in his arms, Daklin lifted her chin. Warm rain sprinkled on her upturned face. He lowered his head to block the rain and his warm lips brushed hers. "I don't want anything to happen to you."

Wrapping her arms around his neck, River reached up to kiss his bristly chin. "Something pretty amazing *did* just happen to me." *Please don't kill my brother.*

He took his time with the kiss, as though savoring every second of it. Then he broke away. "Let's get out of here." As they walked back to the car, his limp more pronounced, which didn't surprise her.

She stopped him with a hand on his upper arm. "How will you get to safety tonight if you can't run?"

He arched a brow. "Worried about me?"

"Every freaking *thing* about what you're planning scares

the crap out of me." She was afraid for herself, too. But that was a given. "I know there's got to be a plan in place for you and your men to get the hell away from the explosion. But you'll have to run like hell to get out of the way." She drew a deep breath then decided now was not the time to be delicate or worry about his ego. "With your leg..." *His chances were slim to none.*

Now she understood why he kissed her and made love like there was no tomorrow.

He isn't planning on there being one. River sucked in a breath. "No! Taking down Xavier. Destroying him, his operation, and the explosive stuff in the mine, and avenging your brother's death? You're going ahead, even if it means you don't live through it."

"Smart as well as beautiful."

"Is this a suicide mission?"

He didn't miss a beat. "The job has to get done."

"That wasn't the damn question."

"River, I'm the best man for this job. I'd be the best man for the job uninjured, and I'm still the best man for the job. The reality is, there's a good chance I *won't* make it out alive. That's part of the job I do. Part of the risks I and the others take every day. It's not good or bad. It just is."

"Damn it, Ash! *Promise* you'll get out. *Safely.* That you'll have an exit plan when you're setting the explosives. That your focus on avenging your brother's death won't be your end goal."

"I can't make that promise."

227

"Then at least promise me you'll *try*." Gripping his biceps, she got up on her tiptoes to look up at him, so close she saw specks of darker blue in his pale irises. "Because you're scaring the hell out of me right now. God." She punched his arm. "How dare you make me feel anything at all for you, when you're not even factoring in your own personal safety tonight."

He gave her a smile that ripped at her heart. Something changed in his eyes. Some of his coolness disappeared, and she saw a glimpse of yearning. "You'll be waiting for me? No matter what this means for your brother?"

"You'll see to it that Oliver is treated fairly?"

"I'll see to it that he gets what he deserves. He's made his bed, River." He brushed his lips over hers, then stepped out of her hold.

Her arms dropped to her sides as he turned back to the car. She blinked rainwater from her eyes.

"We need to get you out of the valley and far the hell away from any fallout."

Good enough. At least he'd said "we."

"Trust me, I'll drive as fast as this little car can get me over that hill."

"Let me get us to the junction, then you can take over." He grimaced as he climbed into the driver's seat, positioning his legs into the space that was much too small for him. "The rental company should be paying you to take this heap."

"She's been an adventure, that's for sure." River didn't care about flat tires, bullet holes, or driving on the rim. All she'd remember about the little red car was making love in it with Ash, in the middle of the jungle, with a monkey watching their every move. Epic.

As they headed down the mountain, he slung an arm across the back of her seat, absently toying with her hair. His touch was casual. So light it was almost inconsequential. Yet, painfully aware they had at most fifteen more minutes together, she felt every brush of his fingers deep in her core.

A quick glance at his face showed him alert and vigilant as he drove. "Do you sleep with one eye open?" she asked.

"It's the nature of my job to always be alert to danger."

"Even at home?"

"I'm rarely there, but yeah. Being hyperaware comes naturally. It's who I am. Always."

"Must be exhausting."

"Invigorating."

River twisted to face him, propping her bent leg on the seat. "I can see how the constant adrenaline rush would be addictive, but it must be draining, too. Do you have any down time?"

"Six weeks the first time, eight with this." He indicated his left leg. "More than enough vacation to last a lifetime."

"Turks and Caicos would be more relaxing." River visually traced his features to store in her memory for later. She hadn't noticed before a little bump on the bridge of his nose. She fought the urge to touch it. A slight wave in his dark hair as it dried gave him a deceptively softer appearance. It wasn't necessary to know him for long. Just on their short acquaintance, she knew he was dedicated, single-minded, and determined. He didn't just *like* his job, he *was* his job. Unlike herself, he clearly didn't make time to enjoy the fruits of his labor.

River was a realist. She could see that there was no room in his life for anything or any*one* else.

Enormous trees towering and dripping on either side of the narrow road shaded most of the trip down the mountainside. It made for a steamy green tunnel as the car limped along at a snail's pace on the rim of the back tire. Finger combing her wet hair off her face with both hands, she was tempted to get out and walk. It would be a lot faster. "God, I miss my Tesla. We'd be zooming right now."

Ash glanced at her, dark lashes spiky, eyes very blue. A lump formed in her throat and a hard pressure constricted her chest. Because she desperately wanted to reach out and stroke his arm, she clutched her fingers together in her lap. God, how stupid. She missed him already.

"We'll switch at the turn off, then you take the car and head up to my people. Someone will take you to the airport and deal with the car." He pointed toward the trees and the direction of the windy mountain pass, which would take her north to the city and airport. "When we're in range, I'll contact my team and give them the head's up you're on your way. They'll meet you a couple of miles up the road, and get you there safely. You have your passport on you, right?"

"I always do when I travel. That's a long walk back, though. Are you sure?" He'd walked miles already, pole-vaulted into the car, and had wild monkey sex in the confines of a bucket seat. His leg must be killing him.

"I want you gone. Walking a few more miles won't kill me."

He believed he was invincible. But it didn't matter what he believed. She'd seen his leg. "What if your communications are still on the fritz? Won't they shoot me on sight?"

His smile, because it was so damned rare, was riveting. "They know who you are. They'll make sure you get home safely."

"Thanks." There was absolutely no point asking when and where she'd see him again. If he survived the night, he'd implied he'd find her. Or maybe that was just wishful thinking.

It was foolish to miss the last opportunity to touch him. It wasn't as if she had anything to lose. Unclasping her fingers, she reached out and placed her hand on his muscled forearm. It felt like warm steel with a brush of crisp dark hair under her fingers.

BOOM.

"Holy crap. What was that?" The blast sounded so close, River expected the tall, swaying trees lining the narrow road to topple over. The air resonated, and the road vibrated, sending shockwaves up through her spine.

The world shifted, the air pulsed, but the man next to her went still. Calm. He watched the trees, assessing visual cues, as he appeared to measure the earth's tremors with his senses. He turned to her, gave her a reassuring nod, and pumped the accelerator of the hopelessly slow car. "We'll be fine." Flocks of red and green parrots shot out of the tree canopy, adding their cries to the cacophony of surround-sound noise.

Yelling to be heard, River shot him a glance. "Was that like the other explosion that killed the people at the mine?"

He nodded. "Someone screwed up again. I doubt that was a calculated, timed blast. E-1x is volatile as hell. Extract it from the rock the wrong way and you get that." He indicated the mountain, where the echoes of the explosion still reverberated down the valley.

Above the tree canopy, plumes of dark dust shot into the sky, indicating that the explosion had happened miles from their location.

"What if Franco sends people up here to check on the explosion and sees us?" she asked, instead of speculating aloud about how many people had *died* in the explosion.

"Doesn't matter. I doubt he'll bother. Explosions are par for the course in any mining operation," Ash's voice was dry. "He wouldn't be able to tell a planned explosion from a fuck up."

Adroitly missing a trio of small hairy pigs squealing as they trotted across the road, he said, "I'll take you up to the pass, and hand you off."

Like an unwelcome package? "Great."

They got down to the T-junction: left, down to the village,

232

right, up and over the pass's tight curves heading to the airport. Ash turned right.

River had a momentary fantasy of him accompanying her home. Only her imagination wasn't that good. She could only manage to get him as far as the *Santa de Porres* airport.

THIRTEEN

D elta One, to you," Daklin said into his lip mic only to be rewarded with dead air. Dust-thick air made navigating the winding, narrow, nine percent grade road, with its thousand-foot drop-off into the valley below, treacherous as hell. There was no guardrail. If he veered too far over, they'd plummet to their deaths. Keeping to the center, he concentrated on not getting them killed.

River covered her nose and mouth with the sleeve of her jacket to avoid breathing in the dust. She offered him the other sleeve. "Want to share?"

"I'm good." He'd inhaled worse.

Daklin had promised her fair treatment for her brother, and made a mental note to pass along the message. Everyone's interpretation of 'fair' was different.

They were getting closer to the point of the explosion. The force of the blast had snapped thirty-foot-high trees like twigs, which littered the road's slope-side like giant, discarded toothpicks. Fortunately, none blocked their way, but Daklin still had to play dodge-em with branches, rocks, and dead animals. From his vantage point, it was impossible to see where the explosion had originated, but mentally pulling up the schematics of the mine, he figured it had occurred in one of the north to south shafts they hadn't had time to explore earlier.

Someone had surely lost their life, and detonated a goodly portion of Xavier's revenue stream, thereby doing part of T-FLAC's job. It was all good except that now he had to negotiate an obstacle-rich road in a four-cylinder car with no pep and three bald tires.

The wreckage on the twelve-foot-wide stretch of road got thicker, bigger, and harder to navigate the higher they climbed toward the pass. Daklin took the next hairpin curve slowly and with care. Intermittently, terrified animals streamed across the narrow road to get away from the still-trembling ground. The after-effects felt like the aftershocks of an earthquake.

"I think we've seen just about every animal in the jungle in the last fifteen minutes," River said, as a spotted jaguar streaked across the road ahead of them, its coat the color of old gold in the sunlight. "On the up side, at least we're not being shot at anymore."

Two more miles and he'd consider her safe. His men waited in a blind around a hairpin bend to help evacuees as they slipped out of the village. They had enough firepower to repel the full force of Xavier's army, but he hoped to hell that it wouldn't be necessary. He wanted River far away from any possibility of crossfire. "For the moment. The day's still young."

She shot him a look. "You think they'll come after us again?"

"Chances are Xavier's people are more concerned with the aftermath of the explosion than with chasing us down. If they haven't found us by now, I figure they'll stay put. Stay alert."

"Trust me, if I was any more alert I'd be--Uh-oh. I think we have a new problem," River murmured, staring at the mountain of mountain spilling across the narrow road.

No shit. An avalanche of rocks and vegetation four stories high blocked their path.

"Fuck." No way to pass. The good news was his comm suddenly crackled to life in his ear. "Delta team, this is Alpha One." The comm crackled, faded in, faded out, came back. "What's your status?"

"Half village saf. . . transported to a . . .fer location."

Crackling swallowed more of the words, and then cleared up. "...to evac...rest. . . assistance. . . Marcus. Spotty comms playing havoc with. . . plans."

Fortunately, everyone knew what they were *supposed* to be doing, having been trained to think on their feet. The unexpected was always expected. "I'm on other side of a rock fall. Have Dr. Sullivan's sister with me. Need you to transport her to the airport ASAP."

"Can't access. . . your location. Road's blocked. Have no way to do airport transport. Copy?"

"Copy." Fucking *loud and clear. .* Daklin got out of the car to inspect the problem and weigh the options. Picking up a six-foot limb, he prodded the surface of the rockslide. Rocks, and branches immediately tumbled down and he had to jump clear.

He returned to the car.

"I think I can climb over that," River said calmly, her attention on the rocks and shale still tumbling and bouncing onto the road in front of the hood.

The color was high on her cheeks, making her soft gray eyes wide and clear as rainwater. Blonde strands of chin-length hair had fallen precisely back into her former smooth bob as her hair dried. Looking fresh, sexy, and desirable, she was dangerously tempting. She wasn't nearly as fragile as she looked; clearly, not even this was going to get her down.

He wasn't sure if the race of his pulse was disappointment that he wasn't getting rid of her as easily or quickly as he'd anticipated, or sheer fucking delight that he had a few more hours to spend with her. Daklin stepped over the low door to get behind the wheel. He ignored the screaming agony of his leg. It was nothing new. "*Nobody* can climb that. It's too unstable." Unless he could catapult her over the mini-mountain blocking their way, he was out of options. He started the car. It didn't sound any happier than he felt.

"Now what?"

Backing up, he made a tight U-turn. "Now we go back to the hacienda and pretend nothing's happened, until I can get you out." If he hadn't already said enough to convince her she wanted to be far, far away from there, the explosion certainly did.

"*Today*, right?"

"Only if they manage to clear the rock fall, and the chances of that are pretty damn slim. Sorry, honey. We can't risk a chopper flying in to get you. That would alert Xavier and his men."

"I don't suppose there's anywhere else for me to stay tonight if I don't get rescued, is there? That place gives me the willies, and Franco—-"She gave an exaggerated shudder.

"My people will have you out of here before then, don't worry."

"You and your men are awesome." She braced a hand on the shattered dash as a medium-sized Brocket deer leapt across the road in two jumps, disappearing into the dense vegetation on the opposite side. "But sorry, you guys have a completely different agenda that's far more compelling than me. I've always taken care of myself, so forgive me if I don't bank on anyone else saving my ass if and when the shit starts hitting the fan."

They passed the turn off up to the mine, and he kept going. "Did your brother take care of you after your parents died?"

"Oliver having my back has always been the illusion we both clung to," River told him. "But it's always been me, in the present, keeping things together when my absentminded older brother forgot to eat or pay his bills. Or amassed multi-millions in his checking account."

Daklin had figured that much. "What about your husband? Didn't he take care of you?"

She turned to give him a cool look. "I'm quite capable of taking care of myself, Ash. I never needed either Oliver or my ex-husband to take care of me. Devon loved my strength when he married me, but he wasn't so gung ho about it *afterwards*."

Daklin had no fucking idea why he was suddenly irritable. "Very civilized." The sun shone brightly on her pale hair and lightly tanned shoulders and sparkled off the diamonds in her ears. The temperature was rising, but currently no one was trying to kill them, and he could inhale and smell her unique scent. He'd be able to identify her in a dark room amid a hundred women by the smell of her skin alone.

The grade started to level as they approached the valley floor. There was no indication here of the explosion. While narrow and winding, the road was clear of detritus. The sun's heat had dried their clothes, and still caused a steamy mist to rise off the foliage on either side of the road. Not quite a sauna, but damned close.

The tires bit into the cobbled street in the village. "Will the roadblock interfere with getting the rest of the villagers out?"

"Working on that, too." Ash slowed as they got closer to the hacienda. Father Marcus stood outside, watering his flowers. Ash pulled over and stopped. "Morning, Marcus."

Father Marcus turned off the hose at the nozzle. "An interesting morning, I see." He gave the shot up car a cursory glance, fixing his gaze on River. "I heard the explosion. Are you all right, my dear?"

"The car looks a bit like how I feel," River said with a smile. "But I'm unharmed, thanks, Father Marcus."

"Your Excellency?"

"River knows who I am, Marcus. She was up at the plant.

The guards didn't take too kindly to her visit. The car took the brunt of it. We're unharmed. As you see, the convertible wasn't as lucky. The blast brought down the north side of the mountain, blocking the road and pass. No one in or out. I was able to communicate briefly with the team. They'll work on it, but for now, we're sealed in. We'll figure out a way to evacuate the rest of you," Daklin assured him. "Hang tight and wait for word."

Marcus gave him a worried look, but didn't ask specifics. Good thing, because right now Daklin didn't have answers.

"Leave the car here," Marcus told him. "I'll have Jorge come and fetch it. How long do I have to get the rest of my people out?"

"I'll keep you in the loop, don't worry."

"It's my job to do so. And now I'm deeply concerned about River's safety as well."

"Don't worry about me, Father. I can take care of myself. You can also count on me to help you when Ash tells us to move. We'll all go together."

"Thank you, my dear. That's commendable." He glanced at Daklin. "Better go in. Franco asked about you fifteen minutes ago. I told him I thought you'd gone for a run. Leave the car where it is. Go have breakfast. Keep me informed. Now more than ever."

"Copy that." Daklin climbed out of the low-slung car with some difficulty. He didn't allow himself so much as grimace, but River slowed her steps slightly to accommodate his limp as they walked up the driveway of the hacienda.

Only Franco's bodyguard was around when they went inside. He greeted them with a nod, and they went upstairs.

"We'll go down for breakfast together. How long do you need to clean up?"

"Half an hour. Going at a hundred miles an hour, and forgoing mascara." Her smile did some weird shit to his heartbeat. "But honestly? I'm not going down until it's time for me to leave. I don't want to make nice with Franco. I'm not that good an actress."

But I'm not ready to tell you goodbye yet.

That reality shocked him as much as the unexpected explosion had just rocked the fucking mountain. Because he couldn't seem to help himself, Daklin stayed at her doorway, stroking his hand down her arm. Her skin felt soft, smooth, and cool to the touch. "I'll have something sent up." Tempted to follow her into her room, and make use of the wide, soft bed, he gritted his teeth. Once would have to hold him.

He had to make do with River as a snack, and not fall on her like a ravenous dog, and consume her like the meal he craved. It took every ounce of self-control to release her and step away. "We'll keep you updated."

"Great." She inserted the key in the lock, her head bowed. Her nape looked pale and vulnerable. He wanted to lay kisses along the soft, fragrant, delicate curve.

"Fine." Damn it, his feet seemed glued to the carpet.

She pushed open her door a crack behind her. "I caught that we, Ash. Will I see *you* again today?"

"Me, or one of my people."

The light in her eyes dimmed. "Oh, right. Okay then." Moving to enter her room, she turned. He was still standing in the middle of the corridor. "Stay safe, please."

He stuffed his hands in his back pockets so he didn't grab her. "Lock your door."

She turned and slipped into her room, closing the door with a snap.

Standing there in the dimly lit corridor, Daklin heard the click of the key turning in the lock.

Fuck. With the door closing on the soft light and beauty that was the essence of River Sullivan, his harsh reality descended upon him. It felt more as if he was locked out than she was safely locked in. What the hell was wrong with him? He wanted her bad enough that he could fuck up this op.

Let that be goodbye, dumb fuck. You know you're not coming off that goddamn mountain tonight. Regretting that you're never going to see her again is just going to mess with your head.

Which is messed up enough.

Goddamn funny how when you're with her, everything seems perfectly clear. As if she's holding a crystal ball, in which you see a fucking future. His feet heavy, he turned from her doorway and went into his own room.

He was a fallen agent, and T-FLAC had given him one final chance for redemption. The reality was he had a vital mission. Seeing River again would only remind him of how fucked up his life had actually become, because T-FLAC knew, and he knew, that the likelihood of his survival was pretty damn slim.

Remember why you're here, asshole. You can't give her more. Let that be goodbye.

#

Eyes closed, River leaned against the locked door, her heart beating as hard as if she'd run a seven minute mile. "That went well," she murmured sardonically. All her girl parts sparked and sizzled on high alert.

For no freaking reason.

While *she'd* felt hot and bothered, and been acutely aware of the sexual tension arcing between them for the last hour, Ash was wholly focused on his job and seemed oblivious to it, which was only right.

He should be. She should too. Her job was to find her brother. She'd always been able to be pinpoint focused. What the hell was going on to turn her brain into silly, girly slushy mush? And, why did it unreasonably aggravate her that his brain seemed perfectly intact?

Opening her eyes, she pushed away from the door, and then muffled a startled scream when she saw a figure slumped in the easy chair beneath the window.

The woman—-a girl, really—-didn't stir as River approached, her footsteps silent on the thick carpet. "Please don't be dead," she whispered. After the morning's events, anything was possible. As she neared, she realized it was the frail, young maid who worked there. Ah. Juanita. The underwear thief.

Not dead, but her face appeared gray with fatigue. She had one skinny arm wrapped protectively over her slightly rounded belly.

"Juanita," she whispered. The young woman's chest rose and fell rhythmically. She was asleep. Probably exhausted. River's heart ached for this tiny, fragile young woman. Making a living cleaning houses while pregnant, and subjected to the deviant sexual desires of Francisco Xavier, brought out all River's empathy.

She'd bet the girl didn't enjoy being with Franco. Heat flushed into her cheeks just thinking about that. Anger and empathy. One for the monster, the other for his innocent victim.

A quick glance around the room showed the big bed half made, and a pile of used towels heaped on the floor outside the bathroom door. The poor girl had started to tidy the room, then apparently sat down and fallen asleep.

She hoped.

"Juanita?" River said softly, crouching beside the chair, afraid to touch her in case she scared the crap out of the young woman. No doubt, she'd been scared a lot in her life. Red-rimmed, brown eyes fluttered open. It was clear by the confusion there that, for a moment, Juanita had no idea where she was. Then she jerked upright, a flood of apologetic Spanish falling from her lips

River put a hand on the girl's arm. "It's okay. It's okay," she murmured softly in Spanish. "Stay where you are. Can I get you anything? Water?"

This was followed by another spate of wild-eyed Spanish, almost too fast to understand as Juanita apologized for accidentally falling asleep in River's room. She'd merely come to clean and leave a gift. River got to her feet. "Stay where you are, I'm going to get you some water. Don't move," she warned as the girl started to get up.

Going into the spacious bathroom, River filled a glass with tap water and hurried back. If the "gift" was the underwear the girl had taken and used in Franco's kink room, she really, really was going to lose it. She certainly didn't want it back.

"Sip this slowly," she said, handing the glass to her visitor. "I'm not letting you go until I know you'll be all right."

Juanita burst into silent tears. It was heart wrenching because the tears were so quiet. River was an advocate for noisy sobbing, a lot of pacing, and talking herself out of her misery while she cried. In grief, Juanita resembled a terrified, cornered animal, one with no hope of getting past the despair.

River slid into the big chair with her, wrapping her arms around the far too skinny girl and rocking her gently as she smoothed a hand down Juanita's narrow back. "It's okay. Everything is going to be okay. Trust me."

It took several minutes for Juanita to stop crying, but that was only because, River suspected, the girl was too exhausted to cry more.

River's Spanish wasn't quite up to the task of the words

pouring out from the frightened girl. However, she got the gist, and as she did, anger welled up inside her. *El Jefe* had put the baby in her. *El Jefe* made her do things that shamed her. *Jefe* was a monster. He hurt her. Because of *Jefe*, Juanita was going to hell.

"I promise, you are *not* going to hell." *Francisco Xavier is going to hell, hopefully sooner rather than later.* But River would leave that to Ash and his men. "Here's what we're going to do." River brushed Juanita's bangs off her sweaty forehead. "Don't leave this room. You're under my care now. Rest for a little while." River gripped the girl's hands. "Yes?"

Juanita gave a slow nod.

"Take a little nap while I grab a quick shower, then I'm taking you away from here."

Untangling herself carefully, River persuaded Juanita to lie down on the unmade bed, covered her with a light throw, and dashed into the bathroom with a change of clothes.

After a quick shower, and changing into a tank-style maxi dress, River returned to her room to find Juanita curled into a little ball in the middle of the bed, fast asleep.

She was safe here for the moment. After drawing the drapes so the sun didn't shine directly over her, River reviewed her limited options.

Number one priority was to remove Juanita from Franco's hacienda. Since Ash was determined to blow up Franco's mountain and possibly half the valley with it, River herself had to leave. Yet keeping Juanita with her until she figured out how to do that wasn't a viable option. The girl would still be under her abuser's roof.

The only safe place River could think of was with her family, and if they'd gone, with Father Marcus. If there was a way for him to get Juanita, and the rest of the villagers, out of Los Santos, he'd know it. If not, then Ash and his guys would help him figure a way. Marcus could end up being River's way out, as well.

Grabbing the suitcase she'd packed the night before, River separated a few essentials from the case into her small carry on tote. Juanita would need some clothes wherever she was going. River added most of her cash as well. Juanita would need that, too.

After checking that Juanita still slept, River went into the bathroom to apply makeup and dry her hair. Armed for any impending battle, she returned to the bedroom to find Juanita still sleeping.

River picked up her phone to see if she had any bars. Nope. Not having the use of her phone was disconcerting. Oliver might be trying to call her, she'd promised her friend Carly she'd call her, and who knew what was happening with her business while she was out of touch.

She inhaled deeply. Being out of contact wasn't the end of the world. She had competent managers and Devon was good at problem solving. Her ex may have been a lousy match for her, but he was a great people person, and an excellent business partner.

Carly would imagine River had run off with a handsome stable master, and wouldn't worry for at least a few more days. By that time, River would be home. Turning off the phone to save battery life, she tucked it into her back pocket, and went to get her book out of her carry on.

Since she wasn't going to leave the room until Juanita woke, she might as well catch up on reading. Juanita slept deeply as River took a delightful trip to Regency England for a couple of hours.

Putting the book aside when Juanita sat up and reached for the glass of water, River rose. "Do you feel a little better?"

Juanita nodded shyly, her face coloring up a little.

"Is there a way to leave the house without anyone seeing us?" she asked in Spanish.

Apparently, there was a servant's door off the kitchen. Perfect.

"Is there anything you want to take with you?"

Juanita shook her head. "My mother—"

"I'll make sure she knows where you are." Franco would certainly search for her in the most obvious place. No going to her family. River wasn't even sure if Juanita's family was around. They might have already left the valley. Father Marcus was her best bet. River suspected he could handle a little lying if it was to protect the innocent.

"Ready to go?"

Juanita threw her legs over the side of the bed, pausing with a worried frown. "*Jefe*, he *wants* this baby. He will find me."

"He won't. I promise." It wasn't a false promise. River had resources and wouldn't hesitate to throw a protective net over

Juanita and her child. She could certainly use the money given to her by Oliver to secure a good life for them.

Despite having heart palpitations the entire time, she and Juanita managed to leave the hacienda through the servant's passageway, silently slipping into the rectory next door.

They heard the music before they rounded the church at the front door of the rectory. Procol Harum belted out *A Whiter Shade of Pale*. The song, out of context for the grimness of the day, startled River, reminding her poignantly of her mother. She saw herself standing on a little stool behind the counter at the convenience store so she could carefully watch her mom ring up purchases at the cash register. Then, after painstakingly taking out the customer's change and being allowed to hand it over, her mother's pride as she hugged her for being such a clever girl to count out the change so well.

Oliver hated the shop, refusing to waste his time there, but River had loved it. To River, the more time spent with her parents, the better. Now she was so grateful that she'd had those years with them before they died.

Not much of a religious person, she nevertheless whispered a silent prayer to her mother as she guided Juanita to the rectory door. *Hey Mom, Oliver needs you today. Well, truth be told, we both need you today. Do your Mom thing and send some guidance this way.*

"River. Nita." Dressed in jeans and a black shirt, with no clerical collar in sight, Father Marcus opened the door wide, and gave them a welcoming, but slightly puzzled, smile.

"Come in." He had to raise his voice over the music. "I was just about to have a little lunch. Join me."

He led the way to the back of the house. "Would you?" He indicated the radio, and River turned down the volume as he casually pulled the curtain with strawberries on it over the lower half of the window so no one could see inside. Then he took out two more plates.

"Raizia Sosa makes the best lasagna," he told them cheerfully. His cheer seemed a little strained, but River gave him points for not telegraphing the end of the world. "I was just about to defrost this but worried I'd end up wasting most of it."

Since he was pulling the casserole dish out of the small freezer as he spoke, River doubted that's what he'd planned for lunch. He stuck the dish into the microwave and hit a few buttons.

As he turned to address Juanita, River noticed the small communications device in his ear. So, like Ash, he was in communication with the others. Good news! Did that mean Ash and his team could now communicate? River's heart leapt. Was the pass already clear? Could they leave now? If so, it would be the best news she'd heard all day.

Catching Father Marcus's eye, she indicated her ear, and raised an inquiring brow. He shook his head. Damn it. No open communication after all.

"Nita," he said evenly in Spanish. "Would you fix us a nice green salad, my dear? Here. Use this, and this, and this." He efficiently handed the girl a large bowl, then took lettuce from the refrigerator, and tomatoes off the windowsill. He set her up at the counter near the sink.

After taking down three glasses, and removing a jug of lemonade from the fridge, he sat opposite River, and gave her a questioning look before pouring their drinks.

As calm and as easy as he appeared, River could feel the tension pulsing off him in waves. He was worried for his people, for the lives he felt responsible for. Now she was delivering another soul into his care.

"Juanita has decided she doesn't want to work at the hacienda any more. I suggested you could get her safely out of town and that she could *rest* here until you can. The suitcase is hers, and I've given her a little spending money until she's settled."

"No, no. You've done enough, Miss River."

"Accept a little help from a friend," River told her firmly. "Father, if you could let me know how she's doing, I'd appreciate it. I don't want to lose touch."

He nodded.

When Juanita turned to the kitchen sink to rinse the lettuce, River whispered, "By rest, I mean hide. You're aware that Franco is a monster?"

Anger pinked his cheeks, and made his eyes glitter. His mouth tightened. "This only came to light recently, but yes. I am now painfully aware."

"She mustn't be exposed to him again. Her mother needs to

join her, because I'm worried Xavier will use her mother to get to her. Juanita says he wants the baby."

"Her mother waits for her in Abad; she left last night. I have a message for her from her mama."

After exchanging the information, it was amazing how effectively she and Marcus could communicate nonverbally in between their verbal conversation. He would get Juanita away with the others. In the meantime, she could stay in the rectory. He'd make sure River knew where to send money if necessary.

"I'm hoping to leave for Santa de Porres later today," he told Juanita as she brought the salad to the table, and sat down. "There's a bit of a problem right now getting through the pass, but I hope it'll be cleared before dark."

"Me, too," River muttered, helping herself to lasagna that was still more than half frozen in the middle. If the road was still impassable, did Ash's plan to blow up the mine tonight still hold? Surely, he could wait another day?

Juanita lay her fork down and yawned.

River shot her a smile. "I think Little Mama here needs a nap. Is there somewhere?"

As Juanita got up from her chair, her legs wobbled. Father Marcus rose to his feet and put his arm around the girl. "I have a very comfortable sofa in my office. Come along, my dear."

Juanita didn't protest much as she was ushered away. While they were gone, River put away the leftovers and started washing the dishes.

"Do you think they'll be able to clear the pass?" she asked when Marcus returned. Then she stopped and pointed to her ear, giving him an inquiring look. "You sure Franco can't hear?" she mouthed.

"Don't worry." Marcus shook his head. "I sweep for bugs every day. There are no listening devices here. But I can't say the same for the main house."

"Franco bugs his own house?"

"*T-FLAC* has the house under surveillance. Daklin ordered your room to be clean. You can speak freely there."

"Okay, that's creepy. Are you sure I wasn't seen or heard in that room?"

"They removed surveillance the night of your arrival."

"Whew. Good to know. Okay, where were we?"

Father Marcus smiled. "They're bringing in large earth moving equipment all the way from Santa de Porres. However, it won't get here until tomorrow. Early, yes, but still tomorrow."

"But Ash said he is exploding the mine tonight. Can his plans be postponed?"

"No, my dear, unfortunately, it cannot. I'm not at liberty to divulge the reasons, but trust me when I say, this operation is time sensitive, and of utmost importance. Imperative even."

"But the rest of the villagers..."

"Daklin is *the* best explosives engineer there is. Under normal circumstances, he'd engineer the detonation to the last rock that would fall. He's *that* good at what he does. He has the hands of a surgeon when it comes to explosives."

When it came to a woman's body, too. "Then why take such drastic precautions to evacuate the town?"

"Because in this instance, he *can't* control the blast. The mountain is riddled with veins of E-1x. It's impossible to know where each vein is, or how much explosive is hidden deep inside the rock, unseen. There's absolutely no way to anticipate how big or far reaching the explosion, or the chain reaction from one will be. As you saw with this morning's event."

After drinking deeply, he set his glass down with care, his eyes somber. "I'm hazarding a guess that this morning's explosion was accidental. Assuredly, people lost their lives because they weren't careful enough when removing the substance from the rock. E-1x is volatile and extremely powerful, and so far, it is impossible to defuse once ignited." He drank the rest of his lemonade. "So it's very possible, no, *probable,* that the annihilation will extend not only to this valley, but to surrounding areas for hundreds of miles."

And Daklin would be at the epicenter of it all. With an injured leg. Unable to run far enough or fast enough to get away. River went ice cold from head to toe. She drew in a deep breath. "I can't just sit around and wait. Put me to work, Father."

FOURTEEN

The ghost of her scent was everywhere.

But she was gone.

Suitcase, clothes, River herself.

Fuck, fuck, and triple fuck.

Because he didn't want to raise suspicion, Daklin had suffered through the rest of the morning with Xavier, when all he'd wanted to do was spend his last day with River. The thought of her, the scent of her, consumed him, and engaging in idle chitchat with the man he was going to destroy in a few hours, wasn't nearly enough distraction. He'd finally made his excuses under the guise of writing his reports on Xavier's apparition for Rome.

Only to find her room empty.

It was God's last laugh. Just when he resigned himself to his fate and ready to die, he met a woman like River Sullivan who made him want to live again. In his head, a timer counted down the minutes. He didn't want to waste a second that could be spent with her.

His men knew their roles. There was no more planning necessary. Now it was a waiting game. He'd played it on ops dozens of times. It had never bothered him before. Today i t fuckingwell did.

Charlie Kytta, leader of Delta Team, and his men worked diligently to clear the slide, and get the rest of the villagers——and River——a safe distance from the valley. Where the hell could she have gone? No one could leave via the pass. She wasn't equipped or experienced enough to take a long fucking walk through the jungle. Especially alone.

He imagined her attempting to climb the rubble at the pass, because God only knew, she was stubborn enough, pissy enough, to give it a real shot. Slipping and sliding down the shale, plummeting to the valley floor a thousand feet onto jagged rocks below. To her death.

He rubbed the center of his chest. No. She wasn't stupid. Stubborn. Determined. But not stupid.

Had Father Marcus figured out a way to circumvent the slide and get everyone else clear of the valley?

Daklin made a slow turn in her dim, empty bedroom, the very air redolent with the smell of summer rain and flowers that he'd always associate with her. Not that he had a long time for such an association. His ending was a mere hours away. Which made River's absence in this last moment he might ever have to see her un-fucking-acceptable.

She'd showered, and from the appearance of rumpled covers on the bed, taken a nap, and left.

Scowling, he glared at the rumpled covers on the half-made bed. A nap wasn't who River Sullivan was. She was a woman of action. A planner. She was no coward.

Therefore, the bed was unmade from when she'd left to go up to the mine early this morning.

He checked the enormous teak wardrobe, opening the double doors to see what, if anything, she'd left behind. Daklin frowned. The only thing inside was a long, sheer garment hanging from a padded pink silk hanger.

Frowning, he rubbed the thin material between his fingers. The garment held a musty, faded scent. He held out the garment— a full-length, shift style dress of sheer fabric. Hell, he could clearly see his hand through two layers of material. The thought of seeing River in what looked to be a transparent peignoir set his pulses racing, and made him semi-hard. She'd brought it all the way to Los Santos with her for some bizarre reason. But if it was important enough to bring, why leave it behind?

Daklin closed the heavy, carved doors, and stalked into the bathroom. The steam had long since dissipated, but the scent of her, the femaleness of her, lingered in the air. He picked up her hairbrush, tapped it on his palm as he scanned the feminine articles neatly lined up on a clean, folded towel on the counter. Makeup. Hair crap. A cold flat iron.

A large tote bag sitting on the edge of the sunken tub.

Air rushed out of his lungs.

She wasn't gone.

Unless she'd walked away, leaving all this behind.

Or? This time his heart galloped. Had she been taken? Had

someone walked in and whisked her away? The same someone who'd possibly taken her brother?

Daklin had just left Xavier downstairs. If not Xavier, who could have taken her? And why? Was he just being alarmist because of who he was, and had the knowledge of just how bad people could be? How despicable men like Xavier tended to be?

Yeah. Maybe.

Or maybe not.

He'd find her and find the fuck out.

When his comm buzzed in his ear, he drew up short. Damn thing had been silent too long. "Alpha One," he snapped, returning to the bedroom. "Speak fast."

"No shit." Kytta, leader of Delta team, knew as well as Daklin the vagaries of communications in the valley. "Just got word: Eyes on our package. Secured in container and en route. It cleared Panama Canal, and is now mid-Atlantic. Congested shipping lanes. Will advise when contents neutralized."

"Copy." That was news to Daklin. If Delta team had received word, the comms were better on the other side of the mountain. The line went dead, and then crackled hopefully. Whether he received word directly, or not, this was excellent news. They found the truck they'd been looking. Transported in plain sight, the Nuts of E-1x, concealed in a giant container, on a ship filled with similar containers, and couldn't just be blown to shit in transit.

"We've found your Nuts, Dr. Sullivan. Now where the fuck

are you?" Both Sullivans were now missing.

"-TA for earth movers 0500." Kytta sounded loud and clear as his voice came back on line. For the moment. "And FYI, target made same request for heavy equipment. And of interest, target left urgent message for Spawn One. Party plans for tomorrow. Intel is checking chatter for next big bang. Go? No go?"

Go figure. It seemed that Xavier wanted that pass cleared as fast as the T-FLAC teams did. Spawn One was Xavier's son, Eliseo, who was now in their custody. And whatever the hell Xavier had planned was still scheduled for tomorrow.

"Go." The outbound E-1x had to be deactivated ASAP. To do that, they needed Oliver Sullivan's help, whether he gave it willingly or not. If he couldn't be found in the next eight hours, they'd attempt to clear the shipping lane and detonate instead of defuse. That shipment could not be allowed to reach land.

Delta team signed off, followed immediately by Kai Turley. "Copy that. Eyes on Xavier. You must've bored him to tears. Dude's asleep in his office."

"Stay alert. Keep eyes—" The comm died. Par for the course, and no less annoying even if it was expected. It just made things that much more complicated when there was a breakdown in communication between the teams.

Daklin sensed someone outside the door before he heard the grating of the antique key in the lock. River? Someone else? Glock raised, he moved quickly and silently across the room to stand between a glass-fronted bookcase and the closed door.

River.

Turning, she locked the door, then stood there, her back to the room, head bowed for several seconds. She wore a soft-looking blue and white print ankle length cotton dress, which bared lightly tanned arms and back, and, judging by her height, high heels.

Jesus, did she have no self-preservation instincts? How could she not be aware of him standing two feet away with a loaded weapon?

"And then," she whispered, her head still bowed as if waiting, tension humming in the air. "The scary bishop with the gun..." Slanting him a wicked smile, River taunted, "Did...what?"

God. She made him smile. It was starting to feel almost natural. Laying his weapon on the top of the bookcase, Daklin stepped behind her and swept aside the silky strands of hair at her nape. He inhaled the clean floral scent of her skin deep into his lungs and held it there like a drug.

He let out a sharp laugh. "You don't seem terribly afraid." Lowering his head, he brushed his lips over her soft skin and rewarded as she shuddered.

"You have no idea." River reached up, then pulled his hand down between her breasts as she pressed her sweet ass against the hardness of his dick. "Feel how hard my heart's racing."

Daklin nestled his open hand between the gentle swells as he kissed the side of her neck. She tilted her head to give him better access, as he traced the swirl of her ear with the tip of his tongue. "How much time do we have?"

"Hours." Three. He'd have to live the rest of his life in those hundred eighty minutes.

Turning in his arms, River looped her own arms around his neck, pressing the hard peaks of her nipples against his chest.

For a second, her gaze held his. Open, pained honesty flooded her eyes. Maybe it was just wishful thinking on his part, or maybe it was just in the waning moments before the most important op of his life, but he wanted someone to give a damn about him. Someone who would remember him when he was gone.

It was selfish of him to look to her for that.

But she did acknowledge him and, better than that, her gaze was wise, knowing, and forgiving. When in his life had he ever been able to know what a woman was thinking, or even care? His heart ached with that knowledge and the total certainty of it.

Yeah, he knew that she knew.

She knew he wasn't likely to come off that damn mountain, no matter what he told her. And, because he wanted so badly to see it, he saw forgiveness in her eyes, as she stood on tiptoe, set her teeth on his chin and gave a little nip that jolted down the length of his body like a detonator cord and elongated his dick even more.

"Hours, huh? I can think of few things to keep us occupied."

Like the very air that surrounded her, she was keeping things light. Refreshing. This is what happiness felt like, he thought, as she nipped again at his lower lip.

Her fingers fisted in the hair on the back of his head,

causing a sharp, stinging need to flood his body as she nibbled small kisses wherever she could reach. "The door's locked," she said, her voice throaty and low. "And there's a bed over there."

He walked her backwards, his fingers on her hips, bunching miles of unnecessary fabric up her sleek legs. "The wall's closer."

"We'll get to the bed--" She paused as he pulled the dress over her head. It landed somewhere behind him with a soft plop. "--eventually, right?"

Her underwear was a deep sky-blue this time, not more than a curve of a strapless bra that barely covered her nipples, and what passed for a thong but was merely a small panel of lace over her mons, with a thin satin ribbon at each hip. Sliding his palms between skin and the ribbon, he tore the anchor free, delighting at her closed-eyes shiver as he pulled the wisp of fabric from between her legs, leaving her wearing only the scrap of a bra and high-heeled sandals.

Eyes all pupil, she looked up at him, hands busily undoing the fly on his dress pants. "You have on way too many freaking clothes, Bishop Daklin." Unerring, busy fingers tugged at the zipper. It was a challenge, he was sure, since he was so large and unyielding behind the confinement.

"Kick them away," she ordered, shoving down his pants. "Oh, commando." Her eyes glowed hot and wicked. "What an interesting fashion choice for a man of the cloth. I'm a little shocked." She grinned and stroked a hand up the length of his penis, lingering at the moisture welling at the tip. "

He ripped off his shirt and clerical collar. Buttons bounced on the hardwood floor. He pressed his naked chest against the softness of her breasts, loving seeing her in nothing but diamond earrings, the sheer dark blue fabric of her bra, which did nothing to hide the pink of her nipples, and those fuck me heels. Gliding a hand down her thigh, he hooked her behind her knee.

Curling her leg over his hip left her fragrant and open. "Take me in your hand, River. Bring me home."

#

Ash tasted of salt, his skin blazing hot against hers. His fingers tightened painfully on the globe of her ass as he urged her to take him. Holding her up, he pressed hot kisses to her throat as he tightened his fingers on the under curve of her butt, pulling her flush against him.

The desire in his eyes left her breathless. Her nipples tightened and her skin felt shimmery, as if static electricity flowed through her veins. Slapping a hand on his chest, she crowded his body with hers, twisting, and turning so she could slam him against the wall.

Panting, his eyes narrowed to slits of electric blue, Ash's voice was rough as he said thickly, "Really?"

River tightened her fingers around his silken, throbbing length. He was rock hard, pulsing, and eager. "Think I can't?"

"I was hoping you w—"

To taunt him even further, she took his mouth. Hot, slick, delicious. The very air crackled around them as River tasted him, while her hand learned the length and breadth of his penis. The muscles in his lower belly flexed as she removed her hand, delighting when he groaned his frustration.

"Good things come to those who wait." She was imprinting him in her memory, running her fingers along his skin, memorizing the hardness of his muscles, the smoothness of his skin here, and roughness there. The puckered scar of a bullet wound on his hip. The long knife cut, just beneath his rib, where uneven stitches had pulled the skin.

He wasn't invincible. He was flesh and blood, her wounded warrior. River couldn't even bear to think about what he had planned for later that night. She couldn't bear the thought that he was going to go through with it, with the odds stacked against him. The idea of Ash no longer existing, of never being able to touch him again, was too horrible to contemplate.

Her throat tight, she splayed her hand on his chest, then lowered her head, kissing her way across his hard pecs, tonguing one hard flat nipple, then the other. Inhaling the heady scent of his clean skin and the salty flavor of him under her tongue, she explored his chest with her lips, teeth, and hands.

Dragging her palms down the battled-scared skin at his sides, she slid both hands down over the rock hard ridges of his abs. "Wow. A twenty pack."

He laughed out a curse, then muttered. "Can't count."

He was tensile steel covered with smooth skin roughened by dark hair. Following the dark trail down below his navel, she tasted his saltiness, breathing deeply of the scent of his skin, profoundly aware of their shared urgency and need.

She was burning and pulsing from the inside out. But this was it. The last time. The only time she had left, and damn it, she wasn't about to waste a single second. She was going to savor every moment if it killed her. Then she'd lock it away in her memory. Anticipation had never felt this good.

Sliding to her knees, she trailed kisses down his left thigh where scars and raised flesh puckered his skin. Old surgeries, new surgeries. So much pain. So much regret.

Her hands lingered, learning, empathizing, tracing the marks, his badges of courage.

"That leg's had all the attention it needs," he murmured, cupping the back of her head to redirect her.

His fingers tangled roughly in her hair as she took him into her mouth. She heard the back of his head thud against the wall as she gripped the base of his penis and twirled her tongue around the glans. His breathing became more ragged, his grip in her hair tighter as she increased the torment.

Gliding her hand along the base of his erect penis, so thick and alive, she clamped her fingers around the pulsing length, then stroked her tongue along the throbbing vein on the underside before circling the hood with her lips.

Ash tightened his fingers in her hair and sucked in a breath as she stroked his length with the slick warmth of her tongue. Silk over steel. River took half the length of him into her mouth, creating a wet suction that had his breath ragged. His hips jerked, driving him deeper into her mouth.

Stilling him with a hand on his hip, she curled her fingers around to cup his butt cheek and hold him where she wanted him.

Where she wanted him was Portland. As far from Los Santos, explosives, and Francisco Xavier as possible.

This moment was all she had. Ash, and the moment. No morning after. No future. It was a useless endeavor wishing for the impossible.

Using her tongue, she lapped and sucked, swirled and used teasing flutters to drive him mad. She loved the taste and texture of him. Loved the power she had to make him moan as he stood there and let her drive him to the breaking point. Loved that she was about to break his self-control. That was power.

Deepening her strokes and pulls, she drew him into her mouth as deep as she could. She reveled in his harsh, ragged breathing and the almost painful grip where his fingers wound tightly in her hair as his body tightened and shook.

He might have been enjoying the hell out of what she was doing, but she knew he had considerable self-control and he wasn't about to lose it.

Cupping her face gently in both hands, he firmly drew her away from his penis.

River blinked up at him, lightheaded with lust.

"I want to come inside you," he said softly. "Not here."

"Not here? Not here in this room? Oh!"

Hands under her arms, he hauled her upright. River wobbled on weak knees. Without missing a beat, he scooped her up. She'd forgotten she still wore her heels, and her shoes thudded to the carpet one at a time as he carried her to the bed, leaving her sprawled on her back wearing just her bra.

"Here," he murmured, positioning himself between her outspread legs, using his hips to push hers even further apart. "Now."

He surged inside her to the hilt. The sudden sensation of fullness brought with it an exquisite, full-body shudder as he seated himself so deep, River felt him in every nerve cluster in her body.

With a throaty growl she tightened her arms around his neck as he stopped for a second, lifted his hips slightly, then surged impossibly deeper.

As he started thrusting, she managed to formulate real words, her breath ragged and raspy with clawing need "This is killing me."

Eyes dark with lust, he groaned in response. "Me too."

River clamped her legs around his pumping hips, her arms around his broad shoulders. She met each movement he made with equal force, holding on for dear life as, breathlessly, they came together. He swallowed her moans with a kiss. Then, when they both could move, he flipped her over, positioning her so that she lay on top of him. He stayed inside of her, cupping her butt with his large hands, keeping their hips joined. Time passed. Neither made a move to separate their bodies. As though every second counted, they kept kissing. Soft kisses. Long kisses. Hungry kisses. And still, he stayed inside of her. It was as though he never wanted to leave. For a while, he was only semi-hard. Then he lengthened. Hardened. Their need built again. She moaned when he pushed deeper inside of her again.

This time, he moved fast, flipping her to her stomach, pinning her to the bed, and thrusting up, deep and deeper still, taking her breath with his hunger. Having her flat on the bed beneath him wasn't enough for him. He pulled her hips up to his, so she was on her knees, with her face buried against the pillow.

"You okay?"

"Better than okay," she moaned. "Feels like . . . heaven."

With each hard thrust, her walls tightened more and more. Biting the pillows, she felt his fingers brushing her clit, as he thrust in and out of her with more power than anyone had ever used with her before. She came, hard, with a climax that started deep inside of her and continued, until she was moaning his name. "Yeah," he said. "Say it."

"What?" she managed to ask.

"My name."

So she did. Over and over again, as he kept thrusting. Until, too soon, he was still, gripping her hips tight. She felt him spilling into her, filling her.

"Where have you been all of my life?" he moaned, lifting her, and once again draping her over him, so that her legs were spread over his.

"Portland."

He chuckled, then pressed his hips closer to her, pushing his penis further in again, threading his fingers through her soft flesh where they joined, toying with her clit, trying not to slip out of her. "I love the way you feel. I'm sorry to see this end."

"Hmmm," she said. "Don't let it end."

"Think about something else for a few minutes. Let me regroup." He moaned as he slipped out of her.

"How's this for something different, Ash? How the hell is everyone going to go over that pass?" River asked, dropping a row of kisses across his shoulder.

"We have large earth movers on the way in."

Twenty feet overhead, the lazily circling fan sluggishly moved warm air over their damp sweaty skin. River was still sprawled half over his body as they lay in a post-coital glow. She had one leg over his, her hand splayed over his chest, head tucked under his chin. Both of them too spent to move. With her breast pressed against his chest, she felt the steady, strong beat of his heart. Her bra was on the floor, and she'd lost an earring in the tangled sheets.

River knew that far too soon, this quiet interlude would be over. She needed a game plan. She was no one's responsibility. Oliver was long gone, and Ash had his own agenda. An agenda that had far reaching repercussions way more important than her safe exit. In this life and death situation, she was on her own.

"They'll clear the road at dawn, but honestly," Ash lazily trailed his fingers down the middle of her back, making her shiver, his soft touch at odds with his harsh tone. "that's too damned late. Marcus and my team on the other side of the slide are working on a way to get you and the others out before I go up to the mine tonight. We have a couple of choppers coming in, but not enough to move a hundred people, and not without alerting Xavier and his men that we're here. It's not that we couldn't handle them, but I don't want to put you and the villagers in the crossfire." He stroked her butt cheek.

"I told Marcus I'd help him do whatever's necessary. I took Juanita." When Ash gave her a puzzled look, she clarified. "Pregnant maid at dinner the other night?"

"Ahh."

"The baby's Franco's," River told him, sifting her fingers through the strands of his dark hair then trailing them down the strong column of his throat. "And according to her, he wants it. That'll be over her dead body, apparently. She's really terrified of him, which really, really, really makes me want to punch him in the balls."

"He'll get worse."

"Excellent. Too bad I won't be around to see it," River told him with asperity. "Juanita's with Father Marcus now. He'll hide her in case Franco comes sniffing around."

Ash tucked her hair behind her ear, his warm fingers lingering on her cheek. She loved the way he touched her, as if she were fine china, but he'd made love to her as if she was his equal in strength and power. He'd given and received as enthusiastically as she had. They'd both have bruises tomorrow. She didn't care. She felt alive, and greedy, and she'd make love to him a hundred more times through the day and night if they could.

Their time was almost up, and they both knew it.

"She'll be safe with Marcus. He'll ensure both of you get out in time. I hate like hell not being able to take you myself."

"I can take care of myself. I've been doing it a long time. Don't worry about me, okay?"

"Yeah. I know how tough you are," he said, and he wasn't teasing. "I don't know many woman who could've done what you did today without freaking out. You were incredibly cool under pressure. It was a hell of a thing to watch you drive while we were under heavy fire."

"I figured screaming Stop! Stop! Stop! at the top of my lungs and getting hysterical would have zero effect on the guys trying to turn us into human sieves."

"Most women would've folded."

"I'm not most women."

"No. No, you're not, River Sullivan. Not only beautiful, but also cool under fire. I admire the hell out of you, you know that?" Over her head, he tilted his wrist to check the time. Ash didn't have to tell her that it was rapidly running out for them. "Did you come across anything interesting when you went sneaking around last night?" As he talked, he stroked her back, tunneling his fingers through her hair.

River closed her eyes for a moment, enjoying the quiet moment, adding it to her memories for later. "Other than the kink room, and that my pricy lingerie was being used for bondage? Not really. Wait. Maybe." She thought about the envelope of pictures she'd found hidden at the back of a drawer. The redhead, from baby to adult. "He might have a love child somewhere. Would that be of interest?"

"Anything about his business, about him, could be useful, especially if it reveals anyone involved in his enterprises. A name or location might help us with decrypting a cloud site we found. Any business associates, partners. Does your brother have any aliases?

River made a rude noise. "Aliases? My brother didn't have friends, let alone an alter ego. His middle name is--"

"Michael. We know."

"I hope you're not implying Oliver had a hand in running things here? If you'd seen my brother trying to manage the store after our parents were killed, you'd know he has no business acumen whatsoever. Maybe the illegitimate daughter is involved?"

"Why are you so sure that he has an illegitimate child? In case you haven't noticed all the photographs around, he has a dozen kids."

River folded her arms across his chest, and rested her chin on her forearm to look up at him. "I found photographs of a woman with red hair. Gorgeous in a scary, I'm-a-Black–Widow-spider, kind of way."

"Another girlfriend?" Ash suggested with a slight smile as he traced her lips with his thumb, as if fascinated by the shape.

River bit the marauding digit. "I assure you, Juanita isn't his "girlfriend," and I didn't come across any pictures of her. There was an ultrasound picture. But the baby looked to be too big for Juanita's; she is only a few months along. So I presume the baby in the ultrasound is of one of his many other children."

"To my knowledge, he doesn't have any redheaded daughters. All his kids have black hair."

River shifted, so she could place a lingering kiss on one of his abs, then straightened. "Maybe he had a redheaded mistress? Still, even for Franco, that would be weird taking pictures of her as a baby, and then—- Nah. Too gross. But that girl must've had a mother. She was the mistress, maybe?"

"If so, he's been remarkably secretive about it. We've looked into every aspect of his life. I'll have my people look again, trying to identify the redhead and find out who she is to him. We've apprehended his wife and youngest son. They were taking a crapload of money as a gift to the Vatican. We got his other two sons and a non-nun daughter. We're rounding up the rest of the family, nuns and priests included. Even with the mine annihilated, we don't want any member of his family to take up the family business when this is all over."

He stroked her cheek. "I'd like a look at those photographs. Maybe something in one of them will ring a bell. Tell me where they are, and I'll get them later so we can try and ID her."

"There's a small drawer on the right side of his desk downstairs. Blue envelope about this big, shoved to the back." She indicated the size. "If you have his whole family in custody, maybe someone can identify her?"

"We'll run her through T-FLAC's facial rec system, first. We should be able to find out who she is to Xavier, and if she's important. After tonight, Francisco Xavier and his enterprise will be done, once and for all. I don't want loose ends."

For a moment, River included himself in that. Perhaps Ash had too many demons and he thought death was the better option. "Why not just take him now? The thought of sitting down to dinner with that creep again gives me the freaking willies."

"We have a few hours. He has an army there, give or take a hundred well-armed men, dogs, and long-range guns. The surrounding area, as you saw, has no cover for miles. Going in under cover of darkness will even the odds."

"You think you and your handful of men, against a gazillion soldiers, is evening the freaking odds? You're kidding, right?"

Ash smoothed away her scowl with his fingertip. "We're damn good."

"I sure hope you're not being braggy. You'd *better* be damn good."

"You don't have to come downstairs at all. As far as he's concerned, it's business as usual. I'll go to dinner and keep him occupied until it's time to take him out. We need the time between now and then to finish evacuating the village. I'm going to leave Ram here to watch your back until you're clear."

"No. You need everyone with you." River replied adamantly. "How many of you are supposed to go up there tonight?"

"Six."

"Well if that was the plan, for God's sake, stick to it. I'm pretty damned sure you can't afford to be one man short. I'll be with Marcus and the people who come to get us out. I'll be fine. Really."

"That depends on when we get Xavier airlifted out. If he's still here, Ram will stay to watch him, anyway."

"Can I have a gun?"

"Do you know how to use one?"

"Point and pull the trigger, right? Honestly, no. But I don't have to be an expect marksman, do I? Can you show me the basics so I can at least protect myself?"

He smiled. "It takes a bit more training than that. I'm sure you'd excel at shooting, but there won't be any need for you to be armed tonight. My men on the pass will have your back the whole time, and Marcus used to be an operative. He's smart and sharp."

"And armed?"

"Oh, yeah." He tucked her hair behind her ear.

River stroked her foot up and down his good leg. She didn't give a shit about Franco, and really, she was only half listening.

She just liked watching his lips move, and the way his deep voice resonated through her.

"What about the redhead? Do you think it's worth tracking her down?"

"You read too many spy novels."

"Pfft. I don't read any spy novels. Regency England is my favorite genre, and I don't like spies in those either. It is a logical question, isn't it? The redhead must be someone important to him if he has so many pictures of her, especially if he took her on a trip to Moscow or Disneyland. She could be anyone, but my vote is that she's his love child. A secret one, since she'd been relegated to the back of a drawer, and not given one of the silver frames he has everywhere. Don't you find that odd? And interesting?"

"You're not going to let this go, are you?" Ash sat up, stuffing several pillows at his back, then hoisted River up beside him. She slid her foot up his calf. Tucking her against his side, he kissed the top of her head, then murmured, "How old would you say she was?"

She gave him a narrow-eyed look, and tugged at the hair on his chest. "Are you humoring me?"

"Not in this instance." He covered her hand with his, then rubbed her fingers back and forth over his chest. She loved the springy tickle of the dark mat trailing down to his groin, and the warmth of his satin smooth skin. She slid her hand slowly down his belly, enjoying the flex and play of muscles under his smooth skin.

"I don't know if something's important until it fits or doesn't fit the jigsaw puzzle of this op," he continued. "There's nothing to suggest Xavier has a business partner, or another female in his life, other than his wife and daughters."

"Maybe she's his boss?"

Daklin laughed. "Whomever she is, or was, she doesn't fit the profile of Top Dog in this scenario."

"That's pretty damned chauvinistic of you. There's nothing that says a beautiful woman can't be Top Dog in all sorts of things. I'm Top Dog of my lingerie company, and I can assure you, I'm smart, savvy, and can be ruthless."

He smiled. "Ruthless?"

"In an affirming way. Sure, if I have to be." Trailing her fingers down his chest, she rested her hand low on his taut belly, brushing the tips of her fingers along his lengthening penis. His abs contracted.

"Don't count this woman out, is all I'm saying. One of the pictures was dated on the back. It was taken four years ago. She looked to be in her late thirties, early forties maybe? I didn't see any pictures after that date. But that doesn't mean there weren't any."

The soft white drapes on either side of the shutters billowed in the breeze. She felt the warm zephyr on her skin like ghostly fingers. Time ticked away their minutes together. River wanted to stop the clocks, barter with someone for more time, and plead with Ash not to blow himself up.

As he played with her hair, goose bumps rose on her skin. "I don't suppose there was a name on any of pictures you saw?"

"On one of them, where she looked to be in her late teens, I saw the name, Catalina. From the background it looked as if it was taken in Russia." She grinned. "Or Disney World. *Somewhere* with brightly painted minarets."

"Moscow. The Cathedral of the Intercession. Better known as St. Basil's cathedral. He has a rosary from there in his private chapel."

"That's pretty innocuous, right? He made a pilgrimage there with this girl? Still, odd, don't you think? She was young. Too young to be his mistress then."

Asher arched an eyebrow.

Her stomach twisted. Remembering who they were talking about, his kink room, and what he'd done to Juanita, she shook her head. "Maybe not."

"Perhaps she was his mistress or, perhaps even then, he was selling E-1x or its precursor to the Russians."

River frowned. "Would he take a young girl with him to sell explosives to terrorists?"

"Depends who the girl was to him. Maybe. God knows the man's a certified grade A psychopath. With Xavier, anything's possible. Maybe this Catalina is a nun. Several of his daughters are. And he's got several sons who are priests. I'll get my people to look into her, see what we can dig up. If she's involved, we'll find her."

"I'm still curious." River dragged her hand lower, closing her fingers around the tensile heat of his erection. "Should I just ask Franco flat out?"

His penis leapt in her hand, and he growled low in his throat when she tightened her fingers.

"Great idea. When he asks how you know about her, tell him you were just skulking around the house in the dead of night and accidentally fell over the pictures as you rifled through his drawers and personal papers. Good plan."

Tightening her fist around his erection, she slid up his chest and brushed her mouth over his. "I could accidentally fall on this. That would be an excellent plan."

Laughing, Ash tumbled her onto her back

FIFTEEN

A sh stopped talking abruptly, glanced at the door, and swung his legs off the bed. River cocked her head. She didn't hear anything. Gloriously naked, he picked up his gun from the bedside table. She loved the taut flex of his butt as he walked across the room.

Sliding off the other side of the bed, she picked up her discarded dress, pulling it on over her naked body.

Ash scooped up his scattered garments with one hand as he kept the other hand steady, gun raised. Then he stepped to the left of the door where he dropped his clothes, out of sight. The fact that he wasn't dressing, his urgency and alert posture, shot up her heartbeat.

It was strangely arousing seeing a naked man with a big black gun in his hand standing as still as a statue. It was incredibly arousing when that naked man was Ash Daklin. Broad chest, ridged abs, narrow hips, almost every inch of him toned and fit, with rippling muscles and satin smooth skin. Every inch except his mangled leg, and the multiple scars indicating just how dangerous his job was. Even relaxed, his penis was impressive.

He hadn't moved. River frowned. She still didn't hear—-

A brisk knock. "Miss Sullivan?"

Franco.

Her eyes met Ash's. "I'm dressing, Franco." Well shit, she probably shouldn't've put that image in his head.

"One of the girls was tasked with giving you my gift this morning. The white dress? It would please me if you'd wear it tonight."

"A gift?" The gift Juanita had mentioned earlier?

"A confirmation dress I had made in Paris for one of my daughters," he said through the heavy door. "She never had the opportunity to wear it. You'll look lovely in it and I'd deem it a great honor if you'd wear it down to dinner later."

Ew. "That's--" *Damned creepy.* "--kind of you."

"Do you have it?"

She raised an inquiring eyebrow at Daklin who jerked his head in the direction of the tall, intricately carved wardrobe on the far wall. River crossed the room. Opening the heavy door, she saw the dress on a padded pink hanger. "I do, thank you. Um, isn't a girl confirmed into the Catholic church as a child?"

The long dress looked small, with delicate white on white embroidery across the scooped neck and down the pin-tucked bodice. The garment looked deceptively innocent until she held her palm under it.

River rubbed the thin fabric between her fingers. She knew her fabrics, and this looked to be nun's cloth. An incredibly fine wool, woven in plain-weave, with the softness and transparency of muslin. She'd used it in her *el velo* collection last year. And, like mist, the dress was completely freaking see-through. Awesome for lingerie; not so awesome for a dress a young girl would wear for a religious ceremony, or one given to her by her father.

"The age of reason is anywhere from seven to sixteen," Franco said through the thick door, his voice slightly raised. "I had the dress designed for Ca-- my daughter, when she was fifteen."

Lovely. He thought she was going to wear his teenager's see-through confirmation dress for him? Disturbing to the max. "It's very pretty. Unfortunately, it looks too small for me." She noticed a couple of Bishop Daklin's buttons lying on the floor, and put her bare foot over them, just in case Franco burst into the room. Of course, he'd probably notice a naked Ash before he saw the two buttons on the floor.

"You're slender and full-busted. I'm sure it will fit you perfectly." The heavy wrought iron door handle rattled as he twisted it from the outside. "Try it on."

Even though Franco was on the other side of a thick slab of wood, and Ash was a few feet away holding his gun, River's heart leapt into her throat at the absurd, and somewhat threatening, suggestion. The fire in Ash's eyes told her he felt exactly the same way.

"I don't want to tear this beautiful fabric. It's so delicate and pretty," River told her creepy host. River had absolutely no intention of trying on, let alone wearing the damn thing to dinner. Not if Franco paid her a million dollars.

"I know you'll handle it with care. Please try to wear it. I'll see you downstairs for drinks in an hour." She'd skipped breakfast, then had an inedible lunch that seemed like hours ago, followed by a marathon of lovemaking. She was starving. But starving enough to sit across the table from Franco? No, thank you.

"See you then." What else was she supposed to say? No, I'll sneak into the kitchen and find a chicken leg to gnaw on while Ash and his men round you and your fellow bad guys up and do whatever they have planned with you?

"I'm looking forward to hearing how you spent your day."

Getting shot at and rained on. Having a lethal snake fall into her lap. Indulging in wild monkey sex in the front seat of a convertible? Almost killed by a rockslide? Finally, rolling around in bed with the bishop? Yeah. She'd get right on filling him in.

River glared at the door without responding. For a few pregnant moments, she held her breath. There were no footsteps indicating Franco's departure. "Have you seen Bishop Daklin? I haven't seen him since breakfast."

I'm looking at every magnificent inch of him right now. "I think I heard the shower running in his room a few minutes ago."

"Ah. I won't disturb him then. I'll see you both downstairs in an hour."

She pulled a face. "I'm looking forward to it." *Liar.* But she did perk up at the bonus hour he'd just given them.

Asher held up his hand when she was about to say something to him. Pulling the dress over her head, River dropped it to the floor, then sat down on the foot of the bed and took in the delicious specimen of manhood that was Ash Daklin.

"Another hour," she said.

"Priceless." His voice was gruff, making the word come out like a growl.

Leaning back, she braced herself on straight arms to wait. "Do you think I'm 'full busted'?"

Stalking toward her, he dropped the clothes he'd just scooped up. "I think you're perfectly busted. He placed his knee between her spread thighs, pushed her flat, and kissed her as if he hadn't seen her in a month. River curled her legs around his hips, placed her crossed feet in the center of his back, and welcomed his hard, powerful thrust.

#

"We know that Xavier doesn't have a legitimate daughter named Catalina," Daklin told River as she watched him dress. "He has five daughters: Rosario, who's a nun; Esperanza and Esmerelda, twins who are teachers in Santa De Porres; Ana, another nun; and Deifilia, who worked for him at the plant. There is no redheaded Catalina."

"Would it help if I managed to get a picture for you? Maybe you can ID her."

"Not just no, but hell no! I don't want you snooping around the house of a known terrorist. He's not only a psychopath, but a deviant as well. If you can handle it, come down for dinner. If not,

284

I'll make your excuses and you can wait here until it's time for you to leave with Marcus."

"Did you know Oliver when you were both at MIT?" River asked, propped against the pillows, bathed in stripes of white moonlight and black shadow. They hadn't bothered turning on the lights after they'd made love again.

"That wasn't a response to my request."

"It wasn't a request, it was an order. An order I'll take under advisement."

He chuckled, despite himself. He loved her sass, even though he had no business liking her at all. *Goddamnittohell.* This is a suckass, but fitting, way for an operative to exit. Only now, he didn't want a drink before the end. She was what he wanted his last memory to be. A crystal clear and vivid memory of River, relaxed from their lovemaking, her bright eyes gleaming in the semi darkness, content and sassy to the end.

It would be a good memory to hold on to when he traveled through the mine tunnels in a few hours.

"You haven't answered my question. Did you know Oliver at MIT?"

"Only marginally," he said, dressing as slowly as he dared, prolonging his time with her. He wasn't going to waste time with a shower before he went downstairs. He wanted the last thing he smelled to be River. On his hands. On his face. The taste of her on his tongue. He stored the memories, imprinting her with all five senses.

"I was a few years behind him, but everyone knew of him. His theories for creating new explosives for mining operations were considered original and cutting edge." Daklin sat down on the other side of the bed to put on his shoes.

Two minutes, tops, was all the time they had left. Once downstairs, he'd be Bishop Daklin until he retired to his room, later tonight. And an hour after the house was asleep, he'd leave to go to the mine. She'd be gone during that hour. Daklin got to his feet, facing her, drinking in the sheen on her skin, memorizing the way the icy moonlight, slotted through the shutters, gleamed on her pale hair. "He was brilliant."

Forget about me when you return to Portland, River Sullivan. Find a nice guy who loves you more than his next breath. Someone stable, sober, and in his right fucking mind, who'll build his life around you and worship the ground you walk on.

She wrapped her arms around her upraised knees. "He's still brilliant."

No dangerous job, okay? A banker maybe. Yeah, a banker. Or an accountant. "Yeah, he is." *If he's still alive. Jesus, she'd be bored out of her mind with some accountant in a three-piece suit.*

Daklin racked his brain to think of someone who'd be perfect for her. Everyone he knew was an operative. They sure as shit weren't stable family men. Okay, maybe Navarro. He seemed to be doing good with Honey. They even had a baby on the way. Then there was Jake Dolan. He'd been married, hell, forfuckingever. Both were still operatives, both seemed stable. Others had made it work.

None of them were alcoholics with fucked up legs who were about to blow up an entire mountain.

It was a little fucking late for a Hail Mary now. There was no time to reevaluate his decision. He had to open his clenched fist and set her free. She deserved every scrap of happiness she could get her hands on.

Asher Daklin was the last thing she needed.

"I'm so glad he isn't here. But you'll find him, wherever he is, won't you?"

Daklin nodded. "My men won't give up until they do." She watched him as he came around to her side of the bed.

He wouldn't touch her. And he sure as hell wouldn't kiss her goodbye. He'd see her over dinner. Daklin swallowed a mirthless laugh, the last fucking supper, then he'd walk away. But only because his leg prevented him from running like hell.

Don't. Touch. Her.

She got up on her knees amid the rumpled sheets, a pagan goddess shadows painted shades of black and white across her pretty, perfectly-sized-for-him breasts and the pale heart-shaped fluff at the juncture of her thighs.

He felt the heat of her skin. Tasted her breath on his lips.

Do. Not. Touch. Her.

Her smooth cheek felt warm in his palm, the cool brush of silky strands of her hair a kiss to his senses. Daklin's chest ached, a physical pain to rival the pain in his leg. It felt as though someone was carving his heart out of his chest with a rusty spoon.

You are fucked, Daklin. Absolutely fucked. Say goodbye. Stop damn well touching her. Go.

River cupped her hand over his, holding it against her face. "Please tell me your people won't kill him." *Be done. Finish this. Now. Before she learns to hate you. Before you deserve her hatred.* "I won't make you any promises, River. Right now he, with Francisco Xavier, tops our most wanted terrorists list."

"It's really, really hard to wrap my brain around that label. It isn't who I know him to be. It just isn't."

"People change." Her hair felt like cool silk spilling between his fingers; he stroked her as one would a cat. "Money corrupts, and Xavier has been making billions from this explosive. He's got the market cornered. It's impossible to believe that your brother—-who, dollars to doughnuts, *invented* it and knows how to defuse it--isn't taking a huge slice of the pie."

"They're planning a series of seven, earth shattering, Armageddon-type explosions tomorrow. We don't know where. We have to get that intel, and we have to get it fast. Both T-FLAC and Interpol are searching for him. We will find him, no matter where he's hiding. I'm sorry. But that's *my* reality. We need him alive, so we won't injure him intentionally. But this is a dangerous op with a lot of highly volatile, moving parts. Shit will happen, and people *will* get hurt.

She kissed his palm. "How do you stop something if you

don't know where it's happening?"

"No idea. All we know is that it will occur, simultaneously, at seven different locations, at fifteen thirty-three. And they'll be using E-1x. Three clues. We've worked with less, I assure you, but it isn't easy. But T-FLAC is good."

"I'm sure they are." Her eyes darkened as she searched his face before asking quietly, "Is this a suicide mission, Ash?"

"Asked and answered."

"Asking *again*. You're going to blow up an entire fucking *mountain*, and you can barely *walk*. How far are you going to go into the mine? How much time have you allowed yourself to get out? Or is your strategy to go in and not come out?"

"I know what I'm doing."

"That wasn't the question."

"I'm not suicidal." *I'm a fatalist, and up until a few days ago, I didn't give a flying fuck if I made it out alive or not. Now, though--* "My job's dangerous. There are inherent risks."

"So you play Russian Roulette with your life every time you're in the field."

"I work with explosives, so yeah. But I'm highly skilled, and damn good at my job." None of which answered the fear and worry he saw in her eyes. "I'm going to try my damndest not to die." Knowing that was a promise he couldn't--*shouldn't*—make, he curved his hand around her nape and pulled her in for a chaste kiss.

No tongue. No juicy smooch. Dry had never tasted so

erotic. He kissed her again the same way, then straightened, gratified to see even that soft brush of lips left her pretty gray eyes a little glazed.

"Hundreds of our best researchers and tech people are following cyber chatter and processing it," he told her, stroking his thumb up and down the sensitive nerves on the back of her neck, loving the way she shivered at his touch, and the way her head dropped so that her hair curtained her face. He wanted to nibble her there, at the soft slope where her neck met her shoulder, he wanted to lick the rim of her ear where a diamond glittered.

He dared not get started again.

"They'll find one clue, and then another," Daklin said, clearing the lust from his throat, and removing his hand from temptation. "Time's running out. We have eyes on Xavier twenty-four-seven. We'll take him at the last second, hoping he'll put in a call to your brother."

Relieved not to be touching her, he stepped back, his body half-turned toward the door. The exit was just yards away. Too bad his feet were still pointed at River. They didn't fucking want to go anywhere.

Thank God, Sullivan was gone. Because, as much as T-FLAC wanted Dr. Sullivan, Daklin didn't want to be the one to kill him if push came to shove. That was a mark his conscience would never recover from, right up there with killing his own brother.

"He might be on some tropical island sipping a mai-tai right about now." *Or manufacturing more E-1x. Better still, he could already be in custody, hopefully spilling his guts.*

"From your lips..." Putting a hand on his chest, she leaned in. "We'd better get ready to go down. One kiss before you go."

Daklin shook his head, moving out of reach so her hand dropped to her lap. "Just don't wear that fucking dress."

#

"I'm disappointed you didn't wear the dress I gifted you, my dear." Franco said, sounding more annoyed than disappointed.

River didn't give a rat's ass. No way would she have worn the revealing dress of a daughter Ash claimed Franco didn't have. Instead, she'd opted for a swingy, white dress with a cherry print, fifties-style with a scooped neck, and nice roomy pockets. It was one of her favorites and one of the few things she hadn't packed for Juanita. Tonight she'd paired it with black strappy high heels and pearls to keep the vintage-inspired look. Usually the dress and lingerie made River feel fun and flirty. Tonight, it felt like a misstep.

She should've worn black jeans and a black shirt for her escape later. "It's beautiful, but unfortunately it didn't fit. It's so exquisitely made, you should save it for a future granddaughter to wear."

"As you say."

He was pissed. Too bad, so sad. She forked up a morsel of gooey appetizer, *Arepa con Carne y Queso.* The melted cheese didn't help the sautéed beef, onions, and peppers go down her constricted throat. She took a sip from her water glass to wash it down, setting her fork on the side of her plate. She couldn't eat tonight. Her stomach was too tied up in knots.

She should've opted to stay in her room, but missing more time with Ash was unacceptable.

Franco's crisp white shirt, worn open-necked with a light gray suit, dazzled in the candlelight in comparison to the other two men's somber garments. When he wasn't eating, he'd place his hand over his phone, which lay beside his plate. Every now and then, when he thought himself unobserved, he'd nervously touch the blue tooth earpiece hooked over his right ear. Clearly, he was waiting for a call. She wanted to suggest he invest in a freaking operable cell tower. She hadn't been able to get a hold of anyone since talking to her friend Carly the day she'd arrived. But that wasn't nearly as dangerous as Ash and his men not being able to communicate.

An elderly woman removed their plates. Only Ash had cleaned his. The meal was interminable, yet Ash, wearing his full bishop regalia, appeared perfectly relaxed and engaged in the conversation between Franco and Father Marcus. He gave no indication that he wanted to race out of there. No indication that he was about to put his life in jeopardy. No indication that behind the scenes, his people were attempting to evacuate a hundred civilians from the village right under Franco's nose.

Father Marcus, wearing all black, relieved only by his crisp white clerical collar, seemed tense. River wasn't sure if Franco noticed, or if *she* did because she knew what was about to happen.

The serving woman returned, bearing salad plates on a big, and clearly heavy, black lacquered tray she could barely carry. Setting the tray down on a nearby table covered with framed photographs, she took two plates at a time and, head bent down, shuffled to the table to deliver them. First to Ash, then Franco, and finally, to Father Marcus and River. She shuffled out without a word.

River stared at her plate as though she'd never seen a salad before. How was she even going to *pretend* to eat? She stabbed a piece of avocado smothered in raspberry dressing, then slid it off her fork. She tried a slice of tomato next, attributing the tension in the room to Franco. But was she right? Was it *Franco* who was nervous as they ate their crisp salad? Or was it her own tension making her imagine everyone else at the table was twitchy? Whatever it was, it ratcheted up her nerves even more.

Franco couldn't possibly know that T-FLAC operatives surrounded both Los Santos and the mine by now, or that, within hours, he'd be in custody, and the mine and surrounding area would be blown to hell and gone. He *couldn't* know. Could he?

She shot a glance across the table at Ash, who was in the middle of a conversation she could barely hear. "—authenticated, will bring believers from all over the world to Los Santos. Something to take into serious consideration."

His head was turned to address Franco, and River had a few moments to drink in his profile. Would she ever have the opportunity to touch him again? Was this the last time she'd *see* him? God, what a depressing thought.

Depressing or not, that was her reality. Damn it, she missed him already and he was still within arm's reach. Still breathing.

"Whether I authenticate it or not, Franco, you are free to believe in it, even without the Church's approval, as long as the apparition contains nothing to contravene faith or morals. However, having witnessed it myself only twice, I cannot authenticate it, yet." He took several drawn out minutes to spear his salad, eating each bite with apparent relish.

Ash was holding Franco's apparition hostage, using Franco's own vanity.

"It is to be expected," Father Marcus chimed in. "The Church never gives approval on an apparition without repeated and exhaustive investigation." A glance at his plate showed River that he hadn't touched a bite, either.

Franco watched Ash as if every word falling from his lips was sent from God, his salad ignored. "I understand, Your Excellency. But the Church surely believes there's enough evidence. They sent you."

"Yes, the Church believes there's enough evidence to warrant commitment of its resources to consider your claims. But this is just the starting point of a long investigation." Ash rubbed a finger to his temple, and gave a small grimace. Of pain?

Having seen his injured leg, he wasn't a man who gave in to discomfort, and if he had a headache, she doubted he'd telegraph that weakness to Franco. "I have explained this." He allowed a little impatience to color his words, surprising River, who'd never seen him lose his cool. Resting her fork on her plate with the speared tomato still on it, she sat up a little straighter.

Ash bit into a carrot. Swallowed, paused. "This cannot happen overnight. I must establish that the facts of the case are error free."

"They are!"

Asher put up his hand and kept talking as if Franco hadn't interrupted. "The person receiving the message must be balanced psychologically. And of course they must be honest, moral, sincere, and respect the authority of the Church."

Franco didn't qualify for any of those, except that last little bit. River picked up her fork and bit into the tomato. Swallowed. It settled like a lump in her stomach.

"Doctrinal errors are not attributed to God, Our Lady, or a saint," Ash told him. "Theological and spiritual doctrines presented have to be error free, and moneymaking is not a motive involved in the events." He took another bite, before he glanced back at his host. "This is delicious. My compliments to the cook."

Then he continued. Beside him, Franco was enraptured. "Be aware: once this information goes public, and it will, there's no way to keep something this big a secret. You will have to prepare for thousands of people to descend into the valley. You will have to provide food and shelter because the faithful will not leave to travel across the mountain to Abad to find housing. Because the apparition is in your home, it will become a holy shrine. People will be lined up to see her, every day. Are you prepared for this, Franco?"

"If you authenticate my apparition, Your Excellency, I will, of course, welcome the faithful and make accommodations for them."

Or more likely keep it a deep, dark, freaking secret and keep it to yourself like all the other freaky stuff that happens in your home.

"Good, then we will continue on this path."

Franco's fingers tightened around the phone on the table beside him, indicating his tension. "Thank you, Your Excellency."

Did he know what was about to happen?

River wished *she* didn't know, quite frankly, because the knowledge was a hard knot in her throat and made eating the tangy, raspberry dressing drenched salad almost impossible.

The elderly woman took her plate and Marcus's plate and returned them to the tray on the sideboard. Then she shuffled around the table to clear the other two plates.

"Send Juanita in with the wine. Even *encinta,* she moves faster than you do, old woman," Franco snapped impatiently as the woman started her return trip with the main course. His foul mood was apparent in his impatient tone, flushed face, and wild eyes. He spent the next few minutes berating her for being a sloth, and God only knew what else, in rapid-fire Spanish as she attempted to serve a steaming chicken and rice dish.

The woman returned the two plates she'd just picked up to

the tray, and turned to stand stoically, her hands clasped tightly at her waist. Tears glistened in her eyes as she informed him in almost a whisper that Juanita wasn't well. She was resting.

The cords of Franco's neck distended, and his face flushed. Holy crap, was he about to have a screaming fit?

He motioned her forward to bring the food. "Get one of the men to help you serve the next course. Go. Go." Franco impatiently waved her away, and addressed Ash, sitting beside him. "I apologize, Your Excellency." He cast a cursory glance across the table. "Father, Miss Sullivan. It seems the stomach illness affecting many people in the village has afflicted my household staff as well."

"You didn't give her a chance to serve us," River said, unable to remain quiet a second longer. "I'm sure she was doing her best."

"My presence makes her nervous," Ash inserted smoothly. "Would you like me to go and reassure her?

"Thank you, Your Excellency, that isn't necessary. She knows she's old and slow. She will try harder, and bring back one of the men to help her serve the next course."

River wanted to lunge across the table and grab the bastard by the throat. Instead, she clasped her fingers beneath the table, and kept her mouth shut. It was as though the very air was filled with invisible gasoline fumes, and one match would ignite the entire polite façade and blow everything to hell and back. She could bite her tongue for another hour.

A few minutes later, the good-looking bodyguard came into the room, and efficiently set a plate before each of them. "Thank you." She gave him a smile. He was a counterterrorist operative, not a freaking waiter.

"*De nada*, Miss River."

A few minutes after he left, and when she couldn't stomach the sight of the food any longer, River dropped her napkin on the table and got to her feet. "Excuse me, I need to powder my nose."

The men rose with her. She invited them to return to their seats with a flutter of her hand. "I won't be long. I believe there's a restroom to the left of the foyer?"

"We'll hold dessert for you, my dear."

"I'll be right back." She hadn't been able to meet Ash's eyes during that bullshit with the old lady. Now she desperately wanted to look at him, to memorize his face. It took everything in her to turn around and walk from the dining room.

The bodyguard who'd just served her meal, one of Ash's men, gave her a slight smile as she passed him where he was stationed outside the door. "Thanks for jumping in—-"

"Ram Ortiz."

"Would you cover me for a few minutes? I have--I'm going to—-Just cover me, okay?"

"As long as I don't have to leave my post. Not tonight."

"I understand. Just shout or whistle or something if anyone leaves the dining room."

He smiled. "I'll do my best to alert you."

"Thanks. Oh, and if you're the one clearing the table, I'm done with my meal. This isn't the night to eat, drink, and be merry, is it?"

"It is not."

River hesitated.

He raised a brow. "Anything else?"

She wanted to say, *Don't let anything happen to Ash.* "No, I'm good." Walking quickly through the living room, she went into the vast entry hall and turned left. Franco's study was beyond the bathroom. Her heart beating a rapid staccato, she ran the last few yards, then slipped inside and shut the door quietly behind her.

SIXTEEN

S tanding in Franco's study in the dark, her heart pounding, and mouth dry, River whispered, "Don't get up from the table. Don't get up from the table."

She heard a sound. Whop-whop-whop. Her heartbeat must be in overdrive. No wait. Whop-whop-whop? No! That was the faint sound of a helicopter!

Who was on it? Was it coming for her and Marcus? If so, how were they going to get out of the hacienda without Franco wanting to know where they were going? Was it big enough to carry everyone left behind? Did they even make a helicopter that size?

Or was T-FLAC sending in people to take Franco right now?

Oh, shit, she didn't know what she was supposed to do.

Breathe. Focus. Make a plan.

First, get the damn photos.

Nervous perspiration prickled her skin. Without turning on the light, she used her phone's light to guide her to the enormous desk.

The helicopter didn't sound as if it was getting closer, but neither did it sound any fainter.

River pulled open the correct drawer. She found the envelope containing the pictures in the back, where she'd last seen it. Debating whether to take the original, or use the phone to take a picture, she chose one of the redhead as an adult to show to Ash when she could.

She took a picture with her phone, then slid one photograph aside to click off a few more. Her fingers shook. It didn't help that she was in a dark room, afraid to turn on the lights, in the hacienda of a sexual predator/terrorist. Or that he was waiting for her to join him for dessert while a helicopter hovered overhead.

When she slipped the phone into her dress pocket, River felt the sharp edge of another piece of paper. Taking it out, she unfolded the scrap of paper, shining the light on it.

Come to Rectory. 11:10 pm. It was signed M.

How the hell, and when, had Marcus slipped the piece of paper into her pocket? Or had Ram done that at some point? Either way, she hadn't felt anything, which proved T-FLAC operatives, even retired ones, were resourceful.

A glance at an ormolu clock on the fireplace mantel showed it was just after ten o clock. Another hour to wait. They'd have to peel her off the freaking ceiling when the time came.

Exiting Franco's office, she nipped into the bathroom next door with a sigh of relief. River ran her fingers through her hair in lieu of a comb. The strands fell neatly back into place. Even though she'd spent an extra ten minutes doing her makeup, she still looked too pale, and her smoky eyes looked overly dramatic. Instead of giving her the hint of cool glamour that she normally accomplished, the pewter eye shadow and charcoal liner accented her wide-eyed terror.

Only because she wanted to see Ash, did she reluctantly return to the dining room. Her heart sank to see his chair empty. "Where's Bishop Daklin?" Her dinner had been replaced with a bowl of vibrant, orange-colored ice-cream.

"Unfortunately, he had a migraine and had to retire to his room," Franco told her, his tone less than sympathetic. "Luckily, he has his medication with him. I'm extremely disappointed that he won't be able to bear witness if the apparition appears tonight."

"There's always tomorrow." River avoided meeting Father Marcus's eyes. All this lying and subterfuge must weigh heavily on him. And even though he was a former operative, that was no longer what he was. Tonight he looked ten years older than he'd appeared earlier that day.

"She doesn't come every night," Franco said bitterly.

"But I'm sure she'll return. As Bishop Daklin said, you must be patient." River was pretty sure Ash hadn't said anything of the sort, but he could have. She forced a positive and upbeat note into her voice. "Are these your daughters?" she asked, pointing to a nearby buffet table massed with silver framed photographs.

None of them had red hair, and all were of varying degrees of unattractiveness. They also all had the busty, child-bearing-hips body type. She'd seen other pictures of them, from when they were babies through adulthood. They were healthy eaters. None of them, by any stretch of imagination, could ever have fit into that white dress. Not even at sixteen.

She listened for the helicopter, but the pulsing beats of the rotors were silent. Had it left? Or landed nearby?

"My angels," Franco said proudly. "God has blessed me with eleven living children. Two nuns. Two priests. "

"I'm sure you are blessed." Was Ash on his way up to the mine as she moved melting, pumpkin tasting, lúcuma ice cream around her bowl? He wouldn't set the explosives until Marcus got everyone out of the village, she knew. Was that happening now? Was Marcus biding his time until eleven to get her out? "I'm sorry to have missed them."

"You're aware, I'm sure, of the landslide blocking the only road out of the valley? I have people coming in from Santa de Porres at first light with earth moving equipment. The road should be clear for your departure in the morning."

"Thank you for your hospitality, Franco. I've overstayed my welcome. I was just so hopeful Oliver would've returned by the time I got here."

"I'm sure your brother will be in contact when he's ready."

He didn't deny that she'd overstayed her welcome. And when Oliver was ready for what? To stop worrying her to death? River was going to kick his ass when he eventually showed his face, or sent her a damn postcard from Bora Bora.

Throwing down his napkin, Franco got to his feet. "Father,

I'm sure you have church business to attend to. If you'd excuse us, I'd like to take Miss Sullivan for a turn around the garden before bed. The light from the full moon is beautiful tonight."

Over her dead body. "As lovely as that sounds, my shoes aren't made for that uneven paving, and I really do need my beauty sleep before an early departure." River rose. "I'll say goodnight and goodbye now, in case I miss you in the morning."

Franco came around the table and took her by the shoulders as Father Marcus rose, too. "You're a fascinating woman, Miss Sullivan. If only we'd met under different circumstances."

River had just a split-second to brace herself as he pulled her in for a shocking, and unwelcome hug. Worse. His wet, open lips landed on the corner of her mouth before she realized what he intended. She reared back, resisted slapping him, and took a giant step back.

Instead of engaging with him, River looked through Franco to address Father Marcus who looked as appalled as she felt. "Good night, Father Marcus."

Turning on her heel, she practically ran upstairs. Locking her bedroom door, she dragged a heavy, ornately carved, velvet-covered side chair across the wide expanse of the carpet and rammed it under the door handle.

When she was sure no one could push against it, she flopped down in the chair, her heartbeat manic. It was as if she'd just fled from a hungry man-eating lion. With Juanita gone, did Franco consider her his next tasty morsel? She shuddered as she stared sightlessly at the gory painting of dead animals over the fireplace.

God, she wanted to get the hell out of here. Now. Home to Portland where things made sense, and counter-terrorists didn't make love to her as if she were their salvation.

Her phone chimed, indicating a text message, and scaring her so badly she let out a shriek. "Dear God. I need a freaking Xanax." Or Ash.

River slipped her phone out of her pocket to check if anyone had called her while she'd been in Los Santos.

She recognized Carly's number. But that was it for calls. Then she checked her text messages. There was only one, but she didn't recognize the number. Then she opened it.

"Oh, shit, shit, shit!" It was from Oliver.

> *I told you NOT to come!*
> *being held hostage in mine lab.*
> *can't escape*
> *send help.*
> **Dangerous* Do. Not.*
> *Come. Yourself!!*
> *Go home River.*

She read it twice. "What do you mean you're being held freaking hostage?" At the lab? The same location where Ash and his men were, right this second? The same location that was going to be rubble in a few damned hours? "Shit, Oliver!"

Breathe. Text him back. Warn him. River punched the

phone number on the text as she jumped up from the chair. It rang twice before going went dead. "Damn it to hell!"

This freaking no-phone zone was driving her insane. She pushed all the buttons on the side of the iPhone in the vain hope that something would make the call go through.

Nothing did.

Pacing, she typed a return text.

O. Call me.
Text me.
Tell me exactly where to find you.

She paused. Should she tell him that the mine was going to be blown-up tonight? What if the person holding him hostage read his messages? Clearly her brother was already scared and desperate. How would telling him help him right now? Okay. No explosion warning.

River pressed send, stopped moving aimlessly around the room, and looked at her phone, willing him to answer. Please. Please. Please.

A red exclamation mark popped up on the screen indicating the text was undeliverable. She resisted throwing the useless phone across the room.

Now what was she to do? Find somewhere in this godforsaken town where she could get a signal? There was nowhere, apparently. If Ash couldn't get a signal on his communication devices, she sure as shit wouldn't get anything on her iPhone. Even if she did get a signal, was calling her brother's phone a good idea? Did his captors now have it? Were they monitoring it?

Think.

She had to do something. She couldn't just sit around in her room hoping the cell phone gods allowed Oliver's texts to get through to her. Crossing the room, she slipped off her belt, dropping it as she went. As she kicked off her sandals, she reached behind her with the other hand to unzip the dress. She tried calling the number again. "Come on. Come on."

Feeling the frantic drumbeat of her pulse throughout her entire body as she disconnected, she tried the number again as she stepped out of the dress, leaving it in a puddle on the floor.

Digging through her carry-on bag, she pulled out jeans, a black T-shirt, and running shoes. Thank God she'd kept these clothes back when she'd been giving things to Juanita. She'd pretty well given her everything else.

"Holy shit, Oliver," River muttered, yanking on her jeans, and hopping on one leg as she pulled them over her hips. "It isn't the freaking cavalry on its way up the damned mountain. It's Ash and his men coming to blow up the building you're in!" And half, more than half, of the Qhapaq freaking mountain range with it!

The explosion was going to be cataclysmic. She was already worried sick about Ash. Now she was freaked out about Oliver being in the middle of Armageddon. Ash and his guys weren't even aware he was in the building. The good news was T-FLAC wanted him alive. The bad news was they didn't know he was exactly where they were going to set the explosion. They'd inadvertently kill him.

"Who's holding you hostage, Oliver? And why?"

River pulled the shirt over her head and shoved her bare feet into her running shoes. Oliver had always lived in his own little bubble, but it would be hard convincing anyone else that he could be working five feet away from World War 3 and not hear a thing going on around him.

She knew her brother was just that oblivious. If he denied knowledge of Franco's terrorist acts, she'd believe him. His single-minded focus, his ability to rule out all external stimuli, could make his deniability plausible. Despite the small fortune he'd sent to her, she knew in her very heart that he was too good a person to be mixed up in any of Franco's evil acts, so he damned well needed a heads up from her on how much trouble he was in.

She had to get up there before anyone did anything. At this point, having Oliver alive and behind bars waiting to explain his actions and prove he wasn't a terrorist, outweighed having Oliver dead. Surely, they could hold off on the big bang until Ash helped sort things out. Hopefully.

Going up there tonight was insane and she damn well knew it. If there were any other choice, she'd have jumped at it.

"I need a car." Sweaty hands made her fingers fumble on the zipper and button as she fastened her jeans. "Faster than ASAP. And a damned phone that works, as well as a loaded gun." And Ash. She really, really needed Ash. Now.

Hyperventilating, River stopped dead in the middle of the room and closed her eyes. She had none of the above. Freaking out was not an option.

Breathe. Focus. Make a plan.

Breathe. Focus. Make a plan.

She was smart, resourceful, and motivated.

She couldn't go tearing through the house searching for car keys, although she would bet if she looked hard enough she would likely find a gun. No, that would alert Franco, and possibly end up endangering Ash and his men.

Holy shit! Ram, the guy who'd helped at dinner was Ash's man. He not only had a gun, he'd have a way to communicate with the men at the mine. He also might have a vehicle. The problem was, as Franco's bodyguard, he'd be with Franco. Or if he was part of the group blowing up the mountain, he'd be with Ash. Shit. Either way he couldn't be with her.

He would help her, though, if she saw him, and if he was alone. Good. If not, she was on her own and had to get out of the house and next door to the rectory to find Marcus.

Breathe. Focus. Make a plan.

"Find Ram. If not Ram, Marcus."

A good start.

Okay. She had a plan. A shaky plan, but a plan nevertheless. "Go!" River dragged the heavy chair away from the door, opening it enough to look down the well-lit corridor. The sweeping staircase was between the guest wing and Franco's private wing. The corridor was empty.

She ran, down the long, carpeted corridor, then down the stairs, taking them three at a time. She skidded to a stop in the vast marble entry hall to listen. No sound of voices. No Ram, but no Franco either.

She silently moved to the heavy, carved front door, opening and closing it quietly behind her. Sprinting, she vaulted down the shallow stone steps and onto the street. The air smelled of rain and the streets were wet, dark, and eerily quiet as she ran.

The wrought iron gate to the church and rectory stood open. River jumped over the abandoned, half-coiled hose, and darted down the path to the rectory. She pounded on the door. "Comeoncomeoncomeon."

No response. "Shit." The door swung open when she turned the handle and stepped inside a dark house. Taking out her phone, she turned on the flashlight app. "Marcus? Are you here?" No answer. She checked the time. 10:17. He must be out rounding up the villagers to get them to safety.

He was expecting her, she knew, but she was early. In her head, a metronome ticked away the minutes as loudly as Big Ben. No, that was her manic heartbeat. "Please walk through that door right now."

No Ram.

No Marcus.

Oliver in serious peril.

What the hell was she going to do?

Go.

She had to go.

But she wanted someone to know where she'd gone, and she didn't want Marcus or Ram to be searching for her, potentially putting the lives of the other villagers at risk.

The priest could be any-freaking-where right now. Oliver didn't have much time. None of them did.

It was as if Ash, with his grim indication of what was going to happen that night, had planted a timer in her head. Now it was ticking off the minutes. Loudly, and with each minute, booming louder. She'd never been more acutely aware of time's passage.

She looked around. "What the hell am I supposed to do?"

She still needed a car, a phone, and a gun. Not necessarily in that order. This was insane. But she was going to find someone before they inadvertently blew up her brother.

Breathe. Focus. Make a new plan.

"Beg, borrow or freaking steal a car."

#

22:30

The temperature had dropped only a few degrees after sundown. It was now a balmy 81 degrees instead of 85. Daklin breathed in thick air, made muggy by heat and the dense cover of surrounding vegetation. Darkness pressed in around him. A mile ahead, beyond the thick tree line, four thousand watt stadium lights surrounded the outer fence of the mine and plant building. The blinding white LED flood lamps illuminated the compound and the surrounding vegetation within a three mile radius.

The five of them had walked up from the bridge, cut their way through dense understory, and come up on the left side of the vast, gravel lot. Deep in the thick underbrush, Daklin and his men lay belly down in the flattened grasses and leaves of the jungle floor. They wore ghillie suits over their LockOut to blend in with their background. The dense black material making up the LockOut suit was impervious to just about anything. Climate controlled bulletproof armor, it was a head-to-toe jumpsuit.

Usually, the strips of burlap of the ghillie would be covered with local vegetation as an effective camouflage. But in this case, vegetation was fucking non-existent between their location and the mine and building. Before they got to the steel gate protecting the entrance to the mine, they had a mile of cleared land, without the protection of even a blade of grass. The dirt-colored burlap strips of the ghillies were covered with sand and pebbles, and the men's faces were mud-streaked.

They watched movement on the guard posts and behind the fence through powerful binoculars.

"Thirty-ish?" Daklin pitched his voice to Aiza, belly down beside him.

"Yeah. They'll patrol until--" Aiza tilted his wrist to look at the big black watch strapped there. "--between 2300 and 2310. Then they switch out. They're no slouches. They switch out pretty fast. We'll have mere minutes to get in undetected. Ten minutes to cross without getting shot first. Diversion there and there." Aiza used two fingers to point where he and Nyhuis would cause a distraction so that the other three men could get by the guards without notifying a hundred-plus men of their intentions.

After the charges were set, the issue would be moot.

Aiza ignored the glistening thumbnail-sized bug crawling on his sweaty cheek. "You, Gibbs, and Turley get in under the north fence. I carved a space under that rock overhang two hundred yards to the left. See it?"

No, he didn't. The lights were too bright, and the enormous rock overhang cast a deep shadow, but that would work in their favor, later. Exactly as planned. The five men would meet up inside the mineshaft at 24:15--2 hours and 45 minutes to detonation. They'd have to move fast.

Turley, on Daklin's left, touched a fist to Daklin's shoulder. "Let me take lead on this, boss——"

"Asked and answered. Same goes for the rest of you. I'll tell you when to get the fuck out, and when I say go, you haul ass. That's a non-negotiable order. The chopper will do a quick round trip and return after taking Marcus and River to Abad. It'll be there when you get to the village at 02:00." Plenty of time for them to evacuate before the first explosion at 03:00.

Something sinuous and slow moving curved and twisted over Daklin's right calf. A snake, and a big one, judging by the weight of its sleekly shifting body. He remained still, barely breathing.

"Fuck." Nyhuis shielded his eyes. "We're gonna be sitting

ducks out there."

"If you know a way to teleport in, have at it," Daklin told him, his voice low as he glanced at the faintly illuminated dial on his watch. The rest of the snake's body slithered free of his leg. In thirty minutes, River would be safely with Marcus. Ram was sitting on Xavier like white on rice until backup arrived. Only that backup was still two hours away. Delta team was cutting their way through the jungle to get vehicles into the valley to extract the priest and the rest of the villagers before the mountain blew at 03:00.

A chopper would land in the village square for River and the pregnant girl at 24:00. Marcus would have a couple of hours to get all his chickens to roost. In the meantime, what was happening to River, to the people of the village, was unimportant. His job wasn't there. Worry and dread for them had no part in the job he was here to do.

Focus.

The next three plus hours would go fast. Daklin was damned glad River would be far gone when the first charge detonated.

The men coordinated their watches. 23:05. Detonation--3 hours 55 minutes.

Everyone had their jobs. Nyhuis was the wild card. Because of his tendencies to go rogue and off book, Aiza would partner him, keep him on track should he get a wild hair.

Where it was dark, and in those few pockets where it was

pitch black, they wouldn't be seen as long as they moved slowly. But out there—-fuck. Out there for more than a mile was zero coverage, and the blackness of night now banished, illuminated by giant floodlights. They were smack dab in the middle of the kill zone.

Xavier's security force would see a fucking ant coming.

Daklin had never been a praying man, but he thought three words that were as close to a prayer as he'd ever come. God. Help. Us.

Maybe it was the time he'd spent in the bishop's robes. Or maybe it was just the sudden urge to see River's gray eyes one more time, which wasn't going to happen even if he managed to get his job done. More likely, it was just a strong-ass desire for all to go as planned, so that he could get on the other goddamned side of the brightly lit kill zone and do his fucking job. Avenge Josh's death. Rid the world of E- E-1x.

God. Help. Me. "Let's do this. Move fast, move smart. Go, Go. Go."

SEVENTEEN

11:05 p.m.

Since Marcus was expecting her, River left a quick note for him on his kitchen table.

It would take twenty minutes to get up to the mine office. Twenty minutes to find and free Oliver, twenty minutes back. An hour tops. And somewhere in there, she needed to tell Ash that she was there so he didn't blow her up. She also had to get into a highly secure facility without getting herself killed or giving away Ash's plans.

"Yeah, right." She gave a mirthless laugh, painfully aware that she was in way over her head, and delusional, thinking she could pull this off. If she'd had weeks of planning, maybe. But alone? With no back-up plan to speak of? In an hour?

No way in hell. "All she needed was her superhero cape and she'd be set. Or Ash Daklin's goddamn phone number, assuming at some point on her trek up the mountain there'd be cell coverage. Even if she *had* service, the hottest man on the planet with whom she'd spent most of the day making love, hadn't given her his number. Wasn't that just freaking perfect?

This was mission impossible and she knew it. If there was any other way, she wouldn't even be considering doing something this crazy. Yet she couldn't leave Oliver without a means of escape. Sometimes the ends justified the means, no matter what those means were. "Marcus, where *are* you?"

How the hell was she going to get through those guarded gates alone? How was she going to find Oliver in that huge building? And once inside—-if she got that freaking far-—how was she going to get them *out*?

She was an artist, a designer. She made exquisite and delicate lingerie. She was not, nor did she want to be, now, or at any time in the near future, a damned counterterrorist operative. Nausea churned her stomach, and she stood still, trying to regulate her erratic breathing.

She had a million questions and no damned answers. As organized and methodical as she was in her day-to-day life, there was no rulebook for search and rescue missions. For Ash, this was just another day at the office. *Hell of an office, buddy.* Her nerves were shredded just thinking about what she had to accomplish.

Breathe. Focus. Make a plan.

The four-wheel drive truck that Ash and Franco had taken up to the mine the other day was parked under the hacienda's portico. If there were keys in it, she'd have her wheels. From there, she'd have to wing it.

River dashed out of Marcus's small house, down the path, jumped over the water hose, ran through the gate, and then sprinted up the hill. Guided by no more than starlight, she crouched beside the low wall of the church, her lungs heaving from the high altitude and stress.

Stopping dead, she spun on her heels and looked up as a loud, throbbing *whop-whop-whop* came out of nowhere. The helicopter sounded as if it was directly overhead. It almost *was* right over her head, so low, she could see pale faces of men inside. She automatically ducked.

Woohoo. The cavalry had arrived. About freaking time!

Her relief was profound. Marcus knew this world. With the help of the priest, as well as the operatives on board, she'd be able to find her brother. Oliver had a hell of a lot to answer for, but she'd save her personal argument with him for when they were both safely away from Los Santos and Cosio.

Covering her ears against the deafening sound of the whipping blades, River ran toward the helicopter as it set down, light as a dragonfly, in front of the hacienda. Its spinning rotors just missed the roof of the portico, flattening flowers and shrubs in nearby flowerbeds. Everything not nailed down whirled up into the vortex created by the chopper.

Ducking, River circumvented the helicopter as the door slid open. At the same time, Franco raced out of the open front door of the house, his hair wild, and eyes manic. In his arms, he carried a two-foot statue of Mary as if it were a baby.

Ram was behind him. Leveling a gun at the fleeing Franco, he fired a shot at Franco's feet, which shattered several nearby driveway tiles. Franco stumbled back. "Stop," Ram shouted. "Or I *will* shoot to kill."

Shit, shit, shit. River stopped dead in her tracks.

Franco wouldn't be running *to* the helicopter if it was filled with T-FLAC operatives. Going hot then cold, River froze in the shadow of the still spinning rotors, terrified to move and draw attention to herself. God, she was way too freaking close to the helicopter. Her pale hair whipped around her head as she took a tiny sliding step back.

Franco's laugh was wild as he handed the statue to someone inside the helicopter. "Careful with her. *Careful* you fool!" he shouted in Spanish, then turned his head to answer the operative in English. "No, you won't. I have information T-FLAC wants."

Ram stood in the slice of light from the front door, his expression grim, his stance and voice authoritative. "I don't have to *kill* you, Xavier. I can take out both your legs. Step away from the chopper and give yourself up. There's nowhere you can run now."

River realized too late that Ram couldn't see her, and she was standing far too close to Franco.

She slid her other foot back and redistributed her weight.

Something alerted Franco, and he turned his eyes sideways. Oh, crap. He saw her. River turned to run. In a spider-like half-crouch, Franco reached up and grabbed her wrist. Already off balance, River staggered as he yanked her down low, hauling her in a tight embrace against his side. Her hair whipped in stinging strands around her face as she struggled uselessly to free herself, pulling backwards, and digging her nails into his skin, none of which had any effect on him.

"Here's my insurance policy." Franco laughed, raising her arms with his, his thick fingers painfully shackling her wrist. "You'll know where to find me—-"

As he lowered their joined hands, River yanked her arm close and bit down, *hard,* on his clenched fingers. With a furious exclamation, he backhanded her. Stinging pain flared in her cheek, and her eyes watered. She kicked him as hard as she could. Her foot landed on his shin and she stomped him again, before he had time to shift out of reach.

He didn't let go of the stronghold he had on her with his right arm. "Bitch! You were trouble the moment I set eyes on you." Dragging her with him, he jerked her closer to the open door, where a crouching man inside opened fire.

A stained glass side panel behind Ram exploded in a shower of colored glass.

Ram returned fire. Someone in the helicopter gave an angry shout, firing a volley of shots as Ram retreated behind an enormous marble pillar.

Over River's head, Franco's men kept up a steady stream of gunfire to hold Ram back. Franco shoved her ahead of him. "Take her. Take her!"

No way in hell would she allow them to take her any-freaking-where. Eyes watering from the blow as well as the high wind of the rotors, River fought Franco by kicking, biting whatever she could reach, and trying to pull away from him with all her might. His implacable grip on her upper arm hurt like hell.

Damn, the son of a bitch was strong!

She was at the wrong angle to knee him in the balls, but she got in several good kicks, and scratched the side of his neck when he hauled back and tried to hit her again.

Blocking his swinging hand with her forearm, River yelled, "*Cobarde*!" in Spanish as she wrenched and twisted. "Only a *coward* preys on innocent young girls. Only a *coward* would—-" He swung at her again, this time almost cutting off her breathing when the side of his hand connected with her throat. "Ow, shit!"

Ram fired, the shot coming perilously close to River's head as the bullet skimmed a hot path over her shoulder. It was one hell of a shot, just missing her, and hitting Franco directly over her left shoulder.

The operative was an expert marksman, gauging to within inches of River's height the much taller Franco. He didn't kill either of them. Yay for him, but River was shaken that he'd opted to shoot Franco while she was pretty much in the way. *Take the shot,* a phrase she often yelled at the hero in action movies, would now have new meaning.

Clutching his shoulder, Franco teetered back, still crouched low, shackling her wrist in the vise of his fingers. "Shoot the fucker! Shoot him!" He screamed a string of obscenities muddled with English, Spanish, orders, and threats.

His garbled speech and frantic movements, not to mention the sweat pouring down his temples, and his unrelenting grip on *her*, told her that Franco was clearly unraveling.

From the open door of the helicopter, the loud sharp crack of returned fire sounded like cannons going over her head. River flinched every time a shot was fired. Glass shattered, wood splintered, bullets pinged off stone. They all combined in a godawful, frenetic noise with the *whop-whop-whop* of the blades overhead.

She was disoriented by the danger at such close quarters, as well as her inability to flee and finding herself in the very center of all this chaos. Everything was happening too fast to process. Her shoulder socket blazed red-hot fire as Franco's weight threatened to drag her to the ground. Counterbalancing, she tried to yank her arm free, trying in vain to half-walk, half-crawl away from him, all the while trying to scratch, bite, and claw.

Fifty feet away, near the open front door of the hacienda, was the only person on her side with a gun and skill. Illuminated by a slice of light from the open front door and the lights on the helicopter, she saw blood pouring down Ram's face from a slash at his temple. Shielded by one of the massive stone pillars of the portico, he swiped an impatient hand across his face to get the blood away from his eye, as he continued firing.

His head wasn't the only place he'd been hit. He was covered in blood, but she couldn't tell where it was coming from. Dear God, was he going to die?

"River!" The whine of another bullet from inside the helicopter silenced whatever the operative was trying to tell her. It slammed into the stone pillar inches from Ram's head. Chunks of marble flew.

She tugged and pulled against Franco's hold, kneeing his leg. But all that did was make the cuff of his fingers tighten painfully, twisting the bones in her wrist. "Get your asses down here and take the girl!" he yelled to his men.

Two shots blasted overhead in quick succession.

Ram fired back three shots. The bullets ricocheted off the metal body of the helicopter in a shower of sparks. A blood curdling shout came from inside. A second later, a man fell out, landing with a sickening thud on the driveway, three feet from where River and Franco crouched. He lay still.

Without half the back of his head, he couldn't be anything but dead. River swallowed bile.

"River! Come to me!"

Ramse had a lot of faith in her ability to wrest herself free of a man this determined to hold onto her. "I'm trying to, damn it!"

The cacophony sounded exactly the way she imagined Dante's seventh level of hell would. The beautifully carved front door was now a mass of holes and splinters. Stained glass sidelights were shattered. Glass and bits of wood littered the elegantly curved stairs leading up to the front door.

Still cursing, Franco twisted her arm up and back. River fell to the ground, hoping he'd fall with her and release his hold. It didn't happen. She connected hard on her hip and shoulder. Air escaped her lungs in a loud whoosh.

"Come take the girl. For fucksake, take the goddamned

girl!"

The persistent *whop-whop-whop* of the helicopter blades was pierced by the sounds of half a dozen more shots.

Sickened, River saw Ram go down through a curtain of her own hair. Dazed, she tried to lever her feet under her, staggering unsteadily, trying to center herself so she could crawl out from under the blades to help him. But Franco still had her in a death grip, and she couldn't break free.

Ram was unconscious. Probably dead. Blood from his head wound now puddled, glistening dark red around him.

Suddenly Franco released her. Shocked, River took a running step, only to be brought up short when a man jumped down from the helicopter to scoop her up. *Shit, shit, shit.*

"Get her in. Get her in!"

Kicking, bucking, and screaming like a demented banshee, there wasn't any-freaking-thing she could do to break the guy's hold, no matter how hard she tried to fight. With her arms pinned to her sides, she could do little more than flail and make herself hard to hold onto. She let her legs fold under her, making herself deadweight. The guy just picked her up in a death grip.

Do not let them get you into the helicopter.

If they did, it would all be over. Franco had nothing good planned for her if he had anything planned at all. She was a nuisance and in the way. He'd kill her. The only question was how quickly.

The bear-hugging thug hoisted her up to someone inside

the helicopter who grabbed her arms, almost wrenching them from the sockets as he dragged her half into the helicopter. The coldness of the metal floor seeped into her cheek, and the edge of the threshold to the sliding door dug into her hipbones as she teetered, half in and half out.

River fought to right herself and slid out of the helicopter, backwards. The second man slammed his foot on her back to hold her down. *Ow, shit!* Air left her lungs in a pained grunt. Wrapping both hands around his other ankle, digging her nails into his shin just above his heavy boot, she tried to pull him off balance. She was rewarded with a hard stomp in the small of her back, and a string of unintelligible Russian.

Beside her, Franco was quickly pulled inside.

"Go!" he yelled in Spanish. He lay on his belly on the metal floor beside her. Crimson blood soaked the shoulder of his crisply ironed white shirt, and matted the hair over his temple. She hoped it hurt like hell. A streak of black dirt smudged his cheek as he looked her straight in the eye. "Retribution is mine, saith the Lord. Amen. Lift off. Get us the fuck out of here!"

The guy's foot lifted from River's back. She sucked a breath into her oxygen-starved lungs then kicked backwards before anyone could stop her. As the helicopter rose, she dropped out of the open door. For a few seconds, she fell through nothing but air as the high-pitched whine of a bullet skimmed her ear.

River landed on the shrubs in a flowerbed, flat on her back. It wasn't exactly a soft landing, but at least she hadn't hit the tiles.

Shots fired from the retreating helicopter severed branches, scattered leaves, and lopped the heads off a row of purple flowers.

Her heart pounded so hard, she felt as though a midget was attempting to jackhammer his way out of her chest while several of his fat friends bore down on her deflated lungs. *Calm down. Don't panic.* It was hard not to. Fear dogged her every breath. Gasping, it took several minutes to inflate her lungs and for the dizziness to fade. Profound relief seeped through her veins as she blinked the bright lights on the helicopter into focus, watching as it rose into the starry night sky.

"Stay down. Stay down!" Father Marcus dropped to the dirt beside her, scaring the shit out of her all over again.

Since she'd had all the air knocked out of her, and had yet to drag in a full breath, she didn't have any other option. She tried to blink him into focus. Dressed all in black and without his clerical collar, the priest knelt beside her with a massive weapon positioned on his shoulder. "Here, cover your ears!" He shoved an earmuff-type headset in her general direction.

She managed to fumble the headset over her ears seconds before he fired. A blast of blazing hot air and a brilliant flash of light accompanied an incredibly loud *bang* that made River's ears ring in spite of the protective headwear.

"Fuck. *Missed*!" Ram yelled. She saw him running toward them in her peripheral vision. "We're losing our window. Here, give it to me, Father."

#

"She fell from the helicopter," Franco repeated time. He listened through the head-set as the helicopter left the lights of Los Santos behind, flying now over jungle. A private jet waited for him in Santa De Porres.

"Are you sure she's dead?"

"Of *course* she's dead." The pain in his shoulder where he'd been shot stung like damned fire ants, bleeding a hot, sticky red patch on his shirt. His heart pounded hard enough that he felt each staccato beat behind his eyes.

Adrenaline surged nauseatingly through his body as the helicopter distanced him from danger. He gripped Mary against him to ward off more evil.

His daughter would understand what he was going through. Catarina knew his world so well. Franco's eyes stung and he ached, missing her as deeply now as he had three years ago when he'd learned she'd been murdered. He remembered her as small girl. So intelligent, so inquisitive. If he could've taken her away from her mother to raise, dear Lord, what he could have made of her. But she had grown, with the steadying hand of her father to guide her only from a distance. Franco had been so very proud of all she'd accomplished, proud of her recruitment by T-FLAC—-the very organization that had been dogging his heels for years.

She'd planted a bomb inside the well-protected, secure underground facility of T-FLAC headquarters building. Setting it to detonate years in the future. She'd had no idea at the time that less than a month after setting the timer, she'd be dead.

Murdered in cold blood by the very people she'd worked beside, the very people she trusted. Hate ate at him. He had a prime directive. A God-given purpose.

"And your Bishop?" The supercilious voice of his partner was muffled by the headset. Beneath the helicopter, the jungle was dark, although Franco could see the bright lights of the mine compound off to his left as they flew a few miles away.

Should he lie? "As good as dead." It pained Franco that he'd had to leave behind Bishop Daklin. Taking him as a hostage would have been to his advantage. But he'd been lucky to escape the house with Mary. Where he was going, he needed nothing else.

"As-good-as is not *dead*, Franco. It was a simple order. You'd better be absolutely certain, because if he's still alive, he'll return and tell them."

"Tell them *what*?" Franco demanded. His partner never got his damned hands dirty. "Easy for you to give orders left, right, and center. I'm not willing to kill a man of God. *There*. I said it. If the bishop escapes Los Santos tonight with his life, so be it. Perhaps he'll authenticate my apparition when he returns."

"And how will that help you where you're going, Franco?"

"My children will know. It will be my legacy."

"That man is no more a bishop than you or me. He *duped* you, Franco. Made a fool out of you."

"This is not true. Rome sent him."

"He's a *T-FLAC operative*, you idiot. Did you really think Rome would send someone on such short notice?"

"You cannot know this. You've never met the man."

"I've watched him. Listened to him. Now we know that T-FLAC infiltrated the soldiers. Infiltrated your own bodyguards."

Franco wanted to say it was impossible. Yet there was no mistaking that Ortiz suddenly, and without provocation, wanted him dead. It had to be T-FLAC's influence. There was no other explanation.

Tomorrow he'd fight on his daughter's battlefield.

What his Catarina had set into motion years earlier, mere weeks before she'd been betrayed and brutally killed by the very people she worked beside, was about to bring the counterterrorism organization down from inside its impenetrable walls.

Pretending to be a man of God was a sin.

There was a special hell for Ash Daklin, and Franco would give him the express pass. T-FLAC had no authority over a Godly man like Francisco Xavier, no right to ruin his business, to destroy years of hard work that put food in the mouths of his family. The mercenary army that was T-FLAC was *not* sanctioned by God.

His blessed daughter had been right all along. *They* had called her Catherine Seymour, but to Franco, she'd forever be the child of his heart, Catarina. They had killed his girl. Brutally. Shame on them. Shame on them all.

God was testing him to see if he had what it took to complete the assignment he'd accepted years ago. This was his very own crucifixion. First he must suffer, then die, and then be resurrected to be seated at the right hand of the Father.

Catarina's bomb was on a timer, a timer so clever, so diabolical, that not even T-FLAC's top explosive experts could defuse it before it detonated at 3:33.

The date and time of Catarina—-Catherine's--blessed birth.

The date and time of T-FLAC's death.

Fitting.

Franco adjusted his seatbelt as satisfaction bloomed. A glint of light aiming directly at the helicopter caught his eye. "Dear God."

"What is it?"

"Faster," he yelled at the pilot. "Go *faster!*"

#

A bright flash of light exploded in the night sky. Squinting up, River watched Franco's helicopter explode into a fiery ball. The glowing orb hovered, then plummeted to the tree canopy, trailing fire in its wake across the dark sky.

Holy crap. Ram had shot down Franco's helicopter.

"Good job, my boy," Father Marcus patted Ram's arm. "I guess I've been out of the business too long."

"The sight's a little off, Father," Ram told him.

"The fact that you had a PRG handy is miraculous."

"It was Xavier's. I found it last night and hid it out here to take with me to the mine later."

Ram smiled, his teeth white in his blood-covered face. "It served its purpose earlier than anticipated. Nobody made it out of that alive." He pointed.

A flare of orange in the darkness indicated the trajectory of Franco's helicopter. The fireball disappeared beyond the treetops in a shower of sparks, exploding in another spectacular fiery burst. "Excellent work, my son."

Ram handed the big gun back to Father Marcus before his legs gave way and he started to wilt.

"Ram!" River yelled.

Father Marcus redirected his attention from the sky to the operative. "Ramse? Dear Lord." He grabbed the other man's arm, staggering under his weight. "Here, let me help you."

With a grunt of pain, River half-rolled, half-staggered to her feet. The stars spun, and Father Marcus grabbed her arm to steady her, too. "Can you take his other side?"

"I'll try." She could barely stand upright herself, let alone lift two hundred pounds of solid muscle. She pulled his arm over her neck, digging her shoulder into his armpit to leverage him upright. Ramse was a dead weight between them. She had to lock her knees.

"Why don't you just sit down right here until we can get someone back up here to help?"

Ram shook his head, his throat working before he could speak. "No. Give me a minute. I can walk."

He couldn't freaking walk. He could barely stand.

"How badly are *you* hurt, River?"

River did a mental physical check. Arms. Check. Legs. Check. Back. Check. Yes, she damn well hurt all over. But nothing

331

CHERRY ADAIR

seemed broken, and she was freaking overjoyed to be on the ground and not blown to hell. "I'm okay. But we have to help Ram."

"I'm good." Ram managed to stabilize himself by spreading his feet, but he still wobbled. His face smeared with wet blood, he tightened his fingers around River's shoulder. "I'm okay."

Not. She turned to look at Marcus. "Can you get help?"

"Some of Delta team members have arrived with the truck to evacuate the villagers." Father Marcus looked as pale as River felt. "They're loading the first vehicle now. Your father is on the first truck, Ram. River can go and get him."

"Of course. She had a frightening image of Franco emerging from the flames of the downed chopper like a zombie.

What she feared must have shown on her face. "Nobody could have survived that. God rest their souls." Father Marcus crossed himself.

Good. River dragged in a breath, now tinged with the oily smell of smoke carried down valley on the breeze. She wished her heart would stop racing. Wished she could steady her breathing. Wished every single goddamned noise wasn't amplified, bouncing through her brain with sickening, dizzying volume.

More than being afraid, more than feeling the stomach-turning nausea at the violence she'd just witnessed and smelling the volumes of coppery-scented blood on Ram, she felt an overwhelming sense of dread.

She doubted that in the middle of this jungle there was a

goddamned thing she, Marcus, or T-FLAC could do about Ram's injuries, which looked life threatening to her untrained eyes.

Marcus gave River a serious glance over the operative's bowed head. "I'll get you both to the helicopter waiting in the square, but I'm staying in the village until everyone is loaded and on their way to Abad."

"How long will that be?" River asked, shifting to better support Ram between them.

"A couple of hours."

"That's cutting it too close."

"Don't worry. Daklin's an expert at his job. He has this precisely timed. It'll be fine."

God. He had such faith. But he was naïve to have so much confidence. Ash might be an expert, but he was mortal.

"But the mine's filled with unstable, untested explosives. Ash told me the stuff is not only powerful, it's unpredictable. Evacuate as many people as you can, but *you* must get on one of those transport vehicles. Promise me."

His eyes told her he knew exactly what would happen as he patted her arm. "Run ahead. Have Ramse's father, Señor Ortiz, return to help me get his son to the helicopter in the square. Juanita is already on board. I'd just returned to find you, my dear."

"I'll go for help, Father, but I can't leave the valley just yet. Oliver sent me a text. He's being held prisoner at the plant. I have to go there. I need to get him to safety."

"Held *prisoner*? He's still *here*?" He frowned. "Who could possibly be holding him?" Then he seemed to snap back to the issue at hand. "No. You can't do that." The priest looked appalled, horrified, and incredulous all at the same time. "As you say, leave that to Daklin and the others to deal with. Ramse Ortiz sagged in Marcus's hold. "Sorry, my boy. Yes, sit for a moment." They both helped him slide down the pillar to sit on the ground. "No, Miss Sullivan. I insist you go in the chopper to safety."

"Sorry, Father Marcus. I'm going to find my brother. If you manage to communicate with Ash, tell him."

"Don't count on that," the priest said. "Xavier has been jamming communication since he returned a month ago. Ramse here discovered a red phone in Xavier's quarters, however, which means he had direct contact with *someone*."

"Good, I'll use that!"

"Sorry, Ma'am," Ram said, his voice weak. "It requires a code to activate it. This red phone is a point-to-point encryption device. A secure, encrypted line for two people to communicate privately without detection. Messages delete themselves automatically from the screen after ninety seconds. There's no server. No back up. He could call out, but he was jamming signals to the satellite so everyone else in the valley was dark."

"Well, he's gone now. Maybe all the lines are open again." She took her phone out of her back pocket. The screen was shattered, and there was no signal. "Still no service. But if you *are* able to communicate with anyone who can get a message to Ash, tell him Oliver is alive and trapped up there, *somewhere*."

Father Marcus practically wrung his hands, his brow furrowed with concern. "You must get on the T-FLAC helicopter, River. Daklin will never forgive me if I allow anything to happen to you. I would never forgive *myself*!"

"The helicopter can take me."

"No, ma'am, it can't do that. There's an army up there. The first sound of a chopper and they'll shoot."

"Then I'll drive and walk if I have to. Sorry, Father, but I'd never forgive *myself* if I didn't do everything in my power to rescue my brother. But don't worry. First I'll find Señor Ortiz and send him up here. I'll see you in Abad before everything goes to hell."

Without waiting for a response, she turned and ran back down the hill as if the hounds of hell were on her ass.

#

Taking a circuitous route, belly crawling the entire mile, and sticking as close to the perimeter tree line as possible, Turley, Gibbs, and Daklin arrived at the rock overhang. They'd picked up a couple of passengers along the way, one of which was squirming, scratching, and trying to start up a conversation inside Daklin's pack.

He gave his shifting bag a little pat. "Almost there, buddy." The spider monkey screeched and chattered, but after a few seconds quieted as it settled on top of Daklin's supplies to eat the Camu camu, a small, tart citrus fruit he and his men had picked before they'd captured three of the long-limbed animals. They'd tried for more, but spider monkeys were harder to catch than time allowed. Three would have to do.

Chances were their packs would be full of monkey shit by the time the night was over. But it was a small price to pay if the distraction worked.

No one was more surprised than Daklin that they'd made it across the vast wasteland without being spotted. At least, without being shot at. They were constantly alert to that other shoe dropping, but so far, so good. The other two members of his team were about to make their play.

Perfect timing. Nyhuis and Aiza were just pulling up to the gate in the work vehicle. They drunkenly demanded in Spanish that the gate be opened to let them through. "We've come to part*ay*, brothers!"

Nyhuis did drunk well. Bottles clinked as he and Aiza, who claimed never to have drunk to excess, did a terrific job acting as if they were falling on their asses, boozed to the gills and ready to party until dawn. They only thing that would've sold it even more was if the car had been filled with scantily dressed hookers.

Even if they'd wanted them for the night's performance, there were no hookers in Los Santos. The women of the village would be loading into transportation vehicles right about now, on their way to Abad and safety. Abad. Where River should, about now, be landing in the helicopter, and soon safely tucked into bed in her hotel room. From Abad she'd be flown on the T-FLAC Challenger directly to Portland first thing in the morning.

He'd never see her again.

It was best.

For her.

"Let's do this." Daklin indicated the shallow crawl space beneath the heavy-duty chain link fence, at a thousand feet away, the men in the guard towers joked with their two new drunken friends below. They were far enough away that their voices were muted, the laughter and sound of glass striking glass indicated the two operatives had the guards at the gate engaged for at least a few more minutes. It could even be longer, if the guards started drinking with them.

They had to remove their packs to clear the space, shoving them through first. The damned monkeys shrieked their annoyance. Since the jungle was always vocal, there wasn't much chance of anyone coming over here to check. And, fuck it, if they did, he'd shoot them.

With a hand gesture, Daklin indicated they remove the cumbersome ghillie suits, too, leaving them at the fence.

His leg was FUBAR from running flat out, crawling, and overexertion. This was the serrated knife granddaddy of all pain, and under any other fucking circumstances, it would've incapacitated him. God only knew, it still might. A pain pill wasn't going to make *this* pain disappear. Right now, he could barely walk. He'd faked it up until the last mile.

Even inside the climate-controlled LockOut, he sweated profusely, his jaw clenched so tightly he heard his teeth grinding.

Pain radiated from his leg directly into nerve clusters in his brain. The flask of Tovaritch Vodka in his pack called a siren song to him. Soon. But not yet. He needed all his wits about him for a few more hours. He'd have to suck up the pain. Just for a few more hours.

It already felt like a lifetime of agony. What was three more hours in the grand fucking scheme of things? *Fuck. Don't pass out. Not now. Not yet.* He struggled to breathe through it. His red-rimmed vision grayed. *Fuck, fuck, fuck.* This wasn't the way he'd planned to end it. Not stuck halfway under a fence, too banged up to crawl. *Hell no. He had to end on a high. That asshat Daklin, people would say. Redeemed himself in the end.* All he had to do was get under this goddamned fence, traverse the open area without getting shot, get into the sealed mine, set his explosives, then sit back and enjoy the shitshow.

That's all.

Fuckshitdamn.

"Stay put," Turley said quietly. "I can do it. We'll come back for you."

Daklin shook his head. *He wasn't gonna pass the fuck out. So far so good.* "Three man job. I'm good." It was a *four*-man job. It would have to do.

"You're a fucking liar." Gibbs sounded worried. It was hard to tell behind his NVGs, with his voice pitched barely above a whisper. "You should see yourself, man. You look like shit and you can barely walk. How are you going to get out in time when we have to haul ass? Jesus, do you have a death wish?"

Not a wish exactly. A little fucking late to come to that conclusion. For the good of the team, he *had* considered pulling out. Letting his men do the job. He'd seriously considered it. Not because he was afraid to die. Hell, his job was guaranteed, sooner or later, to kill him. But because there was no one better than himself to do what had to be done.

That wasn't vanity; it was a fact. Because he'd been recuperating back-to-back for almost two years, he'd had more time than anyone else to study E-1x. He was T-FLAC's resident expert, which was the prime reason they'd given him this last shot to make good instead of canning his ass. He didn't know everything, but he had a better grasp of its makeup and properties than the others did.

"We're wasting time. Go."

Turley rubbed a hand over his mouth. "I'm not unsympathetic here, but you'll slow us down. Get us *all* killed."

"If that happens, I'll shoot myself and save everyone the trouble. If I can't perform my job, you'll be the second to know. In the meantime, when I say go, we all fucking-well go."

He could, and *would,* last the next few hours. He'd do his job, not get his men killed, bring down Xavier, and wipe E-1x off the face of the Earth. Not a bad night's work if he pulled it off.

And he would.

More of the mine's perimeter security force were now gathered at the gate where the two drunks were still putting on a show. Nyhuis and Aiza would be tossing bottles of booze up to the guard towers about now. Daklin heard the crash of a full bottle hitting the gravel, and gritted his teeth, thinking how badly he wanted that spilled booze.

He jerked his chin in that direction as he removed his ghillie. "They must be bored."

"Their commander hears that shit and they'll all be shot." Gibbs spoke in a whisper meant only to be heard a few feet away as he got down to crawl. "No fucking kidding. There's no down time on the job."

"True." Turley got down on all fours, ready to slither under the fence. "Means the commander is off-site."

"Let's hope his men accept the offer of a party, and he stays wherever he is."

Nyhuis and Aiza had come well prepared with cases of booze and Cuban cigars in the back of the truck. Maybe Nyhuis wasn't acting. There was a lot of shouting going on as bottles thrown and caught with whoops of laughter, and triumphant shouts.

"Go," Daklin urged his men. They scrambled ahead of him as he guarded their flank. Turley and then Gibbs crawled under the fence. He followed as soon as Gibbs was clear. Halfway under, his leg refused to propel him forward. Breaking out in an ice cold sweat, stars flared in his vision and nausea rose in the back of his throat. Ah, Jesus…

Suck it up, MOFO, suck it up.

"Daklin?"

"Keep moving." Sweating despite the LockOut, he dragged himself through on his elbows, fighting not to pass the hell out right here, halfway under the fence for all to see. By sheer, steely force of will, he got through without humiliating himself or getting killed. Win-win. This side of the barricade looked exactly like the other. A vast, open, gravel area intermittently lit by a rotating flood light. Five minutes light. Two minutes dark. The open ground wasn't as vast as the area they'd just covered, but there were several hundred feet to cover before they reached the long, low building housing the offices on one end, the processing plant on the other.

They had to get to and around the building undetected, and over a thirty-foot tall tungsten steel gate, into the loading area between the mine and behind the processing section on the south side of the building. Then they had to breach the second door, this one blocking the mine entrance.

Daklin checked his watch. 23:36. Detonation three hours and twenty-four minutes. He held up a finger as he tried his comm. It would be fucking fantastic if they had air support, ground penetrating x-ray, and back up. They needed eyes and ears, satellite surveillance, and support.

Hell, they still didn't even have operable comms.

He gave his guys a thumbs down, and then indicated the way he wanted them to go. A huge earth-moving machine, clearly not in use in the last decade, threw a deep shadow bridge between the fence and the corner of the building. Half a dozen smaller, rusted machines lent their bulky shadows as cover. Powerful spotlights strafed the area, but were no match for the size and bulk of the shadows cast by the abandoned machinery.

With hand signs, Daklin repeated the plan. They'd dart from shadow to shadow as the light swept the area every two minutes. Five minutes light. Two minutes darkness. Standing still for five minutes while hidden was going to feel like a fucking lifetime. The ticking time bomb in his head was a given, but these small respites could work in his favor.

Daklin watched as Gibbs moved from shadow to shadow, pausing as the spotlight panned the area, then running like hell to the next island of darkness. Turley went next. Daklin covered their asses as they moved.

The racket of yelling and laughing at the front gate was layered over the rustle of the jungle at Daklin's back, an occasional bird call, something large moving through the undergrowth, and the soft crunch of his men's footfalls as they ran across the gravel. Under all that, the rasp of his own ragged breathing rang in his ears, as he cleared the fence, then rose to his feet.

Gibbs made it into the cone of shadow at the corner of the building. He'd cover Daklin, and Daklin moved fast. Shadow to shadow, to-—— Fuck! A motion sensor light on the building suddenly blinked on between the brilliance of the strafing light. This light wasn't as bright, but it shone directly on the machine behind which he hid.

The levity at the gate stopped. In the ensuing silence, Daklin heard the pounding of dozens of pairs of feet. Night patrols, two dozen strong, crisscrossing the compound, twenty-four seven.

He waited, about to haul ass, when he heard, "Yo. Anyone here? Fuck. There's *never* anyone out here, right, Bagdan." The voice was Russian. Young.

Adrenaline surged through his body. Instinctively shifting his hold on his Uzi, Daklin eased the strap free of his pack, as he listened to better pinpoint their location.

"Better check." This voice was older. Also speaking Russian. "Maybe new guys snuck pretty girls in for us tonight."

"I don't care if ugly girl," Bagdan said. "If I not shooting some person, I want fuck girl."

His friend laughed as their heavy, booted footfalls crunched loudly on the gravel. "Is almost over. We find *prostitutka* in Santa de Porres tomorrow night. Sisters, da?"

Almost over? What was almost over? Their job here? A prickle of unease made the short hairs on the back of Daklin's neck stand on end. A warning, a premonition? Whatever. He always listened, and right now, years of experience as an operative told him there was more going on tonight than what he and his men were doing.

"We here six months, Yuri," Bagdan protested, his footfall getting closer. "No army come. Don't be shooting me by mistake."

Daklin was waiting for the spotlight to rotate again, leaving him in shadows. His hand inside his pack, he curled his fingers gently around the monkey's belly. The animal rewarded him with a sharp bite to his finger, drawing blood. Good thing T-FLAC was adamant about rabies shots.

"Anyone there?" Yuri shouted in Russian, then repeated it in atrocious Spanish.

Daklin tossed the monkey at a low trajectory out into the open. Monkey and men intersected ten feet from his hiding place. All three screamed. Daklin bit back a smile as he crouched, ready.

"Your *podruga*, Yuri? She very pretty. Here, pretty one, here, pretty one." Laughing, the two men stayed put as the monkey darted across the gravel toward the fence and the trees.

The smell of sulfur and two small, brief flashes of light indicated cigarettes had been lit. The stink of strong, unfiltered Russian cigarettes drifted to his hiding place.

He'd been about to run, balanced on his bad leg, ready to take off on his stronger right leg when they'd stopped. The vice-like pain--excruciating enough to cause him to see bright specks of light in his vision--made Daklin fight to remain conscious. *Don't move, dickhead. Do not fucking move an eyelash.*

Knowing the flask was in his pack blurred reason. One slug. Maybe two. Take the edge off. Hell, he'd function better if his brain wasn't clouded and distracted by pain.

A drink would get him through the next three hours.

A drink would mask the pain.

A drink would numb his brain enough to follow through with his original plan.

344

Damnit to hell. No.

He was stronger than the craving to drink.

Fuck. No he wasn't.

Stealthy as hell, Daklin's hand went to his pack. Through the red haze and gritted teeth, he suddenly imagined River's soft gray eyes filled with gut-wrenching disappointment. Curling his fingers into a fist, he struggled to breathe through the wanting. Breathe through the pain.

Gravel crunched as the two soldiers started walking back the way they'd come. "Stop," the younger Russian suddenly whispered. The guy dropped his voice and Daklin heard the familiar sound of a slide racking back on an M4. "You hear?"

The crunch of returning steps. Fuck. Ignoring the sparklers obscuring his vision, Daklin switched direction. The revelry at the gate hadn't abated, as more voices joined in. Still, a gunshot would bring them running. They weren't too drunk to respond to a threat.

"*Da,*" whispered. "Come out here, *bop,*" Louder. More bravado. He, too, racked the slide on his weapon.

The blinding light strafed the area.

No gun. Slowly moving his hand down from his pack, Daklin soundlessly slid the Ka-Bar out of its leather ankle sheath. The custom grip fit his hand as one lethal unit. He counted off the seconds until the spotlight moved on.

The area plunged into darkness.

Now!

Bursting out from behind cover without warning gave him

seconds of surprise. He used those seconds to grab the closest guy around the neck, slitting his throat before he could call out. He dropped the body before the second guy could turn and finish raising his weapon.

Kicking out with his bad leg, Daklin used his good leg as ballast. The heel of his heavy boot struck the guy on the jaw, causing him to stumble, then stagger back, fumbling to right his weapon.

Daklin grabbed the barrel as the guy fumbled for control. Yanking him forward, he elbowed the soldier in the face, hearing the gratifying crunch of bone and cartilage as the man's nose and cheekbone shattered.

Using the M4 as a fulcrum, Daklin swung the guy around as he choked on his own blood, then finished him off by plunging the Ka-Bar up high, into his kidneys.

Eliminating the two threats had taken all of four seconds.

Staggering back into the deep shadows, Daklin fell against the giant earth-moving machine as the world spun. He couldn't pass the fuck out or puke. Dropping his head back, he struggled to remain conscious.

Those bodies had to be dragged into the shadows before the floodlight swung around again.

Sweat beaded his brow as nausea welled.

Timing the light from behind closed lids, he waited. Evened his breathing. Tamped down the nausea. Contemplated amputating his own fucking leg to get rid of the pain.

The light moved.

Dashing out into the open, he grabbed the first guy by the shoulders, and dragged him behind the machine. Then he hobbled out, grabbed the second man by his shirtfront, and pulled him out of sight, too.

He was panting like a little old lady walking up a fucking hill. The light covered the area again. *Breathe. Get a fucking grip. Breathe.* The second the light moved on again, Daklin took advantage of the darkness to dash to the corner of the building three hundred feet away.

"You good?" Turley whispered.

"Had company."

"Saw."

"Move." Daklin didn't have the breath or the energy to have a convo.

A couple of dim lights shone from two windows on the east side of the building. Crouching, Uzis and Glocks in hand, they raced across the gravel, staying tight against the wall in the deep shadow cast by the building. Daklin indicated the lights. "Anyone?"

Gibbs shook his head. "It's lit up 24/7, but no one works at night."

Good, because they'd be dead in a couple of hours if that was the case. Now all they had to do was scale a thirty foot tall, tungsten steel gate that blocked access to the yard between the back of the plant and mine entrance, get into the loading area behind the building and break through the *other* tungsten steel door, this one barring entry to the mine shaft, their ultimate goal. And, accomplish this while in the kill zone of close to a hundred, highly trained, Russian soldiers, bored and eager for action.

"Keep moving, ladies," Daklin urged. "Time's a wasting."

EIGHTEEN

With each step on the mountainous road leading up to the guard gate, River hoped to hell she'd figure out a viable plan before she got there. And Oliver would contact her. And Ash would receive her telepathic S.O.S.

The air, thick with pungent smoke from the helicopter crash, and the burning trees, lit the sky an eerie orange.

She tried her phone every few minutes. Still no text or cell service. The useless device was nothing but dead weight and occasionally, when the darkness freaked her out too much, a flashlight.

She'd hot-wired an ancient, beat-up VW Beatle she had found parked on a narrow side street in town and drove it up the road as far as she dared, using just the parking lights to show the way when necessary. Not knowing what to expect, she left it down by the bridge and out of sight. It was a four-mile jog up to the guarded gates; the same gates where the heavily armed soldiers had tried to kill her.

Four miles.

In the dark.

With wild animals lurking on either side of the narrow road.

With overhanging trees that might harbor spiders, snakes, and God-only-knew-what-else. The night wasn't quiet at all.

Leaves rustled, branches creaked, birds squawked. An animal off to her left kept giving a low, rough grunt that had her heart in her throat and goose bumps on top of her other fear-induced goose bumps.

Franco had made his bed. She wondered how someone so freaking pious could be so evil. She wondered if, now that Franco was dead, Oliver would be free to go? Just walk away? She almost anticipated seeing her brother strolling toward her, hands in his pockets, pale hair catching the moonlight, that typical, slightly quizzical look on his face as he tried to figure out a problem. River wished things could be that simple. Unfortunately, nothing about Oliver was ever simple.

With no starlight or firelight visible, it was dark under the trees overhanging the narrow road, and uncomfortably muggy. She was not a stupid woman. She'd never walk alone at night in a dangerous area. In fact, she never walked alone at night *anywhere*. Yet, here she was.

If the guards didn't ultimately kill her, some wild animal would probably rip her limb from limb. Only Marcus knew where she was. They'd find her bones licked clean on the side of the road come morning. "What were my options?" River's whisper sounded louder than the ambient noises of the jungle. But hearing a voice, even her own, helped. A little.

"Go with Marcus, and return home? Leave my brother, my only family, here to die? *Not* an option. Would it be better to have sent an army armed to the teeth to rescue Oliver? Hell yes. Double hell yes. I'd be thrilled to wait in Marcus's kitchen sipping lemonade."

That wasn't an option either.

One foot in front of the other.

Something nearby made a hell of a lot of noise: branches snapped and leaves whipped in its passage as it screeched, swinging from branch to branch in the nearby trees. Was the damn thing following her?

She picked up speed, going from a fast jog to a flat out run. Everything about the situation scared the living crap out of her. The thought of Oliver helpless somewhere. Ash getting ready to blow up the mountain and himself. A jungle full of terrifying creatures, and a welcoming party of God only knew how many men with guns--or worse--waiting for her.

"Being a lingerie designer did not equip me for thi—- *Fuck*!" She rarely said the word, but a giant pig, a wild freaking *boar,* darted across the road ahead. The animal swiveled its head to size her up as it ran. It looked as if it was going to veer right down the middle of the way-too-narrow road and mow her down.

Responding out of instinct and fear, River opened her arms wide, waving them like a windmill as she stomped her feet. She would've screamed if she hadn't thought more animals, not to mention people with guns, would come running. Finally, the beast lumbered off into the bushes, making a racket as it crashed, unseen, through the underbrush.

"The animals are more scared of me than I am of them." Her spoken voice didn't sound nearly as bracing as it did in her head. And she knew she was lying. If any denizens of the jungle were hungry, *she* was their hot meal for the night.

She started running again, her fast pace steady as her lungs labored for air. Something growled low to her left. She stopped, freezing on a dime as a pair of yellow eyes glittered at her from beneath dense undergrowth, close enough to touch. Standing still, with her breathing quiet, an unexpected and welcome sound greeted her.

Noise. *Drunken* noise. Men shouting, laughing, and glass breaking. It sounded like a frat party. The sound of men having a good time was incongruent to the surroundings, and with what she knew Daklin had planned for the night. Maybe it was all part of the plan, yet another ruse he'd dreamed up, like his bishop disguise.

Deep down, she'd started to question if his interest in her had just been an act in an attempt to get information on Oliver, one that just happened to have some fantastic perks.

The continued party noise amped up her fear as she resumed jogging, then walking, up the hill toward the plant.

There was barely enough starlight to light her way. At least she could see where she was running now, as the clouds drifted off the moon for a moment. She saved the light on her phone for emergencies. She wanted enough battery power so she could keep trying Oliver's number.

The laughter and carousing grew, getting louder and louder, and now she saw pinpoints of light through the trees. Once she walked around the next curve, she'd be in sight of the plant. Then she had another three miles to traverse, out in the open.

Exactly where she'd been shot at yesterday.

Stumbling on the edge of a pothole, her ankle rolled and she almost fell. Taking several hobbling steps, she righted herself before her tired legs stopped her forward momentum.

Hands on her knees, River paused to catch her breath. The stress of the night and the altitude were both wearing on her, and now her ankle burned. That just made her think about Ash's leg and she started to worry all over again, about how he was going to run when he could barely freaking walk.

"*He* knows what he's doing; I'm the one who hasn't a freaking clue." *Great pep talk.*

She hit the number Oliver used to text her again. An animal's sudden screech nearby had her instinctively freeze, prepared for an attack. Heart in her throat, she searched the darkness. Listened. Waited. There was no indication anything was about to jump out at her. Yet.

River breathed deeply to center herself.

Should she walk right up to the gate as bold as brass and get them to take her to Oliver. Not the best idea. Who knew when those men had last *seen* a woman? Taking her to her brother was probably the *last* thing they'd do. Shit. Unfortunately, that was the only plan she had for now. She'd make another plan after that. And another, until they were safe. It wasn't a great plan. In fact it was a shitty, possibly lethal one, but it was all she had.

Squinting against the brightness of the phone screen, she listened to it, then straightened when the ringtone stopped. The line was open. "Oliver?"

"Jesus fuck, River! Go away!"

"You're alive! Thank God, I—"

"I told you *not* to come!"

"Yes, you did." Cold trepidation filled her insides as his words registered. "Wait. How did you know I'm in Los Santos and not at home in Portland?"

"That's immaterial now. Where are you?"

"On the road. Almost to the mine. After the bridge." Dead silence. Shit, had the phone died? "Oliver?"

"There's a reflective stake, about a foot off the ground. Red. It's on your right between where you are now, and the main gate. Take a right. There's a narrow road there, which leads to a side gate. It's kinda rough going. What kind of car are you driving?"

"A beat up 1960 VW Beatle that I hot-wired and freaking *stole* to come and get you.*"*

"How many people do you have with you?"

I wish. "Nobody. I'm alone."

"That's inadvisable. Be that as it may, follow my directions and come quickly."

"I left the car at the bridge, so I'm running as fast as I can."

Slowing her pace, she continued at a brisk walk as a stitch bit sharply into her side. If she was faltering because of a *stitch*, how was Ash managing on that leg? River made a concerted effort to focus on her own situation. She had to trust that Ash could manage. She just didn't have the capacity to worry about all of them at the same time. "Are you badly hurt?"

"Just drive up to the gate, River."

Typical Oliver. Not even listening. "I'm not driving, I'm *running*. Alone. In the middle of the jungle. Sweating." She swiped at her wet cheek. "I'm scared out of my mind, Oliver. Please."

"I have one of the security people on my side. He'll let you in. I'm being held in the lab on the East side of the building. Second door to the left."

Something was *on* her. She brushed off her butt. The something, wet and slimy, stuck to her finger and with a grimace, she flicked it off, impatient to get some damn answers.

"If one of the security people is on your side, why can't *he* help you get out? Oliver? Oliver, damn it, don't you dare cut me off like *that*. I am going to kill you the moment you're safe, you little shit!"

After running for another five minutes, and only because she knew where to look, River saw the small reflector off to the side of the road. Oliver's "narrow road" was a damned dirt-- *muddy* as hell--*path*. Using the flashlight on her phone, she forged up the track, walking as fast as the dense vegetation and slimy mud allowed. Sweat rolled down her temples, and glued her shirt to her clammy skin. The only way she managed to put one foot in front of the other was to block out the knowledge of what surrounded her, block out the sounds and smells, block out anticipation of impending and imminent death.

The sound of the party indicated she must be getting closer. The pungent stink of cigarette smoke was incongruous amidst the damp green smell of the surrounding jungle, and different from the wood burning smoke from the fire. *Someone* was close by. Since her heartbeat was already manic, the knowledge barely caused a flutter. She kept her eyes peeled and stepped lightly on the balls of her feet, redistributing her weight in case whoever it was attacked.

"Who's there?" No response. "If you're leading me on a wild goose chase for some warped reason, Oliver, I swear." She almost walked into the ten-foot high chain link fence blocking her path and let out a choked scream.

"Down this way." A man, his heavily accented voice disembodied, was a darker silhouette against the darkness. The smoker. A cigarette glowed orange, followed by a plume of the pungent smoke, which rose in a paler cloud around his head. She followed the voice. A faint metal on metal noise was followed by a squeak. As it turned out, getting *inside* the compound was shockingly simple. Why couldn't Oliver get out the same way?

Stepping through the gate as the guard held it open, she waited while the guy relocked it using a high tech keypad. In the distance, glass shattered to the whoops and cheers of the men. One guy started singing, badly, to the drunken hilarity of the others.

The soldier towered over her, and River took a few steps back. Holy crap, he was a hulk. "Where's my brother?" She squinted, holding up a hand to shade her eyes as he flicked on a small, powerful flashlight and trained it on her face. "Is Dr. Sullivan injured? Incapacitated?" River had no idea *what* to expect. Oliver had sounded like Oliver. Distracted. Impatient, intolerant of anyone who didn't "get it" right away.

The guard didn't respond.

Blinking to get her vision back, she took in the man as he shifted the beam to check the jungle beyond the fence. "You alone?"

"Yes."

The man had black peach fuzz on his head and jaw, massive shoulders, and a barrel chest barely contained in military fatigues. He was also heavily armed. A machine gun slung across his chest like a cross body purse, a handgun resting in a hip holster, and a large knife strapped to his ankle. Overall, he was definitely someone she'd rather have on her side than against.

Turning off the flashlight, he indicated with a jerk of his square jaw that she was to precede him to the building, which was a paler square about five hundred feet away. Their footsteps crunched across the gravel. Any sounds they made were drowned out as several men joined the singer in a raucous chorus.

"How far are we going?" Darkness pressed around her like a damp wool blanket and her heart was doing calisthenics. *Don't let your nerves get the better of you. Keep sharp. Use your brain.*

357

Be ready for anything.

The sudden staccato pops of guns discharging and shouts stiffened her shoulders. But then they went back to singing off tune. The sound of more gunfire was distant, but she picked up her pace as the singing suddenly stopped. "Is it much further?"

The sound of multiple engines springing to life a few minutes later was jarring. Her head shot up and her steps faltered. "What's happening?" she asked, as muffled male voices speaking what she presumed to be Russian shouted back and forth. Car doors slammed. Tires scattered gravel. Shit. Why the sudden activity in the middle of the night? Had they discovered Ash and his men? Her blood ran cold and her already frantic heartbeat stuttered.

The longer they walked, the more River's concern for both Ash and her brother grew. The shouting, laughing and singing stopped, only to be replaced by tires on gravel, and door slamming. What the hell was going on? And how would this affect Oliver and Ash?

Was Oliver injured? Did he need medical attention? She sure as hell hoped he was mobile. If she managed to get him out of wherever he was, they'd have to run back almost four miles to reach the car. If he couldn't walk or run, she'd have to retrace her steps. Alone. Fast. *Twice.* She shuddered.

As for Ash… No, she couldn't go there. She just couldn't. He knew the risks of what he was doing, knew his own physical limitations.

What he didn't know was how she felt about him. Even she was shocked at how fast she'd fallen. Would that knowledge have made any difference to the decisions he'd made tonight? She'd probably never know, and that made her chest ache.

The humongous soldier rapped sharply on the outside wall, which was covered with siding painted a matte black. Looking twice, River realized there was an almost invisible door in the wall. Above the frame, a small red light betrayed the presence of an active camera.

The door gave a series of clicks and whirs, and cracked open, emitting a muted shaft of yellow light across the dirt and gravel. She braced herself and stepped inside. The dimly lit corridor had been painted white about fifty years ago. Chipped, peeling, filthy, nicotine-colored now, the corridor smelled strongly of corrosive chemicals, and even more strongly of stale cigarette smoke. She associated these odors with her brother.

Her throat closed with fear. Anticipation, horrific, terrifying anticipation was a hard knot in her chest.

There wasn't a picture, or a window, or a sign, or anything to indicate what this place was used for. From the smells, she presumed it was near Oliver's lab. Cold. Industrial. Pretty damned unfriendly. Sweat dried on River's skin. The soldier stopped in front of an unassuming door and turned to look at her with black eyes and no expression. *"Vkhodit'."*

"Go in?"

"Vkhodit'."

359

River twisted the door handle, walked inside, then blinked. The vast room, lit only with the flickering light of a dozen computer monitors, was dim. It was so cold, she shivered.

She braced herself for the worst. Blood. Broken limbs. *God, please.* Had Oliver been tortured? Starved? Was he chained? Restrained? Trepidation filled her mind with a million fleeting, terrifying images gleaned from movies and TV shows, her only knowledge of what being held captive looked like.

"Oliver?"

Her brother stepped out from behind a long table. Tall, thin, rumpled. But not restrained in any way. River took in the room in a sweeping glance to see if anyone was holding him at gunpoint. They were the only two people in the lab.

His black-rimmed glasses were, as always, smudged and slightly crooked. His white blonde hair stuck straight up, as if he'd been running his fingers through it as he worked out a complicated problem. He was no thinner or paler than the last time she'd seen him five years ago. He was unbruised, unbloodied, and damn it, the muscle in his cheek twitched, indicating he was annoyed. That same tic had appeared throughout his life whenever reality intruded on the complex thought processes and puzzles in his head.

Annoyed? She narrowed her eyes. *He* was freaking *annoyed?* Scanning the room, she saw exactly where they were. His damned lab.

His home away from home. She'd been in enough of his workspaces in her life to recognize the tools he used. Computers, monitors, chemicals, and liquids. Mysterious lab equipment. It was his usual scrupulously tidy workspace, and organized in a way that made sense only to him. Inside was his favorite style of black leather ergonomic chair, exactly twenty-five yellow number 2 pencils in the same crooked blue ceramic pot she'd so proudly made for him in fifth grade, the bulky electric pencil sharpener, always on the right and a neat stack of five lined yellow note pads beside the plain blue mouse pad. "What the hell, Oliver?"

"I told you not to come. I thought I'd have more time."

River's temper shot up, flaring through her body like red-hot, molten lava. She walked right up to him and punched him hard in the chest. "Franco's dead."

"I'm well aware."

"You *are*?" Looking past him, she saw an image of the front the hacienda in one of the large monitors behind him. Her attention returned to his stoic features. "You were *watching* us the whole time?"

"Irrelevant. Please don't get confrontational. You know I don't like it. And stop talking endlessly. Here." He shoved a laptop against her chest, and she automatically wrapped her arms around it. "Hold this while I finish backing up the rest of my files."

"We don't have time to do anything but *leave*, Oliver."

"Seven minutes," he told her absently, all his attention on the scrolling text on the largest monitor. "The pass is blocked. How does T-FLAC plan to get you out of the valley? Is that helicopter coming back for you?" He typed a series of commands, as the text kept scrolling.

"Franco's helicopter?"

Without turning around, he snapped, "For God's sake, River. *Focus*. Not *Franco's* helicopter. The one they sent to pick people up in the square earlier. It left. Is it coming back for you?"

"I suppose so." Dear God. Had her brother been watching them, all the time? The thought was chilling. "You *know* counterterrorist operatives are here?"

Fortunately, the question was rhetorical. He didn't answer as he moved to another keyboard and leaned over to type commands with two fingers.

"Where are your captors?" she demanded. "Where are the restraints? The guards with guns? There are no kidnappers, are there, Oliver? That text message was just a load of bullshit, wasn't it? No one is or was holding you captive. You designed this goddamned lab. You can walk right out of that door any freaking time you want to."

She narrowed her eyes, so mad she shook. "It wasn't *me* you wanted up here. It was someone else. Someone you thought I'd tell all about my poor brother held captive, and ask for help. Someone who would come here to 'rescue' you. Who *were* you expecting to come and 'save' you, Oliver?"

Arms loose at his sides, Oliver didn't react to her anger. "Will you lower your voice, and adjust your tone?"

"Probably not." She crossed her arms, giving him a cold look. He was, of course, impervious. Human emotions weren't in

362

his wheelhouse. Due to his Asperger's, and his tendency to ignore others, he didn't understand them. Showing a loss of temper, her frustration, or even how terrified she was, was a waste of time, no matter how strong those emotions were. "I have every damned right to be pissed at you." River stuffed her fingers into her front pockets to prevent herself from slapping him. "Do you freaking well *know* what I thought when I discovered all that money in my bank account and didn't hear from you for more than three weeks?" Her voice choked, and she had to clear the lump in her throat before she could continue. "I thought you were contemplating suicide. I came to Los Santos to stop you.

He didn't look up as his fingers flew over the keyboard. "Why would I take my own life?"

"I thought you were depressed after your girlfriend died."

"Catarina didn't *die.*" He didn't take his attention off the screen for even a second. "She was murdered. And that was three years ago." He kept typing, moving from one keyboard to another. "I'm over it."

"Over?" Her voice died as she looked beyond the overflowing ashtrays, the empty packs of Nicorette gum scattered everywhere, dirty dishes, and his favorite childhood faded blue blanket on the matted brown velvet swayback sofa.

A bank of monitors flickered and glowed in the semi-darkness. Each one showed six views. With a small frown, she turned her back to him to get a closer look. They showed the interior and exterior of Franco's home, the front door of the rectory, and Marcus's kitchen where her note was still propped on the sugar bowl. It also showed the town square from several angles where people were gathered to get into a giant camouflage painted helicopter and her bedroom at the hacienda, with her cherry-print dress left where she'd stepped out of it on the floor in a frantic puddle to get to her brother.

Two other monitors showed Ash in an eerie green light. Alone, inside the mine as he ran cord along the wet floor. Or that's what she imagined his movement to be. She could only see a green image, without any detail.

River's blood turned to ice as she swung back to her brother. Pale and rumpled, he removed his glasses, cleaned the lenses on the hem of his short-sleeved, mis-buttoned, cotton shirt, put them back on, then combed back his hair with both hands. It was a lot of action for Oliver. He was nervous.

River indicated the computer monitors. "What's all this?"

He took her upper arm in surprisingly strong fingers, and started pulling her to the door. "I'll explain it later."

She stopped dead in her tracks, her shoes making a high-pitched squeak on the linoleum floor. "Explain *right now*."

"I've uploaded my life's work to a cloud site. I'm ready to leave now."

"Did you think by telling me you were being held 'hostage' that I *wouldn't* come?"

"I thought you'd be sensible, and tell one of the counterterrorist operatives to come."

"Not when I think your life is being threatened. And how do you know about the operatives in town? Oh, right. You've been keeping your eyes on things. Why do you have surveillance on Franco's house? Why are you watching Father Marcus? And why do you have a night vision camera in the mine?"

Sighing, he pushed up his black-rimmed glasses with a nicotine-stained finger. "Franco is a *terrorist*. He's the one who's been keeping me up here all this time. I accidently came up with the formula for a powerful explosive while looking for the most expedient, contained blast to use in the mining operation. Emeralds are soft. They fracture easily if the blast...never mind. While walking through the mine, I discovered veins of a substance more powerful than any manmade explosive. I formulated it so that he could use very small amounts to blast designated areas.

He glanced around as if looking for something, talking almost absently as he frowned. "When I discovered he was selling that product to terrorists around the world, I was appalled and tried to leave. He stopped me. They've been holding me prisoner here as I worked on a better delivery system. Those guards out there aren't here to keep people out. He hired them to keep me in."

He was prevaricating. "*One* guard."

"Heavily armed."

"Who let *me* in. You could've left at any time, couldn't you, Oliver?" River tried to suppress her temper. Losing her cool would completely shut him down. She couldn't afford for Oliver to shut down. Not here and not now. Still her temper flared hot. She ground her teeth, and breathed in deeply through her nose. Chemicals. Cigarettes. And weirdly, an underlying sweet smell of honey.

Had her brother sat right here this afternoon watching her having sex with Ash? "Why were you monitoring *my* room?"

"That was the bedroom I stayed in when I went to town. I wanted to see if Franco searched it."

"Did you watch me having sex?"

"Of course not. Who would you have sex *with*? Did you bring Devon with you?"

"Of course not. He's re-married and we don't have that kind of relationship. Damn it. Stop changing the subject."

"We've got to get out of here, River." He pointed to the monitor on the left. "That's one of the men sent here to destroy Franco and his business. He's in there to blow the mine. I don't know how long we have, but it's sure to be happening damned soon."

River's attention was glued to the screen, watching as Ash did his job. Even in the grainy image, she recognized him, seeing how he favored his left leg. There was no evidence that anyone else was with him. "Where are the others?" she whispered, observing Ash's pronounced limp.

"Damn it, River! *Gone*. Who cares? Once he ignites that charge he's laying, the whole mountain will be sheared off! And everyone in a hundred mile radius will go with it. Let's *go*. That helicopter they sent back for you will be collateral damage unless we're on it and out of here." His fingers tightened on her upper arms and he tugged at her to get her feet in motion. "*Move*."

Unable to tear her eyes from the screen, she ignored him as Ash stumbled. River's heart stopped. Limping a few more feet, he reached out as if to support his weight, but he didn't quite make it, and fell to one knee. River's heart swelled as he tried to lever himself to his feet. Instead, he dropped to the ground and lay still.

It was bad enough to *imagine* it, but it was devastating to actually *watch* him fall. "How do we get *there*?" Her mouth dry, skin clammy with nervous perspiration, she pointed.

"Get where? Are you *nuts*? *Inside* the mine? To where that guy is? With charges set to blow at any minute? No. We run like hell. There's a company car. We'll take that and hightail it to the village square. *Look*." He pointed at the changed view to that of the almost empty square. The fountain was no longer spraying and the streets were empty, save for the helicopter, its blades spinning.

"Their helicopter is waiting for you. Let's go. I don't know how much time we have. Every second counts. Move it. Damn it, River—-"

"Tell me how to get to where Ash is. You can leave if you want to."

"You know I don't drive." He searched her face, saw she was determined, and threw up his hands. "Are you fucking out of your *mind*?" Oliver's face flushed dark red, and his eyes behind his thick glasses looked wild as he started scooping what could only be emeralds, into a pouch. "No. I won't be party to your insanity."

He didn't look up as he swept various-sized stones into the bag. "And I sure as hell won't stand by while you kill yourself." Pulling the drawstring, he tucked the bag into his back pocket. "Why do *you* give a flying fuck what happens to the guy?"

"I don't have time to argue with you, Oliver." River moved quickly to the door. "With or without your help, I'm going to go and help him." She paused to look back. "And when we're somewhere safe, you'd better have a damn good explanation." Angrily River swept her hand around the room. "For the money, the lack of communication for all those weeks, for *all* of *this*."

NINETEEN

His pulse slowed, and his focus became pinpoint. The only sound Daklin heard was his own heartbeat throbbing in his ears. The dank, dark tunnel smelled of mildew, sweat, and the underlying sweet, honeyed smell of E-1x. He'd ordered his men out, and back to the valley, fifty minutes earlier. There was nothing left for them to do. He'd rejected their offers to stay in his stead. This part of the op was for a one-man band.

It was his responsibility. His penance.

All he had to do was get out, shut the blast proof door, then haul ass.

That was the promise he'd made Turley and Gibbs when they'd reluctantly left him to complete the job. Once initiating detonation, he'd have thirty minutes to get to safety. There was nowhere enough time to crawl his way out. And crawl was about all he could do right now. He wouldn't make it to the fucking door three hundred feet away.

Trapped, for the rest of his--thankfully short--life in the deep end of a mineshaft that was far too narrow for the motorized vehicle, which could've taken him to safety.

He'd tried a couple of times to get to his feet, making a fucking effort to get out. But his leg had given up the ghost and refused to hold him this last time he went down. So be it.

Taking off his NVG's, Daklin closed his eyes in the unrelieved blackness, letting his head drop back to the soggy ground as he listened to the beat of his heart echoing in his ears. Water seeped into his hair as he lay in a puddle formed by the constant drip of moisture from the earthen ceiling. He could roll over and drag himself by his elbows, as he'd done to get under the fence. His leg was a fiery mass of excruciating pain, and even the slightest movement threatened to knock him out cold. It was something he was seriously considering.

Moving was redundant at this point. His rusty laugh bounced off the rough-hewn walls. Nope. The fucking water wasn't what was going to kill him. The LockOut kept water and cold from his body, but Daklin was cold anyway. Cold to the bone.

He'd never cared about living as much as he did now that living was no longer an option. The only good news was that River was far from the blast and safe. He felt for his pack. That monkey had crapped on pretty much everything inside, but his flask was tucked into the outer pocket. Pulling it free, he ran his thumb over the worn leather.

He carried his father's flask with him wherever he went as a reminder. *Think you won't love this bitch as much as I do, Junior?* His father's slurred voice sounded crystal clear in his head. *Think she won't comfort and love you like no other? Think again. You and I have the same DNA. Addictive personalities both of us. Go ahead, take a drink. You'll feel better for it.*

Daklin had been eight the day his father offered him his first drink. Vodka had been his friend ever since.

He unscrewed the silver cap.

You can beat this, Ash. Josh's pleas had resonated, tears sheening his eyes as he'd come to get Ash from some shit hole bar for the umpteenth time. *You aren't Dad. Please. If not for yourself, then for me. For T-FLAC, damn it. They'll fire your ass.*

"Yeah, well, this was my last chance. I'll save them the trouble." His voice, low as it was, bounced off the walls and echoed back to him.

He'd set the automatic timers on the charges. There was no turning back. No way to prevent detonation. Destruction was now in motion. The next thirty-five minutes were going to be the longest goddamn thirty-five minutes of his life.

Bringing the flask to his lips, he dragged in a shuddering breath, his lips an inch from the rim. The faint smell of alcohol made him salivate, and he squeezed his eyes shut on a shudder of need. But was this how he wanted to be greeted on the other side by his baby brother?

Drunk as a fucking skunk on arrival? The curved side of the flask buckled as his fingers tightened. Could he do this sober?

Or not?

Maybe this was the ultimate test, to see if he was capable of maintaining sobriety.

Done debating with himself, Daklin did an overhand pitch, throwing the open flask into the darkness. Considering the weight of the decision, the small container pinged lightly against the rock wall with no fanfare, dropping with a small splash to the ground.

He scrubbed his hand across his mouth, throat aching with the loss. Fuck it. Nobody was going to say Ash Daklin didn't fucking well try.

He started pulling himself along on his elbows.

Sweat dripped into his eyes. Hell, he couldn't see worth shit anyway. The flask was somewhere in the dark, but now, all his concentration and effort was making it through the heavy door at the mouth of the mine. When he died, it would be breathing fresh air, and imagining River's face.

He didn't stop for the galaxy of spinning stars, or the abnormally loud flub-dub-flub-dub of his heartbeat. He just kept dragging his ass through mud, and over rock.

A foreign sound—-a combo of a creak and a thud—-stopped him. He reached back for the Glock. Someone had just opened the tungsten steel door blocking the entrance to the mine.

Cocking his head, he heard running steps. Two people. Light steps, heading towards him. His men coming back to haul his ass out of there, whether he wanted to go or not? Daklin flattened out in the slime on the hard, uneven ground. The movement sent excruciating pain into his thigh, piercing like a lightning bolt directly to every pain center in his brain.

Bright silver stars sparked before his eyes. Nausea welled in the back of his throat. His fingers tightened reflexively on the trigger, although now he couldn't hear a damn thing, and couldn't see anything because his NVG's were somewhere back there in the mud of his almost final resting place.

He hesitated. Death by bullet beat death by falling mountain. Fuck that. He had thirty minutes. He was taking them.

"Stop where you are!" he yelled in Russian, then repeated it in Spanish, and again in English for good measure. He selected Russian for, "You shoot and we all blow up."

By now, he would've normally fired off a round to hold them off, and his finger flexed in anticipation, but he didn't fire. One spark would precipitate the string of explosions he'd set deep into the mine. "Get your asses out of here——-"

"Ash?!"

Daklin's veins flooded with ice as his worst fear was realized. Dear, God. He'd killed her. As sure as if he'd fired a bullet through her heart. "River," he breathed soundlessly.

No! She was in Abad. He knew she was. Marcus would never leave her behind. Daklin expelled a tight breath, and the tension left his shoulders. Warmth returned to his veins.

A hallucination. Thank God.

If he didn't make it out, this wouldn't be so bad if he had her voice in his head.

"Asher Daklin, damn it! Answer me! Where are you? You said he was about quarter of mile down this shaft. He must be close, right, Oliver?"

What the fuck?!

"Or not. I might've been mistaken. Damn you for always

being so stubborn, River," a man snapped, clearly pissed. His annoyance bounced off the walls. "We're going to die here tonight."

How had she found him? How the hell had she passed through Xavier's crack security army? Why the fuck was she here at all?

"Asher?" River's voice broke, and the sound of running footsteps, splashing through water, and squishing in the mud, came closer and closer. The darkness up ahead was broken by light as she ran toward him.

"Get out, River," Daklin yelled at full volume, his throat tight and aching with fear. "Run! Detonation's set. You've got precisely twenty-seven minutes to get off this mountain. Turn around and go! Get the fuck out before it's too late." It was already too fucking late.

"You were right. He's down this way. We're coming, Ash."

"I don't *want* you to come to me, goddamn it!"

"That seems to be a popular freaking theme tonight. Too damn bad. I'm here!"

"Can't you take a fucking hint?" he yelled, hoping like hell to piss her off enough that she'd turn and run from him, instead of to him. "You were a great diversion, but this is my job, and I don't want you around anymore. Fuck off. I have work to do."

"We're not leaving without you." Calm, rational, too damned close. Not fooled in the least. He checked the dimly lit dial on his watch.

Detonation - 27 minutes. No turning back.

She didn't have enough time to get out and return to the valley, out of the destruction zone.

Daklin's eyes squeezed shut, and his cold, dead heart hurt so bad he thought this pain *would* kill him. Fuckfuckfuckfuck. "Don't!"

Then she was there.

Right.

Fucking.

There.

He was engulfed in the sweaty, summer-flowers-in-the-rain, smell of her as she dropped to her knees beside him in the mud and filth. The light brush of her warm fingers on his cheek felt like a benediction. "Oh, Ash!"

Wanting to nuzzle her hand, he jerked his head back, and said harshly, "I don't want you here, River."

"I know. Can you get his other arm, Oliver? That's the side of his bad leg. Be careful."

Somehow, River and the person Daklin presumed to be her brother got him to his feet. So the brother *had* been on the property all along. How the hell this reunion had happened, Daklin couldn't imagine. Not that it mattered now. The three of them were walking corpses.

River and her brother staggered under his weight. "I'm not going anywhere. Get it through your goddamned head. I don't need or want you, here or anywhere else."

"Up you go. Don't put any weight on that leg. We'll help you." She held a light to the ground. Her phone's flashlight.

"Get lost." Stubbornly, Daklin planted his good leg so they didn't have his help. "You have minutes to get to safety. And you've got to move. You understand? Run as fast as you can, get in a fast car, and floor it. You don't have time to waste helping me."

"You said twenty-seven. We need to speed this up, Oliver. Are you good?"

"No. I'm not fucking go--"

"Shh! I wasn't talking to you. Save your strength."

He was walking. By the beam of her phone, his weight dragging down her slender shoulders, he was walking. Limping. Mobile. "What about I don't want or need you here or anywhere else?"

"I tried telling her."

"What if I'm the woman of your dreams, Ash? Don't you at least want to explore the possibility?"

Shitfuckdamn. A boulder of need weighed down on his chest, heavy enough he barely felt his bum leg. "No. I stopped dreaming a long fucking time ago. Trust me."

"Almost there." To her brother she said, "Are you sure this is the right way, Oliver? We don't have time to get lost."

Daklin's eyes had adjusted well to the faint light. The massive door was straight ahead. Looking at River beside him, so close he could've counted her lashes, made his heart clench, and his breath uneven. He'd never smell summer rain again without thinking about how she looked right now; her jaw grimly determined, lips a hard line of concentration, clothes and face covered with mud and smudged with dirt, sweat spiking her hair.

Aw. Hell. He never would smell summer rain again.

He tried adjusting his weight so that he took some of it himself, but his leg caved, and he had to hold onto both of them to maintain his balance.

Sullivan grunted when he adjusted his weight again.

The scientist was tall, skinny, and blonder than his sister. Wearing muddy chinos, a short-sleeved plaid shirt, and black-rimmed glasses with a crack across the lenses, he looked exactly like what he was. Fortunately, or unfortunately in this case, the guy was fairly strong.

"We don't have time," Daklin reminded them. "Period."

River's blonde hair stuck to her flushed cheeks, and her mouth was set in a tight, grim line. Daklin had never seen anything, or anyone, more beautiful. "I'm not leaving without you."

"You wouldn't be so goddamned brave, if you got it through your head that we're all going to be dead and buried soon."

He'd killed Josh and now he was going to have River's death on his conscience for all fucking eternity.

"I'm not brave at all. Inside I'm terrified and sobbing like a th-three year old," she said tartly, bravado leaking out when her voice hitched. "Shut up. Just shut the hell up, Ash. If you can't say anything positive, I don't want to hear it. Is that the door up ahead?

Yes. It is! Almost there."

The door sealing off the mine was just one of a dozen obstacles they'd have to face to get out of there. "Almost where? We're not going anywhere."

Twenty-four minutes. "River."

"What's the protocol here?" Sullivan interrupted, not breaking stride as the passage widened and they navigated ruts and standing water, small equipment, and a half-buried railway line no longer in use.

The pain was so bad, it took every ounce of will Daklin had to remain upright and put one foot in front of the other. Lightheaded, he knew he was about to puke or pass out. Neither was acceptable. He swallowed bile, and blinked away the sparkling lights from his darkening vision.

"The *protocol* is the fact that the charges have all been set." Daklin's voice sounded as weighted down as he felt. "There isn't a hope in hell of us not taking the full brunt."

"The door is blast resistant," Sullivan told him. "Not proof, of course, but *resistant.*" With a frown, he shoved up his glasses as they saw the cracked open door up ahead. "Sealing the door from the outside will buy us time. Not a lot, perhaps ten or fifteen minutes, give or take. Made from tungsten steel, its hollow core filled with six feet of shockproof concrete."

Daklin knew from the weight of the door that was the case, but he hadn't realized to what extent Xavier had gone to contain any accidental explosion from inside the mine. Logical, since the processing plant for the finished product of E-1x was just a few hundred feet across from the mine's main entrance.

"It's engineered for high-pressure blast waves by anything up to and including nuclear detonation." Sullivan breathed unevenly with Daklin's weight dragging him down. "The blast will expand radially from points of origin until it takes the path of least resistance. The frame is bolted to the rock with high strength concrete wedge anchors, as are the anchor bolts. But E-1x is unstable. It's never been tested on this scale."

One Nut had decimated T-FLAC's bomb lab and flattened everything within a one-mile radius. The mountain contained tons of the shit. The sealed door would give them a little more time to get as far out of range as possible.

Breathing hard, River hitched her shoulder under Daklin's armpit.

The three of them shoved the door shut. It still fucking weighed a ton, despite the hydraulics. Sullivan activated the locks.

Daklin leaned against the door to drag in a few breaths of night air as River instructed, "Bring the car closer, Oliver. I don't think he can walk anymore."

Her brother moved toward a black Jeep parked at the mine entrance. How it came to be there, and any explanation on why bullets weren't flying and the security forces weren't raining Armageddon down on their heads could be saved for later. If there was a later.

"Security forces won't allow us through. And even if you

somehow parked a car right outside the front gate, we'll be shot in the process."

River licked perspiration from her upper lip. "The soldiers are gone."

"What do you mean *gone*?"

"Gone as in there's no one here. *Anywhere.* Ah, here's my brother with the car. Not that I want to scare you or anything," River said, "But Oliver can't drive."

This was evident by the way the other man hunched over the steering wheel; he drove as slowly as a grandmother did on her way to church, without turning on the headlights.

River pounded on top of the car the second her brother pulled up next to them. "Out, out, out!"

"Jesus, River." Her brother's scowl reminded Daklin of River when they'd first met. She was fearless, brave, sassy, and just about perfect.

They were going to die here. *She* was going to die here because she was dangerously impulsive and shouldn't have come in the first place. If there was a time to get something off his chest, this was it. Daklin opened his mouth just as River yanked open the passenger door, then ran around the front of the vehicle.

The high beams came on, illuminating the next massive, impenetrable obstacle.

"Help him into the front seat, Oliver. You can ride in the back."

Sullivan grabbed him none too gently by the arm and pretty

much shoved his ass into the seat, then left Daklin to figure out how to get his legs inside as he climbed in back.

River put her foot flat on the accelerator before his door was closed. It slammed shut, almost taking Daklin's good leg with it. He grinned.

"Take it easy, will you?" her brother snapped from the backseat, gripping Daklin's headrest in both hands to anchor himself.

The Jeep rocked as River increased her speed.

"Are we playing chicken, here?" Daklin asked as the gate loomed ahead. Thirty feet high, tungsten steel. It was a hundred and eighty feet and closing. He glanced over at the speedometer. Ninety miles per hour. They had two minutes before they hit.

Man, he was racking up multiple ways to die tonight. Surely, one of them would take, especially now that he had decided he wanted to live. He didn't bother bracing himself. Instead, he just relaxed back and drank in River's pale profile.

"I'm not slowing down, and I never liked chicken. Stop messing around. Open the damn gate, Oliver!"

River didn't slow down and the gate finally slid open. She passed through the opening when it was barely wide enough for the vehicle, like threading a needle, and shot through the other side like a racecar driver. The tires sprayed gravel as she wheeled out of the compound.

She shot him a cocky, strained, grin. "You were saying?

#

River wondered how long it would be before they were blown to smithereens. "How much time?"

"Twenty-three minutes," Ash responded without looking at his watch. Out of the corner of her eye, she saw his fingers, bracketing his thigh, tighten, relax, and tighten again.

Her heart, already racing, galloped unevenly. Twenty-three freaking minutes? It would take almost that long to reach the valley, five times that long to get to Abad.

"Where the fuck are all the security people?" Ash demanded as River floored the accelerator pedal. Oliver, not fond of speed, remained mute in the back seat.

"I think they were leaving when I arrived." She had to concentrate on her driving moving at this speed on the winding mountain road. "They were having a party, then I heard cars leaving about half an hour ago."

"Know anything about that, Dr. Sullivan?"

"No."

She saw Asher's jaw clench. He wasn't used to Oliver's monosyllables, and she had a very good idea that he wouldn't be as tolerant as she was. Armed to the teeth with a machine gun, a handgun ready for action in his lap, and a knife strapped on his injured leg, Ash was dressed all in black. Shocker. But it wasn't just his clothing that made him darker against the night. He was covered from head to toe in black mud. Even his hair was stiff with it.

River's jaw hurt as she ground her teeth, biting back words

she knew would be counterproductive. She'd been stunned to find Ash alone and incapacitated. He'd been lying on the cold wet floor of the mine for how damned long? *Too* long. She was absolutely livid that he was so cavalier about his own life considering how much his life meant to *her*.

She also wanted to aim a few strong words at the men who'd left him behind to die. The mother lode of all questions she would aim at Ash: if he'd sent them away because of the risk, what made *him* so damned special that he had to stay behind to be blown to hell?

This was neither the time nor the pace to ream him out, but later, later. She let out the sigh constricting her chest. There'd *be* no later. Clearly it didn't matter what anyone else said or suggested. Ash wouldn't listen. She refused to watch it play out, which was laughable in a macabre way. He hadn't given her that option, nor, she knew, *would* he. The self-righteous decision was moot.

That didn't mean she wasn't vibrating with the need to yell at him. River's fingers tightened around the steering wheel as she focused on the road. *Move, move, move*. Damn it, she couldn't press the pedal any harder to coax out more speed.

"Would you prefer them to be shooting at us right now?" Oliver asked from the back seat, matching Ash's irritation with his own mild version of sarcasm. "They had rocket launchers and automatic weapons. I'd think you'd be *grateful* we weren't all killed the second you showed your face."

River, already stretched like a rubber band with tension,

was becoming increasingly more pissed with both men. *They* were the ones starring in this shit show. She felt like one of the stagehands in a play, unexpectedly thrust into the spotlight. No rehearsal, hell, she hadn't even been given a script.

Being *shot at* was the least awful thing on the agenda right now. "I'm sure your penises are the same size guys. Lighten up."

"It's illogical to hire a fucking army," Ash said, wondering at the night's events. "only to have them all disappear at the same time. Their job was to stay and protect the facility. So the fact that they left now is damned suspect."

River thought so, too. She refrained from adding her two cents as she concentrated on keeping the vehicle on the narrow, rutted jungle road while going flat out in the amber-colored darkness. She shot a glance at the rearview mirror. Nothing behind them except black night. No showy explosion. And she was going too fast to see any animal eyes glowing in her taillights.

She gave herself a mental headshake. When that mountain blew, there'd be no time to observe anything in the rearview mirror. They'd all be toast.

Tick, tick, tick.

Oliver leaned forward, his forearm resting on the back of her seat, pushing into the back of her shoulder. In the rearview mirror, River observed the familiar tightening of her brother's lips even in the sketchy, dim lights from the dash.

Oliver was holding something back. Even as kids, she knew that face meant he wasn't telling the whole story. His IQ was high genius level, one-sixty-plus. He hated explaining himself to people he considered beneath himself intellectually, including their parents, River, and pretty much everyone else he'd ever met.

His elbow jabbed her shoulder. "Can't you go any faster, for God's sake?"

She was pushing the high-powered car to the max, foot flat on the accelerator, staring unblinkingly at the road, *willing* more speed. "Not without some divine intervention. Know any saints we could pray to?" She flexed her cramping fingers on the wheel she held too tightly, feeling as though a fire-breathing dragon rode her tail. *Tick, tick, tick.*

Trees and thick clumps of ferns flashed by in the headlights as she took one of the curves way too fast. The car shook and tipped slightly, threatening to flip. "Franco was holding Oliver. Oliver, tell him."

Asher addressed her brother without taking his eyes off the road. "Dr. Sullivan, are you going to let your sister talk for you? If Xavier called off his pack of rabid Russian watchdogs, why didn't you leave as well?"

"Apparently it bears repeating. I was a *prisoner*. I didn't know they were gone until River showed up. Before that, I knew even if I had walked out of there, I would have just been eaten in the jungle."

"That's not true," River said, just as Ash said, "Why detain you?"

"Believe me, I *wanted* to leave. He had other ideas. I was

385

working on a new delivery system for E-1x."

"That so? Something other than the Nut?"

"Look," her brother said, going directly to his I-hate-being-questioned-by-anyone mode. "I worked for four months on formulating the most expedient, least invasive explosive devices to mine *emeralds*. Then I discovered the natural explosive in a vein in the mine. A natural, *plentiful*, substance, easy to mine, and in high demand. As soon as I did that, Franco closed down the emerald operation, and marketed E-1x to the highest bidders. Terrorists all over the world." Oliver paused as River pulled a wheelie around another curve.

"I protested the use." His voice was monotone, mildly annoyed. Which meant he was annoyed big time, and was possibly about to have a meltdown. "He assured me he was selling it to countries who'd benefit from the ability to mine safely and cheaply. I realized almost immediately that was bullshit, and what they were doing was criminal. I wanted no part of it. I tried to leave. Franco put a gun to my head and told me the only way I was leaving was in a body bag. If you'd seen the look in his eyes you would've believed him, too. He's held me prisoner for two and a half years."

Wow. That was the longest speech she'd ever heard from her brother. Being taciturn with bouts of total silence was Oliver's usual default. River remembered the small waterfall coming up on the right, and adroitly avoided a sheet of water in the road produced from the continual overspray. The tires skittered, spinning out, before regaining traction.

Too bad Oliver's story was total bullshit. River knew Ash would see through it without her help. Her brother would soon be hanging himself with his lies. River glanced at him in the rearview mirror, trying to warn him to tell the truth. Asher concentrated on the ribbon of road ahead as though he were the one driving.

"Franco scared the shit out of me. He's a psychopath. I just kept my nose down and did my job."

"Do you have access to his customer base? Who has how much? And do you know how to defuse this shit?" He said it as though he damn well expected Oliver to tell him everything. Maybe not now, this very second, but sooner rather than later. River knew her brother well enough to know the other thing Oliver hated: anyone telling him what to do. He had his own way of doing things, and his own timetable.

"And if I do? What happens to me then?"

"Tell the truth. Tell us everything you know, and we'll protect you from Franco's associates. T-FLAC has an impressive reach."

"Franco's dead. So how the hell can you protect me from people whose identity you don't know?"

"Rest assured, with or without your help, we'll know their names soon enough, Dr. Sullivan."

River glanced at Oliver's face in the mirror. His lips were still pinched, corners turned down, his brow furrowed in the tenacious bulldog-look she knew so well. Stubbornness was a

Sullivan family character trait. And from what she'd learned about Ash in the last few days, bullheadedness was a character trait he shared, too. He was the alpha dog, and he clearly didn't take kindly to being less than one hundred percent in charge.

"I don't believe you will," Oliver said.

"Come on, Oliver. Try to cooperate a little, will you?"

The road straightened out. Jungle, jungle, shiny eyes now and then. She'd bet Ash wasn't aware that he was digging his fingers into his leg. The fact that he was not fighting physically fit must be incredibly frustrating to him. Dealing with an unpredictable explosive, something he couldn't control, must also piss him off. And Oliver being uncooperative must be exacerbating his pissed-off-ness. They were batting a thousand tonight.

River didn't think Oliver was going to answer. He didn't, of course. Instead, he merely said, "These are not the most optimal circumstances to have this conversation."

"We might not get another chance. Do you know any names? Places? Anything?"

Ash didn't know her brother was contrary as well as determined. Oliver would say black was white just for the hell of it, then five minutes later, he'd forget he'd had that argument and be puzzled that the other person was annoyed with him. She spared a quick glance at Ash's face, illuminated by the dash lights. His jaw was tight. A muscle jerked in his cheek, and his eyes glittered.

"I know a lot about any number of things. You must be aware that communications in and out of the valley were jammed.

That's because Franco didn't want anyone communicating unless he authorized it. He's always been paranoid that way. He's the only one who had any intercourse with the buyers. He didn't even allow Eliseo or Trinidad to talk to customers."

"If you don't know who Xavier sold to, Dr. Sullivan, then how did you know he was selling to terrorists?"

Oliver gave Ash silence as an answer.

"When you do start talking, you might want to think about your answers. We have the hard drives from all three computers in the house, but they're highly encrypted. I don't suppose you know the passwords?"

"I do not." Oliver missed the sarcasm. "Once I ascertain that the authorities don't consider me accountable for Franco's actions, and with a lawyer present, I'll be happy to tell you what I know."

"Fuck." Ash braced one hand on the dash, leaned forward to get a better look at something that caught his attention in the night sky, and transferred his gripping hand from his own thigh to hers.

Holy crap he had a strong grip.

"Slow down. But be ready to punch it."

What the hell had he seen? River couldn't see further than the edge of the damn headlights in front of her. Her heart ricocheted in her chest. No one back there had taken potshots at them, *so far*, although she anticipated the high-pitched screech of a bullet hitting the car at any moment. She had no intention of slowing or stopping until they got somewhere safe. It took all of her concentration not to flip the car.

"Faster, faster, faster. For God sake, River!" Oliver's voice was tight with tension. "Can't you make this thing go any faster?"

"No," she told him tersely. "I can't." She couldn't afford to spare Ash a glance as the jungle on either side of the winding road flashed by in the high beams. Her foot pressed flat on the accelerator, which, in her Tesla, would've been too fast for her to handle on this narrow, curvy road with its steep grade, potholes and pockets of water. In the truck, though, flooring it meant she could just hit ninety, and that was jarring every bone she possessed.

"River," Ash said urgently, his fingers digging painfully into the muscle of her thigh. "Stop the car."

She wished everyone would make up their damned freaking minds. "Now?"

"Yeah. Chopper's going to land on the road ahead. Angle so that you can go around it if you need to."

"What chopp--?" A familiar *whop-whop-whop* pulsed against her eardrums. "Oh, God." Had Franco's people come back to finish her off in another helicopter? She was concentrating so hard, she'd been oblivious. Now that she *did* hear the familiar noise approaching, fear sliced like a hot knife through her barely-maintained façade of calm. Her palms grew instantly slick on the steering wheel. Remembering the bloodbath at the hacienda, she couldn't breathe.

Instead of braking, she crushed the pedal as hard as she could, flooring it. Not that it did a damn bit of good. "Why aren't you shooting?"

"Stop for fucksake. It's my men. The *good* guys."

"Well, it's damn nice of them to decide to come back for you. About freaking high time!" When Ash said the helicopter was going to land up ahead, he meant *now*. Slamming her foot on the brake, River hoped she could stop in time. The rear end fishtailed.

The same huge military-style helicopter with dull camouflage paint that she'd seen on Oliver's monitor landed lightly in the center of the road. The whirling rotors decapitated small trees and shrubs. Leaves and branches flew in a rain of debris. With annoyed cawing and flapping of wings, a flock of parrots catapulted into the night sky.

Heart pounding, River managed to bring the vehicle to a jarring stop a few yards shy of the helicopter.

"Impressive." Ash popped his door. "Move it."

Armed men dressed in black spilled from the open door of the helicopter and ran to the car.

"She took a defensive driving class for some weird reason known only to River," Oliver stated matter-of-factly.

"I had a psychic premonition that I'd be on the run on a mountain jungle road in South America," River shot back. The engine pinged and popped when she turned off the truck. She glanced at Ash. His face was bone white and sweat made rivulets of dark mud down his cheeks. "Stay where you are. I'll come around to help you."

He held up a hand. "I'm good."

Right. His men were racing toward them. He wouldn't want them to see him as anything other than their leader. River opened her door and got out, while a couple of men went to Ash.

"Ram!" Recognizing him, she wrapped her arms around his waist and hugged him tightly. Like Ash, Ram's body was rock hard and unyielding. She'd been sure he'd died outside the hacienda and she was relieved to see him. He was still covered with dried blood. "I'm so happy to see you," she shouted. "Are you all right?"

He signaled okay with his fingers, then tucked her under his arm and, bending low to avoid the spinning blades, hustled her between car and the helicopter. He hoisted her up to another man inside, as her hair whipped violently around her face. Climbing in after her, Ram helped her get situated on a bench seat opposite the open door.

"Eighteen minutes," Ash yelled as he clambered inside. "Get us the fuck airborne!"

TWENTY

B ranches and leaves thrashed in the rotor's high winds, just beyond the door as they started their ascent. River's eyes watered. "Isn't anyone going to close the door?"

"No door," Ram told her. Was he purposely blocking her line of sight to Ash? He and Oliver, having gotten in, were at the far end of the large open space. She motioned him to move aside, but Ram shook his head.

"He's in a shitload of pain, ma'am. He won't want you seeing him like that."

"I've been with him for the last few days. I want him next to me. Can you make that happen?"

Her hands shook so badly, she kept dropping the latch for her seatbelt. Ram gave her a small smile as he helped her secure the buckle. "Looks like you didn't have to ask. He's headed your way."

Ash, balancing on his feet as nimbly as a tightrope walker in the open space between them, looked at the big watch on his wrist, then spoke into a lip mic. Or maybe he was talking to himself, "Seventeen minutes. We need a minimum fifty miles between us and that blast. A hundred would be better."

The helicopter lifted above the swaying treetops and up

into the star bright sky. The only lights inside where those on the instrument panel, which cast an eerie green glow on the pilot's face.

Sitting behind the pilot, flanked by two men dressed all in black as the others were, her brother looked around nervously. He said something to the man to his left, and the guy responded. It was impossible for River to hear anything other than the rotors and the wind.

Ash spoke into his mic, apparently to the man her brother had just spoken to. "Repeat." He paused to listen. "Supersonic over-pressurization shock wave? Yeah. No shit. Tell Dr. Sullivan to tell us something we don't know. Strap yourselves in, ladies. Haul ass." Within a few seconds, Ash flopped onto the bench seat beside her, his legs extended. She touched his hand to get his attention, then, leaving her hand resting lightly over his, she mouthed, "Where are we going?"

"Abad."

He didn't need to add, *if we make it out of the blast zone.*

He slipped his hand free of hers to rub his jaw. He looked pale, drawn, exhausted. She felt the loss of physical contact as if he'd slapped her. Her chest aching, she swallowed a murmur of disappointment. "Assuming we make it."

"Positive outcome's unlikely." His grim tone matched the faces in the helicopter. Everyone looked tense. They all knew what was about to happen. In her case, River figured ignorance was bliss. "I'm not spending the last eighteen minutes—-"

"Seventeen now."

"Fine. Keep counting. My last few minutes will not be spent, Ash Daklin, thinking that I'm going to die. I'm going to assume we'll live." She could only imagine the ramifications of what a supersonic over-pressurization shock wave actually *meant*. From Ash's tight expression, it wasn't good. "Once we get to Abad, what then?"

"For you? Portland. We have the T-FLAC Challenger at a private airstrip, ready to go wheels up as soon as we load you onboard."

Ah. So he couldn't wait to get rid of the inconvenient luggage that was her. "And you?"

He shrugged. "Wherever work takes me."

"How long until we get to Abad?"

"Thirty-five minutes or so, depending on the blast and the tailwind."

Or until they blew up.

Tick.

Tick.

Tick.

She glanced over at her brother. His pale hair waved around his head, his boney hands knitted in his lap. His glasses had a crack across one lens, and he tapped his foot. Oblivious to his surroundings, Oliver usually tapped his left foot while attempting to figure out equations. Knowing Oliver, he was mentally figuring out, to the second, when the blast would hit the helicopter.

He was family, but he wasn't an easy person to love. Her parents had given her the task to always take care of him, keep him from harm. They couldn't possibly have anticipated *this* bizarre turn of events. She turned to look at Ash. "And Oliver?"

"He'll go to T-FLAC Headquarters in Montana for debriefing. He knows Xavier's business inside and out." His eyes glinted in the semi-darkness, and a muscle clenched in his jaw. "He's got valuable intel for us. With Xavier dead, he's one of the few people who can tell us what we need to know about manufacturing details and Xavier's customer base."

The *whop-whop-whop-whop* of the whirling rotors beat loudly against her eardrums. Strands of her hair stung her cheeks as the wind whipped through the open door.

Reaching up, Ash snagged a pair of headsets off the wall over their heads, and handed her one. When River slipped them on, the sound of the rotors disappeared, and all she heard was her own rapid heartbeat pulsing in her ears.

Leaning over her, he cinched the belt more tightly across her lap. Her lips accidentally brushed his ear. She tasted mud and didn't care. He froze for a second before straightening and reaching up for a couple of facemasks. Taking the one he offered to her, River put it on as he did the same. Over the edge of his mask, Ash's pale eyes looked otherworldly in his mud-smeared face.

The heat of his arm against hers as he pulled his own belt low across his lap, made River realize how cold her skin was. Nerves. It certainly wasn't cold. Hell, even in the middle of the night, the temperature had to be in the eighties.

His elbow brushed her shoulder as he put the noise cancelling headgear over his own ears. Beneath her lashes, as she pretended to fiddle with the webbed belt across her lap, she observed Ash's hands, which he placed on his slightly spread knees. He had beautiful hands, despite a couple of scars and right now, dried mud. She wanted to take his hand and thread her fingers through his. She wanted to lean her head on his arm, so close beside her, and close her eyes.

She wanted him to say a lot of stupid promises he wouldn't mean and wouldn't keep. It was better this way. A clean break.

She envisioned them standing three feet apart on the tarmac, the plane's engine revving impatiently as they said awkward goodbyes. Because, honestly how could it not be uncomfortable? *Thanks for the great sex. Awesome sex actually.*

"Brace yourself," Ash shouted, then said a low, "Fuck it," and shifted to wrap both arms around her, dragging her half way across his body, surrounding her like a steel cage, one large hand covering the back of her head.

Despite the belt still harnessing her, cutting off her circulation, River wasn't about to complain as she slid her arms around his waist. Hanging onto the back of his shirt with both hands, she pressed her face to his broad chest. He smelled of fresh sweat, mud, and a faint trace of honey. Squeezing her eyes shut, she buried her nose against the hard beating of his heart and the dried mud on his chest.

#

"Brace!" he shouted over her head. "Blast wave incoming. Brace. Brace. Brace!"

The explosion was his best yet. E-1x was a HE—a high-order explosive. HE detonated to produce defining supersonic over-pressurized shock waves. The jarring force hit the body of the Apache with the force of a high-speed freight train going at supersonic speed. *Bam.*

Up. Down. Around, sideways, and vertical the bird tumbled in the fiery sky while the passengers and crew held on for dear life.

Spectacularly large, impressively bright, deafeningly loud. Energy released from the explosion radiated outward from the mountain in all directions, at speeds of up to nine kilometers per second. The burst of light flashed and wavered behind his closed lids, and even with the noise-cancelling headset, the supersonic blast hurt his eardrums.

The chopper rocked and rolled, pitching as if on an angry sea. The armor plating might help. *Some.* Only if they put enough distance between themselves and the epicenter of the explosion. If they were too fucking close, nothing would save them.

Not. A. Damned. Fucking. Thing.

His arms clamped so tightly around River, he was afraid he'd break her ribs. It would be the least of her problems; since there was a damned good chance the concussive blast would knock them out of the fucking sky or melt their guts to soup.

With every hard knock of his heart, Daklin waited for the

velocity of the shock wave to impart more energy than the object it passed through, be it a solid concrete wall, or their fucking vital organs.

Were they out of reach? He'd soon know if his body compressed and he was dead. He had no worries for himself, but he definitely had them for her.

Death by his own lethal explosion was his chosen path. In no lifetime would he have taken this route if he'd have known the blast would kill her too. Fuck it all to hell and back.

It would have been one hell of a way to die. Yet River, smaller, lighter, more fucking vulnerable, would die first. He'd be *aware* of her dying. Fate was playing the cruelest of tricks, that he would, once again in his sorry life, know the gut- wrenching pain that came with heartbreak, grief, and regret.

As the blast wave passed over them or near enough to impact them, it would destroy everything. The supersonic wall of air would leave a near vacuum in its wake. Like the sonic wave created by an atomic bomb, it would shatter everything and leave nothing behind. He counted off the seconds before their bodies became severely compressed, followed almost immediately by an equally massive opposing depressurizing force. They were about to become human pancakes or, alternatively, human confetti.

Were they in the triple point? The mach stem formation would occur when the blast wave reflected off the ground and the reflection caught up with the original shock front, creating a high-pressure zone that extended from the ground up to the triple point at the edge of the blast wave.

One.

So fucking far, so good. They weren't pancakes. Yet.

Two.

The explosion wasn't over just yet. Air immediately rushed in to fill the atmospheric void left behind by the blast wave, pulling careening debris and objects past the open door of the chopper and back toward the source of the explosion. The annihilated mountain range.

Three.

Even strapped in, Daklin's body lifted and twisted as the wind tried to rip River from his arms, and tear him from his seat. Her face was pressed against his chest, her arms wrapped as tightly around him as his were around her.

Four.

Barotrauma could destroy any air filled organs—lungs, ears, stomach—and yank at joints and ligaments where tissues of different densities met. Hemorrhaging. Organ rupture. The effects of an explosion of this magnitude on the human body would force bodily fluids into the brain and skull.

Jesus. Daklin's arms crushed River's slender bones against his chest.

Five.

Were they far enough away to avoid the brunt of it? The waves would dissipate as they traveled. The only thing that could protect them from the shock waves was distance.

Her teeth bit into his shoulder as he pressed her head against him. No up. No down. It was like being tossed around inside a cement mixer as the world spun and twisted inside the sun. The chopper bounced on air. Hard.

With River held in a death grip in his arms, Daklin buried his face against her hair. *Don't die. Don't die. Don't fucking die.*

"Clear," he heard the pilot say. The chopper dropped a jarring two hundred feet before it evened out. Daklin's arms tightened around River. He'd loosened his harness so that he could hold onto her through the turbulence. Choking clouds of dust and debris swirled around inside the chopper. They all wore their masks pulled up like bandits. Daklin adjusted River's mask so it came just under her beautiful eyes. His heart clenched with profound relief that they'd made it. *She'd* made it. They were fortunate the blast hadn't liquefied them. Extremely fucking fortunate. "Everyone have solid organs and all their teeth?" Daklin asked through his comm, as he ran his hand over the back of River's head, then lifted the headset from her ears.

"Okay?" he asked.

Eyes dazed, she raised her head and nodded.

He wasn't letting go. Not until he absolutely had to. "ETA?" he asked into his comm. "Seven minutes."

"Make it five. Give me a visual." He needed to see his handiwork.

The chopper turned, angling to give him a view of the explosion site. Through billowing brown smoke, fragmented debris, and thick dust, he observed a glowing, flat plain. It was a new geological feature. Hours earlier, the eight-thousand-foot-high Qhapaq Mountain peak had shadowed the valley. For miles beneath them, as far as he could see, towers of red and orange flame shot into the dark night sky. The air vibrated as another pocket of E-1x exploded, followed in quick succession by a half dozen more explosions from deep within the earth; the gift that kept on giving.

"Fucking A." Feeling the satisfaction of a job well done, he was also painfully aware that his biggest misstep was gripping his shirt, trusting him to keep her safe. He might not have gotten her killed as he'd done Josh, but by God, he seemed to have done just about everything he could to keep her in the fucking line of fire.

Fail. Fail. Fucking epic fail. It wouldn't be fair to voice any of his hopes and desires. Giving voice to what was in his heart would put her in the untenable position of telling him the party was over and that she wanted nothing more to do with his sorry self. What bright, beautiful woman in her right mind would want a broken alcoholic with a dubious future?

His chest ached with pending loss as he brushed his lips over her hair. He took one more satisfied look at his masterpiece of sharp explosions, billowing flames, and annihilation before the chopper peeled away. The pride he felt at the destruction was a reminder that there was *always* collateral damage, no matter how hard he tried to mitigate it. It was a sharp reminder that he shouldn't form attachments to anything that could be destroyed by his actions.

Josh.

River.

"We're done here," he said into his lip mic. "Head out." The helicopter swooped in a wide circle, flying through the dust-choked darkness toward Abad.

#

Even though the motion indicated they'd straightened out, River still kept her eyes squeezed shut against the stinging debris swirling around inside the helicopter. It was one hell of a way to get a freaking face peel.

The viselike grip of Ash's arms was all but cutting off her circulation, and she shifted to get a little more breathing room from his implacably steely grip. Instead of releasing her, his arms tightened. Considering the air quality, breathing was highly overrated, anyway.

"Clear in a minute. Keep your eyes closed."

River forced her clenched muscles to relax against the hard wall of Ash's chest. Despite the mask over her nose and mouth, and her face pressed against the solid column of his throat, she coughed against the toxic swirling mix of thick dust and hot, gritty sand. Everyone on board had the same problem. Coughing and hacking, their lungs being scoured from the inside. Still, there were whoops of triumph as the operatives got a look at their handiwork.

Ears ringing, chest aching, she gripped the back of Ash's

shirt as the helicopter bounced on heated air.

It wasn't just the people of Los Santos who'd had their lives irreversibly changed. The past few days had irrevocably changed hers, too, so much, that now she couldn't imagine walking away from him and never seeing him again.

But did that feeling, that certainty that she needed to see him again, mean they had a future? If they did, what, if anything, could that future hold? A few nights together? No. Not enough. More than that? Zero likelihood. One look at him as he coolly and with great interest surveyed the destruction below them had given her all the information she needed to answer her question.

He was his job.

And once she was no longer connected to this job, she would no longer be connected to him. Their time together had been too short, too full of issues, for him to form the kind of bond she'd instantly felt for him. That visceral reaction had been quick and a first for her. There was no need to put him in the uncomfortable position of fending off her unwanted declarations of love. Dear God. River jerked in his hold.

She was in *love* with this tough, battle-scarred warrior who had several massive freaking chips on his shoulders.

The realization was so huge, that she was still reeling from it when the helicopter landed with a light thump some time later. Ash's arms tightened around her briefly, before he released her. The separation pulled at a level deeper than her skin, leaving River bereft and filled with a combination of sadness and elation.

Sadness that it was almost time for them to go their separate ways, elation that they were at least alive to walk away from each other unscathed. Or, for her part, unscathed physically.

Her foolish heart, another matter altogether, was shattered by what she knew was coming. By the hard set of his jaw, and the steely determination in his eyes, he appeared unaffected by their apocalyptic surroundings.

Unaffected by *her*.

Tall, broad, and filthy, Ash looked like the fallen angel she'd first thought him to be. River drank him in, committing to memory his broad shoulders, the tilt of his head, the way his dark hair spiked as he'd tried to get the muddy strands off his face. The liquid Mediterranean blue of his eyes told her absolutely nothing.

Asher Daklin was the whole package. Her heart physically ached with wanting him. Not just wanting him physically, which was a given, but wanting *him*.

Stay.

The word repeated, over and over in her head, turning the chopchopchop of the helicopter blades into a plea of *Stay. Stay. Stay.*

Want me as much as I want you. If you did, you'd stay.

Of course, he wouldn't. To her, the past few days were indelibly imprinted on her synapses, events etched for life upon her heart, mind, and soul. To him, this had merely been an interlude while he did his job. She'd been an enjoyable bonus, nothing more.

Drawing in a shallow breath, she choked on the hot,

clogged air. The night sky glowed an eerie orange as showers of burning embers swirled from the sky like rain.

Damned if she'd waste the last few precious moments with Ash moping for the unattainable. River unsnapped the harness, and got unsteadily to her feet as he did the same. A thousand questions and pleas fluttered inside her like a swarm of bees. Knowing how useless it would be to voice any of them, especially *now*, the words remained an unyielding, unsaid buzz within her. "Okay to say goodbye to my brother?"

Coughing, Ash readjusted her face mask, then his own. "Wait till we're on the tarmac. You can speak to him then. Wheels up ASAP, the fires are burning this way."

Without a door covering the wide opening, River could look directly over the leaping flames, and realized just how close those fires were. Probably less than two miles away, and eating trees at a furious rate. She'd never seen a fire this big, nor been close enough to a wildfire to feel its scalding heat on her skin. They'd gone from one intense situation to the next with barely a breath drawn in between. Surges of adrenaline and erratic heartbeats were becoming her new norm. She wondered briefly how she'd adjust to sitting at her drawing board listening to the Mamas and Papas once she got home.

The stink of burning wood, wet vegetation, and the unpleasantly sweet smell of burning flesh permeated the air. The sky rained fire. Narrowing her eyes against the acrid smoke, River looked out over fiery chaos. "Can the pilots take off with zero visibility like this?"

"Ours can." A blast of blistering air surrounded them as soon as they cleared the shelter of the helicopter. God, she'd stepped straight into the depths of Hell. The thick choking smoke made her eyes and nose water, despite the mask. The world around them was an inferno, a living, breathing blaze destroying everything in its path.

As everyone disembarked, they ran. More people joined them on the runway, presumably Ash's men who'd been waiting in Abad. The airstrip was in the middle of nowhere. No buildings visible, only the large helicopter behind them, and the white shimmer of two sleek jets parked, ready to take off midway down the runway. The aircraft and humans were right in the middle of a ring of fast approaching fire.

Grabbing her upper arm in a death grip, almost cutting off her circulation, Ash yelled, "Faster!" over the snap crackle and pop of the leaping flames.

Running flat out, he pulled, pushed and half-carried her toward the planes as loud explosions rent the air. Ear- shattering blasts reverberated as the earth was torn apart from the inside.

If they made it out of there, it would be a freaking miracle.

River kept up despite Ash's longer strides. Suddenly he slammed his forearm across her chest, stopping her mid-stride. It was like crashing into a solid brick wall.

"*Shit.*"

Shit indeed. She saw, felt and heard the same thing he did.

407

There was a massive roar and a super-heated blast of air as one of the planes three hundred yards away burst into flame, spewing chunks of metal and debris high into the air, dangerously close to the people on the tarmac.

Wrapping his arm around her waist, Ash switched direction and propelled her toward the second plane. As embers rained down on them, he constantly brushed them off her hair and face. "Delta and Echo teams, take the chopper. The rest of you with me. *Go*, for fucksake.

Men, black silhouetted against orange and gold, reversed to race back to the helicopter.

Ahead, all she saw of Oliver was his pale hair amongst the men in black surrounding him as they ran up the steps of the second plane. Several groups converged to board the same plane as her brother.

Ash shoved her ahead of him, catching her as she stumbled up the steep steps to the plane. "Close the hatch," he instructed Ram, who waited for them. "Wheels up," he said into his comm. Ram pulled the door shut, sealing them inside. "Push it." Powerful engines vibrated beneath her feet, ready to take off. Thank God.

The interior of the private jet was air-conditioned, furnished with plush creams and tans, and as far from the noisy, dirty, explosion-marked helicopter as transportation could possibly be. Ash nudged her to the back of the plane as River took several tentative breaths.

Her lungs protested, but she kept breathing in the clean air as a powerful ventilation system filtered out the smoke and particles that had come inside with them.

"*Go*," he ordered. The plane taxied down the runway even as people found their seats.

The plane seated about twenty comfortably. Four wide seats faced each other in groups on either side of the aisle.

River dropped into the seat Ash indicated, and he sat beside her. When she fumbled with clumsy fingers to fasten her seat belt, he did it for her. Quick, efficient. Then he did his own.

The take-off was shockingly fast, throwing her back against her seat as the powerful engines catapulted them into the sky above the inferno. She was not sorry to see the last of Los Santos, or Cosio. Now, if only her heart would stop beating in fight or flight mode, she'd be able to draw a normal breath.

Ash stood, grabbing a couple of bottles of water from a compartment in the bulkhead, twisting off the top of one, then handing it to her. He drank his own in two gulps.

Barely pausing between swallows, River finished the entire bottle, then wiped her chin as he handed her a second. The membranes in her throat felt parched and it actually hurt to swallow. She felt better after downing the second bottle. "Thanks, I needed that."

The plane was still climbing, and a glance out of the window showed the fire beneath them visible as flicks of orange through a thick blanket of gray smoke. The sky was lit with swirling orange rain even at thirty thousand feet. "It's going to be a while before I even want to *look* at a cozy fire while I drink my hot chocolate."

He gave her a faint smile. "You've held up well."

"I wasn't given options," she argued, loving the way his pale eyes roamed her face, and the slight curve of his lips. Her face must be as dirty as his, but she didn't care. Sweaty and hot, they both smelled of smoke. She'd kill for a shower. Soapy skin. Clean hair. She'd rinse. Repeat. And do it again. If he could be in that first long, hot shower with her, she'd never get out of it. "Is your life always this exciting? It's freaking *exhausting*."

"You'll come down from the adrenaline high soon. You'll sleep really well."

"I figured, but right now I'm still wired. Oh. I almost forgot. I took pictures of those photographs of that redhead I found in Franco's study." Lifting her hip, she slid her phone out of her back pocket. The screen was shattered, but when she turned it on, the phone flared to life. "I don't suppose it matters any more now that he's dead."

He held out his hand. "I'll take a look."

Scrolling through her camera roll, River located the first of three pictures, then handed him the phone. Their hands brushed and her heart kicked into high gear with longing.

As filthy and sweaty as they both were, she'd do him right now, right here. "I presume we're on our way to Montana?" A few more hours with Ash was an unexpected bonus, even if they were in a confined space with dozens of his men surrounding them.

"Yeah. There'll be a briefing." He glanced over at her. "It will be brief, I promise; then you'll be on your way home." His attention returned to her phone. "It's hard to see anything with the screen shattered. Wait! What the fuck! This is Catherine Seymour." His pale eyes glittered in the screen's light. He used his thumb to scroll to the next image.

"Sending image for confirmation," he said, clearly speaking into his comm as he thumbed in a series of numbers and then hit send. "Yeah. Catherine Seymour. For fucksake, *she's* Xavier's illegitimate daughter. Her involvement in this clusterfuck connects the rest of the dots and puts a whole other spin on things. Yes. ASAP. No doubt. It's her."

Tangling his fingers in her hair, Ash pulled her in for a hard and fast kiss. His firm lips left her breathless and wanting more. The kiss, combined with the G-force as they catapulted through the sky, caused her stomach to jump and her heart to race.

"Great job." Smiling, he sat back. The curve of his mouth and the way his gaze lingered on her face made River's heart pinch. "She's the missing link that glues this entire goatfuck together."

Now that she didn't need the massive surges of adrenaline to deal with her body's fight or flight responses, River felt the overwhelming urge to puke, or cry. Too much emotion and fear in a short amount of time had drained her. A good cry would relieve some of the tension that had increased exponentially with each hour of this long ass day. Folding her arms, she hugged herself tightly to stop the fine tremors that were starting to make her shake. "Who is she to you?"

"A long-term T-FLAC operative. A rogue operative and a traitor. She was captured, sent to a super max and managed an almost impossible escape. She was killed on T-FLAC property several years ago. Tying her to Xavier puts a whole different spin on his motivation and his hatred for our organization."

"*She* was also Oliver's girlfriend, I suspect his first." Oliver had been tangled up with not only a terrorist but with Xavier's daughter, a rogue operative. Guilty or not. "You'll throw the book at him, won't you?" she said, hugging herself more tightly as she came down from her adrenaline high. Her trembling intensified.

"He has a lot to answer for."

The answer to her question was yes. She glanced out of the window. Black night, tinged with a rosy glow on the horizon, stretched as far as she could see as the plane leveled out. "We appear to be at cruising altitude. Is it okay if I go and talk to him now?" *Before I fall apart.*

"How about a shower first?"

"Of course, there's a shower on board," she said dryly with a quick glance to the front of the plane. She'd rather do just about anything right now rather than confront her brother. "I'd like nothing more. But I should really talk to Oliver first."

"It's a twelve hour flight." Ash rose. "He'll be available when you've had a chance to freshen up and get some sleep."

"Believe me, putting the conversation off won't make it any more palatable," River said dryly. "But maybe I will clean up first.

Then I'll talk to my brother. Perhaps by then, I'll feel more civil." It would probably take several years for her to feel anything other than livid. But half an hour would just have to do. "Which way?"

TWENTY-ONE

D aklin reached down to help her unsnap her seat belt. Fuck, she was shaking like a leaf. He wanted to wrap her in his arms and hold on to her, to assure her everything was okay now. But he couldn't keep her from talking to her brother, and he admired her for rising to the unpleasant task.

Up front, his men talked quietly, the soft sound of their voices mingling with the hum of the Challenger's powerful engines.

River got to her feet, and he didn't move out of the way, leaving them just a couple of feet apart. She scratched her face with a trembling hand, leaving a pale smear in the dirt. "Is the water in the shower hot?"

He nodded. "Of course."

"Is there room for two?"

Daklin touched her cold, dusty cheek, then slid his hand around the back of her neck to draw her closer. Her grey eyes were as clear as water, despite the glimmer of fear in them. And even though the danger for her had passed, he knew just how fucking close he'd come to losing her. Cupping the back of her head, he murmured, "How're you holding up?" Just because the things he *wanted* to say were dammed up in his chest, and he needed time to process them, that didn't mean he was going to hold off touching her.

Her tired smile sliced into his heart. "Ask me in a week."

In a week she'd be home, and he'd be on to his next op. "I have a more immediate solution. Come with me."

"Anywhere."

They both fucking well knew he had nowhere to take her. Nor should he. He had bugger-all to offer her, except these last few hours. They'd have to last him a lifetime.

He selfishly and helplessly gave in to the overwhelming need to make love to her one last time. Sliding open the door that was immediately behind their seats, he nudged her inside the aft cabin. "Come in here." He slid the door shut with a final *thunk,* followed by a decisive click of the lock. The small room enclosed them in darkness and privacy. Gathering River's face between his hands, he crushed her mouth under his with a hot, open-mouthed kiss. Sweet. Moist. Delicious.

As he wrapped her in his arms a little too tightly, Daklin wanted to give her everything, but the best he could offer was a few hours. He wanted to warm her with the heat of his mouth, soothe her with his body, free her mind by consuming her every thought with his touch.

She was his. For now.

He'd take what he could get. Savor it.

Turning her in his arms, he closed his mouth on hers as he reverse-walked her to the foot of one of two single beds. With one

415

knee on the mattress, he lowered her down, still kissing her, because he couldn't not kiss her.

"We really need that shower," she murmured, breathless when he let her up for air. Her fingers were tangled in his hair, and one slender leg was wrapped around his hip as they lay half on, half off the narrow bed.

"*Eventually*. Going dark," he said, before turning off and removing his earpiece. He'd almost forgotten he was still broadcasting to his team on board and his support team on the ground. That had *never* happened in all the years he'd been an operative. Jesus. She consumed him. Made him irrational.

He tossed the comm in the general direction of the built-in table between the beds. "I love the taste of you," he whispered against her ear, nuzzling the swirls and making her shudder. "I love the smell of your skin." He trailed his tongue down the tendon of her throat, making her neck arch, and her fingers tighten in his hair. "Here." Across her collar bone. "And here." The soft upper slope of her left breast. "And here." He nibbled her nipple through the cloth of her shirt, as he bunched the fabric for better access.

She smelled of smoke, and the underlying, achingly familiar floral scent that would always remind him of her. Of this.

It seemed forever, and almost magically quick before they were both naked. Her skin, warm and resilient, seemed to melt into him as if they were two halves of a whole. A living, breathing entity dependent on the other for survival.

When he slid into her, her body opened, wet and

welcoming to receive him. It was perfect, so fucking right that he had to freeze for a moment to relish what he held in his arms. To treasure this miracle of a woman. "You're perfection, River Sullivan."

"Silly man."

Daklin made love to her slowly, as if he had all the time in the world. He drew it out, loving her, imprinting her on his synapses for all time.

Afterwards she lay on top of him, lazily playing with his hair as she pressed small soft kisses all over his face. "I don't want to sleep, but I might anyway. Will you keep me awake?"

"You can sleep when you get to Portland." God, his voice was unrecognizable. Harsh. Cold. Everything he wasn't feeling.

He felt the subtle change in her body as she responded to the tone of his voice. "You're right." Her voice was brisk as she rolled away from him. "But you need sleep more than I do. You have a big day ahead. I'll grab a quick shower, and come back to join you."

Daklin grabbed her hand when she stood beside the bed. "It's against T-FLACs policy to shower alone on board. Waste of water."

River laughed softly. "You and Ram in the shower together? I can't imagine it."

"*Us* in the shower." He rolled off the bed to lead her by the hand into the small bathroom. Not turning on the light he cranked on the shower, and while the water steamed up the room, he pressed her against the wall to kiss her. It wasn't enough. It would never be enough. He'd never be satisfied, never be satiated.

But this was all he could have.

#

"Can I talk to him alone for a few minutes?"

After a leisurely shower, he'd found her some clean clothes, black on black on black and a pair of boots that almost fit. River wasn't going to quibble. With her hair finger-combed, her cheeks flushed and her mouth tender, there was no mistaking she'd been having wild monkey sex for the last hour. But she didn't give a damn who noticed.

"You can talk, but not alone." Ash smiled.

"What?"

He ran his thumb over her bottom lip. "You look like a bad-ass...until anyone sees this soft mouth."

"This soft mouth is about to tell my brother some hard truths."

He unlocked the door and pushed it open. "You'll have a captive audience."

"Good. That'll give me better odds of him actually *listening*."

They headed to the front of the plane where Oliver slumped at the window seat, hemmed in by three operatives. Others were stretched out in comfortable chairs, footrests up, their eyes closed. River had never seen more unrelaxed men pretending to sleep in her life. They all looked as though they were poised to jump to their feet any moment, guns drawn. She couldn't imagine living on the edge like that. Constantly alert for danger. Perpetually knowing that their job would kill them, probably sooner than later.

She swallowed regret.

The warmth of Ash's hand on the small of her back reminded her that he was alive, and *here*. And she'd better not waste a single one of their remaining hours together.

"Give River and her brother a few minutes."

The men who had Oliver hemmed in rose and passed them in the aisle. They didn't go far, and they all had the steely-eyed focus she recognized as *de rigueur* for operatives.

River shot them a smile, then skirted the aisle seat and coffee table to stand near her brother. She had no idea where to even freaking start.

He hadn't had the benefit of a shower, and he smelled pungently of smoke and dust. Only his eyes showed some life as he swiveled his head, slowly, to look up at her.

There was total disinterest in his gaze. "What do you want, River?"

Even though his attitude didn't surprise her, it still hurt. "To see how you're holding up."

Red-rimmed eyes, a darker gray than her own, telegraphed his annoyance. "How do you think I'm holding up, for Christ sake? My life's work just got blown to hell."

Striving to keep her tone moderate, just as she always had with him, she gave him a steady look. "Your life's work was creating explosives for *terrorists*, Oliver. I would think that's a small price to pay to save the rest of the world."

"Neurotic people like you don't grasp the complexities of what someone like me is capable of. I'm not wasting my time discussing my work with someone who can't even grasp the fundamentals. Go away. You're hovering."

Telling herself that it was the Asperger's making him sound so abrupt and that he didn't mean to be insulting, she swallowed her anger. Just like she'd done all their lives. Any reciprocal rude retort would fall on deaf ears. "As far as these men are concerned your life's work was *criminal*."

Oliver's face was pale under the smudges, but nothing could hide his closed, mutinous expression. As much as she loved him, she wanted to smack that intractable attitude right out of him.

"Still hovering. No. Wait." He got unsteadily to his feet, holding out his arms. "I'm sorry, Riv. This whole situation--it's stressful for both of us. Give me a hug. That'll make us both feel better."

Very much doubting it, River hesitated. She didn't *want* a hug from the adult Oliver, who was someone she didn't know or particularly like. She wanted a hug goodbye from the tall, gangly boy who'd taught her how to ride a bike, who'd taught her to hot-wire a car, who'd been a part of her life when things had been sane and happy. When their parents had been alive.

As she looked at him now, she saw his outstretched arms for what they were. Not a hug. Nothing sincere. Only manipulation, pure and simple. Just like every smile he'd ever given her as a young boy. It was goddamned time for her to say goodbye to the person she'd created with wishful thinking, and see him as the man he was now.

Fatally flawed. And in reality, she knew he'd always been.

Yet she couldn't remember when he'd ever requested a hug from her. Her chest ached as she stepped into his arms and wrapped her arms around his waist, burying her face against his bony chest. Only because she needed the closure. He stank of cigarettes and smoke from the fire. His stiff posture indicated how little he wanted the physical contact.

"Goodbye, Oliver."

The hug was brief and uncomfortable. For both of them.

Surprisingly, he reached out to take her hands in his when she stepped out of his hold. "Don't worry, Riv." He pressed something into her palm, then dropped his hands to shove them back into his pockets, his shoulders hunched. "Everything's going to be okay."

"Everything's always okay if someone *else* fixes it, Oliver. I can't fix this for you. You're in big trouble." *Understatement of the century.* She didn't say international terrorism, but surely he must be aware that that was what his actions were? "Just cooperate and answer all their questions."

He sat down, turning his head to look out of the window. "Give me some space."

Shoving the small leather pouch into her front pocket,

River circumvented the table, and sat across from him. "Better?" she asked.

"*Acceptable.*"

Asher settled on the arm of her chair, his hip against her arm. She loved the physical contact, and leaned against him just a little as she dragged in a determined breath. "You understand that you're in a boatload of trouble, and your story that you were being held captive doesn't make sense?"

Narrow-eyed, her brother glanced at Ash. "According to who? Your boyfriend? It would make sense to anyone with half a brain."

"Let's start with the basics," Ash said, his tone moderate. "Why don't you tell your sister how you knew she was in Los Santos and not in Portland when you texted her. And why did you let her come? You knew she'd move heaven and earth to find you?"

"I'd never put her in danger. She did that to herself."

"She traveled all the way to Cosio to find you. You knew damn well she wouldn't stop until she did just that. You knew damn well she'd come herself to get you after that S.O.S. text."

Oliver shrugged. "I guess."

River's elevated blood pressure throbbed behind her eyeballs. "You freaking *guess*? The mine was stuffed full of explosives, soldiers were *everywhere*, you dropped all phone communication with me, and you *guessed* I'd come for you? Jesus, Oliver! Did you not care that the chances of me getting killed were freaking *astronomical*?"

His lips tightened.

"You knew you weren't going to die tonight, didn't you? You *knew* the soldiers had gone. Talk, Oliver, for God's sake! Franco paid you blood money, and you in turn put it in my account. Why? To salve your conscience? Do you even *have* a conscience?"

Ash rested a comforting hand on her shoulder. His warm fingers provided an anchor to her wildly swinging emotions. Oliver's bland expression was both maddening and terrifying. Ash and his people didn't understand her brother as she did. They hadn't grown up with his detachment. It was who he was, but that didn't make it any less frustrating. Especially now, when so much depended on him being transparent.

Somehow she had to impress upon him, in a way he'd understand, just how much trouble he was in. Her duty of taking care of Oliver, a lifelong obligation for her, was a hard habit to break. Answering her basic questions truthfully and freaking immediately would go a long way toward mitigating the irritation she read in the eyes of the operatives who surrounded them both. So far, Ash was allowing her to ask questions, but she guessed that pretty soon that option would be taken off the table. "What was the plan, Oliver? That I'd come to get you, drive you to wherever and then you'd *disappear* again. Pretend to be dead? Start up somewhere else? Different name, different place, same damned terrorist activities?"

"It's complicated."

"I think I can keep up," she said dryly. The hard thumping of her heart behind her eyes indicated the level of her blood pressure. "I deserve the freaking truth after everything you've put me through."

"You're overwrought and hysterical."

Before she realized what she was doing, River lunged out of her seat and slapped him. Hard. Her hand left a red mark across his pale cheek. Tears of shame immediately sprang to her eyes, and she dashed them away with the heel of her stinging hand. Dear God, her mother would be appalled if she could see how River was treating her handicapped brother, especially when he was already afraid and confused and didn't realize the ramifications of being obtuse.

Or did he?

This wasn't the boy she'd grown up with. His eyes went wide as he touched his cheek, looking at her as if he didn't recognize her. "What the *fuck's* wrong with you?"

Blinking back the prickle of tears and curling her smarting fingers into a fist at her side, she said tightly, "Overwrought and hysterical? Really Oliver? I can show you overwrought and freaking hysterical, but Mom would roll over in her grave."

He waved her away like a pesky fly. "Sit down, you're making a fool of yourself."

"At least I'm not the one making shit that kills innocent people." Damn it, now that her temper was unleashed, it was hard to stuff it back where it had hidden for years. "And *I'm* not the one heading straight to jail. Talk to them, Oliver. Tell them the truth. Stop acting like you're hiding something."

Ash wrapped a strong arm around her shoulders, and handed her a napkin. River looked at it blankly. He took it back and wiped her cheeks with it. Shit. Had she been crying this whole time? River relaxed into the squishy leather seat, her pulse racing through her body like a drunk driving a Ferrari. She glared at her brother through a blur of tears. Losing her temper was counter-productive. Her chest ached and her throat closed as she struggled not to break down sobbing at this whole ball of crap her brother had dumped on her and everyone else on board.

Strong emotions bewildered Oliver, and coming on too strong would make him shut down even more. These were all things she knew, and had lived with all her life. River modulated her tone, and leaned back instead of forward, relaxing her shoulders, and evening out her face. "*I* know you wanted to work on this project because it was challenging, and you thought you were doing something good. How big a role did you play in Franco's business?"

"Just doing my job. For God's sake, River, take a chill pill and get off my back." He sounded like a belligerent lush, his speech slightly slurred, and slower than usual.

The only reason River *didn't* damn the consequences and grab her brother by the scruff and shake him, was Ash's restraining arm on her shoulder. "You can either tell her how you knew she was in Los Santos, or I will," Ash told her brother when he clamped his lips tightly and shut his eyes to close everyone out.

"I saw the monitors in his lab," she admitted. She'd never done an act of violence on anyone, and the fact that she'd been driven to slap Oliver made her feel small and petty. Oliver swigged the last few drops of soda from the can, then crushed it and tossed it toward the table. It landed on the floor. "He saw everything that was said and done at the hacienda in real time. But why, Oliver?"

Oliver didn't open his eyes. "Ask your hotshot boyfriend."

"We have a pretty damned good idea." Ash's fingers tightened warningly on River's shoulder. "Xavier was on his way to Montana tonight, wasn't he?"

"How would I know?"

"Oliver, I swear, if you don't damn well start answering, I'm going to do more than slap some sense into you."

"I don't *know*, but yes. *Maybe* his destination was Montana. But that's moot now, isn't it? Your people killed him."

"How did you meet Catherine?" Ash asked.

"MIT. Final year. She was the most beautiful woman."

The soothing stroking of Ash's hand on River's back paused. "You're saying you went to work for Francisco Xavier right after MIT?"

"No." She glanced up at Ash, then looked back at her brother who was quietly humming under his breath. The sound, the fact that he was *humming*, made the small hairs on River's arms stand up. This, like the rest of his behavior at the moment, was atypical. "Oliver started working for him five years ago, right, Oliver?"

"*Wrong*, River. I'd go from Boston to Los Santos in a private jet. I lived for the times Catherine would visit. She was a naughty, naughty girl, my Catherine."

River could see how a sexy woman showing her brother any interest must've been seductive and compelling. He'd been led by his penis.

"Seymour was a rogue operative of T-FLAC, Dr. Sullivan," Ash answered tightly, rubbing River's back, as one would gentle a frightened animal. "Put one of the world's most dangerous terrorists together with a rogue T-FLAC operative, a trip to Montana with explosives, throw your expertise into the mix, and what do you think we have?"

Oliver lifted his eyes to give Ash a vaguely bland look. "Sup-Supposition."

"We know that there are seven bomb targets scheduled to detonate on the twelfth at three-thirty pm. What are those locations?"

"Catherine's birthday," Oliver smiled, his eyes dreamy. "She would've been thirty-six tomorrow." Slouching down further in his seat, he rested his head back as if it was too heavy to hold up. His coordination seemed off as he tried, and failed, to cross one leg over the other. His features slack, he looked down at his lower body as if he couldn't figure out what he was trying to do.

Was he drunk? No, Oliver didn't drink alcohol. Had he

taken something without Ash's men noticing? It seemed impossible, because they hadn't taken their eyes off him since they'd left Los Santos. God. Had he been bitten by something somewhere along the way? But they'd been in the lab, the car, the helicopter. Still. Maybe.

"What are the exact locations of the devices, Dr. Sullivan?"

"I've been a prisoner for over *two years*, I'm not pr-i-vy to that information."

As annoyed and frustrated as she was, her brother's halting speech and the odd sheen of his unfocused eyes was concerning. "We're all aware you weren't a damn prisoner *at all*, Oliver."

He didn't respond. His attention was fixed on Ash, who said, "We know T-FLAC HQ is one of those targets. What's the location of the bomb, Sullivan?"

Oliver shrugged.

River lifted her butt off the chair to reach over and knock some sense into him. When Ash gave her shoulder another warning squeeze she remained seated, but was still poised to charge. "*Enough!* Don't you get it that not answering makes you look *guilty*? Look around you. Do these men *look* like they want to play freaking games? They already know enough to put you in prison and throw away the key. Answer the questions, and damn well do it *right now*..."

"Shhh-tay out of this River."

"Are you *insane*? Look at us. *I'm* here because of the mess *you're* in. People are going to die, Oliver. Hundreds, possibly thousands of people will die in a few hours' time unless you tell them where those bombs are and how to defuse them."

"I'm not admitting my own cul- culp-culpability. I want to make that crystal clear. I just overheard things."

#

"Spit it out, for God's sake, Oliver!" River was clearly at the end of her rope.

Daklin thought she was holding it together damn well, all things considered. That gentle slap she'd given her brother was nothing compared to what Daklin wanted to fucking rain on Sullivan's head. The law, aka T-FLAC, would take care of Sullivan's crimes, but what he felt right now was a fuckton more personal. If this was Sullivan's usual modus operandi with his sister, he was stunned she'd travelled to a war torn country to find him. The guy was a prick, and clearly didn't give a flying fuck about his sister or the dangers he'd put her in.

Humming under his breath, Sullivan fought the drug they'd administered in his soda immediately they'd boarded. The drug worked best as an injectable, but they'd opted for the liquid form and ingestion in this case. Daklin had never seen resistance like it. His eyes met Ram's. The other man gave a small shrug. They knew it would kick in. Eventually.

"You were brilliant in setting the bombs, Dr. Sullivan. Can you tell us where they were placed?" Daklin kept his tone even, with just a slight hint of authority. Someone under the influence of truth serum--which Sullivan was now fighting for all he was worth--tended to tell the interrogators whatever he thought they wanted to hear. Until he went deeper. For now, the questions had to be specific, while he still had cognizance and before the drug suppressed the part of the brain that made Sullivan assess the questions.

Daklin rephrased. "Where are the bombs located, Oliver?"

Eyes glassy, Oliver blinked him into focus, then said in a dreamy voice. "Manila Ninoy Aquino. Can I get another Coke? S-something to eat. Protein?"

"No," River interrupted. "Keep going."

With a puzzled scowl, Sullivan cast her a look of profound confusion, as if he was trying to place who she was, where he was. "Tehran Imam Khomeini. LAX. Atatürk International. T-FLAC Headquart-" Sullivan snickered like a naughty schoolboy. "*That* was our *favorite* target of all. Haneda in Tokyo. Soekarno-Hatta, Jakarta." His pause seemed endless before he spoke again. "Oh, yeah--Antonio Nariño, Columbia. That's what I know."

Quietly and simultaneously, Daklin relayed the intel into his comm. "Other than Montana, those are all international airports," he noted, casually resting a calming hand on River's hip. Energy hummed through her body, a combo of sustained adrenaline and irritation.

"There are bigger and busier airports," he prodded Sullivan. "Why those in particular?" The death toll at those contested hubs would be astronomical. The Nuts would be almost impossible to find unless Sullivan knew, and divulged, the info in time to defuse the bombs.

Sullivan gave him a sly, albeit sloppy, smile. "*Fault lines. My clever girl. Brilliant. Chaos, high death toll, power. Money.*" His uncharacteristic giggle indicated a loss of inhibition as the serum flowed through his bloodstream, finally becoming effective. "A--" His voice trailed off as his eyes lost focus.

"Fucking hell." Clipped tension tightened Daklin's voice. "Blackmail on a global scale." Detonating directly on a geological fault line would cause tens of thousands of deaths on site. It would also precipitate, for hundreds, possibly thousands of miles along the fault, earthquakes and tsunamis. This was man-made destruction of international proportions never seen before. Bigger, and a hell of a lot worse than any of them would've dared to imagine. And then some.

The scientist leaned back, his eyes closed, and slurred dreamily. "Pay up, or detonate. Simple and b-beautifully executed."

Jesus. "How do we defuse the bombs?"

"Simult--"

"Yeah. We got that. What are the exact locations of the explosive devices in each building, and how do we defuse them, Dr. Sullivan?"

"He's asleep? How the hell--?" River asked unnecessarily.

"Bring him back by whatever means necessary," Daklin instructed his men, his tone grim, as he nudged River into motion. "Keep him awake. Get answers. I'll be aft. Come."

431

As he steered her to the rear of the plane they passed several of his men stretched out, resting, but always alert. "Sorry," he said as they sat down out of earshot of the others. He saw by the rigidity of her shoulders, and the tension around her eyes that the adrenaline that had sustained her for hours, that had kept her alert, had dissipated, leaving her spent and depleted. She needed sleep.

Glancing over her shoulder with a frown, she asked, "For what?"

"For your brother being such a dick."

"Yeah, me too." They shared a moment fraught with things unsaid and questions unasked as they slid into their seats. "He's a sociopath, isn't he?"

"You knew?"

"My parents suspected. We didn't want to believe it." She squeezed her eyes shut, then opened them to give him a steady look that jolted his heart and reminded him just how strong she was. "I've spent my entire life making excuses for him. Trying my freaking damnedest to love him, and feeling guilty as hell because he's always been just so damned hard to love."

There didn't seem to be any love lost on Sullivan's part, either. His team had discovered that the fucker had tried to get Xavier to *kill* her. Daklin had no intention of sharing *that*. "Yet you came all the way to Los Santos to find him."

"He's my brother."

He got it. "What did he give you back there?"

"No idea." River lifted her hip to retrieve the item from her back pocket.

Daklin extended his hand, and she transferred a small chamois leather pouch to him. He muttered, "Fuck," under his breath as he felt the weight and shape of the contents.

"Oh, God." Her gaze shot from the bag to his face. "Is it--?"

Jesus, he hoped to hell not. Opening the bag, he gently dropped the contents into his palm. They both breathed a sigh of relief when they saw the three, walnut-sized, green stones. "*Emeralds,* not Nuts." Returning them to the drawstring bag, he handed it back to her. "Hang on to them. No reason you can't keep them."

"Don't you need to book them into evidence or something?"

He smiled. "We're not the police."

"Okay. But the last thing I want is a souvenir from Los Santos. If I do get to keep them, I'll give them to Father Marcus with the money Oliver stuck in my account." River shot a look in the general direction of the front of the plane. "Did you have to resort to drugging Oliver to get that terrifying information out of him?"

Daklin nodded. "We gave him a powerful truth serum to alter his higher cognitive function, which as you saw, he resisted for longer than I've ever seen anyone resist. We suspected he wouldn't tell us what we had to know in our short window. Not without assistance."

"You suspected right. He takes stubborn to a whole new level. I had no idea things were so bad." She grimaced, and it was so fucking cute, Daklin wanted to grab her and kiss her until she begged for mercy.

"We knew it was bad, but not *this*. The fate of millions rests in his hands. Those airports are on major geological fault lines. The ramifications of a targeted E-1x explosion in any one of those locations will be devastating. A coordinated detonation of this magnitude would be cataclysmic. We're talking earthquakes, tsunamis. We couldn't leave his confession to chance."

Eyes troubled as she turned to face him, River clutched a seat back, her face bone white under the smeared dirt. "Oh God, Ash." She seemed paralyzed with the realization. "I can't even *pretend* that Oliver is a good guy, can I? He's as culpable for all of this as Franco." Storm-gray eyes met his. "More so because he invented those damned Nuts, didn't he?"

TWENTY-TWO

L ooking bright-eyed and achingly beautiful, River emerged from the aft cabin in time to enjoy a hearty breakfast with Daklin and some of his team a couple of hours before landing. With her wet hair slicked back from a makeup-free face, the black pants, T-shirt, and boots she wore gave her a tough edge that she usually kept adroitly hidden under pretty clothes and a sunny smile. She might be a lingerie designer, but she was as kick-ass as they came. She slid into the empty seat beside Ram, directly across the table from Ash. Daklin had planned it that way. Close enough to look his fill, but far enough away, that he'd keep his hands off her.

She'd showered again, and even though the soap in the dispenser was, by necessity, fragrance free, he imagined he could smell the intoxicating scent of summer rain and flowers on her skin. He would always associate these scents with her, no matter where he was, because it was the essence of River. Pure perfection.

Several groupings of swivel seats faced inward, the low coffee tables raised to dining height so that up to twelve people could sit together at the same time. Usually the arrangement was left this way after takeoff. It was where the operatives ate and convened before and after an op.

It was odd to have River here. In his work place, with his

men. Odd, but right somehow. Fuck. He looked his fill, while the ache in his chest seemed to expand exponentially with her every smile. Sunlight streamed through a nearby window, making her clear skin look as though she glowed from the inside. All signs of fear and stress from the night before seemed to be gone. She was as resilient as she was beautiful, and his heart felt as though it had been cut out with a fucking blunt hunting knife just looking at her.

He wanted to pick her up, carry her back to the aft cabin, and make love to her again. And again. "We'll be landing in a couple of hours," Daklin told her as Ram poured her a steaming mug of fragrant coffee. Mike, a crewmember and medic, brought her a plate of eggs, toast, a fat, juicy steak, and crisp bacon. They all ate without conversation. When one never knew when the next meal would be available, one didn't waste chow time.

"Thought you'd like to know," Mike addressed River directly as they finished their meals. "Dr. Sullivan is resting peacefully. I'll wake him before we land."

River smiled up at him, and Mike almost dropped the fresh coffee pot he was holding. Yeah, River's smile could knock a man off his feet and make him stupid between one breath and the next. "I saw him sleeping back there, thank you. Did he tell you what you needed to know?"

Daklin had seen her pause as she passed her sleeping brother. He was stretched out in a drugged sleep. She'd hesitated long enough to gently touch his hair, then walked resolutely between the seats, visibly relaxing her shoulders as she made her way to the front of the plane. "In his own fashion. The info he gave us might be bullshit. Certainly, it's illogical. Unfortunately, we don't have any Nuts at our Montana location to test his theory of disposal." Mike smiled, showing a chipped front tooth, and too much fucking enthusiasm. "Your brother has ba-- Excuse me, he has a strong will, ma'am."

"A family trait, I'm afraid."

Dr. Sullivan's information had been relayed to T-FLAC operatives in each of the location he had identified, in real time, and teams of bomb disposal specialists dispatched. Having the formula and method to disable the Nuts would save countless lives. Daklin had learned about the progress they'd made when he'd emerged from the aft cabin a few hours after River had fallen asleep on top of him like a sweet, supple blanket.

"Give me the coffee before you drop it on River's lap." Ram reached for the heavy pot, lifting it up and away from Mike. "Want some?" He held it over River's half-full mug.

"Thanks."

His buddy seemed to have a crush on River, and looking around at the faces of his operatives, Daklin suspected several of the others did, too. And why not? She was every damned thing a man could want and more in one package. The thought of any other man's hands on her bored straight through him like a drill bit to the brain. He didn't like it, but claiming her wasn't an option. He had just too many damned issues to saddle her with. End of story.

"Just want you to know what to expect when we land," Daklin said curtly, annoyed that he was annoyed by the way River seemed to charm his men without even trying. The fact that he suddenly had the irrational urge to lock her up somewhere where only he got to see her alarmed him. "Your brother will leave the plane first with a security detail. He claimed, under the effects of the truth serum, that he'd ingested a Nut. Until we ascertain if he did indeed swallow an explosive device, we'll hold him at our bomb disposal facility."

It was the same facility where Joshua had died on Daklin's watch. Full fucking circle. River, who'd lifted the mug to her lips, paused to look at him over the rim. "I'm sorry. I thought you said my brother swallowed an explosive."

"So he claimed before he lost consciousness."

Putting down her coffee, she glanced around the table. "Do you believe him? How could he even *detonate* a bomb inside himself?"

"Some sort of remote control device. We didn't find anything on him when we searched him before boarding. And no. Despite the truth serum, we *don't* believe him, but we'll err on the side of caution and have him X-rayed anyway. As soon as we get the all clear, I'll take you for a short debriefing." He would do that only after notification that the twelve story underground facility was bomb-free. So far, the operatives there had found nothing.

They'd been ordered to look harder.

There was a strong possibility it was a ruse to make them

endlessly chase their tails.

Sullivan had given them the exact location of the bombs in six out of the seven locations. He'd left out only T-FLAC HQ. Claiming to be under influence of the serum, he'd said that he had no knowledge of where that one was located. Still, the fact that Dr. Sullivan was aware of precisely where the other six explosive devices were located proved that he was more knowledgeable about Xavier's operation than he'd wanted them to believe.

"Then you can re-board and head straight to Portland." *Shadowed by unobtrusive bodyguards for as long as it takes to confirm Xavier actually died in that chopper.* "Couple of hours, give or take. Unless you'd like to take a scenic tour of all that Montana has to offer?"

Like me.

What the fuck could he show her? His employee apartment——*room*——that contained an excellent sound system and a ninety-inch television? His imagination instead led him to the idea of entering his apartment, not bothering with a light or the scenic tour, but making love to her on his narrow bed. *It's good to want things.*

"Thanks, but I'll pass. I have a business to get back to, and friends waiting for all the gory details." She put up a hand. "Strongly edited, of course." Smiling, she swiveled her chair and crossed her legs as she picked up the mug in both hands to sip her coffee. "It'll be good to be home where I know nothing will blow up. I'll never get used to that. Plus, I'll have to apply for a new passport since I left everything behind."

"That's already in the works," Daklin told her, damning the efficiency of T-FLAC ground staff who'd allow no delay in her departure.

Setting down her now empty mug, she got to her feet. All the men rose respectfully with her. Holy shit, Daklin had never seen that happen. "Thanks, guys. Sit down and finish your coffee. I'll go back and clean up, then come back up here, if that's all right and you don't have covert, secret decoder ring, top secret conversations you don't want me to hear?"

Daklin hungrily watched the sway of her perky ass as she walked away.

"I'm a tit man." Coffee forgotten, Nyhuis watched her with hungry eyes. "But I swear, I'm converted to an ass man right now."

"Convert to keeping your eyes and your thoughts away from Daklin's lady unless you want him to stab you with that steak knife he just picked up," Ram warned, thereby saving Daklin from lunging at the man across the breakfast table.

"Help Mike get this cleaned up before landing," he told Nyhuis, pointing to the dirty dishes. He got exactly the bitching complaints he expected. "Do it anyway," he said unsympathetically. He'd cooked the steaks and bacon, Gibbs had done the eggs, and Ram had made the endless carafes of coffee. It was a fair division of labor, and no one was exempt.

River returned as they were swiveling the large chairs back into position, the tables lowered, and the men seated for landing.

Sitting beside Daklin, she gave him a smile that pierced his heart and made his throat ache. "I'd forgotten I had nothing to pack. It's weird not even having my purse." Curling her legs beside her, she made herself comfortable. "Not to excuse anything, but I believe Catherine was the first woman Oliver ever slept with. Sex is a powerful motivator, especially to a guy like my brother. I suspect he'd have done anything for her."

"She was a Black Widow spider, and yeah. Seymour had a way with men. God help him, if she was his first sexual experience. That would scar any man for life." No doubt, Seymour had introduced Sullivan to a crapload more than 'sex'. She had an appetite for violence and perversion. After her death, the appetites Oliver had acquired had been catered to and fed by Xavier. Daklin suspected it was a means of controlling the younger man in his grief over losing the love of his life.

Too bad Sullivan had turned the tables and gone from learning at his master's knee, to being the puppet master.

River watched him with curious liquid gray eyes. "Did *you* have sex with her?"

"God, no."

She smiled. "That's pretty adamant."

"Seymour wasn't just a rogue operative. She was a deviant, a sexual predator. If she'd set her sights on your brother, he wouldn't have stood a chance."

"He's always been easily swayed, but that means, with the right motivation and encouragement, he can go from bad to good, right?" She frowned. "He's always been as focused as a weapon. Damn, I probably shouldn't tell you that." She waved her hand as if erasing the words. "What I mean is, he's always been hyper focused, and will go wherever he's pointed, be that a math problem, or whatever." She shrugged. "*Whatever*. A woman. A cause. God, I hate saying this, but the truth is, he lacks a moral compass. To him, the world is just a series of complex math problems. This stuff they found in Franco's emerald mine was a new and fascinating problem to solve. I'm sure he never gave any thought at all to the end result. So there's a chance he can be redeemed, right?"

"Yeah," Daklin told her, forcibly not leaning over to kiss her. "Anything's possible." He didn't have the heart to share his doubts about her brother's ability to be rehabilitated. The plane landed on one of T-FLAC's private landing strips. Several black SUVs waited to transport them. "Can I give Oliver a hug goodbye?"

"He's still groggy, but yeah. I'll go with you." Daklin accompanied her to the first vehicle, where four operatives were about to help Sullivan into the back seat. A nod had the man closest to Sullivan step back.

River awkwardly wrapped her arms around her brother's waist and buried her face against his chest. "I love you, Oliver. Please tell them everything they ask you so they know what a good guy you are. When this is over, come and stay with me for a while until you're ready to go to work, okay?"

With a frown, he untangled her arms from around his waist and shoved her away from him. She took a stumbling couple of steps back, and Daklin caught her by the arms, then left his hands there.

"I still *have* a job, River." Turning, he climbed into the vehicle, slammed the door, then rolled up the window and looked straight ahead as an operative got in after him.

Dick. Daklin tightened his fingers on her arms, feeling the shiver that ran through her despite the warmth of the sun.

One look from Daklin to Dan Greeves, the lead operative in charge of Sullivan, instructed Greeves to stay on the scientist for the duration. With a nod, Greeves opened the door, then slid into the seat, keeping Sullivan sandwiched between himself and another operative on the other side of him. The car pulled away.

"This way." Daklin led her to one of the other waiting cars. Biting her lip, her eyes dark with hurt, River held it together as she walked beside him.

When they were on their way to the HQ building a mile away, he said quietly, "Your brother's not himself. He's still medicated. I'll make sure you get to see him again before you leave. By then, the drugs will have left his system." Daklin figured the guy was still a dickhead, medicated or not.

And if he doesn't fucking cooperate further, the second you're wheels up, we'll drug the son of a bitch again.

#

River was unimpressed by the low, one-story building in

the middle of a clearing covered with wild grasses. A small herd of black cattle grazed nearby and there was pretty much nothing else to see. They were in the middle of Nowhere, Montana. In the distance, what looked like a forest of Douglas fir, Lodge pole pine and the bright yellow of Aspen leaves gave a clue about the natural vegetation cleared to construct T-FLAC's headquarters building. Several shrub and tree-covered berms were scattered about, humps against the vast blue sky.

It was nice to breathe fresh, clean air after being cooped up in a plane for twelve hours. The mid-morning sun felt good on River's face, but wasn't enough to drive the chill out of her. It was a chill of confusion and heartache, inspired by both her brother's behavior and Ash's. Her brother, well, she should have seen it coming. But Ash? No way could she have anticipated meeting a man like him. He'd landed in her life with the impact of a meteor.

After dropping them off, their SUV made a U-turn and disappeared down a gravel road. They were alone. She looked around. No people, no cars, and other than the disinterested cows, not a sign of life. "Is today a holiday?"

"We never adhere to holidays." He pointed to a thick, unmarked glass door leading into the single story concrete building.

Great. They were back to monosyllables and hand gestures. It wasn't the most comforting situation, especially given their surroundings. Grays. Stark. Empty. Not even a potted plant to liven up the place. "This is cozy."

"The tip of the iceberg," he said without a smile. The lover of last night was gone. The man in black was back, and in full operative mode. "This way."

He led her into an elevator. Her stomach jumped to her throat as the floor seemed to drop from under her feet a second after the doors closed. Staggering, she grabbed Ash's steel-like forearm for balance. "Did we just *freefall*?"

"High speed elevator. Twelve stories underground."

"Did they find the bomb?" she asked as they exited into a wide, brightly-lit hallway. Full spectrum lighting gave a feeling of fresh air and space. Stunning and starkly beautiful, large black and white photographs of trees in simple black frames lined the walls. None of the doors had plaques or signage of any kind. River wondered what was behind them, but figured with a place like this, if one asked the question, they'd have to kill you once they'd answered. Preferring to stay very much alive, she kept her questions to herself.

Asher shook his head. "No. It could've been a red herring. Your brother was unable to give us any proof that an explosive device was planted here. HQ is as impenetrable as Fort Knox. Stronger than that, even. The only person who could've feasibly set a bomb inside undetected was Seymour, and she's been dead three years."

She glanced up at Ash as they walked. "So Oliver lied?"

"Nuts *were* found, and they are in the process of being defused as we speak, in all the other places he told us about under the truth serum."

Opening a door, he led her inside, where a giant of a man sat behind a modern, metal table. Though well lit, the room was painted a thundercloud gray, and the carpet was the exact same shade, making it look as though the metal table floated weightlessly in a stormy sea.

The somber color made River's mind go to a design for a fetish-style bra and panties. Something in hard gray, but with sheer see-through silk and small silver embellishments. Blinking the room back into focus, she mentally set aside the design, and concentrated on the here and now.

Leaning up against the table within reach, a pair of strange looking metal crutches indicated the man behind the desk had been injured in some way. He half-smiled. Or maybe that was a scowl, she wasn't sure. His mouth was slightly distorted by a wicked looking scar. "River, this is Dare. He'll take your statement. Tell him anything you can. Hell, anything you saw or overheard in Los Santos. Everything's relevant. I'll wait for you outside."

River turned to look at Ash. His features cold, his eyes looked distant and shuttered, void of emotion. His expression was that of a man impatient to get back to work. He'd already washed his hands of her. This was merely a formality before he politely shipped her home.

"Everything?" she taunted, just to get a rise out of him. Any emotion would be good right now. This place was sterile and cold, intimidating in a way River had never experienced before. It was all alien to her, and having a friendly face would've gone a long way to put her at ease.

"Yeah." He met her eyes. "Everything." Turning on his heel, he strode to the door, shutting it quietly behind him. Her throat tight, River felt as naked emotionally now as she'd been physically open to Ash a few short hours ago. Stuffing her hands in her pockets, her fingers curled around the pouch of emeralds as if they were a talisman. The gems clicked softly as she rolled them between her fingers like big expensive worry beads.

Several large, flickering screens illuminated the enormous width and height of the man behind the desk, reflecting small squares of light in his eyes.

"Miss Sullivan." His voice was deep, smooth, and illogically comforting. "Please take a seat." He indicated the straight-backed chair in front of him with a wave of a surprisingly elegant, if enormous, hand. "This will be painless, I promise."

The hell it would. Reliving every day, every moment she'd spent with Ash, just to have him jerk it away, was like having someone peel off your skin while you were wide-awake. Painful wouldn't even begin to describe it.

River glanced around the barren room. There was nowhere for her to go. No way to get there.

Get it over with. She sat down.

Dare tapped his keyboard twice, opening up a blank screen, the cursor blinking expectantly. "Start with the five million dollars your brother wired into your checking account."

#

15:02:08

"Daklin? We just ripped out wall on eleventh floor. We *are* hot," Rafe Navarro interrupted.

Fucking hell. "Hold," Daklin addressed the others he'd been monitoring as he ran to the stairs in response to the news.

Nuts had been located worldwide in each city, exactly as Sullivan had told them. T-FLAC's best and brightest were at each location. When Navarro cut in, Daklin was talking to the six lead operatives as they attempted containment of the devices.

Sullivan, even under the influence of the drug, had refused to divulge a *rational* method on *how* to defuse the Nuts. That lack of information ate at Daklin's gut. This was Josh, times a million.

As the prime conductor of this clusterfuck of a discordant symphony, Daklin was responsible for hundreds of thousands of lives. Lives lost if he fucked up.

Detonation timer set at 3:33.

"On my way. Dare? No. Topside ASAP." Dare suggested taking River to the SCIFF room, built to even more exacting security measures than the entire building housing it. It was on the same floor as the interrogation room, but Daklin wanted her above ground, as far away as possible from a potential explosion.

"Done," the operative assured him.

"Gibbs?"

"En route with Sullivan," Ryan Gibbs responded. "ETA, three minutes. X-ray shows no anomaly ingested."

Not necessarily good news. He didn't give a flying fuck if Sullivan wanted to blow himself up. He only cared how it would impact River. Ignoring the almost debilitating pain, Daklin took the stairs three at a time to the floor above, while River sat beneath a potential explosion, large enough to level T-FLAC HQ and the surrounding area for miles and vaporize every living creature.

He had to trust Dare to get her clear, just in case. God, he hated like hell to depend on someone else to keep her safe. But this was not something he could ignore. From headquarters to London, Barcelona, Moscow, Tokyo, Mexico City, LAX and Sao Paolo—-thousands of lives were in his hands right now. He had to do his job. Focus.

The comm was open so everyone heard what he heard. They'd speak when necessary, but he sensed their tension buzzing through the open line.

15:08:40

Busting through the doors on the eleventh floor, Daklin saw several operatives wearing bomb suits standing by. The air smelled of the spray paint they had used to mark an X on areas already searched. Rafe Navarro, who *wasn't* wearing a suit, held the gear out to him. "What do we have?" Daklin asked, waving away the gear. "No point putting it on. That won't protect any of us if it blows."

"Looked like cat shit on first pass," Rafe told him, indicating part of the wall that had been ripped down to the steel studs. Five dark-brownish black Nuts lay scattered inside the

449

cavity, with cording threaded through each small, one inch round explosive like pearls on a necklace.

"What the fuck." Daklin looked from the explosives to Navarro. "These are *Nuts*."

Rafe raised a brow. "Yeah, so?"

"How the hell did Seymour have access to Nuts four or five *years ago?*" Daklin demanded. "*We* didn't know about E-1x until eighteen months ago ourselves." He hadn't been surprised that Nuts had been found at the other locations. Xavier had been selling the product for years, and any one of his buyers, or he himself, could've set the explosives to detonate at the same time. But knowing Catherine Seymour had left Nuts here that long ago, came as a fucking revelation. Seymour had had connections, intel, and motivation to wipe them all off the face of the Earth. The trifecta of fucked.

Rafe rubbed his jaw as realization dawned. "This means the Nuts were perfected *years* before we learned they even existed."

"Yeah." Daklin crouched down on one knee to inspect what they were dealing with, and responded almost absently. "Which means he's been working on a *different* delivery system for a hell of a lot longer than a couple of years. What the fuck is it? How would we know what we're looking at is a bomb and not a fucking. . .cupcake?"

Hunkering down beside the opening, he visually inspected what they were dealing with. Not just bad. Catastrophic. His watched beeped the countdown. 15.05.00. 3:05 P.M. He automatically synced it, to the second, with the tiny countdown clock wired into the cording.

It showed today's date, and the timer.

Before her unexpected death, Seymour had planned this detonation for exactly this date and time. They'd checked their records. Sullivan was correct. This was Seymour's date and time of birth. "Five Nuts?" A few seconds later he got confirmation from operatives in London, Barcelona, Moscow, Tokyo, Mexico City, and Sao Paolo. In each location, they'd uncovered five Nuts. Same det cord. Same timer set to Mountain Time Zone, which was Montana.

In those population-dense cities, the explosion would go up and out, flattening buildings in a fifty plus mile radius, killing millions upon millions of people. "I have Dr. Sullivan on his way. He's out of time, and out of options. He *will* tell us how to defuse this. Stay with me."

A Nut, half the size of *one* of these, had annihilated the bomb lab and everything in a one-mile radius. The small outlying building, constructed of the same materials as the HQ building, had been decimated, leaving nothing but a smoking crater. That Nut had blasted through high-tech, explosion-resistant concrete walls reinforced with short steel fibers, with a tensile strength ten times higher than normal steel-reinforced concrete. The explosion had sliced through the bombproof wallpaper, titanium doors, and bombproof glass like a samurai sword through a cantaloupe. It had splintered trees, and crushed his truck to sheet metal.

451

That had been just one half of *one* of the Nuts now residing in the wall, eleven floors beneath the ground. There were five full Nuts here. Glossy. Black. Lethal.

The same Nuts were in six other locations worldwide. All set to detonate at 3:33:00 his time.

They had twenty-eight minutes. *Fuck.*

Daklin estimated the size of the crater the explosion would produce, should they detonate inside a twelve story building deep underground. It would create a void of upwards five miles in depth and diameter.

And if it happened in a busy international airport, near a city center? Many hundreds of thousands of people would die today unless he contained the E-1x and got it as far away from HQ as possible in the short time they had left.

Rafe dropped down beside him. "Honey informed me that Seymour had been in for a psych eval and spent the night here. We checked. This floor was under construction five years ago. Once we had the new intel, we decided to rip out the walls."

Pissed, Daklin bit his tongue. There was no point now, but Goddamn it, the fucking walls should've been the *first* place to look. Cunning Seymour had been nothing if not thorough. She would've seized any opportunity to fuck with them. She must be laughing her ass off right now from her home in Hell.

"Rip 'em out on *every* floor that was under construction for the last ten years. She was Machiavellian enough to use the construction to hide more Nuts at various locations. Check for

452

patches, unusual finishes, *anything* out of the ordinary. When in doubt rip it apart. We have less than twenty-eight goddamn minutes, people. *Go.*"

TWENTY-THREE

*M*ove," Daklin ordered two rookie operatives standing back to observe. They ran, speaking into their comms as they went.

15:04:43

"Get that?" he demanded of Control.

"On it."

Daklin shot a glance at the men standing nearby. "What are you waiting for? *Move!*"

Up and down the wide corridor, operatives armed with tools immediately started hacking away at bombproof wallpaper and sheet rock to search between the steel studs inside the walls. Two of Navarro's team arrived at a run, pushing a small flat cart. "Packing's here." They moved the cart into position.

"Ready?" Daklin waited for Rafe to maneuver into a crouched position beside him, balanced on his back foot so they could swivel toward each other to get the bomb onto the cart. "Let's get this show on the road and fuck Seymour's plan." Gingerly Daklin slid his hands under the first three conjoined Nuts as Rafe did the same with the trailing two. So lightweight, yet capable of causing so much damage. There was six inches of slack in the cord between each Nut. They moved slowly, painfully aware that any jolt that caused the Nuts to touch, or a tug on the det cord, and it would all be over. The other two guys slid the cart fractionally closer. They'd padded it with a nest of Upsolite-filled blast blankets. There wasn't enough of the diffuser to mitigate the explosion, but it was a safer way to convey the explosives to ground level where the others waited.

All they had to do was lower the Nuts so they didn't touch, and haul ass up top. Daklin's attention was pinpoint and focused, but he couldn't forget that six other teams worldwide were dealing with massive issues of their own.

"For Christsake, don't let them touch. Slow and steady. Ever see anything like this det cord?" he asked Rafe as they moved in unison and practically in slow-mo.

About 2-mil long and dark green, the plastic-like covering consisted of two strands twisted together like a rope. The thinness of the wiring in no way represented the amount of power it would generate.

"Never. But I'd sure as hell like to get a closer look when we aren't about to be blown to hell."

Yeah, so would he. "Everyone got a plentiful supply of Upsalite?" Daklin did. But it was eleven floors up. For now, this small amount would have to do. He got a succession of yeses from the others on the comm.

Upsalite technology had been in its infancy when Josh had been killed, but a highly motivated Daklin, a group of T-FLAC scientists, and a dozen bomb techs, had worked to perfect the formula over the past eighteen months.

In a larger amount, not only could the beads absorb a massive shockwave, but each bead's surface was also porous. The walls of each one of the millions of beads could absorb a plethora of liquids. The wall of just one gram of Upsalite was over eight hundred square meters, meaning the product could not only absorb eight hundred times its weight in liquid but, theoretically, could dissipate a massive shockwave. The product had been tested on a much smaller scale. And it had worked. Now it was SOP on bombsites. Because of the massive weight of the amount needed at HQ, it hadn't been brought down the elevator to the eleventh floor. But it was on site. All they had to do was get this safely up to ground level where the larger quantity of Upsalite waited.

Daklin knew the quantity of Nuts that each location had discovered. Each location had enough Upsalite on site.

"Where the fuck's Sullivan?"

One issue at a time.

Nuts first.

Nutcase second.

3:05:01

Simultaneously he and Rafe gingerly lowered the string, the Nuts, and the timer onto the nest of blankets.

"Here," Gibbs said quietly.

In his periphery, Daklin observed the scientist's loafer-clad feet beside those of assigned jailer as the bombs came to rest with the gentleness of a mother lowering her child into its crib. He ascertained that there was no possibility of them touching by carefully filling the spaces between them with loose Upsolite beads. After layering the bead-filled blankets over the Nuts for transport, he got to his feet. "Start talking, and no bullshit. It's time to shit or get off the pot, Dr. Sullivan."

Sullivan gave him a sulky look. "What if I want to get off the pot?"

"I'll haul you off by your fucking balls. Detonation is set at 3:33 p.m." Daklin studied him carefully, then added, "Your sister's in the building."

15:07:00

Thank God Dare had by now taken River above ground and had her at a safe distance. The only people still in the building were those ripping the place apart at a furious rate, and the skeleton staff in the Sensitive Compartmented Information Facility down on the twelfth floor. The SCIF room was the nerve center and brains of T-FLAC, and every technology was in play to keep the separate unit inviolate. It was electronically secure, and as blast proof as Fort Knox. But they hadn't fucking known about E-1x when it had been constructed.

Support was still vital for operatives in the field working on unrelated ops worlds away. If T-FLAC HQ was high security, the people inside SCIF were protected by even more bells and whistles. The nerve center had been constructed with the highest of high tech materials.

Daklin knew they'd be transferring intel and personnel to one of their other servers in the subterranean vault inside hidden salt mines in Kansas. They should be able to operate without too long a lag time. In some cases, though, the delay of seconds could mean an operative's life. The SCIF team was determined to wait until the very last minute.

This *was* the fucking last minute.

"Alert SCIF to start evacuation," Daklin said into his comm, his voice low. "Are you willing to kill your sister, Dr. Sullivan? Because in a few more minutes, this will no longer be a theory."

Shoulders hunched and not making eye contact, Dr. Sullivan jingled the change in his pockets. "She shouldn't be here."

And he'd fucking completely missed the point. "No shit. But she's directly below us right now, so you'd better defuse this shit fast."

This was already a goatfuck of gigantic proportions, and Daklin had to depend on a man who'd had to be drugged so they could drag bits and pieces of information out of him. He manipulated his comm, wanting the operatives in the field attempting the same thing to get the info in real time.

He wanted options in case the Upsalite *didn't* fucking work. There couldn't be enough backups in this case.

"You don't want her to die. Defuse this or we'll all die together." He nodded to the two men to take the cart up to ground level. They knew to move at a snail's pace.

"Do me a favor. Kill the fucker. Make it hurt. A bomb blast is too clean an exit for this guy," the operative in Barcelona said in his ear.

3:08:55

"*Oliver*!" River shouted from the other end of the corridor, her voice cutting through the sound of drills and hammers, and the low hum of voices.

Daklin's blood froze and it felt as though his heart stopped. No. She was with Dare. She should be at ground level, far enough to be out of danger.

But fuck no. She was here on level eleven. At ground fucking zero. Her eyes blazing, her booted feet ate up the distance until she stood toe to toe with her brother. Behind her, Dare caught up, looking just as pissed as Daklin felt. They'd have words later.

River white-knuckle gripped a lowered Glock in front of her with both hands. "Answer Ash right freaking now, or I'll shoot you right here, right now, Oliver."

3:09:03

Two-handed, River raised the gun to point at her brother's chest. The gun looked enormous and unwieldy in her slender hand, a hand that shook with nerves and anger. "Talk, Oliver. One--"

"Lower the gun, River. I've got this." The chance of her over shooting and hitting the Upsolite covered bombs was high, especially given the confined space and her lack of skill.

River's attention remained fixed on her brother. Daklin could easily overpower her, but he quite liked the idea of her

459

taking out her dick of a brother. "Go," he instructed the men with the cart as they hesitated. They hauled ass down the corridor heading for the elevator.

15:11:54

#

She wasn't going to lower the gun. The only way River knew to resolve this was to threaten to shoot her brother. He couldn't doubt she'd do it, when she was standing here with a gun pointed at his chest.

River was aware of Ash standing three feet away. He could disarm her with some clever move, but he was just watching her with those crystal blue eyes, his mouth a grim line. Every muscle in his body seemed coiled, ready to spring, but he stayed put.

"He won't respond to you. But he will to me." She met Oliver's eyes, the same eyes she saw in the mirror every morning, but without the light. "Tell him, Oliver. Tell him right Goddamned now, or I *will* shoot you."

"Catherine said you wouldn't understand. Poor, simple, River who just likes pretty things. Can't you see what's at stake? How these people aren't protecting you? They're holding you hostage. You're just their tool. Just like Catherine was."

"Stop talking about your damn psycho girlfriend and tell Ash how to defuse the bomb!"

"You don't know how to hold a gun, let alone shoot one."

River squeezed the trigger. Oliver stumbled back when she shot him in the thigh. She was just as shocked as he was. She'd been aiming for his shoulder.

He doubled over, clutching his bleeding leg. "Jesus Christ, River, have you've lost your-—"

"Two." Her fingers buzzed, and her arms shook. "Oliver Michael Sullivan, you'll tell Ash *exactly* what he wants to know, and you'll do it *right now*. Next time, I'll hit an organ." Or the wall, or Ash. She repositioned the barrel to take aim at her brother's chest.

Blood ran between his fingers, quickly seeping into the leg of his neatly pressed khaki pants, then dripping onto his shoe.

River wished she'd stop shaking, wished the sick fear in her stomach would stop backing up into her throat. More than anything, she wished it hadn't come to this. But wishes wouldn't get Ash and his men what they had to have right now. The time to beg and plead had long since passed. "Talk!" This time, despite the inner nerves, her hands didn't waver.

Ash talked quietly into his mic. Giving quiet orders, he fixed his attention on Oliver.

"Two seconds and then I'll shoot you again. If you refuse to help them, then you're more trouble than you're worth. To them." River paused. "To *me*. At this distance, I'll hit you somewhere vital."

"All right, all right," Oliver said, white-lipped, eyes blazing. "I need a gallon of oil."

"What kind of oil?" Ash demanded.

River shot him a quick look. He *believed* her brother?

"Oliver, if this is your sick idea of a joke. . ."

"Cooking. Engine. Doesn't fucking *matter*. Just bring me a gallon of oil."

Asher didn't quibble. "Cooking. Mess, two floors up. Move it." He waved Ram Ortiz over. "Stand by in case this asshole passes out from blood loss. Operatives?" When they checked in, he repeated, "Oil. Any kind."

"You'd let me bleed to death in front of my sister?"

Ash shrugged, eyes hard. "She's the one who shot you. What do we do when we get the oil?"

Oliver's face was a set, pale mask. "I'll do it."

"No. You won't," Ash informed him, his voice icy. "Tell me what and how, and I'll do what's necessary. River, go topside, and wait for me."

Her jaw hurt from clenching her teeth. "If you and Oliver and all these other people are staying, *I'm* staying."

"3:17:00." Ash noted the time.

River's internal organs contracted with stress.

"I suggest you lay out those instructions fast." He looked down the hall, presumably to see where his men were. River suddenly noticed that far from this drama playing out, the operatives were still tearing the walls apart.

She hadn't even been aware of the noise as she confronted Oliver.

"Where else did Seymour plant Nuts in this facility?"

Oliver's smirk made River's finger twitch on the trigger.

462

"There was no need for more. What you found is enough to take out half of Montana, you moron. She didn't know she'd be long dead and fucking buried before she'd see the fruits of our labor. Don't you get it? Even way back then, she planned to bring down T-FLAC from the inside." Oliver's laugh turned to a grimace as he shifted, and blood welled from his leg. He shot River a menacing look, his features contorted by the pain. "You'll pay for this, River."

River had zero sympathy, and didn't mind in the least watching her brother suffer. "*You'll* pay for this, Oliver. I'm the one with a gun in my hand, surrounded with men with bigger guns and better aim."

Oliver looked back to Ash. "This is Catherine's retaliation for you bastards killing her. She set this one. But I was the one to order the others placed to coincide with *this* explosion." He pretended to raise a glass. "Happy birthday, my darling."

"Most men would get their girl a fucking cake." Ash rose when two rookies came in, each carrying gallon jugs in each arm.

The guy on the left said, "We have olive and canola oil."

"Cut the top off the canola," Oliver ordered. "One will do."

Ash used his utility knife to cut away the top of the plastic container, then set it on the floor.

"This is still in the experimental stage," Oliver told him, his voice surly, eyes cold. "I'm not sure if it'll work."

With lightning speed, Ash grabbed Oliver by the front of his shirt, lifting him onto his toes and pressed his gun under his chin. "Stop fucking around. I don't give a shit if you've made peace with your maker and are willing to die here and now. But trust me, I won't let it be fast, and I sure as shit won't make it painless. Tell me what to do with the oil."

What chilled River to the core was her brother's expression. He didn't give a damn who died here today. Not himself, not her, not hundreds of T-FLAC operatives and personnel in the building. Not the countless thousands, maybe millions, of people the other bombs would annihilate. His gray eyes looked flat. He *wanted* to die.

The knowledge sickened, saddened, and infuriated her.

"Let go. I'll show you."

"In your fucking dreams. Bring back the cart."

Ash had two conversations going on. River got it. It felt like hours later, but was probably only seconds, when two men materialized beside Ash, pushing a small flatbed cart. She kept her eyes on Oliver, the whole time, watching his expression for any sign of what he was going to do. God only knew.

Yes, she knew he was surrounded by professionals, and yes, she was preternaturally aware of Ash standing close by. But he was *her* brother, she *knew* him. River didn't trust him one damn bit, and if he made any false moves, she wouldn't hesitate to shoot him again if she had to.

The men on either side of Oliver held him fast between them. He didn't put up a fight, or argue, but River didn't like the gleam in his eyes, or that small smirk.

Ash pushed aside the covering and picked up the string of little bombs. River's heart stopped beating. Holy shit. . .

"What are you waiting for?" Oliver taunted. "Put them in the oil."

Ash eased the string of little bombs, one at a time, into the liquid.

"Operatives, drop the Nuts in the oil." Ash draped a heavy blanket around her like a shawl, then stood in front of her shielding her with his body, though they both knew it was a useless endeavor. If those things detonated, it would evaporate them all before they knew it. Stepping closer, she rested a hand on his back, welcoming the tension in his muscles as they flexed.

Sweat prickled her skin as the world seemed to hold its collective breath.

"Do it." Stress showed on Ash's brow as he observed how the glow of the timer turned the pale oil an eerie green. "Everyone evacuate. *Now*," he ordered the people nearby. Oil spilled over the rim of the plastic container onto the floor as the Nuts plopped one by one into the viscous liquid, then sank slowly to the bottom. Carrying the jug, Ash headed for the elevator. River stayed with him, close enough to touch. "How much time?"

"Six seconds to the surface. A minute or so to get everyone away from the building." He frowned. "What the hell? Who just went dark?" Daklin listened to Control as he strode down the hallway. "Jesus. Atatürk International just vaporized."

15:28:28

Turkey's international airport's bomb detonated minutes *early*. They hadn't had time to find oil, and they'd been in the process of lowering the Nuts into the Upsalite. *Early,* God damn it.

Reports were being transmitted into Daklin's ear in real time. There was a 9.5 quake in progress, causing a ripple effect as it traveled the active right-lateral strike-slip of the North Anatolian fault westward for a length of fifteen hundred kilometers, creating devastation and destruction on a massive scale.

Daklin didn't state the obvious. Sullivan's suggested method of defusing was not only unorthodox, it was as unpredictable as hell. He also had to consider the very real scenario that River's brother could just be jacking them off for his own amusement. Deep in his gut, Daklin believed that was far more likely given that this sociopathic brainiac didn't give a flying fuck if millions died.

Clustered together, the five dark globes looked deceptively benign submerged in the golden oil.

Daklin held his breath. *This had better motherfucking work.*

He took a second to sweep a glance at the expectant faces around him, all focused on the jug of oil as if it held some mystic secret. It was one thing to contemplate death, another to stare it down, and yet still another to give it an oil bath with your own hands. Sweat dripped from foreheads. Some prayed silently. All they fucking wanted to do was save their asses. He didn't blame them. He wanted to live too. Now, more than ever.

Wasn't that the bitch of it all? Just when you realize what was really important, the universe smacks you upside the head and gives you four and a half minutes to enjoy what you really wanted all along, before snatching it all away.

Daklin rested his eyes for a nanosecond longer on River. Wide, troubled gray eyes rested on *him*. Not on the bomb. Not on the thing that could, and very well fucking might, flash and instantly end all their lives. *Him*. Her lips curved in an encouraging smile as their eyes met.

How can she still trust me to protect her? Jesus, I can't even protect myself, or my brother, or the men in my team if this thing fucking blows. Daklin wasn't a praying man, but he gave it his best shot. *God, please don't let me kill her today. I know I've been a screw-up, and you can take me, but please, please, keep River alive.*

In Daklin's ear only, Control reported the damage in Istanbul--thirty city blocks decimated, estimated death toll one million people. Injured count rapidly climbing.

15:28:57

The numbers on *his* timer still blinked. These Nuts were still viable.

Blood pounded in his ears as he focused on the tiny explosives. He weighed the variables, mapped out a route in his head, and calculated the odds of any of them making it out alive.

Saying the odds sucked was an understatement.

15:28:59

Between one blink and the next, the illuminated digital numbers went black.

Collectively, everyone held their breath.

Daklin's watch continued the countdown to 3:33.

15:30:01

Three minutes to detonation.

The timer was dead.

"Fucking hell," the operative in Barcelona whispered, his relief evident.

In Montana, several people let out their collective breaths.

"Son of a bitch," Moscow said, almost soundlessly. "The timer's stopped."

"Are you fucking kidding me?" Tokyo said in Japanese.

"Got to be a hoax," London inserted, plummy voice skeptical. "Can't be this fucking simple."

Everything in Daklin screamed this oil-dunking crap *was* bullshit. A ruse. But he was now out of options and as long as the timer was on hold, he didn't give a fuck if it was a ruse or not. With minutes to spare, he had to get River and his men out of the building and put as much distance as possible between them and the explosive.

Oil, being a lipid, *stored* energy. He might've just given Sullivan permission to concoct a *gallon* of fucking bomb oil without knowing it.

He had to make a split-second decision: take the oil up top, or leave it here on the eleventh floor?

If he'd just made a goddamned gallon of E-1x and it blew underground, the entire infrastructure, and the *brain*, of T-FLAC would fucking die.

On the other hand, even if he'd just made a gallon of E-1x and managed to get it to the surface in time, he had men waiting topside with a container of Upsalite as back-up and a bomb-proof vehicle to put some distance between them. The people and T-FLAC headquarters would at least have a two-hundred foot protective bomb shield of earth between them and the most explosive shit on the planet. Which gave them slightly better odds of survival.

Above ground it was.

"This gives us a little more time," Rafe said. "Now we can get this outside before they detonate."

"Or we'll lose the last few minutes and blow up now." Daklin focused on Sullivan. The scientist looked detached. It wasn't only that he didn't look interested, scared, or affected. It was that he didn't appear interested in the drama circulating around him, almost as if their panic soothed him. Jiggling change in his pocket, Sullivan's expression, if anything, was slightly bored.

"Yes." Sullivan's voice was flat, without inflection. "Or that."

Detached times a hundred. Who the hell was so blasé about the loss of human life? Unless they were complete sociopaths. The dark thought slithered through his mind, burrowing deeper, confirming Doc Sullivan wasn't all he seemed. "This is only a time buyer, people," Daklin said into the comm to the operatives in the other cities. "If you have the Upsalite, immerse the jug, and get the hell out of there. Dr. Sullivan, how *much* more time?"

Sullivan's lips twisted in a sly smile.

Daklin's heartbeat stuttered. *Jesus--* "Is this oil a motherfucking *accelerant*?"

15:26:00

Sullivan's gray eyes, disconcertingly almost the same color as River's, held a look laced with contempt and something that really pissed off Daklin. Smugness, with a touch of amusement. "I didn't say that at all."

"Everyone stay put! Rafe, let's get this shit topside on the double." Daklin gripped the container and drizzled oil on the floor as he ran as fast as his goddamned leg allowed. "Move! Move! Move!"

He and his key team members dashed to the end of the corridor, to the elevator's open door. "Get this up top and get it packed in the box, then floor that blast truck as far away from headquarters as you can get it," he instructed through his comm, as the door slammed shut. "Remaining personnel, this is a level four lockdown. No one else but the explosives team is to leave base until we're cleared."

Daklin motioned his men to close in around River as soon as the doors closed. River's safety was paramount, but so was protecting the twelve belowground floors, and the critical T-FLAC personnel still inside.

If he had the capability, he'd send the jug of oil--and doctorfuckingSullivan with it--into space. But that wasn't an option. Not in the next few minutes anyway.

TWENTY-FOUR

The six seconds it took for the elevator to travel from the eleventh floor up to ground level were the longest six seconds of Daklin's life. Beside him, River's eyes looked smudged in her bone white face. More than anything, he wanted to wrap her in his arms, inhale her fresh scent, assure her everything was going to be okay, and kiss her until neither of them could breathe. Her arm brushed his, sending a shudder of regret through him. He shifted away, redirecting his gaze to the sleek doors, as if they held the answers to all his fucking problems.

The outcome was not assured, but he wouldn't be around to kick his own ass if this clusterfuck went sideways. He'd have eternity in hell to feel the weight of his guilt. First for Josh, and now, for River.

The elevator doors whipped open to organized chaos. The vast lobby was a beehive of activity, where operatives and support personnel, without hysteria or fanfare, spoke rapidly into comms as they carried laptops, boxes, and equipment to vehicles that were outside, their engines revving. Even for seasoned operatives, this situation was intense. Voices were low and calm, but expressions were grim. This was more fucking personal than any other op. It was on home ground, set by one of their own, with an explosive device that was unpredictable, and, even in the smallest amount, lethal. They knew one device had already detonated early. Everyone waited for the other shoe to drop here in Montana. At ground zero, there was no point running like hell. Everyone present knew that even the fastest vehicle wouldn't get enough clearance IF the nuts were actually going to detonate. Daklin knew it, the operatives knew it. But it was a damn big IF and they were doing their jobs anyway.

Three men joined Ram in surrounding River, and immediately started outfitting her. T-FLAC's state-of-the-art Explosive Ordinance Disposal suit weighed upwards of seventy pounds. The ballistic body armor, similar to the LockOut worn on dangerous missions, was designed to protect the head and body from projectiles and over-pressure.

It was good.

But it wasn't going to be good enough.

15:26:00. Detonation minus seven.

More operatives waited directly outside the elevator doors, a six-foot square, lead-lined box filled with Upsalite on a small forklift between them. Too heavy to take down in the elevator, the lift would move the box quickly and easily from inside the building to the remote controlled vehicle beyond the doors. Incongruously, the sky beyond the glass doors was a clear and brilliant blue, the grassy fields surrounding the building lush and green. Bucolic. Serene.

Daklin had to trust his people to do their jobs while he figured out in the next few minutes what Dr. Sullivan's game really was. "Finish getting River suited up," he instructed Ram as he watched the T-FLAC personnel cautiously transfer the oil jug from its shallow bed of Upsalite and move it to the deeper container. "Then head to Honey's." There was a bomb shelter there. He pretended she'd reach it in time if this fucker blew.

Sullivan, with his own detail, stood nearby, watching the flurry of activity with no expression. They made no move to suit him up. That was a given.

Via his earpiece, Daklin listened to the reports from the other operatives at the various bombsites, as his gaze rested on River now ten feet away, between himself and the door. All he saw was her. Her sunny hair, the grim line of her soft mouth.

"Aren't you putting on one of these?" she asked Ram as he buckled the last strap on her blast suit. "Omph. Holy crap, this is heavy."

"Yeah."

Ash gave a grim smile at her antics, turning once again to the matter at hand. All locations now had the oil submerged Nuts buried in Upsalite. All locations were loading the deadly cargo into remote control vehicles similar to the one right outside the door of HQ.

Oil. God!

Sullivan wasn't stupid, just sociopathic. He was the mastermind behind the entire goatfuck of what they'd thought was

Francisco Xavier's enterprise. Their techs had already started breaking the encryptions of Xavier's cloud storage. The fucker was a perv. Sullivan even more so.

River was far from safe, even in the depths of T-FLAC headquarters.

"Everyone out," he ordered, knowing the order was an illusion and none of the seasoned operatives would fall for it. Knowledgeable eyes telegraphed acceptance. Fuck that.

He didn't trust Sullivan. The oil dunking might very well be bullshit. The very notion was preposterous, but Daklin had been out of fucking options and grasping at straws. And given his experience, he wasn't one hundred percent confident that the containment in Upsalite would work this go round either. Or that the bomb vehicle could contain the blast if it didn't.

Sullivan seemed amazingly resigned about his girlfriend's plan fizzling out in a gallon of fucking cooking oil. Something wasn't adding up. Daklin motioned to Ram, even though he knew it was already too late. "Take her!"

River tried to pull out of reach of the operative, who nevertheless kept a firm, but gentle hand clasped around the thick padding of her upper arm as she moved back, toward Daklin, instead of the door. "No. If it's safe for you to stay, I'm staying, too."

The sound of her voice--scared, yet brave and determined-- pinged through him, setting every nerve afire with radioactive fear.

He'd only ever been this afraid once in his life. But this was worse. "It's my job to stay."

3:31:24

He'd believed he'd die inside the mountain. He'd been given twelve hours reprieve. Twelve hours more with River. Now he'd be responsible for killing her.

"I won't run. Not when so many others have died because of my brother. I'm——-"

"Don't say responsible. Don't ever——-"

She didn't so much as glance at Sullivan standing nearby. "I should've. God. I don't know. Kept a closer eye on him. Done a better job of getting him help. We always knew he needed help."

"Free will, River." A metronome ticked in his head as people passed between and around them, as insubstantial as ghosts, as he and River locked eyes. Outside, the remote vehicle, locked and loaded, shot out of the driveway as if it were jet propelled.

Daklin prayed, actually prayed, that the oil and Upsalite worked. "He's chosen his path and you had nothing to do with it. He'll be staying with me, not you. Sorry, honey. Time's up. You've got to go. Now. Ram will get you back to Portland."

Narrowed gray eyes turned stormy, and her jaw set. "Really?"

"Yeah. Really." *Tell her whatever's necessary. Make her leave. At least fucking give her a chance.*

Sullivan, standing with his four-man detail slightly back, but between them, swiveled his eyes to watch them. He cut in,

476

breaking the deadlock. "Where are the emeralds I gave you, River? Do you have them safe, or did you have to hand them over?"

"For God's sake. Not now, Oliver." She didn't look away from Daklin. "You know if that bomb goes off, even in that, We'll all go up together." She motioned toward the empty spot in front of the building where moments before the bulletproof vehicle had been loaded before it had been driven away. "I'd rather stay with you, than leave without you."

"That's adorable," Sullivan inserted. "I'll just opt to go with these guys, and leave you two lovebirds to decide if you should die together or apart. About those stones, River?"

3:32:18

Even for a psycho, Sullivan was abnormally calm.

Something nagged in the instinctive part of Daklin's brain. The part that had gotten him through countless ops, where he had milliseconds to read a situation and make a call, which usually meant the difference between life and death.

He tensed, replaying Sullivan's words in his mind. Why would Sullivan say die together or apart? Unless the man knew the oil wouldn't defuse the Nuts?

"All locations clear?" he asked Control, his attention fixed on Sullivan, not River. Clear, meaning the oil dunked bombs, encased in magnesium-enforced boxes of Upsolite beads, were being driven to remote locations as quickly as possible.

Control's voice came through. "Negative. You are not rendered safe yet."

42 seconds."

Maybe.

Daklin waited, once again holding River's gaze. It was the last face he'd see. He'd escaped certain death hundreds of times. Working with stoic calmness, where only seconds separated living and dying, death was in his job description. He damn well did it better than the best. On this one, though, as the seconds dwindled to zero, he felt the pain of a million deaths. Because of her.

15:33:00

No big bang.

His heartbeat knocking in his ears, he vaguely heard each country chime in with an all clear.

For some goddamn reason, Daklin couldn't draw that breath of relief he should be sucking in right now. Not even when Control said in his ear, "Confirmed clear."

Turkey had detonated early. There was no reason why one or more of the others shouldn't be late. . .

There was no chance ground personnel could escape the blast now. None. Zip. Fucking zero.

If it went, they all went.

"Riv. Where are the stones?"

The moment the son of a bitch had been living for--for fucking *years*--had just come and gone, and all he did was calmly ask for his emeralds back? What the fuck was wrong with this picture? All Daklin could see, with River encased in the suit from throat to toes, was her face. Her respiration was too fast, her pupils dilated, and perspiration sheened her pale face. Ram hadn't got the helmet on her, and she held it tightly in one hand as she spoke to her brother, but looked at Daklin. Her voice was even, but she was scared shitless with good cause.   "You can't have them back. I'm giving them, and that money you gave me, to Father Marcus."

"Nice gesture." Sullivan held out his arms, preppy casual in his fucking pressed chinos and open-necked golf shirt, every pale hair on his head in place. Not even sweating, even though his leg was still blood-soaked. He had to be in pain, but you'd never know it. "Give me one last hug. This is where we part ways and they lock me up and throw away the key."

He gave his sister a wry smile as Daklin's men, still flanking him, held him back. "Go to hell, Oliver."

Sullivan gave his sister a pleading look. "River. Please."

Daklin's intuition went nova. He leapt forward to intersect as Sullivan lunged for her, his arms outstretched. "No!"

As her brother grabbed her from behind, his forearm across her throat, she staggered back under the weight of the blast suit and the helmet in her hand crashed to the floor.

#

River gagged as Oliver jerked her flush against his chest, pressing his surprisingly muscular arm across her windpipe to yank her off her feet. Her hands automatically curled around his arm, trying to pull free. Her eyes met Ash's, her vision narrowing on him, as if he was at the end of a long tunnel.

Blood drained from her head as her vision filled with black snow. "Oliver, what the hell?" Her voice came out as a wobbly croak.

"I'm staying right here until I take T-FLAC to hell with me."

The confirmation of how dangerously disturbed her brother was terrified her. But it didn't come as a surprise, all things considered. His Asperger's had always masked a more serious diagnosis: psychopath. Her parents had been told that years ago, but they hadn't wanted to believe it. Their mother had always hoped that Oliver would even out with therapy. God. He was a galaxy away from ever 'evening out'

River closed her eyes for a moment. Thank God her parents weren't here to see this. They'd be devastated to know how Oliver was using his genius. When she opened them again, she felt as though she was underwater. Everything around her was a blur. Sounds were muted. "What are you talking about?"

"Where are the stones I gave you?"

Prickles of unease made her skin tingle all over, and her heartbeat ratcheted up to manic. Dry mouthed, she had to lick her lips to answer him. "In my back pocket."

River felt the expansion of her brother's chest against her back as he took a deep, satisfied breath. In her peripheral vision, she saw people closing in as if in slow motion. Her gaze fixed on Ash. The pale blue of his eyes gleamed like the hottest part of a flame as he looked down the barrel of his gun.

"Let's see how well this blast suit contains the explosion when it comes from the inside," Oliver said.

"The emeralds are your new delivery system." Ash motioned his men to move. He stood with his booted feet spread, the gun a natural extension of his arm. He didn't look scared, or pissed. He looked focused and determined. Solid. Competent.

There wasn't a damn thing any of them could do with Oliver using her, in her bomb suit, as a shield. Her skin felt both hot and cold. Her heartbeat sounded unnaturally loud in her ears.

Her brother's breath ruffled her hair at her temple as he spoke over her left shoulder. "Ingenious, right? Who the hell isn't going to be greedy enough to claim a handful?"

"You'll die, too," River told him as she tried to wrench herself free, though that was impossible to do when he was holding her so that her feet were off the damned floor. It didn't stop her from fighting him for all she was worth, however. But the heavy suit hampered her movements. She just hoped her weight, coupled with the bulk and weight of the blast suit would break his hold. All her struggles did was cut off more air to her lungs. Gagging and choking, she kept fighting.

Oliver grabbed her hair, jerking her head back against his shoulder, then tightened his arm across her throat, pulling her more tightly against him. "I died three years ago when these fuckers killed the love of my life."

"All you were to her was a dick with a brain. For all the smarts you have, Catherine led you by the balls, Doctor." Ash lifted the barrel of his gun a little higher. "She was as psycho as you are, as fucking psycho as her father, and a hell of a lot more devious and manipulative than Xavier could ever have been. I assure you, Seymour was incapable of love, affection, or human kindness. She played you, and your ego fell right into her baited trap."

"She loved me."

"She used you. She made sure the sex was explosive and mind-bending, didn't she? Yeah, that's exactly how she manipulated you. The only love Seymour had was for herself. The label of deviant sexual predator was the kindest thing a panel of shrinks could come up with."

"Oliver," River begged, "Don't do this. None of these people had anything to do with Catherine's death. I didn't even know her. I went to Los Santos to help you. Let me go. I'll come with you wherever you like." Brave damned words, but they came out a breathless croak. "We'll start a new life."

He pulled her even further backwards with a vicious tug of her hair. As he tightened his arm across her throat, black snow obliterated her vision. "Shut the fuck up, you stupid cunt."

Bile rose in the back of her throat as she met Ash's eyes across the expanse of the open lobby.

I love you. It didn't sound so improbable and illogical now. She mouthed the words. "I love you," but his focus was locked over her head, as he watched Oliver's every move.

Something burnt a searing path across the side of her neck, shocking the rest of the breath from her lungs.

Without a sound, Oliver's restraining arm fell away. Fighting the weight of the suit with leaden limbs, she struggled to roll over and get to her feet. Since her arms and legs were so weighted and uncoordinated, she lay still. Something hot and wet trickled down her neck, soaking into the fabric of her thickly padded garment.

She dropped like a stone, falling hard on her back with no time to brace for the fall. Faces rushed at her, but blurred in a dizzying swirl. Features were reduced to a kaleidoscope of muted color.

The thumpthumpthump of her heartbeat faded in and out as if she were deep underwater.

"Hurry the fuck up." Ash's rough voice sounded distant, then he said more calmly, "Lie still, sweetheart." His face swam into view. "You're bleeding like a stuck pig."

Rough hands unclasped fasteners with rapid-fire clicks, and cool air bathed her chest as the suit was opened.

How could something so freaking rude sound so nice? "Hardly compl-complimentary. Ow, shit, my neck hurts."

"It hurts because you've been shot." His voice was grim as he used a gentle finger to push her hair out of her eyes, his hand pressing against the fire in her neck, his blue eyes dark with concern.

"You *shot* me?"

"I shot a terrorist. He had a detonation device on him or in him. It was the only thing that made sense. You happened to be in the way."

She turned her head. Several operatives knelt on the floor near her fallen brother. "Oliver?"

Ram looked up from his crouched position beside her brother. "Dead," he informed Ash. "There's no device. No," he addressed someone out of sight. "Rip that sucker's fucking clothes off. Tear his body apart. And make damn sure."

River closed her eyes for a moment. "I'm sorry."

"Jesus," Daklin cupped her cheek. His hand felt hot against her shocky, clammy, cold skin. She wanted to rub her face into his palm. "You're sorry?"

"Sorry that you had to kill my brother. He was evil. You didn't have any c-choice." The light dimmed and she kept her attention on Ash's beloved face, but even so, darkness was starting to encroach on the edges of her vision. "I feel really weird, Ash."

"Where the fuck is that doctor?"

She smiled, wanting to touch him, but unable to move. "Are you allowed to say fuck on your comm?"

Ram dropped down on the other side of her. "Do something!" Ash ordered. "Yes, I can say all manner of things on the comm. Hold still, let Ram take a look. Get her out of this suit."

"You have to let her go then," Ram said.

"I take the pressure off, she's gone. Get me a fucking medic now."

"I am a physician, Daklin. Hey, pretty girl, look at my finger right here. Nope, don't close those beautiful eyes."

There were suddenly hands all over her. It seemed as though a dozen people were stripping her down to her underwear. "Hey!" Cool air dried the sweat on her skin and she broke into shivering chills before someone finally wrapped her in a t-shirt that smelled like Asher.

Ash cradled her head against his chest, his fingers gentle on her hair as Ram poked and prodded, putting something cold and solid against her neck.

"Stitches," Ram said over her head. "Blood loss. Get her to the Med bay, downstairs. Yeah, well, you have to let her go so we can take her."

"Don't let me go," River pleaded, annoyed when her voice sounded thin and weak.

"Never." Daklin rose with her in his arms.

"Oh, God." River buried her face against his chest, squeezing her eyes shut as he strode across the lobby. Intense nausea overwhelmed her.

"Puke or pass out?" he asked as he stepped into the elevator.

"Both."

She did neither, thank God. One moment they were in the elevator, the next a corridor, the next in a brightly lit room. "We're in the hospital," he told her as he gently rested her on an exam table. "Where the hell is the medical team?" He turned as two men walked in a few seconds behind them, both slightly out of breath.

They wasted no time washing their hands and donning blue surgical gloves as other personnel tended to River and yet another brought in a wheeled tray of surgical instruments, lining it up beside the table.

Ash took River's hand, and she clung to it like a lifeline. She didn't like needles, and the ones she saw on the tray didn't instill her with confidence. Ash squeezed her fingers. "I'm hand delivering a VIP patient."

"So I see," the one doctor said. Then he turned to River. "Sorry you had to visit HQ under these circumstances. You've had an exciting few days, haven't you? I'm Dr. Wayne, and this is my sidekick Robin. That was a dramatic finish upstairs just now. Nothing wrong with your aim, Daklin. Nothing at all. Shit, sorry. That was insensitive of me."

River didn't want to talk about what had just happened. Not until she'd had time to process it herself. She let Robin help her sit upright, her legs dangling off the exam table, and took the glass of orange juice he handed her. Her head spun. Ash wrapped an arm around her shoulders to support her, and braced the bottom of the glass on his finger so she could drink. "Batman and Robin?"

Dr. Wayne's white teeth flashed. "Never gets old. Let's see what we've got here. Daklin, move your arm. Yeah, Thanks. Any nausea?"

"She felt nauseous and faint right after I shot her."

486

Glancing up, she gave him a soft smile "You know I'm capable of answering for myself, right?" He was so dear, so concerned, so freaking sweet and attentive. The shadowy guilt in his eyes hurt her heart. Lifting her hand, she wove her fingers with his where they cupped her shoulder.

Robin wrapped a blood pressure cuff around her other arm, and River rested her head on Ash's chest as her temperature and vitals were taken.

Dr. Wayne looked at Ash. "Just a crease."

"To us," Ash responded, his voice rough and grim. "To her it's a fucking gun shot."

"Need a sedative?" Robin asked, his eyes twinkling.

"No, I-"

"I was speaking to Daklin."

"Just do your damned job, and make sure she's not in pain. Are you in pain?"

Of course she was in pain. "I'm fine. Let them do their jobs and I'll be even better."

"A little lightheaded?" Dr. Wayne asked, probably because her eyes were rolling, and a film of sweat covered her skin. "Here, lie down again. Close your eyes. We'll be done in a jiffy. Then you can take a nice long nap."

The wound was cleaned and examined as Ash watched with steely eyes and a grim expression. He kept her hand in his the entire time.

"Clean exit wound. Nicked a small vein but missed the critical carotids," the doctor told her after a thorough exam and stitches. Her neck stung and felt raw, but Ash's aim had been extraordinary.

According to the conversation the men were having as if she wasn't even there, the bullet had creased the side of her throat just above the blast suit, to travel directly to Oliver's heart. He'd died instantly.

"How soon can she fly?"

The doctor snapped off his gloves. "I'd like to keep her in overnight for observation." He turned away to wash his hands again. "This has been a traumatic day." He smiled as Robin held a wheelchair for her. "For all of us. Robin has your chariot; he'll take you to a room and get you settled. I guarantee you'll feel a lot better after a good night's sleep."

Sleep wasn't going to cure what ailed her.

"Can I have a minute with her?" Asher asked.

"We'll be right outside. Don't take too long. A decent night's sleep without drama will be the best medicine."

Ash waited for the men to leave.

"You're going to be okay." Lifting her with ease, he placed her gently in the waiting wheelchair. "You're in excellent hands. They're the best. They've treated more gunshot wounds than they can count."

"I figured as much. Ash?" She didn't know where to go from there.

Crouching in front of her, he placed his hands on the arms of the chair, caging her between his arms. "I'm sorry about your brother, River. Sorry that I was the one to pull the trigger. I couldn't let him hurt you, you understand that, right? Forget everything else he did, that was the clincher. Seeing your face when he told you the bombs were on you, and he'd fucking given them to you, I couldn't."

"Don't. I lost my brother years ago. I didn't know the Oliver you knew. The man you killed was a terrorist. Prepared to kill thousands of people." Touching his hand, she felt the coldness of his skin and the tension in his hands as he held onto the wheelchair with a death grip.

She really, really needed to lie down. Head spinning, the nausea from earlier came back with a vengeance. "I don't blame you. If you hadn't taken that shot, he would've strangled me or blown me up make his point. He didn't care. He wasn't capable of caring." River lifted a hand to touch his face.

Closing his eyes, he brushed her palm with his lips. The action made her chest hurt with longing. Instead of the kiss she longed for, he removed her hand, and put it in her lap.

"I don't blame you for doing your job, Ash. Honest to God. I don't. Now, will you please?" *Kiss me.*

"Robin's waiting to take you to a room." Ash got to his feet, towering over her as he straightened. "Barring complications, Ram will accompany you to Portland tomorrow. He'll get you settled, make sure you're okay."

She wasn't okay now. But a kiss and a conversation would fix that. "I'd rather you came with me."

He limped to the door, his body stiff. Hand on the doorknob, he turned. His eyes were just as brilliant a blue, but now they gleamed cold as ice as he looked at her. "I'm the wrong man for you, River. You'll realize that when you go back to your normal life."

"I'll never go back to my 'normal' life, Ash." She waved her hand. "All this has irreparably changed me."

"You don't want a broken man. You need someone who can make you whole. A hero. And honey, a hero I'm not."

"You shot a terrorist. You saved the world. You saved me. That makes you a hero in my book. When are you going to forgive yourself enough to stop running away, Ash? When is it *ever* going to be enough? What about the life you *want*? Don't you deserve that?"

"I've not good at sticking around. I'm doing the right thing here, giving you the chance at a normal life."

"Why don't you ask me what *I* want? Maybe all I want is a life with you, just as you are?"

His pupils dilated and the pulse in his jaw throbbed faster. "Don't let the drugs talk you into saying something you don't mean."

"Damn it, Asher Daklin, I know *exactly* what I mean. Are you going to shut up and kiss me or, not?"

"I'm walking out this door, River, and won't look back. Have a good life. Be happy."

TWENTY-FIVE

86 days later
Portland, Oregon

From the glass elevator rising to the penthouse, Daklin noticed that River's luxury condo building had a spectacular view of the Willamette River. Not that he was calm enough to admire the fall colors of the trees lining the banks.

He'd considered wearing a suit, then decided against the formality. He'd tried on a dress shirt and dress slacks. They'd been uncomfortable as hell. He'd ended up wearing his favorite jeans and a gray T-shirt because every goddamned day for the last 86 days, he'd thought of River's eyes whenever he'd seen that color. He had no idea how much of his limited wardrobe was that exact hue.

He'd defused bombs with less trepidation than he felt knocking on her glossy red door, clutching a cellophane-wrapped bunch of flowers.

Jesus. He'd never brought a woman flowers in his life.

Asher's defense physiology kicked into high gear. His pulse slowed and his focus became pinpoint as he rapped a little harder than necessary.

The door snapped open. A tall woman with a riot of black curly hair, wearing an oversized purple sweater and green framed glasses, shot him a curious look. "You're not the pizza guy."

"Ah. No. Is this River's place?" Crap. Was his intel right? Had she moved?

The woman stared at him, unblinking, from behind her glasses. "Yes." The way she blocked the door to hold it ajar prevented him seeing beyond her.

In two seconds, he was going to pick her up, move her out of his way, and storm inside. "She here?" Without removing the arm barring him entry, the brunette turned her head. "River? Are you here for tall, dark, and cranky? He brought flowers."

"Carnations?"

Hearing River's voice caused his heart to double tap.

"Orange roses." The woman tilted her head to inspect him, and the roses, with an unnervingly direct gaze. "Fascinated. Bewitched. New beginnings. Intense desire. Three dozen at a guess. Orange is excellent, Riv. He's very sorry."

All Daklin understood was the last bit. "Very sorry for what?"

"Don't know." She gave him an eyebrow arch. "But I bet it's a doozy. Riv, I'm going home. Save me some pizza. The money's here on the table." The brunette slid by to dart barefoot down the carpeted corridor. A door further down the wide hallway opened and closed.

The sliver of living room he glimpsed through the partially open door showed soft pastels illuminated by a wash of gold from the setting sun. Creams and shades of off-white. Pretty. Feminine. Where the hell was she? He pushed the door open.

River materialized in front of him. He was taken aback by a knockout punch of sight, sound, and painfully familiar fragrance. He'd missed her. Yearned for her. Hungered for her. Daklin's breath snagged in his throat. God. He'd forgotten how pretty she was.

Daklin's heart started beating again as he drank her in. Strands of shiny blonde hair escaped a clip to frame her face in sexy, mussed, just-got-out-of-bed wisps. A fluffy sweater, the pale blue-gray of the sky first thing in the morning, showed a smile of silky skin between its hem and her jeans. Her bare feet sported red nail polish, a guaranteed turn-on.

Hell, everything about her turned him on.

He glanced beyond her, because seeing her again made his chest ache and his vision blur. A couple in freeze-frame on the giant television, a royal blue bowl of popcorn on the middle cushion of a white sofa, two half-filled glasses of red wine on the glass coffee table. Pizza on its way. He'd interrupted a girls' night in.

A steady look from her gray eyes told him absolutely nothing of her feelings, while more emotions than he'd ever acknowledged were pent up inside him like a pressure bomb close to detonation.

She crossed one pale foot over the other. "What are you doing here?"

He controlled the urge to grab her and kiss her. "Did you think I wouldn't find you?"

"Honestly?" She rubbed one foot on top of the other. It was an endearing tell that gave him hope. She was nervous, too. "After the way you disappeared in Montana? And after three months? It never occurred to me that you'd look."

He'd known exactly where she was every minute of every day since she'd boarded the T-FLAC Challenger eighty-six days, nine hours, and eighteen minutes ago. "Are you going to invite me in?"

"Sure." She stepped back, then walked through the living room to lean on the counter that separated the room from the kitchen. The place smelled of her. Summer rain and flowers. She seemed bathed in the honeyed light streaming through the picture window.

Mine.

The very concept was ridiculous. River belonged to no one. She was her own woman, and her very independence was a turn-on. Still, his heartbeat thudded, *mine, mine, mine,* as he filled his senses with her.

But then she folded her arms over her chest. Not a good sign. "Are those for me?"

"Yeah." He handed her the flowers like a kid on prom night. Daklin didn't remember a time in his life—-hell, didn't remember a time ever—-when he'd felt this uncertain.

"Thank you, they're beautiful. I'll put them in water." She rounded the counter and reached up to a top cabinet to take down a clear glass vase. Daklin got a quick glimpse of the small of her back, and the swell of her butt cheeks before she straightened. "Carly's a florist," she told him as she filled the container with water. "She's one of my best friends."

He didn't give a rat's ass. Then he realized that anything, everything, having an impact on River affected him as well. "She seemed nice. Protective." Her small smile did big things to his heartbeat. "You know, if there'd been any other way--"

The smile turned to a frown. "Are you talking about Oliver?"

"Yeah. Let me get this out and then we never have to talk about it again."

"I don't think there's much you could tell me about Oliver that would surprise me. I heard you saved the day and defused the emeralds."

"I have a good team."

"Tell me what you want to tell me about Oliver. I'll hold my breath until you finish. When I turn blue the conversation will be over."

Daklin felt some of his nerves begin to unravel. God, he wanted to touch her, taste her, tell her. But first things first.

"Xavier was scared shitless of your brother. And that's saying something since Xavier was one sick fu-- Perv. From what we pieced together, Xavier sent his daughter, Catherine, after Oliver while he was still at MIT. She seduced him, both literally and figuratively, to work for her father. With him having little or no sexual experience, Seymour was a smorgasbord of sexual opportunity."

She grimaced, putting up one hand to stop him. "Turning blue here."

"Seymour targeted him right from the start. She did nothing that wasn't calculated. He was easy pickings." Their intel had painted a dark and twisted picture, and Daklin had learned more than he'd wanted to know about the rogue operative, and how she used sex to manipulate River's brother. Catherine had used Sullivan's dick like a pull toy, leading him wherever she wanted him to follow. She'd introduced Sullivan to BDSM, controlling him by his dick. When she left Los Santos, Xavier took up the teaching role to ensure Sullivan stayed. Over time, the student had become the dominant to Xavier's sub.

It was way the fuck more than Daklin had wanted to know, and he had no intention of sharing any of it with the man's sister. The reality was, Sullivan had taken to Seymour's machinations like a duck to water. He'd been no victim. In fact, he'd turned the tables quite neatly on both Seymour and Xavier and taken over their enterprise right under their fucking noses.

"Let's just say she taught him things, and when she left, Xavier stepped in to continue."

"Dear God, Ash! Not just no, but hell no." River grimaced and put up a hand. "I do not want to hear about his sexual exploits. Not now, not freaking ever."

He didn't blame her. Fuck it all to hell. He hadn't flown to Portland to talk about her brother anyway. That unpleasant convo out of the way, Daklin fought to tamp down the riot of emotions that had been torqueing his heart for the past months without her.

It was ironic that they'd shared just days together. He'd missed her longer than he'd been with her. Daklin had hungered for her every waking and sleeping moment in that time. All he wanted to do now was inhale her. His chest felt the pressure, his throat closed, and his heart pounded so loudly, he was surprised River didn't comment.

Daklin rounded the island to enter the red and white galley style kitchen, crowding her against the counter while closing his hands gently around her upper arms. Her sweater was as soft as kitten fur. Daklin inhaled the painfully arousing scent of summer rain and flowers on her warm skin. "I couldn't stop thinking about you."

River gave him a steady look from clear gray eyes. She wasn't going to give an inch. Whatever he gained today, he was going to have to work for. "I wish you'd come to tell me yourself that you were safe instead of having Ram do it."

He had a million reasonable answers to that one. "He made sure you got home safely." Daklin glided his thumb back and forth over the fluffy fabric of her sweater, feeling the taut muscles in her upper arm as he stroked her skin through the soft yarn.

Her breath smelled of popcorn as she tilted her chin to look up at him. "That isn't the point, Ash. If you couldn't make time to come and tell me in person, I would've appreciated at least hearing your voice. I was worried sick when you didn't come back."

"I shot you!"

"Oh, that's just a bullshit excuse! If you hadn't done what you did, we wouldn't be having this damned slow-moving-get-to-the-freaking-point-conversation."

Was she mad? Daklin tried to read her. Hell, she had the best damned poker face he'd ever seen. "I had my hands full." He'd managed to remain conscious until he'd ascertained that River's injuries weren't life threatening, ensured that the emerald Nuts were defused, and was certain that the Nuts removed from the walls, didn't detonate. Then he'd passed out from the pain in his leg. They'd taken him in for emergency surgery while River was on en route to Portland.

Because she deserved an explanation, he said gruffly, "I had surgery. Went well. Almost no limp." He'd lain in that fucking hospital bed, in the bed where hours earlier she'd been treated, and the pain of missing her exceeded the post-surgical pain. He hadn't allowed himself to call her during his lengthy rehab. He sure as shit didn't want her pity, and he wasn't willing to tempt fate. He'd

499

doubled up on his physical therapy, pushing himself to recover at super-sonic fucking speed so that he could walk in and sweep her off her feet.

Her eyes softened. "How's your leg, now? Really?"

"Good. Really." But he'd done a number on it in the field. The powers that be had reamed him out for faking his healing so he could go on the op, then reamed him out again for doing his job. He'd almost lost the leg. The sixteen-hour surgery had knit everything back together. It had given him more scars, and the prospect of several more surgeries to complete the work the surgeon had done.

He'd had a shitload of thinking time.

He woke every morning longing for her, and finally slept at night only because then he could be with her, if only in his dreams. He'd been a shit patient, and they couldn't wait to get rid of him.

"Yay." Her hands slid up his chest, pausing for a moment over the rapid, hard knock of his heart, before she circled his neck with her arms. "Good for you." Her eyes called him the liar that he was. "You can run in and out of mines and blow up mountains with ease now." Daklin felt the brush of her fingers in his hair. "I've been talking to Marcus, did you know?"

"Yeah." He managed a smile, even though this also wasn't what he was there to talk about. "I kinda liked that my handiwork rained emeralds down into the valley." He'd been in constant contact to make sure a new village was being built in another nearby valley that has escaped the worst of the blast. "He tells me you have quite the cottage industry going with most of the women sewing sexy lingerie for you now."

"Their needlework is exquisite. I'll charge a premium and share the profits with them. It's a win-win. Marcus filled me in on everything you and T-FLAC are doing to restore the miner's jobs. The co-op is a terrific idea. We talked about things that could be done with Franco's hacienda. We're thinking a boarding school with housing for good teachers."

"Sounds good. It would draw kids from all over Cosio." But that wasn't what he wanted to talk about either. "The op in Los Santos showed me two things," he murmured as he cupped her jean-clad butt in both hands, then drew her more tightly against his chest. "Two things I had no control over. E-1x and booze."

"You seem to have mastered that explosive," she said crisply. "The world didn't blow up, thanks to you."

He looked beyond her, hoping for divine intervention. Color, books, pillows, and beautiful artwork filled her living room. A perfect setting for the jewel that she was.

He adjusted his focus so that her beautiful face filled his view. He'd met with the Presidents of three countries, talked to the Pope, spoken at summits, dissuaded terrorists, and defused bombs. This was the first time he'd ever been at a loss for words.

Daklin cleared his throat, and made himself bare his soul. "I don't enjoy not being in control. What I do and who I am demanded that I maintain control in just about every aspect of my life. My drinking put me out of control. I hated myself for not being able to control it, for allowing myself to weaken. That weakness killed my brother."

"As tempted as I was in Los Santos, giving in to that weakness would have meant putting people I cared about in danger. Then you showed up, and I had three things out of my control, putting you in danger."

"So your control issues are the reason you haven't called me in three months? Fortunately," she said with a little bite, "I was not yours to control or otherwise. I never will be."

"I didn't want to control you, River. But I needed to control the situation we were in. You're as free and wild as the wind, and I'd never want to tame that. But you were an unknown quantity. A mysterious question mark I couldn't get rid of and couldn't dismiss out of hand."

"You think I'm mysterious and a puzzle. And yet I'm pretty simple and uncomplicated." She cocked her head, assessing him.

Heart full, Daklin shook his head. "You're complex and fascinating." Perfection is what she was. "I bought a house," he blurted out with zero finesse. "A small ranch, really. Cattle, horses. Pigs. A pond."

Her eyes danced as she stood on her toes, tilting her head back so she could look at him. Taking a page out of his book, she didn't crack a smile. "I bought green bananas and a dozen bagels at Costco."

She was going to make him work for this. His heart smiled. So be it. "I thought you might help me pick out furniture. Sofas and pictures. A bed."

"I don't think Portland's the place to buy furniture. Shipping it from here to Montana would be cost prohibitive."

"Are you trying to drive me nuts?"

"Clearly I don't have to try very hard. Use your words, Ash Daklin." The smile that started in her lively eyes now curved her lips. "We're not getting any younger here."

"You don't just meet your perfect match and then say I love you after less than a week."

Her teeth sank into her lower lip and her eyes danced. "Okay."

"Our lives don't mesh. I live in Montana, your business is here in Portland."

"True"

"You're clean and. . . *Clean.*"

This time she frowned. "I took a shower this morning."

"I mean I'm an alcoholic, River."

"You're dry now."

"But that temptation, that hunger will always be there. I'll stumble, maybe fall."

"How stressful was being eleven stories underground in your place of business with a bomb?"

"A bomb and you. Stress to the max. It was the worst experience of my career, bar none."

"And yet, you didn't take a drink."

"There wasn't time or opportunity. Trust me, the desire was there."

"Taking a swig from the flask in your back pocket would only have taken a second," she told him.

"Maybe I *would've* if I hadn't tossed it at the mine."

"I believe that even if you'd had the means, you wouldn't have jumped on the opportunity Ash. You didn't act on it in the mine under the most terrifying and dire circumstances. And today, instead of relying on alcohol, you used your brains and diplomacy to defuse an untenable situation. Sober."

Yeah, there was that. T-FLAC had commented much the same way, lifting his probationary status. "Yeah, well."

River brushed his jaw with her fingertips. "Apparently this conversation is extremely stressful." Her lips curved. "And you aren't faltering, are you? Did you take a drink before you came here? A swig at the airport? How about outside my front door? Or when my back was turned?"

"No."

"Why not?"

His stomach twisted. *Tell her. Get some fucking courage, and spit it out.* "Because of you. I want to be better. In ways I never thought possible. You inspire me to think of all the possibilities I imagined were impossible for a man like me: A home. A family. A life. I want it all. You inspire me to want it all.

You inspire me to work for it all. You're the key to all of that." He dragged in a deep breath.

Be more honest.

Hope crumbled with his harsh reality. "I have a long way to go." Because if he didn't touch more of her he'd die, Daklin threaded a strand of her hair between his fingers, and rubbed the silky length. "I was this close to getting my ass fired before Los Santos. I still have at least three more surgeries. And every time I look at death, which is often in my line of work, I want a drink and have to fight off the urge. You need to know all of this to make an informed decision."

Expression serious, she said, "You're fearless. You have integrity. You give a damn about people, whether they want you to give a damn or not." Combing her fingers through his too-long hair, she eased his head down, and whispered a breath away from his lips, "Is there a question in there?"

Resisting the pull, because no matter how desperately he needed to kiss her, he had to get it all out first. "I can't ask you to marry an alcoholic who's still facing a couple more surgeries and a long road to recovery."

"Hmm. I have an awful temper."

"Really?"

She nodded. "And I'm stubborn."

"Yeah. Got that."

"I love to shop online in the middle of the night, and I don't plan on getting out of bed to do it."

"That's all you've got?" He could only narrow his eyes. "What the hell does any of that have to do with anything when I just asked you to marry me?"

"Just an illustration that the broken, crazy bits of our fractured lives fit together like a puzzle. You started by telling me your flaws, so I figured I'd give you a few of mine. And FYI, so far you haven't asked me anything." Tilting her hips, she shifted her body just enough to drive him crazy.

Daklin cupped her cheek. "Los Santos will always hold a special place in my heart," he told her, his voice gruff. "It's where I met and fell in love with you. I had no idea that I was waiting my whole life to meet you, River Sullivan." There, he'd just jumped from the highest cliff into the unknown. "Hell, woman. Are you through torturing me?"

Her smile was like the sunrise, with a warmth that soaked into Daklin's bones and made him feel as if anything was possible. She was watching him with such tenderness in her eyes it made the knot in his chest unravel a bit. "Yes."

"Yes to what?"

"Crazy man. I love you. You have no freaking idea how relieved I was to find out I hadn't fallen in love at first sight with a bishop! Yes, to moving my business to your ranch in Montana. Yes, to taking care of you while you finish healing. Yes, to being extremely brave when you go back to work, now that I know what you do. Yes, to helping buy furniture. And finally, yes, I'll marry you, Ash Daklin."

"Thank God," he said roughly, his heart overflowing with love. Inhaling her summer rain fragrance that he hadn't been unable to get out of his mind, he pulled her tightly against his chest, lifting her off her feet. "I want a lifetime with you, River. I love you, more than I ever thought myself capable of loving anyone. You're the only woman I can imagine spending my future with."

"Fortunately for you, I don't share." With a little hop, she wrapped her legs around his hips, circling his neck with her arms, surrounding him with love. "It's not going to be easy. We're both pretty bossy."

"Not insurmountable."

"Want to a make love here, on the kitchen counter?" Tunneling her fingers through his hair, she kissed the underside of his jaw. "Or in the bedroom?"

He angled his head so their lips were a breath apart. Her love filled every empty place in his heart. "Both." Done talking, Daklin kissed her with everything he had. It was a start

Look For These Thrilling Books and eBooks in the

Cherry Adair Online Bookstore.

http://www.shop.cherryadair.com

Fallen Agents of T-FLAC Series

Absolute Doubt – Book 1

Lodestone Series

Hush - Book 1

Gideon - Book 2

T-FLAC/PSI Series

Edge of Danger Enhanced

Edge of Fear Enhanced

Edge of Darkness Enhanced

T-FLAC/WRIGHT FAMILY

Kiss and Tell Enhanced

Hide and Seek Enhanced

In Too Deep Enhanced

Out of Sight Enhanced

On Thin Ice Enhanced

T-FLAC/BLACK ROSE Series

Hot Ice Enhanced

White Heat Enhanced

Ice Cold

T-FLAC SHORT STORY

Ricochet

Cherry Adairs' Writers' Bible

Available Exclusively on the Cherry Adair Online
Bookstore. Connect with Cherry on CherryAdair.com for info
on new releases, access to exclusive offers, and much more! I
love hearing from readers – wherever you may find me. on,
Twitter, and my beloved Facebook.

CPSIA information can be obtained
at www.ICGtesting.com
Printed in the USA
LVOW01s1210060317
526274LV00001B/96/P